Small Fires In The Sun

Herbert R. Metoyer, Jr.

A Cane River Saga

An adventure based on the life of Louis Juchereau de St. Denis,
The Natchez Indians, and the African slaves

Cover Art: Herbert R. Metoyer, Jr.
Cover Models: Milicent Metoyer-Finister-Souser
Mary Metoyer Rachal

This novel, although based on actual events, is a wholly
fictitious work created by the author to navigate from one mile-
stone in Louisiana's Colonial history to the next.

Manufactured in the United States of America

Published by
Cane River Media
25785 Catalina Street
Southfield, MI 48075

www.CaneRiverMedia.com
www.CaneRiverColony.com
www.HerbMetoyer.com

Dedication

This book is especially dedicated to my wife (Geraldine Williams Metoyer), my mother (Ruby L. Metoyer), my brother (1st Lt. Bryford G. Metoyer, KIA Vietnam 1964) and to my children (Hermes, Angelo, Yolanda, Michael, Valerie and Jeffrey), and to their children,
.....and the children of their children.

How a person perceives life depends wholly upon which side of the mountain that person happens to live on.....

iv

Acknowledgements

Organizations:
  Mary Linn Wernet, Head Archivist
  Cammie G. Henry Research Center / Watson Memorial Library,
  Northwestern University, Natchitoches, Louisiana.

  The Detroit Writers' Guild
  PO Box 21633
  Detroit, Michigan 48212

  Historic New Orleans Collection's Williams Research Center
  410 Chartres Street
  New Orleans, Louisiana 70130

  Melrose Plantation
  Natchitoches, Louisiana
Editors:
  Geraldine Metoyer   Delores D. Metoyer-Finister
  Denise Crittendon   Linda Manuel
  Sandra Miller
Proofreaders:
  Diane M. Lockett   Yolanda Metoyer
Supporters:
  Professor M. L. Liebler of Wayne State Unversity
  Professor Melba Boyd of Wayne State University
  William Finister
  The Cane River Creoles
My best friends:
  Dr. Anthony Rene, Al Goode, Mayon & Mackie Weeks, Steve &
  Diana Biggs, Vince Martin, Angie Cummer, Lena & Bill Fields, Steve
  Schroeder, Cas Jaworowicz, James Llorence, M. L. Liebler, and Mike
  Law (VHPA).
Models:
  Millicent Metoyer-Finister-Souser / Mary Metoyer-Rachal /
  Geraldine Metoyer-Baker / Felicia Hart

Special Thanks:
  To my soul sister, cousin, and author, Linda S. Manuel, for encour-
aging and inspiring me to complete this book.
  To my birth sister, Delores, "Thanks for all your input and
assistance."

About The Author — Herbert R. Metoyer, Jr.

Author, Artist, Musician & Poet

Herbert Metoyer (a Creole of French, Choctaw and African ancestry) has a BS Degree in Liberal Arts from Southern University, Baton Rouge, LA. where he graduated at the early age of nineteen (19). He is a retired military officer and helicopter pilot, and a retiree from General Motors where he served as a Test Engineer in GM's Testing Laboratories.

He has been a member of the Detroit Writers' Guild (*a non-profit literary organization*) since its inception in 1984. As a founding member, he has served as Senior Editor, Creative Writing Instructor, Executive Editor, Chairman of the Board, and Executive Director. He is also an excellent artist and is the person who edited and designed all of the text layouts and covers of books published by the Guild.

In 1994, his story, "*The Awakening of Hanna Lee*" won top honors in "The Metro-Times All State Short Fiction Contest." He was also instrumental in the publishing of "Paradise Valley Days" a photo, poetry and history book that documented Black Detroit from the 1930's to the 1960's. This book earned the Guild an award from the State of Michigan.

His works have also been published in "Ebony Eyes," "Day's Dawn", "Paradise Valley Days," "Pumpkin and the Praying Mantis," and "Before I Wake."

Herb is also a musician and composer with an interest in Jazz, Country, and Urban Folk Blues. His vinyl album recorded in 1965 by MGM's VerveFolkways label entitled "Something New," received a Four Star rating by Billboard Magazine and has become a classic folk album.

Currently, Herb has three CD's to his credit. His 2010 release of "This Is the Time" garnered him an "Asante Award" from the City of New Orleans Asante Foundation.

Herb is an amateur historian and a dedicated community servant with a special interest in the education of children in literary and life skills.

To learn more about Herb visit: www.HerbMetoyer.com.

———

Prologue

When I started this project, my intent was to write a fiction-alized story about the matriarch of our family, Marie Thérèse "Coincoin" Metoyer and how she, a slave, gained her freedom and built one of the largest plantation conglomerates in Colonial Louisiana.

Much has already been written about Coincoin, but very little about the parents who instilled in her a desire to overcome her station. All I discovered about her parents were their names, and the fact that they were servants to *Louis Juchereau de St. Denis,* founder of Natchitoches, the oldest city in Louisiana. That being the case, I decided that if I told the story of *Louis Juchereau de St. Denis,* their master, I would be essentially tell-ing their story also. As a result, *Small Fires in the Sun* came into being as **Book I** of a trilogy concerning the birth, the rise and the fall of Coincoin's dynasty.

About The Natchez....

The first Europeans to encounter the Natchez were probably the remnants of Hernando de Soto's expedition in 1543. This group reported that as they passed a complex of some forty vil-lages on the banks of the Mississippi River during their return journey to Mexico, they were attacked and pursued for several days by a band of hostile Indians.

No other contact was reported until 1678, when René Robert Cavalier de La Salle completed his trip down the Mississippi River to its mouth. Eight years later, La Salle's assistant, Henri de Tonti, repeated the same journey. Both visited the Natchez without encountering any unusual problems. There was, how-ever, no prolonged contact with the Natchez until the broth-ers, Iberville and Bienville, planted France's first settlement in Louisiana in the year 1699.

All accounts, however minor, mentioned some facet of their unusual social order and physical features which was reported to be different from all other American Indians. The Natchez's skin tone was reported to be more bronze in hue as opposed to red and their facial features more handsome than other natives in the vicinity. Le Page Du Pratz in his journal, The History of Louisiana (1774) stated:

"The Natchez may then justly be supposed to be descended from some Phoenicians or Carthaginians who had been wrecked on the shores of South America. In which case, they might well be imagined to have but little acquaintance with the arts, as those who first landed would be obliged to apply all their thoughts to their immediate subsistence, and consequently would soon become rude and barbarous. Their worship of the eternal fire likewise implies their descent from the Phoenicians; for everybody knows that this superstition, which first took its rise in Egypt, was introduced by the Phoenicians into all the countries that they visited. The figurative stile, and the bold and Syriac expressions in the language of the Natchez, is likewise another proof of their being descended from the Phoenicians."

Because the Natchez were sun-worshipping headhunters who practiced a severe form of head-shaping, and often sacrificed children to their God, many other historians and observers speculate that they might have been distant descendants of the Maya or Aztec.

The most abundant source for the clay, palygorskite, used to make the Mayan Blue paint used for sacrificial rituals, is in the Southeastern United States.

The question of their origin will never be known. All we can say for certain is that they were distinctly different in every aspect from the other cultures of North America.

———

The Natchez were a matrilineal society composed of four classes: the ruling Sun Class, which included the sons and daughters of the Sun females; the Nobles, which included primarily the children of the Sun Class males, their families, and a few warriors of the War Chief rank; the Honored People, which included the families of the lowest class who had distinguished themselves in battle or some unusual service; and the lowest class, the Earth people[1], or Stinkards, as they were commonly referred to by the French.

Any person, male or female, could raise their station, and the station of their family, one level higher (but not to include the Sun Class) by sacrificing a small child at the death of a Great Sun. Their tenure, however, was limited to the span of their lives. At death, their family members automatically reverted to their previous level.

Custom required all persons, regardless of their station, to select mates from the bottom of the social order. This practice prevented close intermarriages and inbreeding without interrupting the charter bloodlines. Except for the children of the Sun Class females, all other children were born one class lower than that of the highest rank held by either parent. For this reason, the son of the chief, who is born a nobleman, was prohibited from serving as a Great Sun.

Since the Sun Class females were the procreators of the ruling class, they were given a great deal of latitude in the mate selection process. They chose mates from among the Earth People who were handsome, brave, and above all, intelligent. If a Sun Class female later discovered that her choice had been less than desirable, she was free to have her spouse killed or replaced with another. As her slave, her mate could not eat nor sleep in her presence. He never challenged her decisions, or offered advice, and was required to shout loud praises at her every remark.

Although the Sun females had no direct role in the government of the Nation, they did exert a strong, behind-the-scenes influence upon its activities. The older females were especially influential since they were responsible for selecting the successor to the position of Chief. This, in most cases, was accomplished well in advance so that the young incumbent could be molded and trained to accept his responsibilities at the proper

---

1. *The name "Earth People", used to identify the lowest Natchez class, was coined by the author as an alternative to the name "Stinkards", which I believe was a derogatory title used by the French to express their contempt for certain groups of unmanageable savages. Du Pratz also reported that the Natchez found this name offensive.*

time. This custom also prevented other problems that, in all probability, would have developed had such a delicate decision been delayed until the candidates reached adulthood. As children, innocent and free of jealousy, they were more apt to accept the judgment of the council without contest. As a result, many times, older brothers became servants to their younger sibling.

Besides their unique social order, the Natchez were also unique in the manner in which they constructed their lodges. A majority of the Indians of the area used branches to form a circular framework which they covered with skins or thatch. Natchez hovels were square with all of the saplings bent toward the center at the top to form a dome-shaped roof. Their larger buildings, such as their temple, utilized logs, 9 to 12 inches in diameter, buried upright in the ground to form a rectangular framework. Branches and small, slender saplings were then woven laterally between the logs and the intervals between them filled with *bousillage*, a mixture of mud, moss, straw, and deer hair.

While the outside walls were usually left rough or covered with cane mats, great care would be taken to smooth those on the inside. Larger saplings, covered with thatch, formed their dome-shaped roofs. Many of the structures were also whitewashed with lime or finely-ground, white, oyster shells. Because of the durability of their buildings, this basic method of construction was quickly adopted by the French and widely used throughout their settlements.

The Natchez community consisted of several villages from as few as twelve, by one account, to as many as forty as reported by de Soto. (*It seems that the number reported varied with the speed with which the traveler passed through their territory, as in the case of de Soto's men, who did so quite hurriedly.*)

I, however, suggest that the Natchez community may have been an empire of sorts at one time, and that de Soto's men were more accurate than inaccurate in their estimate. I base this theory, in part, on the fact that by the time the French dropped anchor in 1699, the Natchez Empire had split into at least three different tribes — the Natchez, the Avoyels, and the Taensa, all of whom spoke the unique Natchezan language. There is also the possibility that their numbers were reduced by diseases as a result of their initial contact with La Salle and de Tonti.

Be that as it may, only five known primary villages were still extant when the French arrived. These were — the Great Village, and the smaller villages of White Apple, The Hickories, Grigra, and Tiou.

The Great Village was the largest and served as the center of all major activities. It rested beside a small river called St. Catherine's Creek that emptied into the Mississippi River. The village was dominated by two huge structures perched on mounds eight-to-ten-feet high. One was the residence of the Great Sun, supreme ruler of the tribe, and the other, a larger one, was the Temple. Between the temple and the Great Sun's lodge was a plaza, a large, open area used for social activities. Clustered around the plaza were the lodges of the Suns and Nobles. Beyond that were the lodges of the general population.

The Great Sun was considered, in all respects, to be a God with absolute power over the life and death of his subjects. He served as a visible communication link between the earthbound and his celestial brother, the Sun. As such, his feet were never permitted to touch the ground. Whenever he had reasons to leave his quarters, he rode in a special litter chair or walked upon mats which were rolled out ahead of him by his servants.

Below the Great Sun were the War Chiefs. Each village had three or four. They were commanded by a Great War Chief, who was usually a blood brother or a close relative of the Great Sun. He and the War Chiefs were solely responsible for all matters relating to war and to the security of the tribe.

Responsibility for other matters concerning the government of the Natchez rested with a council of Noblemen (and women) with representation from the War Chiefs.

These arrangements freed the Great Sun from such routine activities and enabled him to devote his full attention to his primary duty — that of worshipping his celestial and spiritual brother, the Sun.

Of all the tribes that inhabited the Louisiana territory, the Natchez were probably the most independent. They displayed an affinity for the African slave and were quick to provide sanctuary to runaways, despite the laws of the French. Unlike the Choctaw, they also refused to assist the French in their political wars. For these reasons, they soon lost favor with the French.

Another item that I found especially intriguing was the custom that required the wife and servants of the Great Sun to accompany him in death. A similar custom existed in ancient Egypt and China. Like the Egyptians and the Aztec, the Natchez believed in an after-life and were concerned with the preservation of the dead, especially their leaders. But since the climate and humidity did not lend itself to mummification, the Natchez chose the next best solution, that of preserving the bones of their deceased. I suggest, too, that the building of earthen mounds might have been substituted for pyramids in a land where building stones were not readily available. Archaeological evidence also suggests that conch shells were used widely as currency for bartering and trading, much as it was in the primitive tribes of Africa. What connection, if any, that might have existed between these cultures, worlds apart, I dare not speculate. Suffice it to say, the Natchez were a special and distinct breed.

And... what might have been learned from them regarding their origin was lost when they were exterminated by the French in 1731.

There has been very little recorded about the Natchez, only bits and pieces, much of which is often contradictory. These bits and pieces, however, were enough to excite my imagination beyond bounds. In the process, I fell victim to their mystique, and, subsequently, developed a profound fondness for this savage band of noble heathens.

Herbert R. Metoyer, Jr.
Amateur Historian

The CHARACTERS

The French —

Louis Juchereau de St. Denis: A fearless adventurer, explorer, and founder of Natchitoches, the oldest city in Louisiana. Although he seeks material gain like most men of his day, he is a man of high ideals who has earned the respect of Indians and slaves alike. He believes in the church and family. But despite his salient character and good intentions, he is often plagued by many untimely setbacks.

Emanuelle de St. Denis: The compassionate, Spanish wife of St. Denis. Usually level headed, she can be very outspoken when prompted.

Jean Baptiste Le Moyne, Sieur de Bienville: Governor of Louisiana. Related to St. Denis through the marriage of his brother, Iberville, to St. Denis's sister. Haughty and egotistical, he rules with an iron hand. He is wise in some matters, ignorant in others. Prone to be spiteful if offended.

Etienne: A young French trapper who has fallen in love with the Natchez princess, Morning Sun. His allegiance is divided.

Commandant Chepart: Commandant of Fort Rosalie. He coveted the lands of the Natchez for his own use — lost his head in the process.

Marguerite: An obese murderess who escaped to the colony. She is coarse and vulgar. She hates Indians, especially the females who have taken French lovers. Her fate is tied to a burning tree.

Claudette: A former prostitute, condemned to plying her trade despite the fact that she yearns only for a husband and a family. She finally achieves her aspirations in the arms of a Natchez warrior.

———

The Natchez —

Two Dog: A teenage boy and one of several guardians responsible for maintaining the Perpetual Fire of his nation. He commits the one unpardonable sin — lets the fire go out. This act sets the stage of impending disaster for his tribe.

Morning Sun: A princess of the ruling Sun Class, and mother of the youth chosen to be the next chief of their tribe. She is haughty and high strung, and although she has a husband, she has fallen in love with xiii

the young Frenchman named *Etienne*. Her gravest concern is the preservation of her tribe.

Tattooed Serpent: Morning Sun's brother, the Great War Chief of the Natchez nation. He is shrewd and cunning. Yet, despite all his wisdom, he is unable to protect his people from the wrath of the French and the eventual annihilation of his tribe at a small lake in North Central Louisiana known today as *Lake Sang Pour Sang (Blood for Blood)*.

Black Hawk: Morning Sun's son, and the boy who would become the next chief.

Fani Mingo (Squirrel Chief) Coutee: A Choctaw War Chief who hires out to assist the French in their wars.

––––––

The Slaves –

Kiokera: Christian name François. A young boy brought to Louisiana in chains aboard the slave ship, Marianne. A favored slave living in the care of his protector, St. Denis. Although he is loyal and devoted, he yearns for freedom even if it means the death of his beloved master.

Mukta: Kiokera's former black slave-master aboard the slave ship, the Marianne. Un-expectantly, he is sold into slavery. He escapes through a peculiar chain of events to wage his own personal war against the French. He lives among the Natchez, who rename him Mukta No-Talk because he speaks with a hoarse whisper, the result of a throat wound received during a fight with Kiokera on the slave docks of Algiers, Louisiana. He seeks retribution.

Zolare: An older female slave in the service of St. Denis. She fell in love with François the moment he arrived from the dark Continent. She, however, is rebuked by François. Her enemies are age and time.

Marie Françoise: The young girl that Kiokera eventually marries. She is the maidservant to St. Denis's wife, Emanuelle.

––––––

Genesis

———

Small fires blaze where strangers gather
To share its warmth and space.
While I think of the road behind,
And how far we've traveled to reach this place

Silently, I listen as the Old Ones speak
Of ancient times, and places rare.
And I'm stricken with the fever,
For I long to visit there.

When the smoldering fire loses its brilliance,
Strangers, now friends, part to go their separate
way,
Circling the circled circle,
Each prompted in a programmed way,

To follow the retreating horizon,
To search each blessed day,
For that silent, mystic land
So far.. far.... away......

TABLE OF CONTENTS

March of the Calumet
(*Public Domain, The History of Louisiana , Le Page du Pratz, 1774)*

PART I

Cross Roads

A Slave Ship
(Herb Metoyer, 2009)

Chapter — One

May 1724 —

"LAND AHEAD! LAND, AHEAD TO PORT!" Mukta heard the crow nester yell above the noise of the gentle surf. "Louisianne!"

Somewhat expectantly, Mukta raised his large, muscular-gone-to-flab body from the short stool upon which he sat and slowly ambled toward the rough plank stairway that led from the lower deck of the Marianne, a hastily converted frigate. A few moments later, he emerged shielding his eyes from the brightness of the morning sun with his thick arms.

A beautiful day, he said to himself. *Almost too beautiful.* But then, landfall was always a beautiful sight, no matter what the conditions. He hated the sea and always would, even if he was forced to sail it for the rest of his life. But hopefully, his ordeal would end soon. And when that time came, he would jump ship, leave the bitch, Marianne, and return to his homeland deep in the interior of Africa.

Suddenly, he sensed something foreboding — something that sent an ominous chill coursing through his body and causing him to shudder despite the warmth of the morning sun. He lifted his nose and sniffed audibly. What remained afterward was a fleeting odor that reminded him of burning hair and rotting snake eggs. *Not good,* he said to himself. *Diablo, is it your presence I smell? If so, be gone. I'll have no business with you this day.*

Almost reverently, he reached down and touched the small leather pouch that he wore tied to the waistband of his filthy, canvas loincloth. Within it was his life — his past, present, and future; a few small gold trinkets and pieces of silver that he had managed to scavenge over the past five years. Droppings left behind by the crew. Someday, when the sack was full, he would jump the Marianne and return to his village a wealthy man. There, he would settle down, resume his life, take several wives, and father a hundred children. This was his dream, the only thing that gave purpose to his otherwise worthless existence.

But before he jumped ship, there were three dogs of Hades that he had marked to die. Three — he had sworn to kill with his bare hands. Mendoza, the "Portuguese," would be first. Then, Cecil, their homosexual cook, followed by the grand Capitaine John Thomas Fortierre. The Portuguese would die because he was the one who had gotten him drunk and shanghaied him into slavery five years ago. Cecil would die because the scurvy, little, rotten-tooth weasel would not give him his daily rations except in exchange for sexual favors. The Captain would die just because he happened to be Captain of the unholy Marianne.

With some remorse, he recalled the terror of waking from a drunken stupor to find himself shackled and chained in darkness, deep within the bowels of the Marianne. He was frightened and sick, and almost driven mad from the incessant slapping of the sea against the ship's hull. He could still hear the Portuguese and several others laughing at him in the shadows.

"Aye, matey, look what I catched me-self with a bottle of rum. What would have cost the Captain ten stout men and a few broken skulls, I catched with a small flask of rotgut."

"And right you are. An ape that size ought to bring a better than fair price on any block."

He had strained on his shackles, but it was useless. The irons were stout and strong. Finally, he gave up, his spirit crushed. In the shadows of the swinging lamps, several of the slaves began to discuss mutiny. A few days later, their plans were finalized, and the mutiny was set to take place the next time they were taken up on deck to exercise.

In the beginning, thoughts of freedom made his blood race. But soon after, the initial elation faded away. And the thought of a mutiny by slaves, who had no knowledge of the sea, or the instruments necessary to navigate its vast domain, frightened him even more than did his uncertain future as a slave. So, out of concern for his own safety, he warned the Captain, believing that the Captain would only alert the slaves that he was aware of their intent and thereby discourage any further attempts.

Nothing, however, could have prepared him for the slaughter that took place two days later. The Captain had not warned the slaves. Instead, he had prepared and lay in wait until the slaves made their move. Then, he and his officers swooped down, cutlasses swinging, and pistols firing aimlessly into the innocent and guilty alike. Within seconds, it was over.

Once the mutiny was quelled, the Captain brought everyone on deck and forced him, Mukta, against his will, and in view of all, to identify everyone who had participated. Then, he, along with the rest of the slaves, watched while bodies were whipped with *cats*, and hands, breasts, and penises were hacked off. And when that was finished, the still screaming souls were chained together and tossed from the sides of the ship into the shark-infested, blue-waters of Hell.

As compensation for his role in saving the Captain and his crew, he was made Master of the Slaves. His reward, however, was not without a price. The burden of guilt weighed heavily on his mind for a long time. Many times in the night, when the wind was just right, and usually at the third glass of the dog's watch, he was still plagued by the cries of those he had doomed. And each time he lay his huge body down to rest, he was forced again to watch in horror, the visions of black, faceless bodies struggling to stay afloat in a fast reddening sea.

As time passed, however, so did much of his guilt, but not all. Most of it, he supposed, would remain with him for the rest of his life. Normally, he was not a violent man. He was, however, a survivor, doing what he had to do, when he had to do it, in order to persist. At one stage in his life, he was a humble and gentle herder of cows, trying to survive on the vast, arid savannas of Africa. Content, he was, without malice toward neither man, beast, or God — not even when the beasts killed and plundered his herd, or when the Gods held back the blessed life-sustaining rains.

The Marianne and her crew, however, soon altered that phase of his life. He was something else now. Something more in the eyes of some, something less in the eyes of others. Yet, the fact that he was only one small step removed from the fate of those subservient to him did not, in any way, diminish the zeal with which he pursued his duties. Any compassion he might have had for his unfortunate charges had long ago been secreted away in a place inaccessible to him and mortal man.

But, because of his heavy hand, the Marianne was never again threatened with mutiny, not once in all the five years he had served as her Slave Master. Usually, by the time they had completed a crossing, even the noblest of warriors had been reduced to something less than a sniveling pup.

So, it was with pride that he went about his task deep in the bowels of the superannuated vessel. The Captain ruled topside, but below decks — he, Mukta, was supreme.

"Channel ahead! Fifteen degrees right, then straight as a boar's prick," the crow nester yelled to the helmsman.

Mukta raised his head and looked up at the crow's nest, resting high, near the top of the foremast.

"All hands on deck," shouted the boatswain. And suddenly, the deck was filled with hurried activity as the swarthy, ragged, unkempt seamen hauled in the yards of mainsail, coiled the rigging, and stowed the spit-kids tightly beneath the spar deck. Only the small topsails and an aft spanker were left aloft to propel the vessel up the channel to the mouth of the Mississippi.

Mukta glanced out over the starboard side and noticed the deep emerald and blue color of the sea slowly changing into a soft muddy brown, a sure sign that they had entered the correct channel that would lead them up the illusive and mysterious river.

This would be his second trip into the French port of New Orleans. Most of the time, they sold their slave cargo in Cuba, or Haiti, and sometimes along the Eastern seaboard. Yet, of all the places he had visited, he found the Louisiana coast the most intriguing — especially the swamps and marsh lands, crowded with thick growths of willows, mimosas, tupelo gums, ungainly pines, and marsh elder. Cattails, great cane breaks, and palmetto thickets grew rampant along the water's edge. And interspersed within, were giant cypress trees with feathery, green foliage and cone-shaped trunks that rested on huge knobby roots that reminded him of someone's knees. Hanging from their branches were long masses of gray moss-like hair that everyone called "Capuchin's beard". He had no idea who Capuchin was, but the sound of the name seemed more than fitting.

The wind caused the topsails to snap, shattering the stillness, and rousing flights of pelicans, herons, swans, and egrets from their nests and feeding grounds in the nearby marshes. Mukta marveled at the spectacular sight, thousands of water fowl of every species, stretching their long necks and filling the hazel-blue sky. When they were gone, he stretched his massive arms and scanned the shoreline, hoping to spot an alligator or some other type of reptile sunning or swimming lazily among the lilies and irises.

Suddenly, the hair on his neck stood like the hackles of a dog. He turned quickly to see why, and found the cold, gray eyes of Captain Fortierre staring directly at him.

"How many dead?" the Captain asked solemnly.

"Four," Mukta replied.

"Damn. One would think my job was to feed the sharks, rather than make a livelihood. Well, step lively and get the bastards over the side. We'll be in port soon."

"*Oui*," Mukta grunted as he turned and lumbered back down into the hold. He had almost forgotten to perform his most important daily chore, that of throwing the bodies of those who had died during the night over the side.

At the bottom of the stairway, he closed his eyes tightly to adjust them to the darkness. Then, he crossed to a short ladder and crawled up into the t'ween deck. He stopped before a young mother and attempted to take the dead body of a small boy from her arms. The woman resisted, cursing, and calling him vile names. Then, she made the mistake of spitting directly into his face. Without another thought, Mukta drew back his massive arm and swatted her heavily across the mouth. She released the child quickly, and just as quickly, buried her bloody face in her shaking hands. Mukta then picked up the cold, stiff, little body and carried it topside leaving its mother to cry softly in the darkness.

Once topside, he avoided looking at the child's face. In fact, he never looked any of the dead in the face. Not that he was afraid or felt any pity for them. It was just a matter of doing his job, and he could do that very well without having to look into their glassy eyes, or their infected, blotched, scaly, black faces. Handling their stinking, maggot-ridden bodies was enough — *wasn't it?*

He was just about to pitch the body over the side, when a wheel pin struck him suddenly, and hard, across the upper muscles of his left arm. He yelped, dropped the body to the deck, and spun around into a defensive posture. He cowered immediately, however, once he saw it was the Portuguese.

"Stupid swine. The Captain would carve your black rump if he knew you were throwing his good irons to the fish," the Portuguese said, pointing to the single, rusty shackle still fixed to the child's ankle.

Mukta looked down, grunted in acknowledgement, then stooped to remove it, his eyes watchful, should the Portuguese decide to strike him again. The Portuguese snarled, then sauntered off. After he was out of range, Mukta picked up the dead body and heaved it angrily over the side. *Yes, Portuguese, you will be the first to die. Then, I will drain my bladder down your slimy throat,* he promised himself as he returned to the hold of the gracious Marianne.

As Mukta went about his tasks, he was ever mindful of evil eyes staring at him in the darkness from every quarter, watching his every move. *Stupid bunch of mongrels.* It wasn't his fault that they were in chains. And it wasn't his fault that he was the one tasked with the responsibility of beating some sense and respect into their black carcasses. Fate had done that, not him. Didn't they realize that he was trapped just as they were? That he was confined to the hold of a stinking ship when his heart yearned for home and Niema, the girl he was supposed to marry? *No,* he supposed not. Well, it did not matter. It still would not change one thing. As the wind blows, so do the sands of the desert. Besides, they deserved no better, he rationalized. *And you, you deserve less than that,* he said with his eyes as he glanced over at a young Mali boy who called himself Kiokera. What fool in his right mind would beg aboard a slaving vessel for a look-see. *Well, you got your look-see all right — a look-see at Hell.*

Mukta did not like the boy. In fact, for reasons he could not adequately explain, he hated the boy almost as much as he did the Portuguese. Maybe, it was because of the embarrassment he had sustained on the day the boy was first lured aboard — the way the youth had kicked him in the groin. He could still hear the crew laughing now. Then too, maybe, it was the boy's eyes, the way they slanted like a snake's. *Evil, want-to-do-me-harm eyes.* Evil eyes, waiting in the dark. *For what? For me to fall down the steps and break my damn neck?* Mukta chuckled to himself at the thought.

When he had finished throwing the last body over the side, he returned to his stool and sat down weightily to rest his sweating body. A large, thick-furred rodent caught his eye. He watched unconcerned as it crawled slowly in and around the huge hand-hewn timbers that formed the ribs of the bloated vessel.

When it was out of sight, his attention shifted slowly to a young girl lying, unchained, on her side near the forward bulkhead. Naked from the waist up, her dark reddish skin glowed amber in the sunlight that filtered from above through the cracks in the floor of the deck. Quietly, a subtle warmth settled in his groin and slowly spread throughout his body. With deft hands, he reached down and massaged himself as he surveyed her well-proportioned body, her full breasts standing like they had been carved from ebony, the outline of her ample buttocks, tightly wrapped and straining against the small piece of broadcloth that barely covered her nakedness.

Silently, he wished that she could have been his own, or someone like her. This one, however, would never do for a mate. This one had been ruined. Barely a week out to sea, the Captain ordered him to bring the frightened girl up to the quarterdeck where he ravaged her. To make matters worse, the Captain had forced him to stand and watch, knowing that his balls were aching and burning like fire for want of a woman.

After that, it seemed as if every other day, he was directed to bring her topside where other officers and privileged crew members took their pleasure. It happened so often, that he stopped bothering to replace her chains. She wasn't the only one forced to submit. They did it to some of the others, too. The younger, the better. She, however, quickly became their favorite, primarily because the little bitch had started to enjoy her excursions. And before long, she was nothing but a wicked, little conniving whore, using her woman's wit indiscriminately to maintain her favor among the slimy bunch of lice-ridden cutthroats. This had both surprised and angered him — to see her smiling and grinning up in their faces and switching her tail around like some bitch-dog in heat. Then, what really angered him further was the fact that the girl had rejected his advances, forgetting that he was the one, in the beginning, who had nursed her bruises and tried to make her comfortable after her initial ordeal. Well, he took care of that. *Had to knock her around a little to get her attention.* But once that was accomplished, from then on, it was nothing but milk and honey. *Milk and honey.*

Normally, he was not allowed to enjoy liberties with the slave women in his care. That right was reserved only for the Captain and a chosen few. But occasionally, when the need was severe enough, he accepted the risk and stole a few moments of pleasure. Most of the time, however, he was forced to obtain relief through the services of Cecil, their homosexual cook. He detested this liaison with a passion. But had he refused, Cecil would have withheld his daily rations of salt pork and biscuits. Just thinking about the act made him sick to his stomach. And there were many times, when he was laboring over the cook's, *red-like-a-monkey's backside,* that he had to restrain himself from snapping the filthy, little weasel's neck — *like a chicken's.*

The throbbing urgency of the turgid growth in his loins again demanded his attention. Casually, he glanced up the stairs. The moment was opportune. All hands were occupied on deck. And if he hurried, he could take his pleasure now, without undue risk.

He stood up, glanced quickly up the stairway again, then made his way over the bodies to where the girl lay. She looked up at him apprehensively, her arm half raised as if she expected him to strike her. Then, her eyes dropped to the pulsing protrusion beneath his loincloth, and he could see that she knew what he wanted. Without prompting, she rolled onto her back submissively and raised her knees. Mukta smiled in satisfaction as he stroked his hugeness into a hard mass.

Well, my cunning, little she-devil, tomorrow it will be some other bewitched fool who will be praying at your dark, sacred altar. Then, he lowered his huge body awkwardly between her dark thighs and rubbed the head of his soul across her moist portal. Suddenly, he plunged deeply. She groaned in pain, but did not attempt to escape. Instead, she gritted her teeth, forced herself to relax and following thereafter, was the slapping sound of flesh upon flesh — a sound not unlike the snap of the wind against a high-flying canvas sail. *Milk and honey. Nothing but, milk and honey....*

Kiokera lay on his back, his hands shackled behind and above his head. Silently, he watched the motion of Mukta's huge, ashy-black rump rising, and flaring between the girl's outstretched limbs; his obscene grunting and snorting not unlike that of a wild boar rooting in the bush.

Such a sight, under different circumstances, would have started the sap flowing through his fifteen-year-old body. But at the moment, all he could think of was the aching in his swollen joints and the burning pain centered around his rubbed-raw wrist and ankles. His buttocks were numb. He attempted to turn over onto his stomach, but his rusty chains made it difficult. Giving up on the idea, he changed his mind in favor of his side, positioning his head carefully in order to keep his face out of the dried vomit he had deposited there several times during the voyage.

On one side of him lay Tuanu, another boy from a village several miles west of his own. Tuanu had been having a difficult time, and several times during the voyage he was sure the boy had died. Diarrhea had drained his body of all fluids, and now, all he did was sleep.

While he felt a deep compassion for Tuanu, all he could feel toward himself was blinding anguish. Anguish that was born of his own stupidity. Because, unlike Tuanu, he had not been run down, chained, and dragged aboard the Marianne. He had walked aboard willingly and of his own accord — like a lamb right into the mouth of the lion's den. How he wished his parents had never moved from Mali to live on the West Coast of Africa.

He had been fishing at the time, riding the gentle swells of the surf, when the big ship glided into view and dropped anchor several hundred yards offshore. For a while, he had sat and watched as the men went about their duties, furling the sails and securing the rigging. Afterwards, several swarthy sailors lowered long boats into the water and paddled toward the shore with what he assumed were casks for water.

Finally, curiosity got the best of him. So, he pulled in his nets and paddled closer for a better view. He was awed by the size of the vessel, its length and breadth more than ten times the length and breadth of the largest canoe he had ever seen. Barnacles, other clinging sea life, and green algae covered the hull near the water line. Dry, aged, pitch oozed from the cracks along the edges of the long lengths of planking. And painted in green, on both sides of the bow, behind and below the hand-carved, weather-beaten image of a woman's head whose eyes stared sadly out to sea were the words, *Marianne*.

He heard laughter and looked up to observe several rugged-looking seamen leaning over the bulwark.

"Ahoy, down there," he heard one say who spoke his tongue. "Come aboard, if you like and see what a real canoe looks like."

Kiokera smiled and waved back at the seaman. He had seen tall ships like this several times before, drifting silently and majestically along the coast with their yards of off-white sails filled with a stiff breeze. He, however, had never seen one up close, not like this. So, when the opportunity to actually go aboard presented itself, he could not resist. Elated, he paddled quickly alongside and climbed the rope that had been thrown over the side for that purpose.

The friendly seamen helped him up and over, then stood back and watched amused as he wandered open-mouthed about the holy-stone scoured deck. Occasionally, one would say something to the other in a tongue he did not understand. Then, they would look at him and laugh.

He was gazing up into the rigging supported by a tree-tall mast, when a huge black fist slammed into his neck just above the shoulder from behind. He went down heavily. He was scrambling to his knees when he saw the frightening giant for the first time, large as two men, with huge gargoyle-like eyes, his black, sweaty body glistening in the heat of the glaring sun. He jumped to his feet and sprinted for the sides. But, several seamen gathered quickly and blocked his escape. Trapped, he stopped and turned again to face the stalking monster of a man. He waited on guard, and when Mukta was in perfect range, he closed his eyes and kicked with every ounce of strength his body could muster. Mukta groaned, grabbed his groin, and doubled to his knees in pain.

He was about to sprint away again, when someone else struck him with a club across his back, almost cracking the bones of his shoulder blades. He went down again, crying out loudly in pain. Then, through the fog, he watched as the angry giant picked up a short length of rope with a knot in one end and swung. On the first blow, the knot struck him beside his face and tore open the insides of his mouth. Unable to do anything else, he crawled into a ball, covered his head with his arms, and remained there until mercifully, unconsciousness came and rescued him....

From that day forth, his life had been a living Hell. One fueled by the flames generated by the ever-growing hatred that was shared equally between him and his black slave master. And while he lay aching in the steaming void, reeking of unwashed bodies, urine, vomit, and feces, most of his waking hours were spent conjuring up ways for Mukta to die. Sometimes, it was by an axe. Sometimes, impalement. Sometimes at the feet of a herd of elephants or in the mouth of a starving lion. And sometimes... it seemed as if Mukta sensed his thoughts. For on those occasions, and for no other apparent reason, Mukta would suddenly turn and send his whip snaking out to bite him in the darkness like a horned viper.

Still, he dreamed. He had once seen a harpoon in the hands of a seamen. It was this wicked-looking instrument that became the favorite weapon of his fantasies. Deep down, however, he knew he would never get the opportunity to do such a thing. And even if he did, he doubted that he could actually take another's life. But, thinking about the possibility helped. It made the time pass, and took his thoughts off the pain and misery of himself and the others around him.

Suddenly, he heard Mukta's groans taking on a higher pitch.

Wearily, he turned to watch the big black's wide hips flailing away between the girls far-flung legs, gaining tempo with each crushing blow. Abruptly, Mukta's body came to a straining stop. The muscles corded along his neck and rolled up the back of his bald head. Then, he released a long, tortured groan and fell away limp.

For a moment, Kiokera stared at Mukta in open contempt, his anger swelling and growing. Soon, he was retreating again into his fantasy world to conjure up yet another way to rid the earth of monsters like... Mukta.

———

Milk and honey, Mukta said to himself as he lay between the girl's legs, resting and basting himself. And when the basting was done, he arose, wiped the sweat from his brow, and walked away on legs like shaky pillars. He felt them before he turned to see them... *Eyes. Evil snake-eyes, staring, always staring.*

He stopped, looked at the boy and scowled. He considered putting the whip to his young ass again, but then decided that they were too close to their journey's end. Instead, he just smiled at the boy contemptuously and continued his way back to the bottom of the steps. There, he turned his face up and breathed deeply of the fresh sea air from above, momentarily forgetting the ghoulish odors of human evacuations and rotting flesh that permeated the bowels of the lady Marianne.

Yet, despite the air's refreshing effect, he suddenly found himself wishing they were back at sea, headed in the opposite direction. Something wasn't right. Above, he could see dark clouds sliding beneath the summer sun. In the distance, he could hear the somber rumble of thunder. Something was different about this day. *Something bad — not good*, he said to himself. *Diablo, stay your distance. Do not pester Mukta this day....*

———

Chapter — Two

Two Dog sat half asleep on the dirt floor of the Natchez Temple watching the hypnotic flames of the perpetual fire. At fifteen-summers-old, he was the youngest of the seven guardians assigned the duty of maintaining it. They were supervised by a priest they all referred to as the *"Old Guardian"* in his presence, and *"Old Frog-eye"* behind his back.

At the moment, he was alone. Four of the guardians had gone into the forest to replenish their stock of hickory and oak logs. The two most senior guardians and the priest had gone with their chief, the Great Sun, and the Great War Chief to the Natchez village of White Apple.

Normally, the four youngest guardians maintained the supply of wood while the more senior guardians usually sat around watching the fire, playing games with sticks or rocks, or telling tall tales. This day, however, he had not been feeling well, and for this reason, the "Old Guardian" had decided to leave him in charge. This suited him just fine. He didn't like foraging in the forest anyway... *Too many ticks and other jumping vermin about.* Smiling to himself at his good fortune, he brushed his long, stringy, unkempt hair back from his slender, gaunt face, bit into a half ripe apple, and relaxed in the shadows of the smoky, ancient temple.

The temple of the Natchez empire was a large, rectangular structure 30-feet wide and 60-feet long with walls that stood 10-feet high. In spite of its size, there was only one small entrance. Above the entrance perched three handcrafted, flat-planed, wooden eagles painted red and white. One was in the center at the apex of the roof, and one on each side of the doorway.

To enter the Temple, one had to pass through a break in the mud, palisade wall that surrounded it. Perched on stakes embedded in the mud wall were the skulls of enemy warriors whose sightless eyes watched the perimeter guardedly. In piles to the right of the passageway were the excess skulls for which there were no stakes, and to the left, stacks of short lengths of hickory and oak firewood. This wood was used to sustain the perpetual fire.

Between the wall and the front entrance of the temple rested a large, round, wooden block. Braided around its base was the hair taken from the scalps of enemy warriors. Upon the top of the block, more braids had been woven to form a facsimile of a flat basket. During the spring, flowers, seeds, eggs, and eagle feathers were placed in the braided basket; during the harvest season, offerings of maize, hominy, berries, and melons; and during the winter, nuts, and small portions of dried fish and wild game.

The inside of the temple was divided into two parts. The center of the first part, and the larger, contained the fire. Further to the rear, was a crude, hand-hewn altar upon which rested the sacred calumet and several other religious artifacts which included a two-foot-high figurine of a pregnant woman, a mummified frog, two chalices, a leather tobacco pouch, and five arrows with golden tips. Hanging from the wall, suspended by two leather thongs, was a large wooden disk, two-feet in diameter. This disk was highly polished and painted to resemble the sun with red and yellow rays radiating from its center. On each side of the disk, on pedestals, were fire pots filled with bear oil. They also burned both day and night.

Along the walls of the first and the second part were shelves upon which nestled the bones of previous Great Suns with those of their wives and servants stored neatly in meticulously woven split-cane baskets. Strange red and white markings in a language known only to the Old Guardian identified each.

In order to sustain the fire, a chute had been constructed at a sixty-degree angle. It held short logs, two- to three-feet in length, end to end. As one log burned away, another automatically fell into its place. It was the guardian's sacred duty to keep the fire burning.

Failure to do so, by law, resulted in the death of all, including the high priest.

According to legend, the fate of the Natchez depended upon this flame. As long as it burned, they would prosper. Two Dog wasn't sure if he believed the legend or not. The fire burned continuously, so there was no way of verifying its validity. Not to say that he was inclined to find out, he was just mildly curious like all young boys and wondered sometimes... *Just what would happen if, for some reason, the stinking fire did go out.*

Off in the distance, he heard thunder. It was the rainy season, and numerous thundershowers were to be expected for the next several weeks. *Good,* he said to himself. *Maybe, the rain will cool things down some.*

During the winter, attending the fire wasn't so bad. But during the summer, it was the worst job in the world. The heat within the mud walls was almost unbearable, and the temple felt more like an earthen oven deep inside the bowels of Hell rather than a hallowed resting place for the dead.

Still, he supposed as he glanced around the wall at the baskets filled with bleached-white bones, it wasn't the worst job around. The job of a Turkey Buzzard man had to be at the bottom of the heap. When a Great Sun or his wife died, they were laid out in the dead house or buried until their bodies could decay. Then, the bone picking Turkey Buzzard men would go to work using their cane or stone knives and long, claw-like fingernails to remove as much of the flesh as possible. From there, the bones would be taken in cane baskets and placed on anthills. Three days later, when the ants finished, the bones would be spotlessly white. No, there was no way he would do that job. Just the thought made him want to puke.

He really wished that he could have been born into the Sun class, the highest of the four classes in their society. Then, he would really have it made with full-time servants and anything else he wanted. But that was out of the question. To be a Sun, you had to be born one. He had been born an *Earth Person,* the lowest of the low. So low, that the land-stealing Frenchmen who wandered up and down the Mississippi like deadly river serpents often called them

Stinkards. To escape their birth status, his mother decided to donate his services to fill a vacancy on the guardian staff. This act elevated him and his mother up one step to the level of the *Honored People*. This was about as high as a guardian could expect to go without becoming the high priest. Beyond that, only the most courageous warriors could ascend to the next higher rank of the *Noble People*, and that took a lot of tattoos — one for each enemy head brought back for the temple wall.

All in all, he had not done too bad as a guardian. The most he had to do was go out and cut wood every other day, and he could live with that well enough.

Two Dog's eyes began to grow heavy and he found it increasingly difficult to remain awake. Drowsily, he reached over and poked into the fire with his poking-stick, moving the embers about and watching the sparks ascend erratically toward the rafters like swarms of reckless fireflies.

A gentle rain began to fall. So, he lay back on his mat and listened to the light, rhythmic pattern that sounded like thousands of tiny feet dancing upon the thatched roof. It was peaceful and relaxing. So peaceful, that he soon fell fast asleep....

———

Somewhere in the vicinity, lightning struck, and the mud walls of the temple trembled, startling Two Dog awake. There was an unusual smell in the air, not unlike burning feathers. He shook himself fully awake, glanced quickly about, then panicked. The fire was almost out. One of the logs in the chute was stuck and had not fallen as it was rigged to do. *Just in time,* he thought smugly as he adjusted the log. *A few moments more... and I would have been standing neck-deep in dog dooky.*

That crisis abated, and thankful that *Old Frog-eye* had not been there to witness the little mishap, Two Dog removed a piece of apple skin from his widely spaced teeth and settled back down on his cane mat.

Several peaceful moments passed. Then, Two Dog noticed

that the wind was slowly growing in intensity. Minutes later, it was randomly lifting the thatch from its sampling anchors and allowing moisture to enter the sacred place. Several drops struck the fire and exploded — popping like over-roasted hickory nuts. Two Dog sat up, mildly concerned now. This type of trouble, he did not need. Silently, he poised on his haunches and watched those leaks closest to the fire. They did not appear to be getting any worse. Certain now that it was only a moderate shower that would soon pass (*and wishing it would*), he allowed himself to relax.

He was just on the verge of falling asleep again when he discerned a distant, strange noise, one that he had never heard before — like a herd of horses or a swarm of locusts headed in his direction. Its magnitude frightened him. He got up, walked to the single entrance, and peered out. The rain was now falling in torrents and the day was dark as any night. He could see nothing.

Without any further warning, the storm struck like an angry bear slamming into the side of the temple. The wind howled, ripped the thatch from the roof, and scattered debris everywhere. Rain fell freely into the temple through the huge gaping holes and lashed meanly at the fire. Outside, he could hear trees groaning in pain as their roots were yanked from the soil, their branches snapping like twigs. And beneath the mask of the storm's fury, faintly discernible, he could hear screams and wailing from the village.

For a moment, he was disoriented, with no idea of what he should do next to protect the fire. *Where is everyone?* he wondered. *Can't they see it's raining hard enough to put this stupid fire out.*

For lack of something better to do, he started spinning around and around, turning on his heels, his face and severely sloped head lifted into the darkness and howling repeatedly like a lone wolf in distress, hoping that someone would hear and come to his aid. He grew dizzy, so he abandoned his spinning. When he came to a stop, he happened to notice the large altar. Frantically, he rushed to it and swept the religious artifacts off with the back of his arm. Then, gathering all the strength his young body could muster and still howling, he dragged the heavy, hand-hewn object to a position above the fire. It helped some, but the wind and rain continued to take their toll.

Where is everybody?... Damn-it! Why don't they come and help me? he said to himself in anger and frustration as he attempted again to nurse the fire. *I never wanted this woman's work, anyway. This was my crazy-assed mother's idea. I wanted to be a warrior.... And where is that old, frog-eyed, know-everything priest? This is his job. All I was supposed to do was cut the fucking wood.*

Scrambling about the muddy floor and howling painfully, he did what he could to preserve the fire. He tried to protect it with his thin body. He tried adding more pine kindling, but the kindling was too wet and would not burn. He tried to keep the embers stirred with his stick; tried to blow life into them with his slender, hollow reed. But, his efforts were hopeless. The last flame flickered, then died. The fire... was out.

Two Dog looked down at the soot and ashes that covered his half-naked body and fell to his bony knees. He was exhausted, and his howling now was nothing more than a hopeless whimper.

The pain of failure was excruciating. In resignation, he watched as dark, threatening shadows emerged from the corners and cracks, and drifted across the floor of the ancient temple like angry ghosts demanding revenge and clamoring for his blood. He was frightened and his heart pounded wildly with fear. He had done all he could. Still, he had failed. Soon, his head would be added to the growing pile of skulls stacked outside the entrance. One more among so many others. The Turkey Buzzard men were probably sharpening their claws at that very moment. No, he supposed, there would be no legends of bravery told about him around the fires, nor about anyone in his family. His name was destined to live in disgrace. All he could hope for was that his death would be swift and painless. Silently, he began to cry, his head bent in humility as the wind and rain lashed at his unprotected body.

Suddenly, it was over. The storm passed. Then, as an after thought, it stopped, reached back, and slapped the temple with one last parting blow. The ensuing gust of wind knocked several of the split-cane baskets filled with bones to the ground. Unexpectedly, a hollow-eyed skull rolled menacingly between Two Dog's knees. He yelped and scrambled back in terror, his rear bouncing like a retreating crayfish.

It was then that he realized that maybe some of the cane baskets on the lower shelves might still be dry. With a spark of hope, he leaped to his feet and raced along the walls, searching the shelves for dry baskets. He found several. Working hurriedly, he dumped their contents to the ground, ripped them apart, and dropped the pieces into one that was only slightly wet. Then, he fell to his knees and searched among the ashes until he found several smoldering embers with faint red cores. Carefully, he gathered them up with two sticks and dropped them into the basket on top of the shredded cane. He next searched for his slender reed, found it, put it to his mouth, and patiently nursed the coals until they were hot enough to ignite. Suddenly, the fire blazed. Two Dog was jubilant. He howled in joy as he quickly added more of the cane strips. Soon, the fire was hot enough to dry and ignite the pine kindling.

Next, he searched deep into the firewood pile and found a relatively dry log which he split into several smaller pieces with his adze. He was adding them to the flames when the Old Guardian priest entered. Two Dog froze momentarily, then hung his head in shame as the Old Guardian surveyed the chaos in silence. Water was everywhere. Bones, thatch, and debris littered the muddy floor. Uncertain and still frightened, Two Dog slowly looked up at the Priest, his trembling mouth agape — his large, doe-eyes pleading hopeless innocence.

"I see, but I fear my eyes are deceiving me. Everything has been destroyed," the Old Guardian stated angrily as he surveyed the devastation.

As he did so, Two Dog lowered his head in shame. Tears flowed freely from his eyes as he waited for his death sentence to be announced.

After a moment, the Old Guardian came alongside and placed his hand on the boy's shoulder. "It is truly a miracle that you were able to keep the fire burning in all this storm — a miracle. I will speak to the Great Sun and tell him of your bravery and how you have distinguished yourself this day. Your courage has saved our nation from certain disaster. Many generations will remember this day and speak of you with great honor."

Two Dog, with some effort, managed to force a meek smile to his face, but inside he was still frightened and hurting. He knew — he had failed. The fire had gone out, and now, despite the comforting words of the Old Guardian, he could hear the silent voice of impending doom ringing in his ears like thunder. Suddenly, he felt very cold. Uncontrollably, he began to shiver as wave, after wave of violent chills passed through his frail, child-like body.

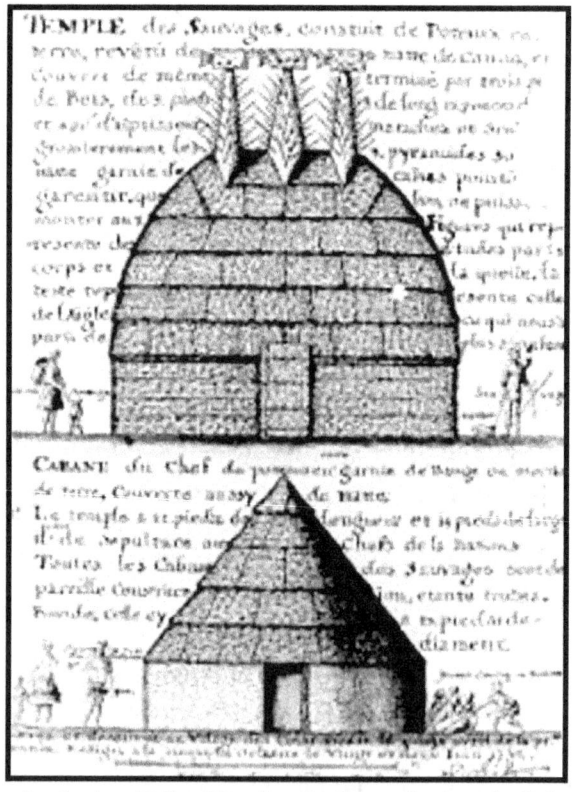

Acolapissa Tribe Temple, similar to the type built by the Natchez. Natchez buildings, however, were square with a dome roof.
(Public domain. The Great Temple and chiefs cabin as drawn by Alexandre de Batz, circa 1735.)

Chapter — Three

ST. DENIS YAWNED, STRETCHED HIS ACHING LIMBS, then dipped his oar back into the muddy Mississippi River. It was not the best day for traveling. Clouds hung low on the horizon. His clothes were damp from the heavy moisture in the air, and he shuddered as the coldness passed through his body. He wasn't sure if he would ever get used to the weather in this godforsaken place. One minute it was stifling hot. The next, a squall or severe thunderstorm would appear suddenly and boldly upon the horizon. Many times, hurricanes hovered just off the coast, waiting to ravage the countryside at the least provocation.

Still, in spite of his complaints, he was quick to admit that he was possessed by the magic of the Louisiana wilderness and fascinated by its unpredictable whims.

Louis Juchereau de St. Denis was Commandant of the French Post of *St. Jean Baptiste des Natchitoches,* a post he had built on the western edge of the Louisiana territory to retard the eastward expansion of the Spanish. He, his valet, and a French soldier were enroute to *Nouvelle Orléans* to visit his sister's brother-in-law and, if possible, to purchase a few more slaves for his plantation.

His valet, Medar Jalot, had been with him for more than twenty years. Besides attending to his personal needs, Jalot served as a surgeon in war and kept everyone entertained with his quick wit and practical jokes. Jalot was also a great storyteller, and he enjoyed telling tales about their many adventures. And with the aid of a little wine, he was not above exaggerating to obtain the desired effect.

While Jalot was of a short and stocky build, St. Denis stood more than six feet tall, almost twelve inches above the height of the average man. Usually, he dressed in brilliant colors that tended to accent his forty-seven-year-old stature. Although he did not consider himself particularly handsome, he knew he presented a very imposing figure — a fact which served to his advantage on any number of occasions, especially where Indians were concerned.

Ahead in the light mist along the east bank of the river, he noticed the obscure details of several forms taking shape — three Indians, young ones from their posture. Two were armed with lances and bows, and the third with a firearm.

Jalot, who sat in the center, noticed them, too. "Stinkards ahead on the left," he shouted quietly.

"I see them. Looks like three. You count more?"

"Only three, so far. Should we give them a wider berth?"

"No. Hold our course. No good to let them think we're shy. Just keep your eyes open and your weapon close," St. Denis directed.

Although most Indians were peaceful at the moment, St. Denis knew that one could not be too careful. While he respected, even admired some of them, he knew from experience that they could be as unpredictable as the weather and twice as treacherous. He would never forget the time he arranged for the Natchitoches, who lived in the community surrounding his post, to live with the Acolapissa tribe on Bayou Castine while he was away on an expeditionary war against the Alabamas. This had been necessary because the gentle, humble Natchitoches had become totally dependent upon him and could not have sustained themselves during his absence. Both tribes had been friends of long standing. But, when he returned after the war to pick up his favored Natchitoches and move them back to his post, the Acolapissa went into a jealous rage and slew over half of them before he and his soldiers could react. They did manage, however, to save the chief and the remainder of the small tribe. From that moment on, he had found it increasingly difficult to trust any Indian, no matter how innocent he appeared to be.

As St. Denis and his party approached, the Indians paused and watched in curious silence, their faces emotionless and, except for an occasional shift of weight from one foot to the other, their bodies were perfectly erect and still.

"Hard to tell if they're friendly or not," said Jalot.

"No matter. Three of them — three of us," St. Denis said as he sat upright and assumed his most commanding posture. Quickly, he adjusted the fringe of silver braid that draped his broad shoulders, hoping the charm of his scarlet breeches and yellow surtout would be enough to impress the wily savages.

When they were almost abreast of the Indians, St. Denis smiled and raised his hand casually, palm out, in a traditional greeting. The Indians neither acknowledged, nor replied to the gesture, but continued to watch, somewhat aloof and detached.

"We got us some arrogant bastards here," Jalot said under his breath.

"Looks that way," St. Denis replied.

"Us in this narrow-assed boat and them high on the bank is not the best place to be should they decide to start something," added the soldier who sat in the front.

"I know. Just ignore them and keep your course," St. Denis replied as he lowered his arm apprehensively and brushed back a lock of his auburn hair that had fallen over his close-set eyes.

From the tattoos on their bodies and their slightly pointed heads, St. Denis readily identified them as Natchez. Tattoos were the Natchez fashion for displaying their war medals. Each time a brave killed an enemy, he earned a tattoo. Since the number of tattoos determined one's position in their military hierarchy, young braves, eager to prove their prowess and courage, were easily provoked.

St. Denis was still trying to second-guess their intentions when, suddenly, he realized that one of the braves had a freshly-severed, human head suspended from his waistband, its bloody neck stump still wet. Alarmed, he glanced down quickly to reassure himself that his musket was within easy reach.

Not wanting the Indians to know how deeply he was concerned, he glanced quickly again at the swinging trophy and determined that it was the head of another Indian. And for that, he was silently thankful.

"Looks like the Stinkards have been out playing with their axes again," Jalot stated with distaste.

"Well, let's hope they got their quota for the day," St. Denis replied.

They drifted past the stolid Indians uneventfully, so St. Denis turned his attention back to maneuvering his craft. He was about to say something more to Jalot, when a deafening howl suddenly split the heavy moisture-laden air. St. Denis yelped and lunged forward, crushing Jalot and almost upsetting the narrow craft — expecting at any moment to hear Natchez arrows whistling through the air.

After a long second of silence, Jalot grunted and said, a little perturbed, "Damn it, Louis, could you ease up a bit? I need to catch a breath."

Sheepishly, St. Denis gripped his musket, raised his head cautiously, and looked back over his shoulder. To his relief, the amused Indians waved, and then turned on their heels to continue their journey north.

"Sorry, I dumped in on top of you like that, Jalot," St. Denis stated as he returned his weapon to its resting place on the bottom of the boat. "My concern was for my back. Too big of a target for those young heathens."

"No harm done. Better your back than mine. Why do you think I always ride amidships?"

St. Denis nodded his head in acknowledgment, then made a quick mental note to make some adjustments in their future seating arrangements. "I suppose, instead of going for our heads, the Stinkards decided to have a little sport — at our expense, of course."

"And that they did," Jalot said matter-of-factly as he dug his oar deep into the murky water and heaved.

"Me, I almost abandoned ship," the soldier said with a chuckle.

St. Denis chuckled, too. But his mind was still on the Natchez, remembering the time he and Bienville had visited them several years back.

———

He had been a young man at the time, out to seek his fortune and carve his name in the annals of history. First, they visited with the Bayougoulas whom they had met earlier. Then, they proceeded up the Mississippi until they came to a wide turn in the river with high bluffs on either side. Just around the bend was a landing with a steep incline that led to the top of the bluff. A road led inland to the Grand Village of the Natchez which nestled between two small creeks.

As they approached, they paused to admire the beauty of their village site. Large areas were under cultivation with maize, beans, tubers, figs, papaws, and persimmons. Interspersed among the shimmering green foliage were their thatch-covered lodges and the white-washed walls of their rectangular Temple. Peach and plum trees were in bloom at the time, and their pink and white colors added another distinctive, artistic dimension to the beautiful land-scape. He knew then, that the Natchez were an unusual tribe with a culture far superior to that of any other they had met.

There was much excitement as they arrived. Curious adults smiled openly, waved their arms, jabbered, and made gestures to one another. Children repeatedly approached, to a point, then would scamper off laughing, each in a different direction.

He fondly recalled one young, would-be warrior who decided to stand his ground, his arms crossed, determined to prove his brav-ery for the sake of his comrades. It was clear, however, that the boy was struggling desperately to conquer his fear.

As fate would have it, a metal helmet accidentally slipped from the hands of a careless soldier and fell to the hard earth. The impact resounded like ringing thunder. Fear triumphed and the youngster bolted, gaining twenty paces before his frail legs stumbled to a halt.

The Natchez, in their own unique way, were probably the most handsome of all the tribes they had encountered, and their women, the most beautiful — especially the young, naughty ones who were notorious flirts. Nothing like the Choctaws, whom they had met the year before. The Choctaws rarely bathed, usually went naked, and instead of wearing their feathers about their head in the traditional fashion, they wore them tied about their waist so that they protruded like the rear plumage of a turkey. They were also tenacious fornica-tors, and that act took precedence over all else. Even in the heat of battle, it was not unusual to see several braves set aside their arms for a hasty romp with some willing or unwilling female.

Laughing to himself, he recalled the time they had stopped to visit the gentle, free-spirited Bayougoulas accompanied by some thirty Choctaw guides. Within minutes, each had corralled a female. Fornication was rampant and feathers were everywhere.

Four days later, when he and Bienville were ready to resume their exploration farther North and West, not one brave had the strength to stand on his own two feet. Bienville was so angry and disgusted that he ordered the expedition to leave without them. Several days later, the braves caught up with them. All, however, were experiencing acute exhaustion.

The Natchez, on the other hand, were a proud people who reminded him of the dark complexioned Moors he had once seen as a young boy in the ports of Marseilles. Each had strong aquiline noses, high-sloped heads, shaped during their infancy with wood compressors, and rich bronze skin. And, even though this trait was shared by all, it was still very easy to tell which of them belonged to the ruling Sun Class. Their deportment was different, aloof, and just a little more aristocratic.

While the men wore their hair in numerous bizarre fashions that accented the slope of their heads, the women wore theirs long and loose, hanging, in many cases, below their waists. Robes of doeskin, that covered their bodies from shoulders to knees, were worn by the women. Young girls, without undergarments, wore facsimiles of skirts made of bark fibers fastened about their waists with two tasseled strings. Above the waist, they were bare with innocent, budding breasts that titillated even the staunchest of men.

Children, for the most part, ran about naked during the summer. But, during the winter, all, young and old alike, sought the comforts of animal hides and swans-down blankets.

Young maidens tended to be promiscuous until they married. And it was not unusual to observe both married and unmarried couples copulating whenever and wherever it was convenient for them to do so. Once married, however, a female risked being beheaded even at the slightest suggestion of infidelity. This rule, however, did not apply to the Sun Class females. They were above the law and did whatever they pleased. As a result, many of the Sun Class females often had several husbands or lovers.

In spite of the beauty of the village, there was one item that caused the French party a great deal of concern. That was the inordinate number of human skulls displayed around the perimeter of the Natchez Temple. Curiously, several of the skulls had remnants of hair suggestive of European coloring. Despite the fact that he had observed this sight with his own eyes, St. Denis still found it extremely difficult to believe that these gentle people, so humble and childlike in appearance, could be capable of such savage atrocities — atrocities that would strain the imagination of any man, sane or insane. Their ferocity was well known, and even though they were a small nation by comparison, both the Chickasaw, to the north, and the Choctaw, to the south, were careful not to offend them.

But, what had annoyed St. Denis even more than the Natchez's fascination with heads was the constant stream of comments concerning their nefarious nature by Father Du Ru, the French priest who traveled with their expedition.

"Heathens... all heathens. Surely, Satan must have his stronghold here. Sin, everywhere. In every quarter.

"My God! How can men go about their duties when there is so much flesh being flaunted about.

"Look! Just look at the depraved manner of those young girls cavorting in front of us. Those are the hands of Satan that I see beckoning. We must be strong, my friend, or temptation will surely conquer us both."

St. Denis looked at the girls as they made obvious sexual suggestions with their hips and coy smiles. Rather than being offended, he found their flirty antics amusing. Under different circumstances, and in different company, he might have considered responding to their overtures. Instead, he had replied, "Let them be, Father Du Ru. They are only children, innocent and totally ignorant of our God and laws."

"Children of Satan, they are. And although I dread it, mine will be the task of changing them. The Lord's work must be done — and soon, before we bring French women into this country."

"Changing them will not be an easy task. This is their way, and I am not all too certain that they should be forced to accept our way of life."

"But change, they must. That is why the church has sent me here — to teach them what is sinful, to tell them to clothe their bodies properly, and refrain from their licentious behavior. It was not intended that man should fornicate without shame in full view of others. It's the females who must be converted first. They are the key, my son. Once they are converted from the ways of that heathen whore, Jezebel, the males will follow along meekly like lambs."

"And how would you propose to accomplish such a formidable task?"

"Oh, have no fear. The Lord deals with a strong hand... and a whip, if necessary. A few well-placed strokes can be quite expedient in these matters."

"I admit that the whip can be useful in subduing a man's body, but I have my doubts as to whether it can ever re-weave the fibers of one's soul."

"That's because you have no experience in the art of applying the whip. To gain the best advantage, you must be aware of several rules. First, you never use the whip alone. You hold the whip in the one hand, and a suitable reward in the other. And second, you must use the whip with a clear purpose. To do this properly, one must make a list of the known sins. Then, the number of strokes to be meted out for each. The number, of course, would vary with the seriousness of the infraction. Much in the same way you would teach an animal or a child."

"And what reward would you give them in return for their obedience?"

"My blessing, of course... and the privilege of keeping the skin on their stinking backs," the priest said with emphasis, then laughed at the wit of his statement. "Don't you agree?" he added.

St. Denis looked at the priest, but did not answer. He did not approve of the priest's implied methods of conversion, and he felt himself growing angry. In spite of this, he knew that acculturation of the Indians would take place. That phase was an integral and mandatory part of their charter — the key element that enabled them to obtain the blessings of the church and the financing necessary for their expedition.

Father Du Ru had waited patiently for a reply. Upon realizing that none was forthcoming, he stood, stretched his limbs, and said with resignation, "Well, it doesn't matter to me if you agree or not. It will be done, even if I have to break the back of every heathen in the territory. Now, I must retire and seek counsel with the Lord. I will be dependent upon His good graces if I am expected to succeed in this great task He has placed before me."

As Father Du Ru ambled away, St. Denis watched him knowingly, certain that the good priest was retiring to seek counsel of a different sort. *The sort best acquired by one in the privacy of his own quarters when pleasures of the flesh have been denied.*

Two days later, after ignoring their initial arrival, the Great Sun, supreme chief of the Natchez, finally acknowledged their presence and granted them an audience. By then, Bienville was frothing at the mouth. And it was clear, even at that early stage, that he and the Great Sun were destined to become bitter enemies.

When the aging Great Sun did appear, he appeared not unlike an ancient emperor, his dark face adorned in a magnificent bonnet constructed with huge, bright, yellow and black feathers that fanned out above his head like the rays of the sun. About his shoulders was a beautiful, white cape of woven swan's-down decorated with patterns of yellow, black, and red designs. Young servants went before him spreading out mats of cane, lest his feet might touch the ground. Behind him, followed the lessor Chiefs and several elders. The magnitude of his charisma dwarfed that of anyone in the French party. And for the first time in all the years since he had known him, he saw Bienville humbled by the mere presence of another human being. A situation, however, that created an even further degree of resentment on the part of Bienville.

Following the introductions and a brief ceremony that included smoking the sacred calumet, the Great Sun retired and left his Great War Chief to host in his stead. This concluded their official welcome. Immediately after, there was a celebration in their honor which commenced with a spectacular parade led by the ranking members of the Sun Class — all dressed in their finest and accompanied by servants who carried the banners and insignia that represented their respective clans and villages. Behind them followed the Nobles and Honored People. Last, was the parade of warriors, all in full battle dress, but without their paints of war. Conducted, he was sure, as a method of displaying their military strength.

Following the formal exhibition, the men played a vigorous stick-ball game to the cheers of the bystanders. When the game ended, the Indians refreshed themselves. Male and female alike, bathed naked in the river, playing in the water like children. Next, there was dancing. This phase of the celebration was initiated by the young unmarried girls, all bare-chested and seductively dressed with belts of beads hanging around their necks and across their shoulders. At the sound of a loud howl, they proceeded in a line, ten abreast, swinging their tasseled hips in an undulating motion, the line moving forward obliquely to the left, then obliquely to the right. Then, a whistle blew and the women split and took places opposite the men, each keeping cadence with a pebble filled gourd in one hand and a cluster of white feathers in the other. Several deerskin drums and an equal number of reed flutes provided the music. The whistle blew again, the women regrouped, and continued dancing as they had before.

After the dancing, there was a banquet which concluded with the offer of a woman for each man for the duration of their stay.

Bienville, in an obvious effort to reassert his authority, declined the offer haughtily. In the process, he insulted the War Chief by telling him that it was not good for white skin to mix with red. Had he not interrupted the two and quickly heaped compliments upon the Chief for his many other hospitalities, a crisis most certainly would have developed. One that could have very easily, resulted in a few more heads for their temple walls.

Suddenly, he remembered her — the one who had come to him in the night, on a subsequent visit with the Natchez, like something out of a dream. He called her *Night Bird* for he never learned the name given her.

It was a warm, humid, quiet, small-mooned night. Everyone had retired. He had been restless, so he got up and walked to the perimeter of the village to relieve his bladder. He was leaning with one hand against the trunk of a huge oak when he felt her presence. He glanced over his shoulder and there she was, standing sassily in the shadows, her arms crossed, watching him solemnly and quietly. Not one word was spoken. She did it all with her eyes, the way she stared at him, and the way her eyes lingered caressingly upon his exposed privates. Within moments, he was fully aroused — more aroused than he had ever been in his whole life.

Without covering himself, he slowly turned and walked toward her. When he was near, she looked below at his manhood, smiled pensively, then lifted the hem of her robe until it was high above her waist, holding it there as she slid gently to the ground. For a moment, he stood immobile, completely captivated by the mystic moon shadows that danced invitingly about her shapely thighs. *To Hell with Bienville,* he recalled saying under his breath as he fell upon her and hammered out his passion.

When it was over, she got up, dropped her robe dispassionately, and left just as quietly and anonymously as she had arrived — leaving him exhausted, too weak to stand, his ego wounded and torn to shreds, and wondering why it was that she had not heard the thunder or felt the earth shake on its foundation as he had.

To this day, he never discovered the woman's identity. That she was of the Sun Class, he was absolutely sure.

A light drizzle began to fall. Ahead, the clouds grew darker and the huge river began to take on the appearance of the open sea. Cautiously, St. Denis cursed and edged his boat closer along the eastern shoreline. For a moment, he considered stopping, but decided against it, since they were only three or four hours from their destination. He knew they were going to be drenched, but at least tonight they would be able to rest in the comfort and safety of the barracks. Tomorrow, he would visit his sister's brother-in-law, *Jean Baptiste Le Moyne, Sieur de Bienville,* Governor, The French Territory of Louisiana.

Louis Juchereau de St. Denis
(Bust located in Downtown, Natchitochs, LA)

Chapter — Four

GOVERNOR BIENVILLE STOOD AT HIS FAVORITE SPOT, looking out of the window of the room that served both as his parlor and office. From there, he had a clear view of the singularly most important building in the colony — the *"Powder Magazine,"* the place used to store his weapons and ammunition. The magazine represented power — his power. The anchor that served as the strength of his command.

It was mid-morning and the low angle of the sun caused its rays to burst into a rainbow of colors as they passed through the irregular, hand-blown window panes. Bienville glanced down at the kaleidoscopic patterns and quietly admired his highly-polished, decorative wood floor, one that had been constructed from the planking of a salvaged vessel. Recently scrubbed and oiled, the morning sun highlighted the depth of its natural grain.

In a few months, he hoped to retire and turn the reins of the colony over to someone new. He wished he knew who that someone was going to be. But, as of yet, that person had not been named. St. Denis was the only person, currently in the colony, the ministry had considered for the job. He, however, had objected and advised them to look elsewhere for a suitable replacement. Not that he had anything personally against St. Denis. St. Denis had been a friend and ally of long standing — had been with him from the beginning when they first explored the Mississippi. The problem with St. Denis was that he had no class or connections to the continental bureaucracy. He was just a country boy who was good at stomping through the forest and settling Indian affairs. No matter how hard he tried, he could never visualize St. Denis in the role of a statesman. Besides, as of late, St. Denis seemed to be more concerned with feathering his own nest rather than serving the colony. This matter disturbed him greatly. But hopefully, by the end of his visit today, maybe he could get him back on track.

In any case, he hoped that the new governor would be a man of some stature and influence, someone who had the ear of the ministry or the king.

What shall this day bring to torment me more? he wondered as he surveyed his sparsely furnished quarters. He doubted that the new governor would find his quarters very appealing. But then, that wasn't his problem — *was it?* The place suited him just fine. Since he was rather conservative by nature, he did not feel that elaborate or expensive accoutrements were necessary. His only requirement was that they be functional and comfortable — like his favorite chair. It, like his floor, had not cost him one piastre. He had confiscated it during the Spanish War of 1719 when he overran one of the Spanish strongholds in Florida. He loved the chair and often wondered about its origin — the woodcarver who was responsible for its intricate, ornate design, and the weaver who wove its beautiful, black, red, and yellow tapestry-covered seat.

A large table in the center of the room served as his desk. Upon it rested several quills, an inkpot caked heavily with dried ink, and several stacks of official papers aligned neatly along one edge. Around the table were four simple, straight-backed, split-cane-seat chairs.

Despite the warming glow of the morning sun, there was a slight chill in the air. So, he walked across the room to a bookcase, which stood against one wall, and took down a light, neck-shawl from a peg wedged into its side. He threw it casually around his shoulders, then walked slowly back to the window.

The bookcase was probably the most valuable of all his possessions. It overflowed with books in several languages and included several volumes by *Luis de Gongora*, a noted Spanish poet, whose style he admired. Although his duties prevented him from reading as much as he would have liked, he continued to collect important literary works — promising himself that he would catch up on his reading as soon as he retired.

He looked at the crude map of New Orleans that hung on the wall opposite the bookcase and wondered if his brother, Iberville, would have approved of the progress he had made toward bringing their dream to life. He would never know. Iberville was dead, died of the fever in Havana, Cuba.

Unlike his brother, Iberville, he had never married. Iberville had married St. Denis' sister. Now, she was a widow, still living in Canada, alone, and lonely. All of which served to solidify his conviction that men of destiny could not afford the luxury of a wife and family. He considered himself such a man, and his convictions in this matter were so strong that he had inadvertently made a lifetime enemy of the former Governor, Antoine de la Mothe Cadillac.

He had been a few years younger then, in 1713, when Cadillac came down from Canada to assume duties as Governor. All went well until Cadillac's overweight daughter *with her phony aristocratic airs* began to make advances. He had, of course, rejected her. Not to be outdone, the young woman then asked her father to intervene on her behalf. In compliance with his daughter's wish, Governor Cadillac invited him to dinner, and during the course of the meal, made his proposition. As respectfully as he could, he had again rejected the offer of marriage, explaining his reasons in detail, and assuring the Governor that his decision had nothing personally to do with his daughter.

The Governor, however, did not take the rejection of his daughter lightly and had all but openly accused him of being a homosexual. From that moment on, the governor did whatever he could to complicate his life. He even tried to get him killed by sending him on a suicide mission into the Natchez camp with only four men to punish the whole tribe for the death of two French citizens.

But Cadillac had underestimated his ingenuity. He survived the encounter and returned to New Orleans triumphantly with the heads of several Natchez War Chiefs and a runaway slave for good measure — all hanging by their hair and strung out like dead fish on a pole.

But, that was long ago. He was older now and starting to bald. He sucked in his small, but growing potbelly, re-tucked his white linen shirt into his green twill breeches, and called out to his valet. "Jason, warm the *café*. We have a visitor approaching — M'sieur St. Denis."

A middle-aged man, who stepped with a light foot, hurried excitedly to the window, seemingly, to verify the guest for himself.

Bienville scowled, and Jason quickly retreated to prepare the café in a flurry of spontaneous activity.

St. Denis was about to knock on the door of Bienville's quarters with a mallet provided for that purpose when the door opened, and he was greeted by the smiling, slightly-pudgy, oval face of the governor.

"Louis! *Bonjour*. How good it is to see you." The governor stated as he stepped aside and allowed St. Denis to enter.

"*Bonjour*, Governor," St. Denis replied as he started to enter, but suddenly stopped when Bienville looked down at his muddy boots and scowled. A little self-consciously, St. Denis quickly removed his boots and left them outside near the doorway.

"I assume that your journey was uneventful?" Bienville asked as he led the way into his parlor.

"Not exactly. We almost got swamped yesterday trying to get here in all that rain. Luckily, we made it before the main storm hit. I never knew it could rain so hard. Felt like I was being pelted with a cat of nine tails."

"Well, at least you arrived safely."

St. Denis was genuinely pleased to see his old friend. They had met in Canada when Bienville and his brother were trying to get their first expedition together. Since then, he had developed a respect and admiration for the governor that was equal to none. He supposed the respect between them was mutual, but sometimes he had his doubts —like now — as he wondered if Bienville would nominate him for governor. He deserved it, especially since he had served him so faithfully over the past years, keeping peace along the Spanish border, and settling sensitive Indian affairs. He had been much younger then. Now that he was older, he needed some stability in his life. The type that came with the position of governor would have suited him just fine.

So, as friends, they sat at Bienville's table and discussed the things that friends discuss, inquiring about each other's health, family and friends, and the latest news. They discussed the colony, its progress, and, of course, its many problems.

Jason entered and went through an unnecessary ritual of placing napkins and arranging the settings for the café. While he was doing so, St. Denis crossed his legs self-consciously and pretended to study the map of the city that hung on the wall to his right.

"Just pour the café, Jason!" Bienville all but shouted.

A little unnerved, Jason shakily poured the coffee and quickly withdrew.

"*Mon ami,*" the Governor spoke, "how I wish that you could be two persons. I need another commander like you to take command of Fort Rosalie."

"Why? Do we have a problem there?" St. Denis asked over the rim of his cup.

"Not at the moment. But, mark my words, there will be. Fort Rosalie lies in the midst of the Natchez Indians. Of all the savages in this country, I think I detest them the most.

Snakes are what they are, and snakes they will always be. They are peaceful now. But as you know, they are capable of irrational behavior. They are the most civilized of all the heathens on this continent, and that fact alone, makes them a dangerous lot. They are a race different and apart from the other savages. You can see this in the pigmentation of their skin. They do not fraternize with the others of this land, and they seem to have an affinity for the Africans. They grant them sanctuary without question and in direct contempt of our laws. Their Chief, the Great Sun, has absolute power over his subjects. When he dies, his wife and all of his servants commit suicide to accompany him into his next life. Do you have that kind of power over your subjects?"

"Not with any that I know of," St. Denis said with a chuckle. "There are a few who would gladly assist me on my way. But none, that I know, who would join me."

Bienville laughed heartily. "And neither have I," he said between laughs. "But then, our subjects do not consider us Gods — do they? That is why I am so concerned. Think of what you could do in battle if you had but one company of soldiers with that depth of devotion. You could conquer the whole of Europe in a week. The Great Sun, barbarian though he is, has that kind of power. So, he must be handled carefully. To keep the peace, one must deal with him fairly, but on terms that he can understand — an eye for an eye. If not, believe me, he will consider you weak and treat you accordingly."

"I understand well what you mean. Still, I have never known the Great Sun to abuse his power," St. Denis said as he uncrossed his legs and inadvertently struck the leg of Bienville's table with his foot.

"That...," Bienville stated as he leaned over and visually inspected the leg for any damage, "that is only because I have not allowed him to do so. Sometime ago, a small band killed two French subjects, you may recall the incident. I retaliated immediately and killed six of his War Chiefs. The Great Sun quickly sued for peace, but only after he saw that he was no match for my weapons. Anyway, I granted him peace only under the condition that he brought me the heads of his three remaining War Chiefs and the head of the runaway slave who was living under his protection.

"Two days after I released him, he brought me the four heads. One was that of his brother, Old Hair. He had only to ask, and they voluntarily put their heads before the axe. Devotion of that type is rare — and could, if not held in check, wreak devastation along the Mississippi."

St. Denis knew of the episode in 1713. He also knew that the Natchez had not sued for peace. Bienville had used treachery by inviting the Great Sun to his camp for peace talks. Once there, the Great Sun was captured and tortured until the Natchez War Council submitted to his demands. He had obtained this information from the Indians several years after the incident had occurred. Now, he felt an over-powering urge to correct Bienville and set the record straight. But instead, he resisted the temptation, and only nodded as Bienville continued with his version.

"... The old Great Sun and I had an understanding and peace has been maintained. Now, the old one is dead, I am leaving for the continent, and his nephew, the new Great Sun, doesn't seem to fear our weapons anymore. This concerns me greatly. So, as you can see, I need a strong commander there. Someone experienced. Someone dependable — and someone who won't hesitate to wipe the bastards off the face of the earth at the first sign of trouble. Jason?" he turned and called out. "Refresh our cups."

Jason entered with fresh coffee and set a tray with several hot, buttered biscuits on the table. St. Denis took one quickly and held out his cup. After Jason had filled it and moved on to fill Bienville's, he took a sip, then remarked, "Jason, you brew the best *café* on this side of the sea."

Jason acknowledged the comment with a small smile and departed.

While Bienville sat sampling his beverage in silence, St. Denis pondered the question put before him. It was quite obvious that Bienville was waiting for him to volunteer for the Ft. Rosalie assignment. *Amazing,* he said to himself. *The post of governor is open, and all I am offered is a command in a den of rattlesnakes.* He had no intentions of spending the last few years of his life in a rattlesnake pit. If he couldn't be governor, he decided, he would be better off if he remained where he was. There, at least, he might be able to make a few coins by trading goods with the Spanish. At Natchitoches, he was only fifteen miles from the Spanish border and the Spanish were quite eager to trade despite the state of war that existed between the two countries.

To avoid any further discussions along that line, St. Denis decided to change the subject. "There is word about that you have submitted a proposal to the Ministry to ban the importation of slaves. Is this fact? And if so, do you consider this wise at this stage of our growth?"

"Yes, in my opinion — very wise," the Governor stated haughtily as he rose from his tapestry covered chair and walked toward the window with his hands clasped behind.

"But surely, with the colony growing, don't you think there will be an even greater demand for slave labor?"

"I am sure there will be. But, that is not the problem. If this colony is to survive, it will not be on the backs of slaves, but on the industry of French citizens. Slavery can do nothing but cripple our progress. Mark my words — if we continue to steer our present course, I wager this colony will be in chaos within ten years."

"Still, I find it hard to see your point. Our numbers are few, and there are many tasks to be accomplished. How can a person be expected to forage the wilderness cutting trails and fighting wars, and still be expected to labor the land."

"You said the right word. The word is numbers. That is the key. Look about you man. Look at the ratio, now, of slaves to French. If this continues, before we realize it, the slaves will outnumber us. And while you are looking — take a careful look at the African. He is strong. His will to survive exceeds that of any other that I know, and he learns fast. The harder he works, the stronger he grows. And all the while, we're sitting on our asses growing fat. God help us, if ever they should align with the Indians. We are playing with fire here! Even you should recognize that... or, can you?"

"Well..., certainly I see your point," St. Denis stammered, sorry now that he had launched Bienville into another one of his preaching tirades, "I just feel that your decision is a little premature."

"Premature? You're starting to sound like the rest of the thick skulls who offer me their advice. What we are building here is a French colony, populated by French citizens, on French soil. My purpose here is not to build another damned African State. And for some reason, the ministry, too, seems to be ignorant of our ultimate purpose. They are still hoping to find the riches of the East here. There are none! When are the bastards going to realize that? What we need to prosper are farmers, trappers, artisans, and fishermen, not slaves. And most of all, we need decent females suitable to serve as mothers and teachers for our children. Instead, they send me privateers, convicts, and whores off the streets of Paris.

"Three years ago they sent me one hundred of these despicable women. Some were diseased, some without their full mental faculties, and none desirable to look at. The ugliest lot of bitches this side of Hell. To this day, only a third have been married. And here I am, left with the burden of supporting the remainder while the eligible men are still bedding slaves, filthy Indians, and... God knows what else. And that malady is not confined to the commoner. There are a great number with noble blood, traceable to the royal family, who seem to prefer the warmth of a black wench to that of their own kind. Some are even bold enough to live in open placage with their black wenches without shame, in open challenge against both State and Church. The evidence is everywhere. Just look at the number of half-breed children in bondage. Half-French and half-ape or half-Indian — mules. God made no provisions for a race of that kind, and it is a sacrilege that man should do so."

St. Denis looked at the governor, somewhat surprised. He was surprised because the current practice had grown out of a previous one initiated by the Governor, himself, during a time when it was advantageous for him to do so. It was at his advice that young men were encouraged to live with the natives in order to learn their language and cultivate better relations between the two races. The practice was referred to by all as *"Wintering with the Indians."* Of course, during that time, when they first arrived, Bienville was more concerned about conserving his own meager supply of corn, rather than offending the Almighty. Silently, St. Denis admitted to himself that Bienville was starting to develop certain inconsistencies in his old age.

In a more subdued voice, the Governor continued, "I, for one, also do not believe that any man should be in perpetual bondage to another. Even if the African is a heathen, it is my opinion that slavery, in any form, is a crime in the sight of God and all that is Holy. That is why I moved the location of that industry across the river to Algiers. Someday, the world will acknowledge this error and set them free. What then — shall we do? And who will accept the responsibility of caring for them?" He paused for effect. "That is why I must return to France. There, I may serve the colony better. There, maybe I can convince the Ministry of our needs for decent citizens, priests, and educators. And above all, I must convince them of the evils of slavery... and Jews, I have no need of stinking Jews in this colony."

"Jews?" St. Denis repeated, half asleep, and wondering at what point had the conversation changed.

"Yes, Jews. I stand firm on this."

"But why? From my experiences, they appear to be quite harmless."

"No Jew is harmless. But then, you have always been gullible. If I could, I would rid the world of their kind. They are a worse problem than slaves. Satan is their guardian, and their greed pushes them to strangle an economy. To prosper, money must flow freely — not into the pocket of some damn Jew. Jews be damned!" he said as he struck the table with the base of his fist. "Some... sometimes I get so frustrated, and so angry, that I bring on the fever.... Jason!" he yelled. "Jason. Open the windows and let some fresh air into this damned place."

Visibly unnerved, Jason hurried into the room to do as he was told.

"Rest easy, Governor. You worry too much about too many things. It's time you learned to relax."

"Of course," the Governor stated while taking a deep breath. "Of course, you are right. Enough of this talk. I am weary of the affairs of state. It is my sincerest wish that the ministry will appoint a replacement for me without undue delay. I must be gone from this place before I am called to join my dear brother before my time."

"I am sure the ministry appreciates your many years of noble service and I, too, hope that you may retire soon." Saying this, St. Denis rose from his chair, embraced the Governor, and excused himself from his company.

———

Outside, St. Denis leaned against the wall and inserted his long, thin feet into his tight, damp boots with some difficulty. When that was done, he took a deep breath, stepped off the gallery, turned left, and walked down Rue Bourbon, and across Toulouse stepping carefully between the numerous puddles of muddy water. When he got to St. Peters, he turned right and walked toward the river.

The city had grown considerably since his last visit. It now boasted more than 1,000 French citizens and about 300 servants and slaves. A church with a sanctuary for the priest had been built. To its left, there was a guardhouse, and a prison. In front of the church, between it and the levee, was the *Place d'Armes* or parade ground. It was adjoined near the river by a flourishing market place.

Except for the government buildings, most of the homes were constructed of upright logs filled with bousillage, a mixture of mud and deer hair. This method of construction was one the French had borrowed from the Natchez, and homes built in this fashion were called *Maisons de poteaux enterre*. Many of the roofs were covered with cedar shingles, but a few were still thatched.

Along one side of the primary streets *banquettes* had been built. These were primitive sidewalks constructed of rough wood planking. They were especially useful since the earth was almost always moist and muddy. In addition, the whole city had been encircled with a low levee to hold back the unpredictable Mississippi River and inhibit the excursions of alligators, serpents, and other notorious wildlife that frequently wandered into the city.

At Chartres Street, he turned right again and proceeded toward the Intendant. It was there that he observed two mulatto children at play in the muddy street. He stood for a moment watching them in silence, suddenly conscious of the Governor's comments regarding slavery. Was it really possible that this colony may, one day, become a colony of mulattoes?

Upon realizing that he was procrastinating, he did an about face, walked quickly back to St. Peter, and continued to the levee. There, he bought passage on a skiff and crossed the river to the slave trading post in Algiers, a small French settlement on the opposite side of the Mississippi River that Bienville had established strictly for the business of bartering human flesh.

Since the importation of slaves would probably be banned, St. Denis reasoned it prudent to take steps to obtain mates for his three single female slaves. If Bienville was successful, then prices would soar, and those unable to breed their own slaves would surely suffer.

———————

Chapter – Five

APPARENTLY, OTHER CITIZENS WERE AWARE OF BIENVILLE'S INTENTIONS REGARDING THE IMPORTATION OF SLAVES. The market was unusually crowded with planters and businessmen seeking to make purchases. The atmosphere was quite festive. While many wandered about, others stood in small groups gossiping or discussing continental politics. One cluster stood around an overturned barrel gambling. Although most were French, St. Denis did notice several Spanish and a few displaced Englishmen in the crowd. Beside them, squatted several Choctaw Indians sharing a jar of cheap cane rum in silence.

Above, seagulls circled playfully, swooping down periodically to search the moist earth for tiny bits of food and shiny, alluring pebbles. Hawkers, mostly black females clad in brightly-colored clothes, plied their wares with high-pitched, singsong voices that just by chance seemed to compliment the reels of a lone street fiddler. Several ladies of the night, with heavily-painted faces, sat on the sides of buggies swinging their carelessly-crossed legs and conversing coarsely among themselves. Hanging heavy in the humid air was the aroma of café mixed with that of dried fish and human sweat.

"Messieurs... Mesdames, pardonnez-moi," the trader shouted as he stepped upon the weather-beaten, wooden platform. Immediately, all side activities stopped and everyone gathered around the platform where they waited anxiously for the bidding to commence. Quickly, the trader thumbed through some paper documents, then continued. "As you may be aware, this trading post may soon be closed. This ship, the Marianne," he added, pointing to his right, "... has just completed passage this morning. Her journey, however, was long and hard. As a result, over half her cargo was lost. It is, therefore, necessary to raise prices, slightly, in consideration of the expenses involved. I assure

you, however, that those who did complete the journey are the finest and healthiest specimens on this continent."

St. Denis, like everyone else, turned to watch as more than a hundred half-starved, sweating, blue-black bodies were herded into a group to one side of the platform where they were instructed to sit on the moist earth. Some were chained in pairs, but most were chained in groups of three and four.

Slowly, the bidding began, then continued at a fairly brisk pace with prices much higher than St. Denis could reasonably afford. At least forty percent of the slaves exhibited were women and children. The rest were males of various ages. All appeared frightened and sick in both body and spirit. All in all, a sad lot. None appealed to St. Denis.

Near the close of the sale, the trader instructed the black slave master to fetch a tall, teenage boy, one St. Denis had not noticed before. When the boy reached the center of the platform, stood erect, and raised his bewildered eyes regally, the crowd hushed.

Immediately, St. Denis was intrigued. This one, without a doubt, was the best buy of the lot. Around him, he could hear whispered appraisals from others as they speculated and admired the condition of his young, muscular body. Besides his powerful back and slender torso, St. Denis was impressed by the character he thought he saw in the boy's oblong face. In fact, the boy suited perfectly, his unfounded impression of an African prince, tall, broad of shoulders, high spirited, and unbowed.

"Four hundred," St. Denis yelled to the top of his voice.

"Be practical, Monsieur. Four hundred livres would barely cover the cost of the food wasted on this one. A young lad like this consumes double rations."

"Five hundred," St. Denis yelled again.

"Six hundred." Someone else yelled. Quickly, St. Denis turned to identify the bidder and galled immediately. It was Monsieur Genet, an egotistical little man who operated a plantation further up the river. In shoes, he stood barely four-feet, two-inches tall — a stumping little midget. Yet, to spite his size, he had developed an obsession for large things. His house was large. He purchased livestock strictly on the basis of their size. Even his wife was of immense stock, towering a full ten inches above him with huge breasts that strained obscenely beneath her overly tight bodice.

On this particular day, she carried a bright, yellow *parasol* in one hand, while clinging to the arm of her husband with the other.

From her flamboyant dress and the outlandish manner in which she cast her wide hips about when she walked, it was easy, even for the untrained eye, to accurately discern that she once walked the streets of Paris. Her masquerade as a lady might have been successful except for her sickly-sweet *parfum*, and her eyes — which, after years of practice, continued to cruise and solicit the attention of the males in the crowd.

"Six-fifty," St. Denis shouted loud, hoping no one would challenge him and knowing that he could not afford one coin more.

"Seven hundred," a Spanish buyer called.

"Nine hundred," Genet countered.

"Nine hundred," the trader repeated. "Do I hear more? Nine hundred, the noble gentleman called. Can I hear nine and fifty?"

There were no other bids, so Genet took possession of the slave and had his manservant tether him off to the side.

Bidding was at a peak by the time the last slave was sold and the buyers who had not yet made purchases began to get unruly. Shouts of obscenities rang out amid accusations that some of the slaves were being withheld to be sold in other ports, or sold to some other privileged person of high rank.

"Gentlemen," the trader attempted to regain control of the mob. "Please, I assure you. The Captain declares that his ship is empty. There are no more slaves. If you must be angry, be angry at the one who is causing your dilemma. The Governor, not the Captain or myself. We are as much victims as you are."

"Then, why have you not sold the Big-Black there, the one with the cat. I'll offer one hundred for him," someone yelled from the crowd partly as a joke, pointing to the slave master.

If it was a joke, for a moment, no one fully appreciated the intent of the statement, and it was plain to see that Mukta, the Big-Black, certainly did not.

Then as the idea set, first one, then another shouted: "Why do you not sell him?" "He should bring a handsome price." While some laughed, others seemed to consider the question legitimate.

When St. Denis looked at the giant, he had to smile to himself in satisfaction. The smug giant had begun to exhibit visible signs of concern. Sweat suddenly appeared on his wide nostrils and a series of tremors passed through his right leg. Tentatively, with unsteady hands, the black reached down and reverently caressed a small leather sack that hung from his waistband. St. Denis found that somewhat odd, but did not dwell on the matter. Instead, he quickly glanced at the Captain, curious to hear his response.

Captain Fortierre stood in the foreground of the platform. And although he appeared some years junior to most of his motley crew, his face was stern and foreboding. Cold, steel-gray eyes were framed on one side with a livid pink scar that ran from just beneath his left ear to the bottom of his chin. *Definitely not one I would turn my back on,* St. Denis said to himself as he waited.

"Gentlemen," the Captain said in a cultured, but raspy voice, "your request is not without merit. This Black is Mukta, my slave master. Mukta has served me well and faithfully these past years — even more devotedly than a son. He is one of a kind and I'm afraid he cannot be replaced at any price. I, therefore, am obliged to decline."

Upon hearing the Captain's response, Mukta relaxed and reared back on his heels. A slight smile crept across his ashy, black face, then folded slowly into a light sneer, almost imperceptible, but a sneer nonetheless.

"M'sieur, considering the fact that you may not anchor in this port again, would it not be wise to take advantage of an opportunity to make a few extra coins?" asked a Spanish gentleman.

"Maybe the Captain doesn't want your worthless pesos, Spaniard," someone yelled, then laughed.

The Captain, although he ignored both, did appear to consider the proposition as a matter of courtesy.

Monsieur Genet, who had worked his way to the front of the crowd so he could be seen, spoke next. "M'sieur Capitaine?"

"Yes, m'sieur."

"I have a need for a male such as you possess. And I agree, he is one of a kind. For that reason, I will make you one offer. Yours to accept, or reject."

The Captain stopped, looked down at Genet, and scowled. "What offer is that, m'sieur?"

"Fifteen hundred."

The price offered caused St. Denis to whistle under his breath. Fifteen hundred was almost twice the normal for a good strong male.

Mukta, obviously secure in the knowledge that he was not for sale, looked at the little man and smiled patronizingly.

While the crowd waited expectantly, Captain Fortierre pawed at the ground with his foot. After a moment, he glanced at Mukta and pursed his lips.

"In gold?" Captain Fortierre asked Genet.

"In gold — more pure than any in the king's treasury."

"In that case, I accept your generous offer, m'sieur."

The sudden, unexpected impact of these words hit Mukta like a hammer. He opened his mouth as if to voice a protest, but instead, only bellowed pitifully like a big, black, beached whale.

"Chain him, Portuguese," the Captain directed a sailor with a scraggly, red beard and a mouth full of half-rotted teeth.

While a bewildered Mukta stood watching his dreams and hopes for the future disintegrate like a fine mist being gathered up by the winds of Hell, a grinning Portuguese and several others shackled him quickly with a short length of chain between his wrists. Mukta looked down at the chains in disbelief, then raised his arms to the captain, his eyes soulful and pleading for reconsideration.

Slowly, the captain sauntered toward him, smiling as if the whole thing was only a joke. Mukta's face filled with hope. But, instead of assisting him, the captain growled suddenly and quickly snatched the leather sack from his waistband.

That single act broke the spell. Like an enraged bull, Mukta roared. In one moment, he was tossing seamen about the platform like they were children. In the next, his large, coarse fingers were wrapped tightly around the Portuguese's neck — *like a chicken's*. So intent was he in trying to part the skull from the Portuguese's body, that he ignored all else and never saw the heavy club that struck him beside the head and brought his rampage to a halt. Quickly, the Portuguese scrambled to safety where he sat bug-eyed, coughing, and spitting up blood — obviously thankful that his scant thread of a life had been spared.

"And so it goes," St. Denis said to no one in particular as the half-conscious giant was taken and tethered next to the African Prince boy. Humiliated, Mukta lowered his head in shame, trying to ignore the obvious, silent expression of delight that filled the hopeless black faces of his former subjects.

The biggest, most obvious smile, however, was on the face of the African Prince boy. And that one, Mukta, apparently, could not ignore. Suddenly, he snarled in anger, turned, and kicked the youth in the side, bowling him over.

Like a sleek jungle cat, the boy sprang to his feet and retaliated, swinging wildly at Mukta with the chains that bound his wrist.

The unexpected charge caught the crowd off guard and caused them to scatter to safety like a flock of wild geese. Madame Genet led the retreat. With her dress held above her knees, she fled — high-stepping, and screaming like a banshee with a pitch and volume that would have been considered most unladylike by almost anyone's standards.

Mukta warded off the initial blows of the boy's chains with his arms, then caught them and used them as leverage to throw him to the ground.

Like vultures, the excited crowd regrouped around the dueling duo, pushing and shoving each other for the best view.

Monsieur Genet made several attempts to solicit help from the crowd, but was hampered by those who clamored for the spectacle to continue. Within seconds, champions had been selected, bets were being placed, and high above the commotion could be heard the penetrating screeching of Genet's wife, a big woman with a big mouth.

A loud, overbearing Englishman of the type St. Denis detested, approached and pestered him to make a wager. He walked away, but the Englishman followed.

"What's the matter Frenchman, afraid to make a sporting bet? I've got my money on the big one."

"Not today, m'sieur. Only a fool would bet on the boy."

"Now, don't tell me you're cowered by a small bet. I thought all true Frenchmen appreciated a good game of chance."

"That might well be, and you probably heard that. But, I don't think you heard that Frenchmen were stupid. This is no contest. The big one is twice the boy's size."

"Well now, you've got a point there. I'll tell you what... I got five of my money to one of yours that say the big black will let fly the young snot's head."

St. Denis deliberated for a second, debating whether to risk any part of his 700 livres, then said, *What the Hell.*

"Two hundred on the boy."

"This is a gentlemen's bet. Make it worth my time. Four hundred?"

"Four hundred it is, Englishman," he replied as they shook hands. Immediately, he was sorry. He had accepted the wager, not because he thought the boy had a chance of winning, but because of his hatred for Englishmen. The bet was just a convenient, even if costly, way of expressing his contempt.

Leaving the Englishman in his place, he forced himself to the front of the crowd where he had a clear view of the action.

By this time, Mukta, with his superior size and strength, had gained the advantage and pinned the boy face-down in the dirt, his knee in his back, and his wrist chains around the boy's neck in a strangle hold. St. Denis shook his head in remorse. *Damn! Four hundred livres —gone.* Suddenly, St. Denis noticed that the boy was crawling slowly toward the platform. *No, you imbecile*, he wanted to shout. *Don't get trapped between the giant and the platform, you're dead for certain.* But then, after observing more closely, he saw what the boy was trying to do. Just beneath the edge of the platform, barely visible, was the point of a rusty marlinspike. Excited now, he abandoned his normally reserved nature and shouted as loud as he could, "Go! Go! *Continuer!* Go. Go!"

Almost as if he understood St. Denis' words of encouragement, the boy doubled his efforts, dragging the weight of the giant, while at the same time trying to hold the chain off his windpipe with one hand, and reach for the marlinspike with the other.

"Go! Go, damn it. You can do it. Go!"

After what seemed like an eternity, the boy was within a hand's span of the spike when Mukta suddenly realized what he was trying to do. Growling low in his throat, Mukta yanked back on the boy's neck viciously with all of his strength. The boy's eyes bulged, and slowly, his bright red tongue emerged from his slobbering mouth like a piece of soft taffy. Death rattled like stones in the youth's throat, and St. Denis felt his stomach growing queasy. Accepting the fact that the end was near, and deciding that he did not care to witness the boy's final moments, St. Denis turned to search for the Englishman. *Emmanuelle will be pooping hot peppers for a week once she learns how much I've lost*, he said to himself as he walked away.

Suddenly, the crowd roared. St. Denis stopped dead in his tracks and turned, straining over the tops of tricornes, skull caps, bald heads, and flouncing wigs to see what was taking place. Unsuccessful, he threw courtesy to the wind and shouldered his way back through to the front of the crowd. He arrived just as the boy completed his final lunge and grasped the spike with a trembling hand.

The big black saw it coming over the boy's shoulders with widening eyes. In desperation, he tried to remove his chains from the boys neck to protect himself. He never made it. The boy drove the marlinspike deep into Mukta's throat and blood spurted from his neck like a geyser. Quickly then, the boy rolled over and drove the spike into Mukta's upper body several times in rapid succession, striking like a cobra — striking until the giant collapsed beside him. Blood from the wounds showered them both. Mukta's struggling ceased.

The boy, thoroughly winded, removed his head from beneath the giants chains and crawled to the side where he rested in silence, his eyes red and clouded with tears. Mucus ran freely from his nostrils, glided over the edge of his boyish mouth, and dropped softly to the earth.

Barely conscious, the giant weakly raised up on his elbow and looked at his life's blood sorrowfully.

"Diablo," was all he said as he flared his wide nostrils and fell limp. A sea gull squealed. A mongrel barked, and a young, comely slave girl standing near the platform buried her face in her hands and screamed hysterically....

The crowd, except for Madame Genet's delirious screeching, was silent. She raved on. "Murderers. All of them, a lot of stinking, black, murdering barbarians. God save us! No one will be safe anymore."

"Shut your damn mouth, bitch!" Monsieur Genet shouted.

"Don't tell me to shut up, you stinking, little cur. I don't want anymore of those filthy, black bastards near me. You hear me! I do not want them near me!"

Monsieur Genet, frustrated and openly grieving his misfortune, lost his last bit of patience. Suddenly, all four feet of him turned with the fury of a whirlwind and slapped wildly at the face of his wife.

Madame Genet, however, was quite quick for her size. She feinted, and the force of the blow was duly absorbed by her humongous teats — one of which, was almost completely dislodged from its sweaty resting place. In the midst of her embarrassment, ripples of laughter flowed through the amused bystanders.

His actions, however, still had the desired effect. Madame stopped her screeching, but continued, in a more subdued manner, to implore her husband not to take the young warrior to their home.

Monsieur Genet ignored his wife and started an argument with the Captain, hoping to retrieve some type of compensation for his loss. The argument, however, was cut short when the Captain placed a knife to his throat and suggested he take his property and depart the premises. Genet backed away.

While Genet was pleading his case to the rest of the bystanders, St. Denis was smiling broadly, counting his money and quietly admiring the tenacity of the youngster. That tenacity, he was sure, had been critical in enabling the boy to subdue his much larger opponent. He, of course, had not counted on winning. But now that he had, the money would certainly come in handy. The boy's success had netted him a two thousand livre profit — all from the pockets of one surprised, dumb-assed Englishman. He couldn't have been more delighted.

He had just pocketed his money, when he noticed Genet standing over the boy shouting, "You black son of a dung-eating bitch! I should run you through and feed your smelly, black carcass to the dogs!"

"Kill him!" Madame Genet shouted. "Do it, now, chéri. Look at his eyes, they tell all. He'll kill us all the first chance he gets. Do it!"

Genet looked at his wife in indecision for a moment, then pulled a handgun from his waistcoat. Slowly, he took aim at the boy's head. The boy cowered.

"M'sieur Genet," St Denis interrupted, "...spare the boy's life. The fight was fair. You, like everyone here, saw the big one provoke the fight. He got his just due. If you do not care to keep the boy, I have a proposal that might lessen some of your losses and save your virtuous lady from a fate worst than death."

"Don't listen to that bony-assed, bastard, chéri. Finish it!"

Genet looked at his wife and scowled. Quickly, she stepped back out of harm's way. "And what proposal is that, m'sieur?" Genet asked St. Denis suspiciously.

"Sell the boy to me. I am prepared to offer you the full nine-hundred you paid for him. And because I am feeling generous today, I will also give you twenty-five percent of what you paid for the dead one. That, if my calculations are correct, should net you about one thousand, two hundred, and seventy-five livres. Your duty, of course, is to see that the dead one is given a proper Christian burial."

Before Genet could reply, his wife interrupted and pleaded, "Take the money, chéri. Take the damn money and let him have the stinking bastard."

Genet studied for a moment, then countered. "Can you make that an even Fifteen hundred, m'sieur?"

St. Denis balked. Suddenly, he realized that it wasn't his money he was spending. Smiling broadly, he replied, "Fifteen-hundred it is, m'sieur. Fifteen-hundred it is."

When the transaction was complete, St. Denis took possession of the slave.

"You," he said, calling Genet's black manservant to him. The man came, somewhat reluctantly.

"Do you speak his tongue?"

"*Oui, m'sieur.*"

"Then ask him if he is of noble birth."

The man leaned and spoke quietly to the boy as if he, too, was afraid of him.

The boy replied.

"Well, is he a prince?" St. Denis asked, expectantly.

"No, m'sieur."

"Well, what is he?"

The servant leaned over and said something else to the boy.

"Well, what is he?" St. Denis asked again, growing impatient.

The servant straightened up and said, "He says that he is a great fisherman."

"A fisherman?" St. Denis repeated unbelievingly. "A fisherman?"

"*Oui, m'sieur,* a *great* fisherman."

A little disappointed, St. Denis gathered his great fisherman's chain and led the way back to the levee where he paid passage on a skiff to carry them back across the river to New Orleans.

As they shoved off, he heard a loud splash. Instinctively, he knew that it was the body of the big black being committed to the river. Not exactly what he had in mind as a proper, Christian burial.

Still — not a bad day. Not a bad day at all, he said to himself as he smiled in satisfaction. So, even though he was not lucky enough to purchase a prince, he still had a fine, stout black in good health, and an extra 500 livres in his purse. All with the grudging compliments of one truly surprised Englishman. *No. Not a bad day in the least.*

At the post, St. Denis procured soap and water, and supervised while the slave boy bathed his bruised body. As the boy scrubbed, St Denis took the opportunity to complete an unhurried appraisal. The boy was not unhandsome, as far as blacks went, but that wasn't his strongest point. Stronger, were his form and the fluid manner of his body movements. His slightly slanted eyes, neither sad nor un-sad, were quick and sharp, and his hair which had been matted stiff with debris and excrement, and now clean, was still just as matted, and just as stiff.

Two heathen marks on each of his cheeks, put there, he supposed, as the sign of his clan, reminded him of cat whiskers and marred the otherwise smooth texture of his blue-black skin. Handling the soap appeared to be a challenge for him, and St. Denis had to smile at his efforts to keep it under command.

———

It was two hours pass sunrise the next day when St. Denis and his party finished loading their boat for their return trip back to Natchitoches.

"Jalot, you take the bow. Corporal, you take the stern. The boy and I will ride amidships," St. Denis instructed the group.

Jalot hesitated, shrugged his shoulders, started to get in, then suddenly changed his mind.

"What is it, Jalot?" St. Denis asked, anxious to get underway. "Speak up. We haven't got all day."

"Louis, you know damn well, I never ride the bow. Not once in all my life. Besides, I do not like the way that boy sits staring at me. He's got eyes like daggers. I'd feel a Hell of a lot more comfortable, if that savage was in the front where I could keep my eyes on him, instead of his on me."

"Well, scratch my balls. Jalot, you're getting as bitchy as a frustrated, old woman. Switch seats if you care to. But, be quick. Night will fall and find us still sitting here arguing about the damn seats."

"Well, that's exactly what I care to do," Jalot said as he motioned the boy to the front and took his place.

That matter settled, all found their appointed seats, and the low-riding boat shoved off for its long, laborious journey upstream.

———

Chapter — Six

THE EARLY-MORNING SUN PAUSED AND REVEALED AN AIR OF EX-CITEMENT about Morning Sun as she went about her daily tasks. Sometime during the late afternoon, she expected a visit from her French lover, Etienne. Before his arrival, however, she had many chores to complete. Everything had to be just right. She, after all, was a princess, and a princess had certain standards to maintain, especially when entertaining an honored guest.

Earlier that morning, she had instructed her servants to start the time-consuming task of baking persimmon bread. While the bread was baking, other servants were instructed to clean her lodge. Hopefully, by the time that was accomplished, her husband and slave, Tattooed Wind, would be back from the hunt with fresh game. She had ordered him to depart before sunrise with specific instructions to return before midday. Since game was plentiful and her husband was a good hunter, she did not think her request was unreasonable. She was sure he would not fail her. If he did, she would have him flogged in front of all his friends. This day was important to her. She had not seen Etienne for almost three months, and she wanted everything to be perfect when he arrived.

Suddenly, she remembered something she had neglected to do. Hurriedly, she went to the door and called her son, Black Hawk. Within moments, he was standing before her, panting, and waiting for his instructions.

"Go into the trees," she said with urgency, "and gather me some nuts."

The young boy turned without a word and sprinted toward the tree line.

"Only the biggest. Only the best — and the biggest," she yelled after him.

When he had disappeared from view, she smiled to herself in satisfaction and returned to her task. She was proud of her half-breed son. When he was born and she first looked into his steel-grey eyes, she knew then that he would be the perfect candidate to fill the role that she had wished upon him. Being half European, she surmised, would also be advantageous to both of their cultures. To guarantee his success, she had made sure that she did all the right things, at the right time, and in the right sequence, leaving nothing to chance. She still had the two wooden compresses she had used to give his head its distinctive, and beautifully-mitered slope — a process that bordered on torture for her child. It had pained her to see him suffer, but she also knew that a perfectly shaped head was one prerequisite that the council considered absolutely essential. She had also arranged for French visitors to teach him their language so he would not feel handicapped when communicating with them.

Since the Natchez were a matrilineal society, it was from the sons of the Sun Class females that the Great Sun and supreme ruler was always chosen. She had been fortunate, and her son, Black Hawk, had been selected by the council from among several well-groomed, aspiring young boys to serve in this coveted capacity.

That day had been a day of great honor for her. No one would ever understand the pride she felt as she watched the Old Guardian escort her only son into the temple for the Ordeal of the Fire, a secret ritual known only to the Guardians and the Great Suns. When her young son had emerged from the smoky temple covered with a mixture of bone ash, bear fat, red and black pigment dust, and wearing the tattoos that entitled him to all the respect and privileges due a Great Sun, she had jumped and screamed for joy. That signaled the start of a wild celebration, one that lasted long into the night. Yes, when the time came, her son would make a great and noble chief. Of that, she was absolutely sure.

After assuring herself that everyone was busy, Morning Sun

walked down to the river, pass the persimmon and fig trees, almost barren now that summer had gone, to her private bathing area. The place she visited each day after sunrise to attend her morning ablutions. Further downstream, as always, she could hear the activities of other women and children as they went about their daily chores.

Gracefully, she slipped out of her doeskin shift, placed it on a nearby branch, walked to the water's edge, and tested the temperature timidly with her foot. It was cool. She shivered as goose-bumps quickly spread over her arms and upper thighs.

Having tested the water, she took her long, midnight-blue hair, rolled it into a ball, and pinned it up off her shoulders with a long, slender-boned spike; unveiling a slightly oval face with two dark, somewhat close-set, haughty eyes that flitted about jerkily like those of a wary snowbird. Below, and above her proud chin, nestled a pair of beautiful lips that tilted up slightly near their edges. Cosmetic tattoos, in the form of several short, blue lines extended outward from the corner of each eye. A similar line ran from the bottom of her lower lip to the center of her chin. And, hanging from her neck was an uncommonly rare, jeweled, silver medallion. That she was beautiful in her own uniqueness was the consensus of every man who had the pleasure to lay eyes upon her.

Somewhat reluctantly, Morning Sun clasped her arms beneath her ample breasts and waded into the river. For a moment, she stood shivering while enjoying the lemon-sweet contrast of the cool water below and the warmth of the sun above. When the surface of the water settled, she looked down and admired the reflection of her perfectly-formed body. Even though she was almost thirty-three summers old, her breasts were still firm, as were her limbs and buttocks. The only mark on her body was a scar on her left shoulder — the result of a wound received during an encounter with two Attakapas warriors when she was a young girl. They had ventured up from the South where they lived along the coast and tried to abduct her. She fought them off and escaped. That night, she and her older brother, *Serpent Piqu,* (Tattooed Serpent), who was now their Great War Chief, donned red and black war paint and departed without the permission of their parents. Two nights later, they slipped into the Attakapas camp and collected two heads in retribution. For their brave efforts, Tattooed Serpent received the honor of his first tattoos. She, well... she received a severe tongue-lashing from her mother.

During those early years, she had yearned to be a male, so that she could serve as a warrior or a Great Sun. Even envied her brothers in this respect. But, as she became older, she realized that, if she had a son, there was a chance that he might be selected to serve as a Great Sun. If that was the case, then she would be able to fulfill all her dreams through him. So, with that purpose in mind, she tempered her warrior-like nature, selected a mate, and settled down to the role expected of a Natchez princess — that of breeding a fine, high-spirited candidate worthy of being Great Sun of the Natchez nation.

A tingling sensation gripped her loins and subtly reminded her of how badly she needed Etienne and his special talents to smother the fire that raged there. An extraordinary feat, only he had been able to accomplish.

She remembered the first time — the way the first unexpected shock waves of pleasure had devastated and frightened her. She had never experienced a climax before, and she actually thought she was dying.

Afterwards, she cried, embarrassed by the way she had lay helpless beneath him, weeping and wailing while her lover systematically ripped away her aristocratic facade... so inappropriate for a Natchez Princess.

Angry at herself for losing total control, she had retaliated in the only manner she knew, attacking him, clawing, kicking, and threatening to have his head torn from his body. But..., Etienne had only laughed, wrestled her to the floor, and there, explained the meaning of the shattering experience to her.

Since then, she had become addicted to his special touch and had shunned that of her husband's. For months at a time, she suffered, waiting for the moment when he would come to her, take her in his arms, give her the wings of a bird, and send her soaring high among the lofty, white clouds.

Sometimes, when he was not away trapping, she would visit him at the fort and sleep in his bed. But, that was not often. She did not like to go there. Marguerite, the *"Fat One"*, a bloated, unsightly French woman with sickly-white skin and a foul body odor, often called her obscene names. Sometimes, the fat pig even dared to spit at her. One day, she was sure, she would add the ugly wench's head to those already mounted on the temple wall. For now, she was content to endure whatever abuses necessary — anything, as long as she could see her beloved.

At the moment, however, her all-consuming need was so great that she wanted to cry out to the sun and demand that it quicken its pace across the southern sky; to hurry on its sluggish journey so that she could lose herself in bliss beneath the fury of her lover's embrace.

How odd it is, she thought, the way life seems to take charge and chart its own course. At first, she detested the French. Their Great White Chief Bienville had killed several members of her family, then built a fort upon their land a mere three miles from her village. War was spoken for by some of the lessor War Chiefs, but the Great War Chief decided that they were no match for the Frenchmen's smoking iron sticks. As a result, the Natchez had backed off and used their energies instead to win the French's friendship rather than their wrath. Eventually... they learned to coexist.

There were no French women at the fort then. And many of the Natchez maidens took French lovers, especially during the winter, when food was scarce and the frivolous, ill-prepared French were hungry and starving. She also, out of curiosity, once had a brief encounter with one of their chiefs — the one who commanded the fort in the land of the Natchitoches. That encounter resulted in the birth of her son, Black Hawk.

Then each spring, while the Natchez headed for their fields with dibble sticks and crude hickory hoes, most of the Frenchmen departed to search the wilds for gold and lost treasures. And... as soon as the first snows of winter touched the icy-hard ground, they filtered back into her village empty-handed to gorge themselves again upon the fruits and labors of her people. Although this practice placed a strain upon their food reserves, it was not an insurmountable burden. The sun, their devine brother, in his generosity, had always provided them with a bountiful harvest. So, sharing their food with the less fortunate Frenchmen was a small price to pay for the cost of preserving the bond between their shaky alliance.

This pattern continued for several years. Gradually, however, the French gave up their false dreams, and started to clear and plant their own fields.

Then, French women began to arrive, many dressed in robes of bright colors, some so sheer that they reminded her of dragonfly wings. Some painted their faces for war in colors of several delicate shades even though the mere thought of war sent them scurrying like a flight of frightened geese.

One by one, the men sheepishly gathered their accoutrements and moved into the fort, leaving behind their winter wives and their little, half-breed children. Within a short time, they soon forgot about the hospitalities that had been extended to them. They, instead, withdrew behind the walls of their fort, closing their gates, neither offering to share their food nor the warmth of their fire — except at a price.

Now... for them, the Natchez were no longer regarded as brothers, or kindred spirits in the common struggle of survival, but as heathens, and Stinkards — words whose meaning she had yet to understand.

The sun was well on its way toward its zenith by the time Morning Sun had finished her bath. Like an egret, she high-stepped through the water to the bank where she sat on a flat rock. Then, she scrubbed her teeth and gums with a small blackgum twig while waiting for the sun to warm and dry her body. *Etienne, where are you*, she wondered. *Probably still asleep in his bunk at the fort*, she concluded with a sigh.

She did not like the fort. It was not a warm, happy place, nor was it a place of welcome, but a place of refuge, a place for hiding. No, she did not care for the French, and usually, she went out of her way to avoid too much personal contact with them.

Then, Etienne came. A tall, handsome Frenchman with gentle blue eyes that sparkled when he smiled, and yellow hair that was as soft to the touch as the silk of the maize.

But, what had attracted her to him the most, was the ornate, silver medallion with its embedded, blood-red stone that hung on a golden chain around his muscular neck. The unusual beauty of the jewel fascinated her like no other ornament she had ever seen. It was a jewel especially worthy of being worn by the mother of a Great Sun. And its magic drew her like a moth to the roaring fires of Hell.

Although she wanted to possess the jewel with all her heart, she had only asked if she might touch it, to feel its texture, and to test the embers of the cold fire that glowed inside the strange, unfamiliar stone. Etienne, instead, had taken it off and placed it gently around her neck.

"Do you like it?" he had asked.

"Yes, it is the most beautiful hanging stone I have ever seen... even more beautiful than the fire of the setting sun."

"Then you may keep it," he had said as he ceremoniously aligned the golden chain around her neck. "Keep it as a token of my admiration for the most beautiful princess in all the world."

It was at that precise moment that she had fallen hopelessly in love, completely captivated and overwhelmed by the unusual man. Without another thought, she took off her conch shell and fish vertebrae *gorget* (necklace) and threw it to the winds, just as far as she could.

Anxious to repay him for his kindness, she had invited him to dine in her humble abode, slightly embarrassed by its crudeness now that she had heard rumors of the great stone halls and marble structures far across the sea. Nevertheless, Etienne had found her home interesting and asked her a thousand questions about the artifacts he observed there. His compliments flattered her. Whether his graciousness was genuine or not, she had not been certain. Yet, the words he spoke and the things he did convinced her that he was, indeed, a very special person. Not much later, they became lovers. Now, she existed only for him — and, of course, her son, Black Hawk.

Suddenly, she closed her eyes tightly, and pressed the palms of her hands against her sweating temples. An unwanted vision was struggling to surface, pounding and digging into her brain like the point of a dagger, a vision of blood and leaping, roaring flames — white-hot and searing. She closed her eyes tighter, and with some effort, willed the vision back, deep into the dark recesses of her mind. *Forget the flaming blood*, she pleaded with herself. *Forget the flaming blood and the Chicken Man.*

After regaining her composure, she took her robe down from the branch and walked naked back to her lodge. Once inside, she sat on a bench in the big room and directed her servant, Red Bird, to oil her body and comb her hair with a liberal portion of bear grease. Red Bird was an Earth person, the lowest class of their social order. She was a member of a family which had been bound into the service of the Sun class clan since time began. As she now served her family, so would her children, and her children's children — and their children. It was their destiny.

While Red Bird combed her hair, Morning Sun surveyed her surroundings, checking to see if everything had been cleaned to her satisfaction.

Her home was not as elaborate as that of her brother, the Great Sun. It was much smaller, but still respectably larger than that of the average Natchez. Constructed in the Natchez fashion of upright logs and bousillage, it was serviced by a single entrance. Six-inch round holes, three in each side wall, served as windows and cross vents. The outside walls were whitewashed and the roof was thatched. To the left and rear were several cherry trees. It was there, beneath their gnarled branches, that her husband and his friends gathered during the heat of the day to lounge on their mats and cool themselves with their cane fans.

Within were two rooms. The rear and smaller room served as her private sleeping area and the place where she kept her most prized possessions. Among them were a dozen or more belts of wampum from various tribes—some as far north as the Iroquois, others as far west as the Cheyenne. At one time, wampum belts represented great wealth. But, since the Europeans had arrived, everything had changed. Now, the belts were almost worthless. Whiskey, pelts, firearms, beads, and vermilion paint were much more in demand. She used the belts now, primarily as decoration to add color to her smooth, unpainted, mud walls. On the opposite side of the room hung a small tapestry given to her by her older brother, the Great War Chief, and a feather bonnet passed down to her from her mother's mother.

In one corner was her bed, formed by anchoring four stakes in the ground. Between them, split cane had been woven to serve as the foundation. A huge bearskin served as a mattress. At the foot of the bed was a cane basket. Nestled inside, were her neatly-folded clothing and personal effects.

The outer and larger room, where she now sat, was where her husband, Tattooed Wind, and her son, Black Hawk, slept. They did not enjoy the luxury of a bunk. They slept on mats which were rolled up and put away during the day. In the center of this room was a small table, and resting against the south wall was a long, split log supported at its base by six stakes. It served as a sitting bench and was covered with an assortment of small animal hides.

In one corner, on the floor, was a large open basket that contained the personal belongings of her husband and her son. Above hung their weapons of war: an iron, smoking stick, two lances, three bows with arrows, a rawhide combat shield, and an old, rusty, metal European helmet that her husband cherished, but never used. He had found it lying in the mud along the edge of the river many years ago — *so, he said.* A shelf held other curios and artifacts. Among them was a doll made of Spanish moss and... the skull of a small infant.

A shadow appeared in the doorway. Morning Sun looked up and saw that it was Tattooed Wind. "What did you kill for me?"

"A fat turkey bird and a small squirrel, my Princess," Tattooed Wind replied, waiting for further instructions.

"Bring them here, so I can see."

Tattooed Wind entered, bowed slightly, then held out the two animals. Morning Sun inspected both, first the turkey, then the squirrel. "This squirrel is too small. Was this the best you could find?"

"Yes, my Princess. If you wish, I will return and hunt deeper into the forest."

"I do not have time. The turkey bird will do. Give it to Red Bird's mother. You may go."

"Blessing, my noble wife and mother of my son."

"Leave," she directed. "And when the Frenchman arrives, do not disturb me — and do not enter this house until he departs. Do you understand?"

"Yes, gracious daughter of the sun."

Morning Sun watched her husband turn and walk away, his face set. Sometimes, she wondered what thoughts were on his mind, thoughts he dared not speak to her face. And sometimes, she wondered what he would do if he ever decided that he was her equal and challenged Etienne for her affection. It could get messy. Tattooed Wind was high spirited and quick tempered, and it took a firm hand to keep him in his place. But, be that as it may, that was the reason she had chosen him as a potential father of her son.

Still naked, she got up, walked to the door, and glanced up at the sun. It still appeared to be hovering in the same spot it was hours ago. Somewhat bored, she went to her room and laid across her fresh, clean bed where she lingered on the borders of sleep in a world dominated by the antics of one annoying and mischievous fly.

———

Sometime later, an excited servant announced Etienne's arrival. Quickly, Morning Sun got up, slipped on her best robe, and rushed to the edge of the village. Etienne was struggling with his bags when she arrived breathlessly and threw her arms about him. So enthusiastic was her embrace that they almost tumbled over backwards.

"Careful, chéri, are you trying to knock me down?"

"Never. Morning Sun is just overfilled with joy this day. Come, let us not tarry. Give me your bag."

"The bag is heavy. Shouldn't you call one of your servants?"

"No. I do not want Stinkards touching anything that belongs to you," Morning Sun said as she spread her legs and straddled the bag. After raising and lowering it several times to measure its weight, she stated with some concern, "This bag is... heavy. Does that mean that you have a special gift for me?"

"I'm afraid not, Sun Princess." Etienne stated mildly perturbed. "Must I bring a gift each time I visit?"

"Well... no, chéri. In the past, you always have, I just thought...

"Then," Etienne interrupted curtly, "...today is different. Today, I bring no gifts." He paused, then continued in a less acerbic manner, "I have been busy trying to prepare for my trapping excursion to Illinois this winter. Every *sou* I have is needed for that purpose. Next time, if all goes well, I promise, I will bring you something very special. Now, am I forgiven?"

Somewhat disappointed, but determined not to see the rest of the day spoiled, Morning Sun shrugged her shoulders and replied with resignation, "Yes, you are forgiven. Do not worry. A gift is of little concern. It is more important that you have come to be with me. That is the best thing of all."

Without any further amenities and still trying to hide her

disappointment, Morning Sun turned her face away, picked up Etienne's bag, and led the way stoutly back to her hovel — passing directly through and interrupting several children who were playing stick ball. At her door, a setting hen blocked her path. A swift kick, much harder than necessary, sent it scurrying in a flurry of cackles and feathers. She had already set the bag down when she suddenly realized that Etienne was not behind her. Curiously, she walked back to the door and peered out. Etienne was standing just outside her entrance, still as a lifeless tree, silently staring off in the distance with a look of bewilderment on his rugged face.

"What is it, chéri? Is something wrong?"

"My God! I don't know. I can't believe my eyes. I have never seen a man the size of that one in all my life. Who is he? Where did he come from?"

"Who? The Black man?" she asked as she looked at the giant standing in the distance with a rag stained with dried blood around his neck and staring unblinkingly in their direction, "That is No-Talk. He was found by some braves, almost dead. He washed up from the river far south from here."

"That man is a slave — a runaway. Don't you know what you're doing? You must return him to the French authorities. Soon, before they accuse the Natchez of breaking their law."

"No-Talk does not belong to the French anymore. They threw him away… into the river. He is a Natchez now, and the French have no authority here."

"Don't be foolish. You know they are going to be angry when they find out about him."

"Then, let them be angry. Their anger is of no concern to me. And Natchez business should be of no concern to them. And you, you stay your distance from No-Talk. He does not like whites. He will kill you if he gets a chance. Now, come inside, chéri."

Still not believing his eyes, and quietly frightened by the potential danger of No-Talk, Etienne quickly followed Morning Sun back into her hovel.

"Sit. Remove your boots and clothing. You must be tired from your journey. After you rest, you may eat. I have prepared a special meal. One that is sure to delight you," Morning Sun said, trying to regain her enthusiasm.

"It might be a little easier to eat if you would remove that smelly animal skin you call a robe. I find it quite offensive," Etienne said as he sat down heavily on the bed and removed his boots and chemise.

Alarmed, Morning Sun quickly inspected her shift, lifting the hem and sniffing it self-consciously. She was puzzled. Etienne had never spoken to her with such a tone and certainly had never criticized her clothing before. "I do not understand. My robe is clean. It has no odor. It took Red Bird's mother two moons to make it. Does it displease you?" she asked, her pride clearly wounded.

"Have you no ears? Yes, it displeases me."

That did it. Morning Sun dropped the hem of her skirt, bared her teeth, and advanced toward Etienne menacingly.

"Watch your tone, Frenchman. Yes, I have ears," She retorted with growing anger. "But I do not trust what they hear. Do you have eyes? If so, you will see that the robe I wear is the robe of a Natchez Princess — not that of a Stinkard. And... if my robe displeases you so much, white man, take your bag and go back to the fort with your foul smelling, pale bitches before I am tempted to add your head to the..."

"Well," Etienne interrupted before things got out of hand. "If this stubborn little princess would do as she is told, she might look in my bag and find something more fitting for a princess."

A little unsure, still agitated, and breathing heavily, Morning Sun fixed Etienne with her eyes, sauntered over to the canvas bag and opened it suspiciously. While she was doing so, Etienne laid back and watched, pretending disinterest, hardly able to hold back his laughter.

As Morning Sun reached into the bag and lifted out a modest, white-linen dress, her drab expression slowly changed and exploded into one of pure delight. Etienne released his repressed laughter. Joyfully, Morning Sun squealed, ran to him, and smothered his face with kisses.

"Oh, Etienne, you have made me so happy. I knew you had not forgotten. I knew! It is beautiful." She released him quickly, stood, and inspected the dress in detail. Then, she held it in front of her, spun around, and remarked, "You are right. The robe I wear is not the robe for a Natchez princess. Red Bird's mother can have it back," she stated as she slipped out of her old dress and into the new one.

"This dress is beautiful," she said proudly as she spun to model it. "Don't you think I look more lovely than the King's... by what name do you call the King's woman?"

"The King's woman is called the Queen."

"*Qwea...nee*," she tried to mimic his sound. Not satisfied with her efforts, she abandoned her attempts and continued rather sassily. "Does the King's woman wear a robe as beautiful as this?"

"No, little tiger. You're the only one in the world with such a robe. It was shipped all the way from Europe especially for you."

"Then, that is good. It is better that the King's woman do not look more pretty than a Natchez princess. Otherwise, I would have to kick her in the ass."

Their laughter filled the air as Etienne pulled her to the bed and into his broad arms. Gently, he pushed her fallen hair from around her face with the tips of his fingers and looked deeply into her misty eyes. The love he saw radiating there honored him, and he bathed himself liberally in the glow of its aura. *So simple and uncomplicated. Yet, wild and untamable — like the wind*, he acknowledged to himself. It was these things that had drawn him to her. He had been an orphaned street urchin — a beggar and part-time thief when he had signed on as a cabin boy for a ship bound for the new world. He was seventeen-years-old then. Now, at age twenty-two, here he was, lying in bed with a princess, a savage of noble birth, eating her food and partaking liberally of her luscious body. The fact that she was almost old enough to be his mother did nothing to diminish her fascinating appeal. The medallion, the last item he had stolen prior to departing Europe, had been a good investment.

He was still looking deep into her eyes, when Morning Sun took his hand and placed it firmly against her breast. Then, she reached down and touched him, passing the palm of her hand lightly across his swelling hardness. He groaned, reached down, and pushed his trousers away. Excited, Morning Sun sat up quickly and removed her new dress, folding it, and placing it carefully on the top of her basket. Anxiously, she rolled back into his arms, throwing one leg wide and across his hip. Her nipples brushed the hair on his chest and he felt her shiver with anticipation. Softly, he started at the back of her knee and ran his coarse hand up her smooth thigh until he was clutching the roundness of her taunt buttocks.

"Do it. Do me now, chéri," she commanded.

In the next moment, they were locked in mortal combat like opposing warriors — their cries of war resounding through the nearby forest like bull drums intimidating both man and beast alike with their lewd suggestions. Cries of war that he knew would prompt her husband, Tattooed Wind, to leave his mat and walk down to the river, where there, he would sit on its bank like a wounded animal and stare out across its expanse. But, at the moment, that did not matter. Nothing mattered save the heat of the battle and the challenge of his equally matched opponent who charged and counter-charged in reckless abandonment. Finally, when he was filled with the pains of ecstasy and joy, he lifted his adze in rage and delivered a final killing blow. A blow that paralyzed them both and caused Morning Sun to howl and bury her nails deep into the flesh of his sweating back.

Moments later, he collapsed heavily upon her still convulsing body, satisfied, but unable to deliver a suitable cry of victory. For, despite his grand display and show of force, he knew deep within that it was Morning Sun who had choreographed the complete theatrical production — the attack, the battle, and finally, her own defeat. She, like always, was the true victor.

"The black man," Etienne asked after they had rested, "why do you call him No-Talk?"

"Because, he speaks in a whisper — like the wind. Someone cut his throat before they threw him away into the river. Do not go near him. I do not trust him. He is trouble."

"Then, why do you let him live here?"

"That was not my decision. Tattooed Serpent likes him, likes his size and strength. Besides, in other matters, he is also quite useful. He knows many things."

"What could a black, runaway slave know that you don't know already?"

"Many things. He knows the stars. He knows some of your talking marks, and he can sail a canoe across the sea, too — many things. Shall we eat now?" Morning Sun said as she rolled to a sitting position.

"Absolutely. I think I could eat a live bear if one walked through that door."

Morning Sun laughed and called out to her servants to serve their meal. Shortly afterwards, Red Bird and her mother entered, handed each of them one of the metal plates that Etienne had given her on a previous occasion, and sat the pots containing the food on the floor. Quickly, Morning Sun dug in, slopping the food liberally onto their plates.

"This wild turkey you eat, it is good?" Morning Sun asked as she devoured her portion, biting and tearing with her teeth, sucking and smacking, and spitting bones liberally about the recently swept floor.

"The best. It is my favorite bird," Etienne replied with a slight smile on his face.

"Why do you smile?"

"No reason, chéri."

"No one smiles without a reason. What is it?"

"It's nothing, chéri."

"You either tell me why you smile or take it off your face."

"Well," Etienne said as he released a small laugh. "I was just imagining what a spectacle it would be — if, for some reason, the king should invite you to dine with his court."

"You want me to eat with your king?" Morning Sun asked, puzzled.

"It would be a day the historians would never forget," Etienne replied, laughing heartily at the thought.

Etienne's laughter was catching, so Morning Sun joined in. When her laughter subsided, she stopped and said quite seriously, "I would go to eat with your king, but I do not care to ride your canoe across the sea. Too much water. But, if you wish, you are welcome to bring your king here."

"That is impossible, chéri. Besides, I was only jesting. I have no intentions of sharing this bird with anyone. Best I've had in a long time."

"Then, you can thank my husband. He killed it today, long before the sun rose from its sleep."

"Then, I will thank him. He, too, has a present in my bag. Some balls and powder for his old musket. For Black Hawk, I have a new knife."

"I thank you for them. You are very kind..." Morning Sun paused, reached into her mouth, pulled out something inedible, and threw it to the floor. "This King's woman, what does she look like? Is she fat like the bitch called Marguerite?"

"I have never seen her, but I am told she is neither fat, nor ugly."

"I bet she is fat, just like that fat pig. That one, I do not like. She is cruel. She does not like Natchez. One day soon, chéri, I will kill her and feed her fat ass to the Attakapas. They would like that. She could feed their whole tribe all winter."

"Please, chéri. Do not talk about eating human flesh. Not now — not while I'm trying to eat this gamey turkey-bird."

"That should not concern you. Only the Attakapas and Asinai eat human flesh. They eat their enemies. The Natchez —

we do not do such primitive things. We only take their heads. We feed the rest to the vermin of the forest. This turkey bird was fat, maybe he — I mean before my husband killed him, maybe he is one of the vermin who eat the meat we throw away." Suddenly, she heard Etienne growl low in his stomach. She looked up from her plate and saw that his face was turning pale. "Are you well, chéri?"

Etienne said nothing in reply. Instead, he pushed his plate aside, grabbed his abdomen, and lowered his head.

Realizing that their conversation had been disturbing to him, Morning Sun put her plate aside and led Etienne back to her bed. Moments later, the conversation forgotten, they made love again with all the savageness of a first encounter.

When it was over, Etienne collapsed upon her body, thoroughly winded. Possessively, Morning Sun clung to him, gripping him internally, and forcing him to remain within the security of her warm, moist thighs.

"I wish I could keep you here like this with me forever," she said softly as she increased the pressure of her embrace.

"There is nothing I would desire more, chéri."

"Then, why must you always leave? Does Etienne know the pain Morning Sun must endure while he is away from her side? Does he know Morning Sun is condemned to counting each sun, each moon, and each single raindrop that falls from the sky until he returns? Does he know of the lonely nights?"

"Yes, I know, chéri. You are not alone. I, too, bear the same burden."

"Then, why do you not stay and live with Morning Sun? If my house is too small. I will make it bigger. No... I will make it bigger and out of stone, like the houses you spoke of across the sea. You could show me how. And when it is complete, you could invite your king to visit us. We will have many celebrations to honor him. We could be so happy, chéri. There is no need for you to wander through the forest hunting for foul-smelling pelts."

"You do not understand, Morning Sun. It is for pelts that I came to this land. I need pelts to make my fortune. And when that is done, I will be able to buy you many, many beautiful gifts."

"Is that the only reason you leave my bed?"

"Well... yes."

"Then... I will have my husband hunt these pelts for you. Let him go into the wilderness. You stay with Morning Sun."

"No, chéri. That cannot be done. I must make my own way. I cannot have your husband do my labor. It is bad enough that I bed his wife while he sits outside the door. That would hurt any man."

"My husband does not hurt. He does not know pain. He is a great Natchez warrior. Have you not seen the tattoos on his body?"

"Yes, I'm afraid I have, and it concerns me. Tattooed Wind endures only because he is devoted to you. But any day now, I expect to see him coming to lay claim to my head."

"Your concern is needless. He would never offend me."

"Well, I pray that is the case."

Morning Sun wanted to make love again, but Etienne had drifted off to sleep. So she snuggled up close to him and draped her leg over his exposed thigh. When she had positioned herself to the best advantage, she hunched against his leg until she obtained the relief she sought. When she was done, she touched his face lightly with her fingertips, enjoying the sensation of the stubble that defined his white skin.

He is beautiful, she observed as she strained in the growing darkness to see his face more clearly. So unlike the rest of the white men. So strong, and yet so gentle, and so kind....

———

Outside the night was still. The only discernible noise was that of a gentle breeze stirring the drying leaves of the cherry trees that stood just beyond her small, round windows... like Tonkin, the night god, playing quietly upon his reed flute.

Soon, winter would be securely perched upon the country-side. Wild geese will have completed their journey south, and all the brave warriors will have put away their lounging mats and cane fans in favor of a blanket and the warmth of a small fire. And she... she had Etienne and his love to warm and shelter her from the cold wind. For tonight... at least.

Forget the flaming blood, she said to herself as she squeezed her eyes tightly shut. *Forget the flaming blood... and forget the cursed Chicken Man.*

Chapter — Seven

NINE DAYS HAD PASSED SINCE ST. DENIS LEFT NEW ORLEANS. They had spent the previous night with the Avoyels, or *Flint People*, as they called themselves. The Avoyels were distant relatives of the Natchez and spoke the same language. They were also producers and traders of flints and stone projectile points. At one time, they were a growing, prosperous tribe, friendly, and full of vitality. Now, they were a dying breed. Their numbers were dwindling rapidly, and the look of hopelessness that filled their shallow faces saddened St. Denis as he waved farewell and continued his journey upstream.

Traveling upstream was laborious, and a task he truly detested. Paddling even a small boat was difficult and care had to be exercised to keep as close to the river bank as possible. For there, the water flow downstream was much slower. On several occasions, where the river was narrower and the water flow faster, they had to get out and pull their boat by hand with a long rope.

They had been traveling about three hours when they hit a small rapids caused by a log jam. Several times, they almost smashed into the huge roots of the waterlogged trees.

"Damn-it, Jalot, we need an oar in the bow if we are to get out of this alive," St. Denis shouted above the noise of the rushing water.

"Well, what you want me to do about it?" Jalot replied sarcastically as he fought to regain control of the craft.

"Give your oar to the boy."

Jalot tapped the boy on the shoulder and handed him the oar. The boy took the oar gladly and released a sigh of relief. Within moments, the boat was under control and out of harm's way. It was then that St. Denis decided that owning a *great fisherman* rather than some pampered, pompous prince might have some advantages after all.

"Doesn't say much, does he?" Jalot asked, referring to the boy.

"No. He doesn't. But he sure knows how to handle a skiff."

"He knows that, right enough. But if eyes could kill, I say, we'd all be alligator meat by now. I suggest we keep a close watch on this one. Don't know what you got here."

Jalot, unknowingly, had just voiced St. Denis' own concerns. For despite his ability at the oars, this fisherman made him very uncomfortable. He supposed that concern was amplified because of his inability to effectively communicate with the boy. Sign language, although adequate for the moment, was still limited, and attempts to communicate in that fashion were restricted solely to the efforts of himself and Jalot. The boy made none, being content to stare at them intensely like he was measuring them for a casket.

For years, St. Denis had felt secure in his ability to judge men, be they Christian or heathen. Now, he had some doubts. To judge a man, it was necessary to talk to him, make him respond so you could evaluate the depths of his emotions and find out what made him what he was. He needed to know this fisherman boy, and it was important that he know soon.

Once the boat turned west and headed up the Red River, the chore became easier. So, St. Denis turned his oar over to the soldier, settled back in the boat, and let his thoughts drift back to the first time he had paddled up this same river for the specific purpose of establishing a post on its banks near the Spanish border....

———

The year was 1714. He had explored the area several times in the past, trading, and getting acquainted with the different tribes. Wherever he went, however, it was not as a conqueror, but as a friend and benefactor. Besides bringing blankets, trinkets, and other gifts, he brought with him a respect for their language and customs, no matter how bizarre they appeared.

Dealing with the Indians was an art. He learned quickly that they were impressed more by deportment and appearance than anything else. Consequently, he wore brilliant surtouts cut from the finest velvet, taffeta, and damask—all adorned with bright, silver braids and buttons. Beneath, he wore gold-embroidered vests. His breeches were usually yellow or scarlet.

As a result, many of the tribes in Western Louisiana and Eastern Texas often referred to him as the "Great White Father," a title that he revered, and an image that he tried desperately to maintain.

Shortly after establishing the little post at Natchitoches, two agents representing the "Company of the Indies" approached him about a venture into Mexico. He agreed to undertake the project. Together, they approached the then Governor, Cadillac, and convinced him to authorize an expedition into Mexico for purposes of establishing diplomatic relations with the Spanish and to obtain horses and horned beasts, both of which were in short supply. Bienville, however, was totally against the idea, voicing his objection loudly and passionately. He based his argument primarily on the fact that the two countries were in a declared state of war. St. Denis countered that since they were outnumbered by Spanish soldiers east and west of them, the survival and prosperity of the colony depended upon some degree of cooperation with the Spanish in spite of the state of war. The agents for the Company agreed — their interest, of course, being more financial than political.

So, with Governor Cadillac's blessings, the Company's financial assistance, and Bienville's *ill-will*, St. Denis gathered a mule train loaded with goods and departed for Mexico with a contingent of thirty Natchitoches Indians

For a short while, he stopped and visited with the Asinai Nation. It was a difficult and trying experience. When he arrived, most of the braves were out on a war party. After four days, Chief Bernardino, a loud-mouthed, boisterous, square-chested savage and his braves returned. With them, were five captives. They had taken eight, but three had been eaten to sustain their return journey.

The five remaining captives were then taken to the center of the village where they were hung by their wrists from a long cross beam supported by three uprights. Their legs were spread and affixed to stakes in the ground. Each morning, they were turned to face the east and the rising sun. In the evenings, to the west. This ritual was to continue for four days.

Meanwhile, families took turns protecting the entrance to their hovels, armed with sticks, rocks, and clubs. Due to custom, any captive who could escape and gain entrance into one of their homes also gained his freedom, and the unfortunate family whose home he entered was obligated to take him in. Since the food they produced was barely sufficient to sustain them, an additional mouth to feed was an unwanted burden. And so, the reason for their vigil.

On the second day of the torture ritual, a young female captive managed to break free of her bonds, but she was bludgeoned almost to death before she could reach the door of the nearest hovel. Her limp body was then returned to the cross where she rejoined her comrades who were still chanting their haunting songs of death. Shortly after, however, she died and her body was promptly eaten.

On the morning of the fourth day, each family arose early and built fires upon which they heated stones to boil their water. Then gourds were placed beneath the captives feet and their thighs slit with sharp, half-moon stone knives. The gourds, filled with blood, were then given to the oldest members of the tribe. They poured the blood into their boiling water. And when it had cooked into gelatin-like lumps, they ate from the pot with their hands.

The lifeless bodies were then taken to a split log table, where they were hacked into small pieces. Each family head formed a line and was given portions according to the number of his household.

It was the first time St. Denis had witnessed cannibalism, and it made him sick. He would have intervened, but since he was in need of their services to point the way to Mexico, he decided not to risk offending them.

As guests, he and his men were offered the choicest cuts. They, however, respectfully declined.

Two days later, he resumed his journey west accompanied by Chief Bernardino and an additional twenty-five Asinai braves. It was not an easy journey. Besides the numerous, natural barriers they encountered, he and his party found it difficult to sleep nights in the company of the man-eating savages.

In the vicinity of the Colorado river, they were attacked by a hostile group of two-hundred renegade Apaches. Over one half of his merchandise was either destroyed or captured.

After the battle, twenty-one of the Asinai, including their loud-mouth Chief, decided the journey was not to be one of pleasure. So, they decided to turn back. St. Denis, for reasons already stated, did not encourage them to remain.

When he finally arrived at the *Presidio of San Juan Bautista,* the northernmost Spanish outpost, he was well received. But shortly afterwards, he was placed under house arrest pending guidance from the authorities in Mexico City. During that time he developed a special affection for the Spanish Commandant's granddaughter, Emanuelle, a beautiful young woman by any man's standards with long, black hair that she wore pinned like a crown high above her head with several small, jeweled combs. Her smile was broad, and displayed within were perfectly-spaced teeth. Her soft skin had been toned by the sun to a rich golden brown, and the twinkle about her black, fiery eyes never failed to send his heart racing wildly.

Finally, the instructions arrived. To his surprise, the rest of his goods were confiscated, and he was taken immediately to Mexico City where he spent almost two years imprisoned in their rat-infested dungeons.

During that period, St. Denis talked his way out of prison and convinced the Spanish hierarchy to re-establish their eastern outpost in Texas. With that accomplished, he quickly returned to San Juan Bautista and married the Spanish Commandant's granddaughter — all of which suited his ulterior motives of making it convenient to trade. His wife would be his passport into the Spanish Territory. And since their eastern outpost at Los Adaes was only fifteen miles from his post at Natchitoches, his transportation and handling costs would be greatly reduced.

The wedding had been a beautiful, colorful, and gay ritual in the best Spanish tradition. The entire population, including the local Indians, turned out for the gala occasion. Seven priests conducted the ceremony that made *Emanuelle de Sanchez Ramon* his wife. It was a grand affair, and the festivities lasted for a full three days....

————

Now that Bienville was retiring and returning to France, maybe he could get back to the business of trying to make some money for himself and his family. In the past, whenever he was on the verge of getting established, Bienville would call upon him to fight a war, iron out some differences between the Indians, or perform some other errand. Still, he had not done too badly. He had a modest home, an adoring wife, three lovely daughters, six slave couples with eight children, two young girls approaching womanhood, old man Gilbeau, two female Indian slaves, and a maidservant for his wife. And although he farmed on a modest scale, his main business was livestock — horses, oxen, cattle, sheep, and milk goats.

He was just in the process of complimenting himself on his progress when a log struck the front of the boat with a loud thump and interrupted his reverie.

"What the Hell was that?" St. Denis asked while searching frantically for his weapon.

"Just a log drifting downstream. Probably from the great raft," Jalot reported.

"Sounded like a stone wall to me."

Jalot laughed. "Well, there she is... your kingdom, Monsieur Commandant. Just ahead."

Acknowledging their arrival, St. Denis straightened his shirt, and sat up erect as several groups of people gathered along the banks of the river to wave and shout their greetings.

It was good to get home to the frail little Fort. He had not made as much progress as Bienville had in New Orleans, but then, his resources were much more limited. His fort was little more than a landmark with stake walls barely over eight-feet high. There were gates in the east and west walls, and projecting bastions at each of the four corners.

Within the walls, and in the center, was the commandant's quarters where he and his family once lived until he was able to build a larger, more suitable home. Now it served as his administrative building.

Along the north side was a seven-room, dirt floor barracks for the soldiers. To the rear of the commandant's office was a small mission church serviced by the Spanish priest from Los Adaes on special occasions since his church had not yet assigned him a priest of his own. Also within the fort was a storeroom, a stable, a guard house, and two caliber-four, iron cannons.

Adjacent to the fort was a stable and blacksmith shop, a small general merchandise store, and Bertrand's tavern. Stretching out into the distance and in a line behind the fort, were a majority of the homes of the settlers.

It was not a large settlement and consisted only of about one-hundred twenty French citizens, including the children. However meager, St. Denis was convinced that someday the site he had chosen would be a great metropolis and trade center. It stood on the banks of the Red River whose headwaters began in New Mexico and flowed Southeasterly across Texas and Eastern Louisiana to the Mississippi. Of course, there was the problem of the *Great Raft*, the enormous log jam upstream that made the river unusable for navigation. The raft stretched for almost a mile. A mile of vermin-infested, decaying trees. Someday, someone would figure a way to clear it away or open a channel through it. Once that was done, then his settlement would blossom to its fullest potential. But, that was well in the future.

Besides being near the river, Natchitoches was also at the crossroads of all the major trails west, north, east, and south. And St. Denis swore to himself, jokingly, that the *El Camino Real*, the main trail west into Texas, would be large enough for two oxen carts abreast by the time he was finished peddling his goods to the gullible Spanish.

After landing, Kiokera, the slave boy, was given a place to rest in the small stable within the walls of the fort. Later, he would be taught the French language and the carpenter's trade; a trade that was scarce in the colony. And since St. Denis' plans for the future included a great deal of construction, a *great fisherman,* turned carpenter, could be put to many uses.

Having completed his immediate duties at the Fort, St. Denis proceeded to the modest home he had built on the west side of the river, on the high ground, between the fort and the camp of the Natchitoches Indians. His wife had named it *Casa de Sombrilla* soon after they had selected the site because of the many shade trees that surrounded the property — so different from the sand and rocks of her homeland in Mexico.

———

Emanuelle was waiting expectantly for her husband at the end of the narrow pathway that led from her front door to the edge of the main road. One of the village children had alerted her soon after his boat had landed. Behind her, standing on the small gallery in the shade, were her maidservant, Douleurs, with her young daughter, Marie Françoise, and her two cooks, Eula and Zolare.

Douleurs had been her maidservant for many years, for almost as long as she could remember. She had brought Douleurs with her when she moved from Mexico. Douleurs had never married. And as far as Emanuelle knew, she had never fraternized with any males. Yet, eight years ago, at a point well past the prime of her life, the graying woman had turned up pregnant. To this day, she still had not been able to determine who the father of her child was. And Douleurs, of course, never divulged her secret. She speculated that the father could not have been a full African, because her daughter's complexion was a little too light, bordering on a soft brown, while Douleurs was as dark as the darkest night in the dead of winter.

That aside, Douleurs was an excellent servant who also possessed the knowledge of roots and medicines. For this reason, she was a valuable and adored asset.

The two young girls, Eula and Zolare, had been purchased by her husband several years ago to serve as breeders and to relieve Douleurs of her menial chores, so that she could provide more assistance to Emanuelle's children.

"Any sight of the commandant, m'selle?" She heard Douleurs ask.

"No, not yet, Douleurs," Emanuelle answered. For lack of something better to do, she decided to watch for her husband from her flower garden. Douleurs had conceived and constructed it shortly after her home was built. The garden stood on the left and slightly forward of her house, tastefully arranged around a small pool, twenty feet in width. The dominant water plant in the pool was a green and lavender carpet of Japanese water hyacinths that Douleurs had to thin out several times a year. Otherwise, they would have choked out the less productive water lilies. The pool also served as a habitat for an assortment of small fish, a family of ducks, and a turtle, they all called Stink Pot.

Radiating from the pool were three paths that wandered among beds of black-eyed Susan plants, elephant ears, ferns, gardenias, philodendrons, lilacs, evergreens, and roses of several different varieties. And interspersed among the green and flowering vegetation, were two banana trees, a dogwood, and three magnolia trees. Douleurs was an expert where plants were concerned, and her efforts coupled with her artistic aptitude had resulted in one of the most beautiful gardens in the territory.

After what seemed like hours, Emanuelle made her way back to the road where she stood looking off into the distance. Finally, she saw him coming. Short heat waves rising from the hot earth obscured her vision, but there was no mistaking his long legs and loping gait. Excitedly, she announced his arrival to her children. Too anxious to wait, her two older daughters, *Luiza Margarita* and *Marie Rosa,* bolted from the house like young colts and ran down the road to greet their father. Squealing in the high-pitched voices of little girls, they embraced his long legs and hung on tenaciously as her husband playfully dragged them with him all the way back to their home. When he reached the path where she stood, they scampered back into the house.

"Back so soon?" Emanuelle said as she kissed her husband lightly on the cheek. "And hardly a month has passed. I expected you to be away at least two."

"And that month, chéri, was one month too long," St. Denis said jokingly as he started down the path that led to the door of their home.

Emanuelle followed, then dashed ahead when she heard her six-month-old baby, *Marie Douleurs*, crying.

"Welcome home, m'sieur," Douleurs said quickly as she, too, dashed inside, close on the heels of her mistress.

"Welcome home, m'sieur," the two giggling cooks chorused as they took St. Denis' bag from his hand.

"Merci. Merci, girls," St. Denis replied.

The cooks giggled even more.

Inside, while Emanuelle and Douleurs attended to the child, St. Denis removed his surtout, kissed his daughters, then dismissed them out to play.

"And how was your trip?" Emanuelle asked.

"Uneventful, chéri, but painful," St. Denis complained as he massaged his backside.

"And your friend, Bienville?"

"He was well, and sends you his regards."

"I'm sure he did..., the old goat," she said sarcastically. "He was probably wishing that I'd be dead and buried by the time you returned. I can't imagine him having suddenly developed a liking for Spaniards."

"Chéri, you are too harsh. He means well."

"I doubt it. They don't come more treacherous than that beady-eyed, old bastard. And you, I wish you would not put so much trust in him. Sometimes, I wonder where your faculties are. If he is the person you say he is, why is he not nominating you to the post of

Governor? He is leaving — isn't he?"

"Soon, he says. But, I'm sure he knows that I am content to stay right here on this river."

"I still say, you should be Governor. You have done more, and suffered more hardships than anyone else in the whole territory. Yet, he sits on his rear and takes all the credit. *N'est-ce pas* (isn't it so)?" she demanded to know.

"Oh... I don't know, chéri."

"Well, I know. And he knows, too. He knows that if you became Governor, the Ministry would soon realize that you were the one responsible for any progress that has been accomplished here. Bienville would be nothing without you. And the little, fat-assed man-lover knows that, too."

"That's enough Emanuelle. No good can come from calling him a homosexual. It's all rumor. Not supported by one piece of evidence. Besides, even if he did nominate me, I don't know if I would like dealing with politics on a daily basis. I enjoy living with one foot in the wilderness too much."

"Well, it's your life," Emanuelle replied with resignation, "Whatever pleases you — pleases me. If you are happy, then so am I.... Anything else of interest happened?"

"I purchased a male African."

"Good. The girls will be excited. Where is he?"

"At the fort. Safest place for him until I can determine his character. This one is straight from the dark continent, and still wild."

"Is he violent?"

"Well... not exactly. But, it's hard to judge heathens. They can be quite unruly in the beginning."

"I suppose you would be unruly too, if someone plucked you away from your family and sent you to the other side of the world in chains. But, why only one? You know that will cause problems. We need at least two."

"One was the best I could do — and that one for the price two would have cost me a year ago."

"How much?"

"1500."

"1500? Did I hear you correct, 1500?"

"You heard correct."

"Why so much? And where did you get 1500 livres? You had less than 800 when you left."

"It's a long story, chéri. Let's just say, a wager was made, and a very generous Englishman decided to donate 2000 of his purse to my cause."

"Well, I suppose we should be thankful. But, you know how I feel about wagering. Have you told Eula and Zolare yet?"

"No. For the moment, it is of no concern of theirs. Besides, I have not decided if I will keep him or not?"

"That may be your desire, but you will have a difficult task trying to convince them not to be concerned. You made the mistake of telling them of your plans to purchase mates for them before you left. That has been their daily conversation. I'm surprised they did not rip your bag apart to see if one was hiding inside." Emanuelle laughed. "What does he look like — this slave you purchased? Is he handsome?"

"I cannot be the judge of that. I have yet to see any African that I would consider handsome. The best I can say about them is that they are of stout stock. How they endure amazes me. All would be lost if we had to depend wholly upon the Indians. Hard work kills them off faster than the plague. But the Africans, they endure."

"And what of this African, has he a strong back?"

"This one is still a boy. But yes, he is tall and strong. Why are you so interested? All the girls care about is what he carries between his legs. You're not considering a substitute bed warmer — are you?"

"Louis Juchereau de St. Denis," Emanuelle said as she playfully picked up a cleaning cloth and threw it at him.

St. Denis laughed, caught the rag, and tossed it back to her. Then, he stretched, sat down, kicked off his boots, and called her to him. Quickly, she sauntered over and sat upon his knees. With great tenderness and affection, they embraced, each thoroughly thankful that the other was alive and well.

Emanuelle adored her husband. He had brought vitality and excitement into her otherwise somber life. She recalled the first time she saw him, when he and his weary band of travelers had arrived at her Grandfather's post. From the beginning, she had been enchanted by the tall, auburn-haired giant who stalked boldly up to their gates with his long, beautiful legs and demanded to see her Grandfather, Commandant Diego Ramon.

After verifying that his mission was one of peace, her grandfather had invited him into their home where he was fed and entertained. Surprisingly, the Frenchman spoke Spanish quite fluently. And in his strong, quiet voice, he told them of his many daring adventures. Spellbound, they had listened to his many dangerous encounters, and laughed heartily at his carefully interspersed anecdotes. As a result, by the time the candles had burned flat in their dishes, he had already won the shaky confidence of everyone in her family.

She was seventeen at the time. St. Denis was thirty-eight. While he was not overly handsome, she found his oblong face and finely-chiseled features quite appealing—a welcomed change from that of her short, status-hungry, Spanish suitors. And although she had remained in the background and apart from the conversation, she could see in his eyes that he had found her equally appealing.

Since France and Spain were at war, her Grandfather had placed St. Denis under house arrest, secured by a gentlemen's agreement until he could obtain guidance from the authorities. In the meantime, she and St. Denis had an ample opportunity to get acquainted, and... to fall hopelessly in love.

Then, things went to Hell. Her parents thought the age difference between them was too severe. Accordingly, they did everything they could to discourage the relationship. Then, a reply from the Spanish Governor ordered St. Denis to be taken to Mexico City and imprisoned. Although the decree devastated her, she did not remain inactive for long. She gathered her resolve and set about writing letters. And she kept writing letters, seeking the assistance of anyone she thought could help. Finally, they released him. Then, before anything else could go wrong— she married him.

To say she loved her tall, stately husband would have been an understatement. She loved him more dearly than life itself and would have followed him gladly to the end of the world, if he so desired. Although she never complained, she was frightened each time he left Casa de Sombrilla on a new adventure or assignment. Each episode produced long periods of high anxieties and suspense that seemed to drain her body of all strength. She dreaded that part of his life.

Very subtly, she felt the stirring in his loins — undeniable evidence that he still found her desirable. She loved the feeling of power his desire bestowed upon her, and it never failed to solicit a reciprocal response.

"Douleurs," she called.

"Yes, m'selle?"

"Get the girls and take them out for a walk down along the river."

"A walk, m'selle?"

"Yes and take Eula and Zolare with you, too."

"But, m'selle, it's too damn hot out there."

"Douleurs...?" Emanuelle said with an expression full of unsaid implications.

"Yes, m'selle," Douleurs replied once she understood that her mistress wanted privacy. "Well, I suppose this is the best time of day for a walk. The hot sun and insects should make it very enjoyable."

"Douleurs...?"

"Yes, m'selle. We're gone," Douleurs said with a teasing smile.

———

Chapter — Eight

———

"F-R-A-N-Ç-O-I-S," ST. DENIS SPELLED OUT FOR THE SECOND TIME that morning as he drove his finger into the boy's chest with each letter. "You — François."

The boy said nothing.

"Me...," St. Denis said pointing to himself, "Commandant." Then he pointed at Jalot. "Ja-lot. Jalot." The boy nodded. "You... François," he added, pointing again to the boy.

The boy nodded his head vigorously and smiled as if he finally understood. Then, he pointed to St. Denis and said, "Commandant."

Pleased, St. Denis smiled and nodded in agreement.

"Jey-lott," the boy continued, pointing at Jalot.

St. Denis nodded again.

"Kio-kera," the boy said, pointing to himself and smiling broadly.

"No. No, you imbecile! No Kiokera. François. François!" St. Denis shouted as the boy's smile quickly disappeared. "Me — Commandant. You —?" he asked again, pointing at the boy. "You?"

The boy's face froze.

"You?" St. Denis demanded angrily.

The boy still did not reply.

St. Denis was about to poke his finger into the boy's chest again, but something about the boy's eyes caused him to stop short. Instead, he turned to Jalot and shouted, "Damn it, Jalot, take this ignorant bastard to Casa de Sombrilla. Put him up with old man Gilbeau. And tell Gilbeau to tell him that his name is François. And tell Gilbeau, he is to work everyday with the carpenter. And tell Gilbeau, if he can, to teach him how to talk. Of all the slaves in the world, I had to buy me a great fisherman, a great stupid one at that... and take off his damn chains."

"Off with his chains? What if he runs?"

"Then, shoot him! There's no better time than now to find out what we've bought."

Jalot took out his handgun. Then, he removed the boy's chains, and threw them deep into the stable.

"Come along," he said as he motioned with his handgun and walked away.

When they had gone, St. Denis turned on his heels and walked wearily back to his office. Inside, he took off his jacket, sat at his desk, and stared at the paperwork that had accumulated in his absence. He hated paperwork with a passion. So, he sat staring at it and wishing, somehow, that he could make it disappear.

The boy had him worried. Maybe, he was not trainable. And, despite his seemingly passive nature, maybe, he really was a killer by instinct. And maybe, he should have kept him at the fort longer, at least until he could have been more certain of the boy's disposition.

It was his intentions to marry the boy to one of his two older, single females, Eula or Zolare. Zolare was eighteen years old. Eula was nineteen. Eula, however, was overweight, shy, and a little on the lazy side. By contrast, Zolare was a vigorous, matured, full-figured, young woman with wide hips, hefty breasts, and a strong back. She, like François, also had slightly slanted, piercing eyes and wore her hair closely cropped. While Zolare was muscular, she was also feminine. A fact that he, on several occasions, had taken the opportunity to admire, especially the way she walked, sensuously, with a gait not unlike that of a fine Spanish pony.

He had a third female, Marie Françoise. She, however, was only eight years old and of no immediate concern. Zolare, he surmised, would probably make the best mate. Between the two of them and their offspring, he would have the finest stable of slaves in the territory.

At the moment, however, he had no intention of marrying François to either one — not until he was sure the boy would not create any problems. He, after all, still had blood on his hands, and only time would tell if he had been adversely affected by the ordeal he encountered in New Orleans. If the boy did prove to be a problem, as much as he might regret it, he would be forced to sell him or dispose of him in some other manner. Still, despite his immediate concerns, he was praying that everything would work out for the best.

Kiokera inspected his raw wrists and scratched at the infectious wounds made by the insects as he followed the short, squat man called Jalot down a small, dusty road. Although he was thankful that his bonds had been removed, he had some misgivings about the tall man, Commandant. While the commandant did not appear to be quick to use the lash, he was quite unpredictable in his behavior, and — not too smart. Kiokera felt that he was much smarter. He had no difficulty in understanding what their names were.

He wondered where they were going and what lay ahead at their destination. *Good or bad?* He hoped they would not be journeying too far. His body ached and his joints were stiff as ebony wood.

"Mend your pace, boy."

Kiokera looked up. He had fallen several paces behind, so he jogged up on line with Jalot.

As they climbed a gentle hill, Kiokera saw a house in the near distance. Would this be his new home, he wondered. It was different from the squalid huts of his homeland, and larger than Chief Motombu's house, the one that sheltered his six wives and their eighteen children. The roof was high-hipped and slanted toward the front. Across the front was a long porch. Around the house, along its base and bordering the entrance footpath, grew an enormous amount of green and flowering vegetation —

much, too much for his own taste. All were nestled within the shade of several tall trees. That, he liked.

To the right and rear was a large barn adjoined by several livestock pens. To the left was a row of eight small cabins with thatched roofs. And behind them, stretching out in the distance, was a large field flowing green with a crop that was unknown to him. Adjacent to that, was a grove of pecan trees.

"Jey-lot?" Kiokera called.

"Well now, I see you at least got my name right. What is it, boy?"

"What place is this?" Kiokera asked in his native tongue.

"Now look, boy, Jalot don't understand or speak heathen tongues. You got any talk, you save it for Gilbeau."

As they approached, three girl children, one black and two white, stopped their play and ran into the house to sound the alarm.

He and Jalot had just entered the yard when an elegant, dark-complexioned, white woman with a kind face and shining, black hair walked out and stood on the porch. Following close behind her was a large, gray haired, black woman who crossed her arms slowly and inspected him with a silent suspicious eye.

"Bonjour, m'selle."

"Bonjour, Jalot."

"This one is François. The..."

"François?"

"Oui, m'selle. The commandant named him this morning, but I don't think the boy likes it."

"What was his name before?"

"Kio..., something."

"Kiokera," Kiokera interjected quickly upon hearing Jalot's attempt to pronounce his name.

"Kio-kera?" the woman asked with a smile.

Kiokera nodded, but did not return her smile.

"That name suits him much better than François," the woman said turning her attention back to Jalot.

"That may well be, m'selle. But you know how the commandant feels about heathen names. You want to see the ole boy do some monkey-jumping, just let him hear one."

"Oh, don't worry about the commandant," Emanuelle said between laughs. "We'll call him François Kiokera. That should satisfy them both."

"That will be up to you and the commandant. He told me to bring him here and put him in with old man Gilbeau. He's going to make a carpenter out of this one."

"Good. I'm sure Gilbeau will appreciate the company. I worry about him out in his cabin all alone. Has the boy eaten yet?"

"Not today."

"Well, he must be starving by now. Take him out to Gilbeau's cabin. I'll send some food... and welcome to Casa de Sombrilla, François Kiokera."

It was then, that Kiokera first saw them. Two older black girls slightly more than his age, looking out the window, giggling, and obviously talking about him. He looked directly into their eyes. Quickly, they shied and hid behind the curtains.

Jalot jabbed him with the handgun to get his attention. "Come along, young man," he said as he walked off.

Kiokera followed Jalot around the house, across a barren backyard, and down an oxen trail to the second cabin where an old man sat on a log block smoking a small, hand-rolled cigar.

"Bonjour, Gilbeau."

"Bonjour, M'sieur Jalot," Gilbeau said with a soft, coarse voice as he struggled weakly to his feet.

"This one is François. The commandant wants you to make that point clear to him — his name is François. He is to sleep with you, so you can teach him what he needs to know. You have any problems, you tell me or the commandant."

"Oui, M'sieur Jalot."

When Jalot had gone, Gilbeau returned to his seat and motioned for Kiokera to sit beside him on the floor. "What is your name, boy?"

"Kiokera," Kiokera replied, overjoyed to hear someone speak his native tongue.

"That was your name. Your new name is François."

"That name is not for me. I have a name, Kiokera. My name is not good?"

"That name was good where you came from, but not here. The white men do not understand that name. So, you must take one that they do understand."

"These white men, they are not so smart. The women are smarter."

"That may be true," Gilbeau said with a chuckle. "But, it is the men who rule. Doesn't matter what you like. Your new name is François."

"What does this name François mean? Is it a good name?"

"It is a good name. The commandant has named you for one of his ancestors. You should be honored."

"I do not understand why I should be honored."

"Well, look at it this way. M'sieur Jalot called you, boy, and you responded. Correct?"

"Yes."

"You responded because a name is only a word. It does not define who we are, or our character. We remain the same, regardless of what name is assigned to us. I was given the name of Gilbeau. It did not change who I was. My advice to you, take the name and define it by your own character. It is a good name for a young boy."

"Well... since you have spoken, maybe I can learn to like this name. I will take it."

"Good. Now, how did you get here?"

François was about to tell Gilbeau about his many trials when he looked up and saw that the two girls who had been standing in the window were coming toward them with two plates of food. "Who are those girls?" he asked.

"Those two? Eula and Zolare. Eula is the big one."

"Bonjour, Gilbeau," the girls chorused. "We have some

food for the stranger."

"Well, don't stand there. Give it to him. Can't you see the boy's half-starved?"

Timidly, the girls handed their plates to Kiokera. He took them and hurriedly dug in with his fingers. The girls, watching his every move, laughed, and started talking excitedly to each other and to Gilbeau.

"That's enough," Gilbeau admonished. "Let the boy eat in peace. You girls go on back and get about your chores."

Reluctantly, the girls turned and walked slowly back toward the main house, still giggling and glancing back over their shoulders.

"What did those girls say?" François asked Gilbeau.

"They asked where had you come from, what was your name, said you smelled like a turkey yard. And the one named, Zolare," Gilbeau said with a hearty chuckle, "volunteered to give you a bath."

Suddenly, Kiokera was conscious of the way he looked and smelled. "Where can I wash?"

"There's a crock filled with water in back of the cabin. Wash there after you eat. Then, rest. I will explain things to you later."

Kiokera went to the crock and bathed his bruised body. When he had finished, he returned to the front of the cabin.

"Old man, I must talk."

"You should rest. There is plenty time for talk."

"I must talk, now."

"Why?"

"There are things I must know."

"Speak."

"If we are slaves, why is everyone here content? Does no one here desire liberty?"

"Yes, we all desire liberty. But, if liberty was granted, where would we go? We own no ships, nor can we pay passage back to our homeland. Believe me, there are far worse fates beyond the boundaries of this place. The commandant is a good protector.

You are very fortunate."

"How can any slave consider himself fortunate?"

"Are your hands in chains?"

"No, they are not."

"Do you see any person here bearing the wounds of a whip?"

"No, I do not."

"Do you see any person here who is hungry for food?"

"No, I do not."

"Do you understand now, why no one desires to leave this place?"

"Yes. Still, I think I would prefer liberty. How does a person gain liberty in this land?"

"There are only two ways to gain liberty. You can run away and live among the Indians, if you desire. But, most who do so are soon caught and punished. Most times, they are hung from the gallows. The second way is to serve your master well with hopes that he may grant you liberty in return for your deeds. That is the one best way. That is what you should do. Now, get some rest. We will talk again."

Still not fully satisfied, François went into the small, dirt floor cabin, surveyed the surroundings, then climbed into an empty bunk outfitted with a corn shuck mattress and fell fast asleep.

———

The next morning, François awoke early, somewhat anxious to begin his new life.

He was first introduced to Leblec, the French overseer, who issued him two shirts of cotton drilling, two pairs of pants, a metal bowl, and a metal cup. He was then taken to the cook house where he was fed by Eula and Zolare. Afterwards, he was introduced to the field hands. One of the field hands reminded him of his father. His name was Cecil, a mature man whose jovial smile radiated genuine warmth and affection. He decided that he liked Cecil immediately.

After the field hands were fed, the remaining food was placed in a large pot on an outside table where naked children gathered and waited. They did not have eating utensils. They ate from the pot with their hands, shoving and jostling each other like a large litter of pups.

Next, Gilbeau took him to see the slave, Louis, who served as both a blacksmith and a cobbler.

"Well, what you and this Bo-jo want, old man?" Louis asked in a gruff voice that startled François.

"This Bojo is François. He needs a pair of shoes."

"A boy that age does not require shoes."

"Louis, I did not come here to argue. The commandant wants him in shoes."

Louis glared at Gilbeau for a second, then went into his shop and returned with an aged piece of rawhide. He threw it on the ground in front of François, pointed to it, and said curtly, "Stand on this, Bo-Jo, and do not move until I am finished."

Gilbeau relayed Louis' instructions, and timidly, François did as he was told, watching curiously as Louis drew the outline of his feet on the rawhide. Then, while he and Gilbeau waited, Louis took a seat on his stool and proceeded to make him a pair of shoes perfectly suited for someone else's feet.

François put on the oversized shoes, looked at Louis in dismay, and said to Gilbeau, "These shoes are not for me."

"Is that Bo-Jo dissatisfied about something, Gilbeau?"

"He says the shoes you made are not for him — too large."

"Then, just who in the Hell does this Bo-Jo think I made those shoes for?" Louis asked as if he could not believe that someone would dare to question his workmanship. "Wasn't it his foot I marked?"

"Yes, but..."

"Well," Louis said as he stood and approached François menacingly, "maybe, I should show your Bo-Jo how to wear those shoes so they will fit."

"Come along, François," Gilbeau quickly interrupted as

he pulled François away by the arm. "We have other things to attend."

"Why is that man so disagreeable?" François asked after they were a safe distance away.

"He has a wife. Her name is Nadine. But, he loves another who lives on a plantation not far from here."

"Then, why doesn't he marry this other woman?"

"That is not possible. He can only marry someone who lives at this place. The woman he wants belongs to another master."

"If it was me, I would only marry the one of my choice."

"You have a lot to learn, son," Gilbeau said, quietly amused.

Throughout his orientation, Kiokera observed that the slaves who worked in the big house seemed to be much better off than those who worked in the fields. He made a mental note of this fact and decided that the big house was where he preferred to work.

Two days later, Gilbeau introduced him to Cesar, the carpenter, to begin his training in that discipline.

In the beginning, François experienced some difficulty in handling the unfamiliar tools of the carpenters trade. But, due to Cesar's efforts and patience, this did not remain a problem for long. François' fascination and determination to master the carpenter's craft became so strong that he spent many extra hours in the workshop. Once he had mastered the basics, he was allowed to decorate his handiwork with ornate woodcarvings of his own designs. While most of his designs were composed of familiar items of the period such as scrolls, flowers, swirls, and ribbons, sometimes he carved items that were more familiar to him such as lions, gazelles, fish, and shells.

It was also through working with Cesar that François mastered the basics of the French language. And by the time he reached the last stages of his apprenticeship, he could communicate in that tongue very well.

To occupy his spare time, François decided to build a small model of his master's house. Several months later, the doll house was complete, a small replica of his master's house with twigs fashioned to look like logs, and a cedar roof to cover the one story, L-shaped superstructure. It was identical in all respects.

"Now that you have completed your house," Cesar asked, "will you leave it here or take it to your cabin?"

"No... I think I will give it to m'selle. Do you think she will accept my gift?"

"I am certain she will. She will be very pleased."

———————

"Louis," Emanuelle shouted with delight, "come quickly and see François' gift. Put it on the table in the sitting room," she directed François as St. Denis ambled into the room half asleep.

"Look, Louis. Isn't it adorable? It is an exact duplicate of Sombrilla. And inside, he has a small doll family."

"It is that," St. Denis said as he inspected the detail of the house. "François, I must say, you have learned your skill well."

"Thank you, Commandant."

"Now that you are a Great Carpenter, how would you like to become a Great Hunter, too?"

"Will I be allowed to use the musket shooting iron?"

"Of course. That's exactly what I am talking about."

"I would like that, m'sieur."

"Then, I will start your training tomorrow evening after we both finish work."

"Thank you, m'sieur. I will be here waiting for your return."

When François had gone, Emanuelle turned to her husband and said, "You like that boy, don't you?"

"Yes, I suppose so," St. Denis replied. "He is a good boy, and he learns quickly."

"I agree."

The next evening, St. Denis took François to the edge of the field and taught him how to use a musket; how to pack the powder, wadding, and balls; how to dress and place the flint; how to aim and fire; and how to clean the barrel once he was finished.

Within a week, François was as adept as the best marksman in the territory.

———

While St. Denis was pleased with François' progress, other problems demanded his attention. His advice to local settlers to clear the land and engage in farming was ignored. Instead, they continued to rely heavily on the Indians for much of their food. Some, rather than hunt themselves, outfitted Indians with guns and munitions in exchange for half their kill.

Despite all the evidence to the contrary, a majority of the colonists continued to shelter dreams of finding gold and riches. They collected, passed, and re-passed among themselves numerous folk tales of certain Indians who had accumulated great wealth. There were tales of Indians who used gold as tips for their arrows and lances; tales of mountains of gold, where one only had to lift stones to bare nuggets as large as your fist. Many of these same legends had been fabricated in France specifically to lure settlers to the colony. St. Denis had heard them all.

While many were so engaged, others searched for quick wealth through more practical schemes. They concentrated on trapping and the fur industry. In addition to setting their own traps, many used more devious means. They stole or made cheap wampum belts, liquor, and blankets which they traded to unsuspecting Indians for pelts.

St. Denis was convinced that the wealth of the colony lay dormant in the soil. The garden plots that surrounded the little Fort were undeniable evidence, as were the larger areas under cultivation by himself and his administrator, Monsieur Derbanne. Whatever was planted grew uninhibited. Nuts and fruits, in abundance, grew wild. Some crops could be grown and harvested several times in a season. Tobacco was especially promising. Its popularity was growing, and all Europe was eager to buy it.

St. Denis' goal was to reverse the current trend and convince the colonists to take farming seriously. If he was successful, then they would need horses and horned beasts to pull their plows. And, he was the one man who could satisfy that demand. Currently, he had over fifty horses, eighteen milk cows, and fifteen oxen in his pastures, all for sale.

In order to further encourage the colonists in this direction, St. Denis set his slaves to work clearing a larger area for his own plantation, a slow and difficult task.

While work progressed, St. Denis pursued his short-range goal of consolidating his trade arrangement with the Spanish. Besides livestock, the Spanish had access to iron and copper utensils. All of which, were in short supply within the French sector. With them, he traded furs, tobacco, corn, beans, and occasionally, salt pork. In season, melons and fruits also proved to be a favorable crop.

To further ensure his success in this endeavor, St. Denis, in keeping with the standard practices of his homeland, established a monopoly for himself and prohibited his constituents from trading directly with the Spanish. There was some initial resistance to these restraints, but St. Denis took care of that by declaring that it was the law, and promising to punish any person caught violating it.

In addition to his economic problems, St. Denis was also plagued by the lack of religious guidance and the never-ending need of mates for his brood. It was with some concern that he watched as the men continued to bed Indian and African females. Even the widow, Braum, who could not interest a mate due to her age and unkempt appearance, he was sure, had reverted to sleeping with one of her black menservants. That was the rumor, anyway. One good thing about the widow, St. Denis admitted, she was an avid farmer. Since that was in his interest, he conveniently ignored her other shortcomings.

True to his word, in 1727, Bienville was successful in convincing the French Ministry to ban the future importation of slaves. Shortly after, the first *Les Filles a'La Cassette* (casket girls) arrived. These were girls of good moral character who had been trained and groomed by the church. Most of them, however, found husbands in New Orleans and were all spoken for by the time word arrived at the little outpost of Natchitoches.

———

During the year 1728, two days after Etienne de Périer became governor, and despite St. Denis' widely publicized desire for a son, Emanuelle presented him and Casa de Sombrilla with another daughter — *Marie Petronille Feliciane.*

It was also during that year that François reached his nineteenth birthday. It was time, St. Denis decided, for the boy to take a wife.

"How many children would you like to father, François?" St. Denis asked as he climbed off his horse in the late evening.

"I don't know, m'sieur. Maybe a hundred," François said jokingly.

"Well, to do that a man needs a wife. I think the time has come for you to get married," St. Denis stated while handing the reins to François.

"Me? I am much too busy to take a wife. There is too much work to be done. Besides, I do not have a cabin."

"Well, build one. You're a carpenter aren't you?"

"Yes. I am the best carpenter."

"Good. Build you a cabin — a big one."

"But, who is there for me to marry?"

"Are you blind, boy? There's Eula and Zolare. Either can give you a hundred sons. Still, if I had to make the choice, I would take a close look at Zolare. One like her, you could ride from here to Mexico without her breaking a sweat."

"I cannot marry either of those women."

"Why?"

"They are too old."

"Too old? Age has nothing to do with how well a woman functions as a wife. They are both good, healthy women. So, take your best choice. Sleep on it tonight and let me know which one you have chosen in the morning."

"But, Commandant..."

"Tomorrow morning, François. Tomorrow," St. Denis said as he walked away.

Thunder rolled in the distance as François took the commandant's horse to the stable, fed him, then returned to his cabin. Careful not to disturb Gilbeau, who had retired earlier, he quickly removed his clothing and stretched out across his bunk. The thought of getting married intrigued him. A soft rain began to fall on the thatched roof of his small cabin. As he listened, he fell asleep.

When morning came, it was still raining. Slowly, François got up, glanced at the still sleeping Gilbeau, and put on his clothing. Then, he walked out of the one room cabin and stood against the wall beneath the porch.

He loved the rain. He loved watching the thousands of tiny drops falling from their lofty perches somewhere high in the overcast sky, splashing against thatched roofs, and separating sand and stone as they scurried on their way to the sea. He often wondered what the Gods did to cause such a mystical event to take place. Suddenly, sadness overwhelmed him. The rain reminded him of home and the many times he had sat in his canoe enjoying a cool, comforting shower. The best time to fish was in the rain. Rain made the fish happy, caused them to leap and frolic, and it was always easy to spot their whereabouts. He always went fishing when it rained, and the urge to go this day was as strong as it had ever been. Fishing, however, would have to wait, for he had another important matter to attend.

So, rather than wait for the commandant to come to him, he left his cabin, dashed across the yard to the main house, and knocked timidly at the back door.

"Yes, François. What is it?" the commandant asked as he walked out onto the gallery, wiping his wet hands on a well-used rag.

"Bonjour, Commandant."

"Bonjour."

"I have this morning, made my decision."

"Good. I don't imagine that was too difficult. Zolare will make you a good wife — all the sex a young buck like you can handle."

"It is not Zolare that I have chosen, Commandant."

"Eula? My God! I never thought it would be Eula. Eula?" St. Denis asked again with an amused chuckle.

"No. It is not Eula. I have chosen Marie Françoise."

"Marie? Who in red Hell said anything about Marie. I offered you a choice between Zolare and Eula."

"I know, m'sieur, but Marie is the very best choice. Those other women, they are too old. It is a bad omen to marry a woman so old. Give them to Gilbeau. For him it is a good omen. For me, Marie is the best choice."

"You must be mad, boy. Marie is too young, still a child."

"I know, m'sieur, but she will be ready next year. That is the best age for marriage."

"Is this one of your heathen customs to marry children barely weaned from their mother's breast?"

"Yes. Her age is the best of all ages. No man marries an old woman."

"Well, you can just forget that barbaric custom. It will not be taking place here."

"But..."

"No! You do as I say. Take Eula or Zolare, or you can hump cows for the rest of your life."

François hung his head and pawed the ground with his foot. Slowly, he raised his head. "May I ask a question?"

"Yes. Speak."

"If age is not important, why is m'selle not so old as you?"

"Damn it, boy!" the commandant replied, his face a beet red. "My personal life is of no concern to you. Now, get about your chores before I lose my patience."

"It is raining. Not a good day to work. The saw does not like wet wood. Do I have permission to go fishing on the river?"

"In all this rain?"

"It is the best time to fish, m'sieur."

"Oh, I don't give a damn. Go ahead. But, if I catch you sniffing around Marie," he yelled as François walked away, "I'll hang you so high, the vultures will need a ladder to get to your carcass."

"What is it? What's happening?" Emanuelle asked as she peeked out the door. "I heard you screaming. What happened?"

"It's François. I gave him the choice of marrying Eula or Zolare. Now all of a sudden, he has decided that he wants to gore little Marie. Can you believe it?"

"Well, she is growing into a very comely, young woman. I suppose I can understand his desires."

"It's a sacrilege for any man to lust after a twelve-year-old child."

"Oh, I don't mean that she should marry now. But at the rate she is developing, it won't be long."

"Emanuelle, I don't have time or patience to deal with this matter. I have problems of a greater concern. Trouble is brewing, and if we are not careful, we'll have an all-out Indian war right on our doorstep."

"What war?"

"The new commandant at Fort Rosalie has suddenly decided he wants to occupy the lands of the Natchez. Of all the land in the territory, he has to have theirs. You know, and I know, the Natchez will never comply with his wishes willingly. Why the ignorant bastard wants to risk starting a war is beyond me."

"That is dreadful news. I'll wager your good friend, Bienville, probably has something to do with this."

Without discussing the subject further, St. Denis threw a waxed piece of canvas over his shoulders, climbed aboard his horse, and departed for the fort. Things didn't appear to be going as he had planned. His immediate concern was for the welfare of the two older females and the need to increase his slave labor stock. Although he was aware that many planters bred slave girls as young as twelve or thirteen with good results, these practices were in direct conflict with his own personal standards. Marie Françoise, in his opinion, was still a child. And no child should be forced to submit to the rigorous prodding of an adult male. A woman wasn't a woman until she reached eighteen — well, seventeen at the very earliest, he backed off as he recalled Emanuelle's age when he first proposed marriage to her.

In François' case, he decided to give the matter more time. Sooner or later, the sap would start to flow in the boy, and when his balls

reached their bursting point, the older girls would start to look a Hell of
a lot more appealing.

When François arrived at the river, the rain had all but stopped. He
threw out his line, but his enthusiasm was gone. All night he had been
daydreaming about his future with Marie. When he first arrived, Marie
was nothing but a scrawny, little urchin who often got in his way and
interrupted his work, many times on purpose he was sure. But now, four
years later, she had grown into a beautiful, young, long-legged girl with
rich, brown, velvet-like skin, and large, dark, doe-like eyes. Through
the efforts of her mother, she wore her hair long and in the fashion of
her mistress, rolled, and pinned. Marie was the best choice. There was
no doubt. And although he had no desire to offend the commandant,
Marie would be his wife, or he would have none.

––––––––––

That evening, just to speed things along, when St. Denis returned to
Sombrilla, he informed both Zolare and Eula, separately, that François
was of age and available for marriage.

Zolare was particularly excited at the prospect. François had
been the object of her desire from the moment of his arrival, and she
had fallen deeply in love with him. Consequently, she was the first to
take advantage of the information. Quickly, she deployed her plan for
seduction.

First, she tried the eye approach. That failed. Next, Zolare decided
to try a more direct approach. That opportunity arrived one day when
she spied François building an armoire for her mistress, Emanuelle. She
approached, admired his handiwork, and said, "M'sieur François, what
a beautiful armoire. M'selle is certain to be pleased."

"Merci, Zolare."

"You have the hands of an artist, strong and beautiful. I imagine
you could build almost anything. Me, I could never make something
that is so intricate. My talents are in the kitchen and at the loom. Have
you had any of my sweet bread?"

"No..., I do not think so."

"Then, you must. I bake the best sweet bread in the territory.

Everyone says so. You know, the old folks say people of talent should join. That provides that the children of such a joining would also be talented. Do you agree?"

"Well, yes. I suppose so."

"I agree, too. That is why I think I could be quite content if I was lucky enough to be joined with a man of talent. François, do you suppose you could build me an armoire?"

"Your cabin is too small for an armoire such as this, Zolare," François replied.

"Oh, I don't know about such things. Maybe you should come to my cabin and see if one such as this could fit within. I will even bake you one of my special cakes for your troubles."

"No, Zolare. You have no need for an armoire such as this. Besides, I am much too busy. But when the commandant finds you a talented husband, I promise to make you a smaller one for your wedding."

Seeing that she was getting nowhere, Zolare turned on her heels and flounced off in the direction of her cabin.

Zolare, however, was not to be discouraged. She was truly attracted to the younger man, almost to the point of total obsession. She was twenty-two-years-old, still a virgin, and each day she grew more desperate to fulfill her duties as a woman.

The coy and direct approach both having failed, she decided to try a more brazen approach. That opportunity presented itself several days later when she saw François walking in from the fields where he had been repairing a broken cart. Quickly, she hurried out of the cook house and deliberately sat down on the steps in an extremely careless and licentious manner — making sure that her skirts were high enough to permit an unobstructed view of her full figured thighs by anyone who happened to be coming from François' direction. She then, involved herself with the task of shucking corn for the evening meal.

When François was close, Zolare dropped her eyes. And although she could not see him, she knew that he was taking every advantage of her carelessness. A small honeybee hummed to a stop and lighted on her corn. She fanned at it and it flew away. She picked up another ear and pulled back the drying, green husk. Suddenly, she could feel François' eyes. They felt like hands lifting her skirt higher, almost touching her.

She squirmed, trying desperately to resist the urge to slam her knees shut. She was hot, *caliente,* and she could feel the moistness welling between her thighs.

She heard the hum again and saw that the honeybee had returned to hover over the corn bowl. She was about to fan it away again, when it suddenly turned and darted beneath her skirt. Without concern for her well-laid plans of seduction, Zolare yelled, jumped up from the steps, and threw her corn everywhere.

François stood open-mouthed, watching in confusion as Zolare danced about, flipping her skirt, and fanning at the bee until it finally flew away. Once François realized what had happened, he doubled to the ground laughing.

Embarrassed and thoroughly angry, Zolare gave François one of her most unforgiving looks, picked up an ear of corn, and hurled it at him with all her might. "Bastard!" she yelled as she turned on her heels and ran sobbing, back into the cookhouse, almost stumbling over the steps.

For a moment, François considered going after her to apologize, but then changed his mind. Instead, he went to the wood shop and put his tools away. He was headed for his cabin, when Cecil called and invited him to eat with him and his wife. He accepted eagerly. And together, they sat in Cecil's backyard talking about the weather while eating wild game stewed in cornmeal from a small, iron pot. When he finished, François stood and thanked the two. Cecil suggested that he take a portion with him for Old Man Gilbeau. François agreed, took a tin of food, and thanked Cecil again. When he arrived, Gilbeau was asleep, so he put the tin near his bed and went to sleep himself.

———

François had been asleep for several hours when he was awakened by a commotion and the loud screams of a woman in distress. He sat up with a start.

"Sounds like Nadine," Gilbeau said in the darkness.

"She is in pain."

"I would not be too concerned. She and Louis are probably fighting again."

"I hear others. I should see if I can be of assistance," François said with concern as he pulled on his trousers hurriedly and ran out the door.

As he approached Nadine's cabin, he could see that she was still crying deliriously while several women attempted to console her. In front of the cabin, sprawled upon the ground was the unconscious body of her husband, Louis Bodine. Around him, stood several men.

"What has happened?" Emanuelle asked as she and Douleurs hurried toward the gathering.

"It's Louis, m'selle," Cecil replied. "He has been beaten close to death."

"Why... and by whom?"

"I don't know, but he is almost dead."

"It was M'sieur Bectel, m'selle," Nadine shouted. "He did it. He's the one who beat my poor Louis."

"What in the world would Louis be doing over on Bectel's place when he should be here in his own cabin."

"It's Bectel's slut, Cleotis, m'selle," Nadine offered. "Louis leaves me and goes there to see her almost every night. M'sieur Bectel told him to stay away from his women. But, Louis, he don't listen. He don't listen to no one. Cleotis, she don't care. She spreads her legs for Bectel and Louis, and any other man."

"Well, he's fortunate that Bectel did not kill him. François, help Cecil carry him inside. Douleurs, see what you can do about his wounds. I'll have the commandant look into this in the morning."

With some effort, he and Cecil managed to get Louis' bulky body into his cabin. When Nadine lit her lamp, François could not believe his eyes. Louis' badly battered face was almost unrecognizable. There was a tooth missing, his eyes were swollen shut, and his raw back was stripped of flesh and bleeding profusely. For a short time, he watched as Douleurs attended him. Periodically, Louis would groan and babble incoherently while his body trembled like someone standing naked in a chilling wind.

When François returned to his cabin, he was in such a heightened state of awareness that his heart raced wildly and irregularly.

"The beating won't stop him," Gilbeau said after François had explained what the commotion was about. "Bectel is very protective of his black wives. He will not have another male, black or white, on his place. The men who do work there are all his sons and grandsons. I am surprised he hasn't killed Louis."

François nodded in agreement, but did not belabor the point. The condition of Louis' battered and beaten body had brought back unwanted memories of the Marianne and all the suffering he had endured while in her care. Wearily, he climbed into his bunk, and although he was tired, he did not rest well that night. He could still hear Nadine's piercing screams pounding in his ears while a band of angry, red-eyed demons with heads in the likeness of Mukta and the Portuguese stormed into his room and pursued him like hounds from Hell....

———————

PART II

Chilling Winds of War

The Great Sun, Chief of the Natchez Nation

(Public domain. From The History of Louisiana, Le Page du Pratz, 1774)

Chapter — Nine

July, 1729....

AS THE EVENING SUN BEGAN ITS DESCENT TOWARD THE HO-
RIZON, Morning Sun hurried along the hot, dusty path that led
from her village to the French post of Fort Rosalie. Beside her,
an impatient shadow prodded her along and filled her with deep
anxiety. She lowered her head and leaned into the wind, forcing
it to stir and gather the folds of her clean, white linen dress about
her slender torso.

Morning Sun was worried. Things had not been going well.
For that reason, she was on a mission — one not sanctioned by
the Great Sun or the Great War Chief. Still, it was one that she
had to do if there was any hope of preserving the peace. Her
task, she supposed, would have been a lot easier if Etienne could
have been there to assist her. He knew her heart. He knew the
hearts of her people, and he knew the hearts of his countrymen.
If anyone in the world could have accomplished the impossible,
she felt confident that he was the one person who could have
done it. It would have been an easy matter for him to take her
crude words, make them speak the right sounds, and make them
say the things that would convince the black-hearted commandant of Fort Rosalie to withdraw his unjust claim for their lands.

But, Etienne was not with her. He had been gone for more
than three years. The last account she heard, he was somewhere
in Illinois country. He should have returned several springs ago.
But that spring and another had long since passed, and still, there
was no word. She did not know if he was dead or alive — and
he did not know that he was the father of a beautiful daughter,
Red Sun, so named because of her flaming red hair and sea green

eyes.

She hated the tall, thin, commandant who called himself Chepart, an egotistical bastard whose arrogance was exceeded only by his unholy greed. She hated him more than any other person she had ever known, even more than she hated the fat pig called Marguerite.

His arrival at the fort had been like a chilling, icy wind — one that froze the smiles of welcome on their faces and made them feel like running for their blankets even though the sun was blazing hot. It was in his eyes, the way they looked through you and scraped at your very bones. She knew then that he meant trouble, from the way he strutted around, his nose in the air, taking stock of their possessions, and talking over the heads of the village council as if they were not even there. Shortly thereafter, he began to openly covet their cleared, cultivated lands with its many apple orchards, visiting often with charts and feathers that made talking marks.

At first, they had been unsure of his intentions. The dead fish, however, all floated to the top, when he ordered them to pack their belongings and move further north. When they re-sisted, he became angry and fortified his demands with threats of extermination.

Finally, as an alternative, they had requested to remain at least until after the harvest, so they could have seeds and food to see them through the winter. With some reluctance, Chepart had consented, but only after they agreed to pay him tribute in the amount of fifty fowls, four pots of bear oil, twenty baskets of corn, and an additional ransom of at least five pelts a day. And as if that wasn't enough, he also demanded one half of their produce at harvest time.

The terms were harsh, but they had agreed, hoping that in time the commandant would have a change of heart and relent. That, however, did not appear to be forthcoming. And now, the War Chiefs were talking daily of war. Having big Mukta No-Talk around did not help matters either. Mukta had wanted war from the moment he arrived, and several times previously, he had attempted to convince Tattooed Serpent to allow him to take a war party against the French. He was trouble. Many times, she wondered what could have happened to make one man so brutally bitter, so bitter that the bitterness preceded him like the odor of rotting eggs. A silent, brooding man, who spent most of his time alone, waiting and watching, and absentmindedly thumping and bruising the face of the earth with his heavy war-club.

Now, it appeared as if Mukta No-Talk would get his way. Everyone was talking war, even the children. And a war was what she had to try and prevent. For despite all the bragging and boasting of the young warriors, she knew that they could not win — not against balls made of hot iron, and cannons that roared so loud the very earth trembled in fear. Cannons that could, in two belches, reduce the beautiful lands of her ancestors to rubble. If that happened, of course, there would be no empire for her son, Black Hawk, to govern.

She knew that many of her countrymen were troubled by the fact that she had two half breed children. She saw it in their eyes and the unheard whispers voiced behind her back — expressing their contempt while being too stupid to realize that all her actions had been initiated for their benefit and to secure the longevity of their tribe.

At one time, the Natchez Empire stretched for miles in all directions with thousands and thousands of people. There were over 800 members of the Sun Class, and when one died, they took at least 20 servants with them to the next world.

It must have been a grand period in which to live — a time when the Natchez were at the height of their grandeur. Their temple was twice the size of the present one. They even had a large open-air forum with a special altar for sacrifices and other community activities. Lightning from the sky and fire had destroyed it all.

Then, the tribe split. First, there was a disagreement between her great uncle, the Great War Chief, and a lesser War Chief of one of the villages. Following a small counter-revolutionary war, the dissenting group was driven out. They became known as the Taensa. Not long after, those who now called themselves Avoyels became dissatisfied with the number of children they had been required to offer for sacrificial ceremonies. So, they left.

She could tolerate the Avoyels. They were honorable people and still on friendly terms with the Natchez. And — when her son became chief of the tribe, her first order of business would be to see that they were welcomed back into the fold. The Taensa, however, were a horse of a different color. Snakes in turtle shells, just as treacherous now as they had ever been, barbarians in the truest sense of the word. When they were without lands of their own, the Bayougoulas invited them into their camp to live. As soon as their homes were established, the Taensa fell upon their hosts one morning with lances, knives, and axes, killing the majority of them and driving the others away.

The five remaining villages of the Natchez were all that was left of their once sprawling empire. They were the last, and it pained her beyond limits to think that those, too, might be lost in the near future.

When Morning Sun again raised her head, she was standing before the gates of the fort, waiting patiently for the guard to complete his demeaning scrutiny and admit her entrance into the sad, squalid structure. Sad, because there was no happiness there, only vermin who behaved more like a basket of clawing, claw-fish rather than human beings. And yet, it was a fort that her own people, in their innocence, had helped them build.

A little hesitantly, the guard finally motioned her through. At his command, she hurried past, looking neither left nor right, and headed in the direction of the barracks where Etienne normally slept whenever he was within the fort.

"No need to hurry, tonight, Morning Sun," a voice from the shadows startled her. It was Maurice, her lover's friend, a vulgar soldier who often pestered her. "Etienne is still upriver."

"Have you had no word?" she stopped and asked.

"No, only that he is up north, in Illinois. If you are still waiting for him, it's my guess you're wasting your time. If you ask me, I say, he is never coming back. Probably living in Canada with some other heathen wench by now."

"He will return," Morning Sun replied a little shaken by the inference. "Etienne needs no other."

"That is a matter of opinion," Maurice said with a chuckle. "But, the fact remains. Etienne is gone. So, why continue to spurn the affection of someone who really cares for you. I am here. You need the itch in your tail scratched? I will gladly do the job for you," Maurice added for the amusement of several of his friends who stood nearby.

For a moment, Morning Sun considered clawing out his furrowed, deep-set eyes. But today, she had resolved not to allow anything to deter her from her primary objective. Instead, she regained her composure and replied, "Please, Monsieur Maurice, I must talk to the commandant. Tell him, Morning Sun has news of great importance."

"Now, Morning Sun, it is late and you know the commandant does not like to be disturbed while he is entertaining guests. It is best that you come back tomorrow."

Realizing that Maurice would be of no help to her, Morning Sun turned quickly and hurried toward the commandant's quarters. She had leaped the steps and was about to push open the door when Maurice grabbed her and shoved her stoutly against the wall.

"Don't do it, Morning Sun. Believe me, it will only lead to trouble."

Her breath coming in short gasps, Morning Sun gritted her teeth, then relaxed. When she had done so, Maurice released her. She took a moment to regain her composure, then turned and peered hopelessly into the window. Chepart, with his long legs and long, hooked nose, was sitting at the head of a long mahogany table in an unusually large chair. A silver-grey bonnet with a black ribbon rested insecurely upon his sweating head. His guests sat on long benches along both sides of the table. And upon the table lay the devastated remains of the evening's meal along with several empty bottles of spirits. Above the table, suspended from the ceiling, was a handcrafted chandelier that held ten large candles.

Conspicuously out of place for such a crude lodge were the two pairs of oversized damask draperies that dwarfed the small, front windows. Their base color was vermilion with gold and white threads interwoven to form several different, complex patterns.

Among the guests were Monsieur Justin, the commissary officer, and his wife; an unshaven trapper; three military officers; and two French females. One of the females, the smaller, more attractive one, she did not know. But it was easy to tell from the way she sat demurely beside the commandant that she was probably his woman.

The "*Fat Pig*", she did know. Her name was Marguerite, a sluttish, unkempt woman who was rarely without a cigar in her mouth. Etienne had remarked that she was a convicted murderess who had escaped prison and fled to this land. She sat between two of the officers, laughing loud and hearty at the commandant's anecdotes and using each as an excuse to slap at the thighs of the officers suggestively. *An unholy lot of dogs,* she said to herself. As she turned about, she noticed that Maurice had stepped back from the door and was leaning comfortably against the upright post that supported the roof of the porch. Without another thought, she took her chance, and pushed through the door, stumbling to a stop before the table of startled guests. Close behind her heels were Maurice and two other soldiers.

"What the Hell...?" the commandant yelled as he raised from his imported chair angrily. "Wench, how dare you disturb my privacy!"

"Monsieur Commandant, Morning Sun means no disrespect. It is a matter of great urgency that forces me to seek your counsel. I must warn you — if you do not open your heart and withdraw your request for our land, the Natchez will war. You must protect yourself! You must protect my child. You must prevent this war!"

"Protect myself?" the commandant repeated in mock amazement. "No, wench. It is the Natchez who must protect themselves. For as sure as the sun rises in the east, if you and your people have not moved by the end of the harvest season, I will build my plantation over your graves. Now, get this stinkard bitch out of here."

Morning Sun stood speechless — overwhelmed by her inability to communicate with the irate commandant.

Marguerite waddled over to her and deliberately blew smoke into Morning Sun's eyes. Morning Sun blinked and choked. Before she could recover, the big woman grabbed her left breast in a death grip, twisting and digging her nails deep. Morning Sun howled as her knees buckled from the excruciating pain. Holding fast to her breast, Marguerite backed her slowly out the door. Then, an open palm slap from the big woman sent Morning Sun sprawling to the ground.

"Next time I catch you sniffing around this fort after Etienne or any other Frenchman, I will cut off your stinking teats," Marguerite said, adding a well-placed kick to Morning Sun's abdomen for effect.

Chepart and his guests returned to their table as Morning Sun struggled to rise to her feet. And although she was physically hurt, the wound to her pride was much more severe. All around her, she could smell and feel the heat of hot, flaming blood. *What is going on?* she screamed to herself in frustration. *Why are these things happening to me? Has the whole world gone mad?*

She was almost to her knees when Maurice finally decided to assist her. Gently, he lifted her and led her slowly away. But, instead of escorting her to the gate, he walked her to a secluded place behind the soldiers quarters near the stockade walls.

"Now, fair princess, it's all over. I warned you not to disturb the commandant. You would not listen. You're fortunate the old bastard did not slit your throat."

"I do not understand. All I am trying to do is stop a needless war. Why won't anyone listen? Doesn't anyone care?" she shouted quietly.

"Now, don't you worry. There will be no war. Leave those matters to the men. War isn't something a beautiful princess should be worrying about," Maurice said as he pulled her close and comforted her.

His kindness and concern for her was unexpected. So, she relaxed and allowed the tears of sadness to flow freely from her aching body. While she cried, she felt Maurice caressing her and nuzzling her neck while breathing deeply the fruity fragrance of her disheveled hair. At the moment, however, it did not seem to matter. Nothing seemed to matter.

Slowly, she felt his hands wandering down the small of her back until they were resting lightly upon the shoulders of her buttocks. Self-consciously, she twisted gently to the side. But by then, Maurice was massaging and squeezing her bottom with his coarse, calloused hands. Soon, she felt his expanding desire. She pulled back again. This time, a little less gently.

"No, please, I must go."

"Morning Sun, must you forever be cruel? You must know by now how I feel. I love you. I love you more than any other creature under this sun. I have always loved you — even before Etienne."

"No. I cannot. I am for Etienne," Morning Sun stated as she tried to pull away again.

"No... wait. Don't move," he pleaded as he resisted her efforts. Feverishly, he took her hand and forced it against his groin. "You see? You see how desperate I am? Take it out. Touch it. I am driven mad with the need to plant it between your legs."

"Then plant it in the Fat One's ass. I am Etienne's woman."

"Etienne be damned! How can you be so stupid? I have told you — Etienne is never coming back. He may even be dead."

"Please, I must go."

"Look. That dress you are wearing, do you know who pur-

chased it for you? It was me, Maurice. I am the one who made the long journey to New Orleans for it. Not your Lord, Etienne. He was too busy. Do you like it? I can get you another. Ten — if you like. Surely, for such a deed, you can grant me a favor this once."

"No, please. I thank you for the dress. But, it is late, and I must go," Morning Sun said more forcibly.

"How is it that you have a husband and a lover, yet you deny me? Am I so detestable? Am I so detestable, you heathen bitch?"

"You are a dog of a man. Now, let me go!"

Suddenly, from nowhere, a blinding slap turned her head. His lust now in full control, Maurice grabbed her, twisted her arm behind her back, and shoved her head first against the side of the building. With increasing pressure, he forced her to bend forward at the waist. Then, he raised her no longer white, linen shift and kicked open her legs. She felt the serpent slide between her buttocks; felt its tongue flickering about the wrong portal.

"Oh, no! Stop! Damn you. Stop and release me," she demanded, all to no avail. Suddenly, she winced through clenched teeth as Maurice drove his manhood into her brutally like a dog gone mad.

In abject humiliation, Morning Sun buried her face in her free arm and bit into her lip until she could taste the salt of her warm blood. At last, when she thought she could bear no more, Maurice ceased his frantic pounding and released a tortured groan. Cursing, he trembled violently and collapsed, still embedded within her body. With the weight of the world across her back, Morning Sun's knees trembled. No man had ever penetrated her in such a fashion before and she felt herself growing sick.

"Aw, chéri," Maurice said, breathing heavily, "I did not mean to hurt you. Didn't want it to be this way. You left me no choice. I am sorry. Truly sorry, I am. But, it wasn't so bad, was it? Be my woman, and I promise, I will take care of you for the rest of your natural life."

Morning Sun could only moan as she gathered her strength and wrenched her body free. Her unexpected action ripped another tortured groan from Maurice. As he reached to comfort the ache in his groin, she dashed wildly for the gate, running fast — off into the black of the night, chased by the **Chicken Man**, her eyes filled with pools of tears and the brilliant, red color of hot, *flaming blood.*

October, 1729....

IN THE EARLY MORNING, DURING THAT SPACE OF TIME when the earth is in accord with the rest of the universe, a low fog precipitated on the river, then drifted aimlessly across the Great Village of the Natchez Nation. From there, it drifted toward the four other Natchez villages of White Apple, The Hickories, Grigra, and Tiou.

The dampness stirred Mukta No-Talk awake where he lay in his shallow, thatch-covered lean-to that he now called home. Slowly, he raised to a sitting position and stretched. For several moments, he sat in silence, staring out into the gray of the departing night, meditating, and listening to the early morning sounds.

The birds had just begun to stir noisily when Mukta saw the Old Guardian priest step out of the temple with a fire-stick and cross the plaza to Great Sun's lodge.

As the Old Guardian entered the Great Sun's lodge, Mukta took a deep breath in anticipation of the day's activities. This was the beginning of a special day. Today, after completing his ritual duties, the Great Sun and his older brother, the Great War Chief, would go to the French Fort to talk of peace. Hopefully, a peace that would enable them to live without abandoning their ancestral home. Participating in talks of this nature was not one of the Great Sun's normal duties. But, because of the seriousness of the matter, the council had decided that there would be much to gain if he should attend these talks. Mukta, of course, had some doubts as to whether a lasting peace could ever be achieved — not with whites. It was not their way. Their way was to plunder, steal, convert, and enslave, all in the name of their king and their God. Any attempt to change them, in his opinion, was nothing but a waste of good time. Someone coughed nearby. Mukta No-Talk glanced around in an effort to identify the individual responsible, but saw no one.

A few moments later, the Great Sun, adorned in his magnificent bonnet and carrying the sacred calumet filled with freshly-cured tobacco from the Natchez fields, strolled majestically out the east door of his lodge and walked casually to the edge of the ten-foot high mound that served as foundation for his abode. There, he held the long-stemmed pipe with a hollowed-bone bowl to his mouth while the Old Guardian lit it with a glowing stick from the perpetual fire. When that was done, he folded his arms and stood poised, waiting patiently to greet his Divine Brother, the Sun.

Since the Sun did not have eyes to see, it was his responsibility, as the Sun's ordained earthbound guide and brother, to point out the path it should travel to reach the western horizon each day; as long as the two brothers honored their obligations to one another, their Father, the Divine Spirit and Creator of all things, would look favorably upon them and grant them prosperity....

At the precise moment that the first rays of the Sun skipped across the trees to cast its warming glow upon the river, the Great Sun began a small shuffling dance while howling his ritual greeting. Cupping his mouth with his free hand, he shouted the chant that had been passed from Great Sun to Great Sun since time had begun. He shouted loud so that the Sun could hear his voice across the distance and know that he was at his ordained post; loud so the Sun would know that his journey across the heavens had begun.

When the Great Sun finished his chant, he knelt on his mat and bowed his head, barely touching the floor with the tip of his bonnet. He then arose, took a deep deliberate draw from the calumet and blew smoke first, to the south, then to the north, and then to the west. He howled again, took his free hand, reached to the east, and beckoned the sun several times, his arm arching high above his head, marking the path the sun should travel on its journey for that day.

His chores complete, his servants rushed to roll out mats upon the ground along a path that led across the plaza to the Temple. The Great Sun then accompanied the Old Guardian across the plaza and into the sacred structure.

Mukta NoTalk had watched the proceedings somewhat detached, yet, he understood the Natchez's reverence to the sun quite well. For he, like many of his countrymen, also held the sun in high esteem. The sun was the most powerful of all the heavenly bodies. It lighted the day for them to see, warmed the blood in their bodies, and fed them by making the maize, millet, sunflowers, pumpkins, and tobacco grow.

———

Two Dog, the young guardian, sat with two others around the eternal fire in silence. His shift was over. Although he was tired, he could not bring himself to get up and walk the few feet necessary to reach his sleeping mat. So, he sat in the same spot where he had spent most of the night, his cheeks parched, and his heart beating somewhat erratically.

At the moment the Great Sun and the Old Guardian entered the temple, everyone sat up erect and voiced their greetings. Out of the corner of his eye, Two Dog watched guardedly as the Great Sun knelt before the altar to meditate and counsel with the spirits of a long lineage of previous Great Suns — seeking their wisdom so that he could make the right decisions, and speak the right words that would convince the French Commandant to let them live in peace.

Occasionally, and at sporadic intervals, the Great Sun would raise his chin high and howl soulfully, his voice reverberating heavily against the ancient walls of the timeless place of worship. Meanwhile, the Old Guardian walked slowly along the walls, blowing smoke from the calumet upon the bleached white bones and fanning it among them with a feather-like duster.

Two Dog watched the proceedings in silence, poking absentmindedly at the fire for lack of something more meaningful to do. Strong feelings of guilt pained his shallow chest as he self-consciously weighed, and weighed again, the gravity of his actions on the day of the big storm — the day the rains had conquered the Holy Fire. He had lived with his dark secret all this time, knowing that he had no control over the events on that fateful day, and yet, feeling that he was guilty of having committed the one unpardonable sin. Then, just when he was on the verge of convincing himself that the Great Creator had forgiven him and all was well, trouble stepped upon the horizon and cast its dark shadow across their fertile fields. Now, he wasn't so sure.

When the Great Sun had completed his meditation ritual, he stood, turned, and looked deep into the humble and somewhat frightened eyes of the young boy and smiled gently. "I see your eyes. They are filled with too much sadness and worry. You have no need. You have done your job well and should be content. It is I who must worry. Pray that I am equally as successful with my task as you have been with yours."

Two Dog tried to speak, tried to force himself to tell the Great Sun that all was not well; that a dark cloud was hanging over the temple; that it was not his fault; that it just happened; that the fire had gone out. But, while he was staring up at the Great Sun with his mouth agape and his jaws locked like a stick had been rammed down his throat, the Great Sun turned and walked away. When he was gone, Two Dog hung his head in despair. At that moment, someone poked at the fire, and the fire laughed, or so it seemed....

———

In the heat of the mid-morning sun, a large, yellow caterpillar inched its way along the top of an exposed root beneath a mulberry tree, careful to remain on the shady side. As if it wasn't sure of its destination, it stopped, turned around, and retraced its infinite steps. Suddenly, from above, a huge, cypress-knot club hurdled across the dusty-blue sky and smashed its tiny world to bits.

Mukta sat on a stool beneath a mulberry tree where he had a clear view of the temple, waiting and watching with anxiety as he twisted the head of his war club in the dirt to remove the vile, green remains of the crawling creature. He could feel the tension of the moment. It was in the air. The war was coming and all the efforts on the part of the Natchez to obtain a peaceful solution would not change one damn thing. *Just a waste of good time.* The whites will never relent. It just wasn't their way. He had told Tattooed Serpent that on several occasions, but the old War Chief kept right on hoping for something more. *Just a waste of good time.*

Well, after today, maybe they would see that he had been right all along. And, if they did not, and they decided not to war, well... he would start his own war without them. He was tired of procrastinating, tired of running to hide every time a white face showed up in the village unexpectedly. He had only done it out of respect for the Natchez. But the running and hiding was deeply disturbing to him. He would have felt much better just cracking the bastards' skulls and feeding their stinking-asses to the alligators.

Yes, if the Natchez backed down this time, he would pack his belongings and leave. He would live in the bush, always moving, attacking their outlying homes, and liberating slaves until he had an army large enough to do some real damage. The bastards would rue the day they stranded Mukta on these Godforsaken shores. No one would be safe. When he finished, there would be nothing but white men's blood and guts from one end of the territory to the other. Nothing but, *blood and guts....*

When the Great Sun emerged from the smoky temple, several servants rushed to rotate mats before him as he and the Old Guardian walked towards the plaza. Mukta No-Talk stood and followed the somber procession.

At the center of the plaza, the Great Sun was greeted by his older brother, the Great War Chief, Tattooed Serpent. Behind him stood several lesser War Chiefs, the council members, his sister, Morning Sun, a large gathering of warriors, and the eight bearers who would carry his litter to Fort Rosalie, three miles away.

"My brother, what words will you speak to the French today?" Tattooed Serpent asked.

The Great Sun raised his chin proudly, crossed his arms, and stated, "I will say — when you came to this place, we fed you and gave you land upon which to build your fort as an offer of peace. I will say there is much land here. Enough for all and you are welcome to make use of any of it except the land of the Natchez."

"And what if they do not hear you?"

"Then, I will say it once again."

"And if their ears are still deaf to your words?"

"Then, I will close my mouth and my ears. I will neither speak nor listen to the white man again. Instead, I will return to this place and call a council of war."

The Great Sun's statement brought guttural sounds of approval from the Council, and shouts and howls from the younger warriors, many of whom were anxious to go about the business of earning tattoos for their unadorned and hairless young bodies. And as they howled and danced in merriment, Mukta No-Talk thumped his club against the ground loudly and boldly in staunch affirmation.

Tattooed Serpent, Natchez Great War Chief
(Artist Redition, Herb Metoyer, 2014)

Chapter — Ten

COMMANDANT CHEPART AND JUSTIN, THE COMMISSARY OFFI-
CER, were reviewing their stock records when one of the gate
guards rushed in to announce the arrival of the Great Sun and
his entourage. Highly miffed and angered by the audacity of
the Indian Chief, Chepart shoved the papers aside, donned his
jacket, sword, and wig, then walked out to the gallery where he
stood and watched their arrival in open contempt. There were at
least twenty warriors in the party. Some were carrying the Great
Sun's litter chair. Some carried crude ornaments, while others
bore tall staffs mounted with an assortment of flags and banners
made of animal hides and adorned with brightly-colored plumage. All, appropriately dressed for the occasion and marching to
the cadence of two dried cane sticks and several pebble-filled
gourds.

"Do my eyes deceive me, Justin?" Chepart said to the commissary officer as a crowd quickly gathered, "or is that the Great
Sun, lord and emperor come down from the mountain among us
lowly mortals."
"First time that I know of. It must be a matter of some importance for him to come in person. That ignorant savage really
believes he is a damn God."
"Well today, we'll see if we cannot enlighten him — this
arrogant, little heathen God."
The procession entered the gates and stopped five paces in
front of the commandant who watched sullenly as the litter chair
bearers lowered their burden to the ground, then took their place
to the rear behind several War Chiefs. Two other servants quickly came forward and proceeded to cool the Great Sun with large
fans made of palmetto and split cane.

Tattooed Serpent was first to speak.

"Greetings, White Chief. My brother, the Great Sun, Chief of the Natchez, has humbled himself to travel this long distance so that he may speak to you about a matter of great importance."

"And just what matter might that be, Tattooed Serpent?"

"Peace. Peace, so that we both may enjoy long, happy lives in this bountiful land."

"Look, Serpent, I am a busy man, and I have no time for this nonsense. Say what you must, and be gone."

Tattooed Serpent nodded, then stepped aside.

After taking a moment to fortify himself, the Great Sun stated: "Greetings, White Chief Chepart. I bring you blessing from my brother the Sun."

He waited a moment for a suitable welcome response. None came. A little unnerved, he continued, "I have come this day to remind you of the long friendship that your people, and mine, have enjoyed over the past years. But before that time, before the French came, and before the great river found its way to the sea, this land was ours. Not one leaf from any tree here belonged to the Choctaw, or the Chickasaw, or the Attakapas.

"Then, you came, and we welcomed you. You were hungry and had no fish. So, we gave you fish. You had no corn. So, we gave you corn and seeds from the Great Temple. You had no women, and we gave you ours. You had no land, so we gave you this place.

"Now, you say that this is not enough — that you must have the land of the Natchez, too. I say, this is enough. To ask for more is madness. I...."

"Look," Chepart interrupted. "I have said it many times before. Now, I'll say it once again so you can hear it with your own ears. This land, as far as an eagle can fly in any direction, is the sovereign property of the King of France. You, like me, are subjects to that king, and we are obliged to comply with his will. Now, for the last time... the king's *will* is that you take your people and move out of this immediate territory, and he desires that you do this peacefully."

"Then, it is your king who is mad. Always in the past, the Natchez have worked for peace, and always at a great price — and a great loss. Many seasons ago, my braves killed a French man in error, and the French Chief Bienville made war. The Great Sun before me spoke for peace. But the French Chief would not grant him peace until the heads of three War Chiefs and the head of a black man were placed at his feet. This was done. One of the War Chiefs was his own brother, Old Hair.

"It was a high price he paid for this peace, but to this day the White Chief Bienville has honored his word.

"Now, you come, and the White Chief's promises of peace are forgotten. Now, I hear only the voice of a king who you say speaks with great authority. And yet, I have never seen this king with my eyes, or touched him with my hand.

"We have given you this place to build your Fort and to raise your children. Yet, you are not satisfied. This puzzles me greatly, for I fear that even if you possessed all the world, your lust would turn to the stars.

"If you could be satisfied, I would gladly give you my head in exchange for peace. This is within my power to do. But, it is not within my power to give you or your king the land of the Natchez. All would be lost — for you, and for me, if the Sun should rise and not find me at my appointed place to greet him. It is..."

"Fool!" Chepart shouted with rage. "Have you not heard a word spoken by me in all this time? To Hell with your damn Sun. Pack up your temple, all of your rubbish, and move! And if, at the end of your harvest, you have not done so, I will have every man, woman, and child shot! Do you understand me?"

While the Great Sun was searching for more words, Marguerite, who had been standing in the rear drinking from a dipper of water, waddled into the foreground and laughed nervously. Her laughter broke the tension and the rest of the French bystanders quickly joined her.

"If you will not listen," the Great Sun resumed, "then, I must have words with the Great Chief Bienville."

"Well, I guess we will finally get to see if you are really a God. But I suspect you will need something that floats better than that litter if you plan to sail the open sea. Bienville is gone. He is no longer Chief here. I am the Chief. And I say — get the Hell out of this fort, now, before I lose what patience I have left. I will come for the land in three weeks following your harvest. Sergeant! Get these dogs out of here," the commandant added as he turned, walked briskly back into his office, and slammed the door.

The Great Sun started to say something more, but before he could, Marguerite threw the rest of the water from her dipper into his face. "And keep your filthy bitches away from our men," she added as she collected a heavy wad of mucus in her mouth and projected it toward the Great Sun.

One of the War Chiefs reached for his dagger, but Tattooed Serpent halted him just as two soldiers raised their firearms. Reluctantly, the War Chief returned his knife to its sheath.

Everywhere Tattooed Serpent looked, he saw the eyes of his enemy, hostile, and threatening. Even the eyes of the children mirrored that of their parents and caused his blood to race in circles like a devil gone mad. Out of the corner of his eye, he caught sight of Maurice, a friend of his sister's lover, one who had lived among the Natchez for a time. He looked at him, directly into his eyes, hoping that he would come forth and speak in their behalf. But the mouth that had once laughed around Natchez campfires and shared Natchez bread and women was now silent. Only his eyes spoke, and they spoke only of pity.

While his brother, the Great Sun, shook the water from

his face and adjusted his bonnet of limp, wet feathers with deliberate, choreographed movements, Tattooed Serpent took a deep breath and said for all to hear, "I see the white man now with a clear vision — as no other creature has ever seen him before. He has no ears, and no heart. We would fair far better talking to the wind. I say to all, remember this day. For even as it is a sad day for the Natchez, it is also a sad day for you."

Then, in the silence that followed, he collected his belittled, demoralized delegation and departed, their cadence a little less precise, and their steps, a little less certain.

After the Natchez envoy had departed, Maurice approached Chepart's Quarters and knocked timidly at his door.

"Enter," the commandant responded.

Maurice entered with his hat in his hand.

"Speak."

"Forgive me for the intrusion, m'sieur," Maurice stated nervously. "I know this is a delicate matter, but I think you should be more cautious where the Natchez are concerned. I have lived among them for several years, and I know they will never willingly give you their ancestral lands. I know of a better place for your plantation a few leagues north of here. Maybe you should take a look at it."

"To Hell and back if I will. Why don't you go tell the Natchez to go look at it. They are the ones who will be needing a place to live. Did you consider that?"

"No, I did not. That would be wasted effort on my part. They are seriously planning for a fucking war."

"I do not give a damn what they are planning. If it is war they want, then a war they will get. What galls me is the fact that your allegiance seems to be with the asses of their Stinkard bitches rather your own countrymen."

"Believe me, Commandant, it's not about that. It's about killing and getting killed."

"Well, you and the Natchez can go right straight to Hell…, and you both can kiss my ass on the way there.

Guards! Guards!" Chepart yelled at the top of his voice.

Two soldiers quickly entered the room. "Yes, Commandant?"

"Chain this cowardly bastard and throw his stupid ass in the jail!"

The soldiers hurriedly arrested a bewildered Maurice and escorted him out the room.

———————

In the center of the Great Village, in the amber light of a small fire, the War Council gathered and talked....

"Was it for their red, and blue blankets that we gave them our corn, our game, and our fish? I say, we did better with our buffalo skins which were warmer and lasted longer. Was it for their sick breath that kills without the touch of a knife or lance that we gave them the fruit of the persimmon? Or for their whiskey, that we gave them our women? I say, we have lost in every exchange.

"Before the white men came, we lived like brave men, happy with who we were, and what we had. Now, we lie idle and grow fat while our young warriors turn to women — not one tattoo upon any of their bodies.... Now, we live like dogs, crouching at our master's feet, thankful for his worth-less blankets that will not keep you warm, and his foul-smell-ing salt pork that you cannot eat, even lower in his sights than the black slaves he holds in chains; never again to do or go where we please.

"I say we must free the land of the Natchez and turn back this enemy who has no honor. This enemy who seeks to en-slave all nations. I speak for War!"

These words spoken by Tattooed Serpent were followed by similar words from the other members of the council. All spoke for war.

Mukta No-Talk looked on, smiling in satisfaction, and

thumping his club into the ground excitedly with each declaration made by the Chiefs of War.

Yes, he knew it. It had to happen sooner or later. It was time. The time of retribution had finally arrived. Now, maybe he could make things right. Now, maybe he could honor the debt he owed to the black, faceless souls that fell before the blazing guns and cutlasses on the deck of the Marianne following his innocent betrayal. Now, maybe he could rid himself of the demons that had haunted him since that infamous day. Finally, the time had come. *Diablo keep your distance, and Mukta will send a thousand worst souls to nourish your unholy fires.*

Morning Sun, who had been standing aside listening and observing the smile on Mukta No-Talk's face, could hold her peace no longer. And although women did not normally take part in these types of proceedings, she elbowed her way into the circle and spoke anyway.

"You speak of war as if it is a child's game. Do you forget that the French have many muskets and cannons?"

"No, I have not forgotten," Tattooed Serpent responded. "But, we have over nine hundred braves. The French number less than two hundred. One Frenchman — one ball. One Natchez — one lance."

"But there are more in the land of Orleans and the Fort in the land of the Natchitoches. And what of the Choctaw, friends of the French? Do you think they will stand idly by?"

"No, I have not forgotten the Choctaw. I will speak to them for their three thousand braves. With their help, it will be a small task to chase the French into the sea."

"What if the Choctaw betray you and tell the French of your plans for war?"

Tattooed Serpent paused, looked at Morning Sun accusingly, then said sarcastically, "Is that any more or less than you have done, little sister? I know of your visit to the Fort and the words spoken there. Let the Choctaw speak, if they will. Because of you, the French already know of our plans for war. But — as you see, they are not concerned. They are the masters, and no master fears his own dogs."

Embarrassed that Tattooed Serpent knew of her clandestine visit to the Fort, Morning Sun coughed and cleared her throat. She started to say something more, but changed her mind and quickly retreated toward her lodge. At the edge of the gathering, she stopped abruptly before Mukta No-Talk.

"I see you smile now for the first time, and it makes me sick to see you do so," she stated with quiet venom in her voice. "I hope you are satisfied, and I hope that our deaths will bring you great joy."

"I am here only to serve and protect, my princess," Mukta replied devotedly.

"Don't you understand, you black imbecile? I do not want or need your kind of protection!"

With that remark, Morning Sun struck the giant violently across his cheek with the palm of her hand, turned on her heels, and continued stoutly on her way to her lodge.

The slap turned Mukta No-Talk's face to rock, but he did not retaliate. As Morning Sun stormed away, his anger faded and his bruised lips slowly turned into an open sneer.

Once inside her lodge, Morning Sun gave full vent to her frustration, stomping about the room, declaring the stupidity of men and their false pride, ranting, and raving until she knocked over her small table.

The noise frightened her daughter, Red Sun, and the toddler began to cry. Still breathing heavily from her exertions, Morning Sun went to her daughter and lifted her into her arms. As she comforted the child, she strolled casually back to the doorway and peered out. She searched the figures in the darkness until she caught sight of her son, Black Hawk. He was standing on the perimeter of the council. And like everyone else, he too, was caught up in the fever of the excitement. Sadness overwhelmed her, and she could hold back the tears no longer. So, she did not try. She let the tears flow softly, and openly. And while she cried, her innocent baby daughter fingered and tugged at the beautiful, silver medallion which hung from her weary neck like a mountain of heavy, granite stone. *Chicken man... chicken man....*

———————

During the next several weeks, the Natchez prepared for war. The war calumet was removed from the Temple and hung on a post in front of the Great War Chief's lodge. Women and children collected switch cane reeds and dogwood switches for arrow shafts, and stones, chipped bones, and gar scales for the arrowheads. Straight saplings of hickory, pecan, and Osage orange were used for the lances and bows. The men shaped and fashioned the implements, often working late into the night in small groups around small fires, working and listening while their elders recounted past battles and told of the daring exploits of legendary Natchez heroes. In the background, the older women instructed the younger in the treatment of major and minor wounds.

During the day, the warriors trained in defensive and offensive tactics and instructed each other in the correct use of firearms and other weapons. At night, they danced and performed their purification ritual by drinking the black drink, *Ilex vomitoria*, a red berry that made them vomit.

While they were so occupied, the Guardians of the fire prayed in the temple and mixed the paints for war. Red and white for the body, and black for the eyes.

A party of warriors were dispatched to visit the Chickasaws to trade and barter for arms. At the same time, Tattooed Serpent sent a messenger to contact the Choctaws. Three days later, the messenger returned and reported that although the Choctaw were receptive to the idea, they had some reservations. They requested to be contacted again for their final decision.

The Natchez arsenal consisted of eighteen firearms, including six which they obtained from the Chickasaw, and very little powder. A number of the braves, however, had ongoing arrangements with some of the French residents. In these arrangements, they were allowed to borrow weapons for the hunt in exchange for an equal share of the kill. In the past, this practice had benefited both. Soon, it would benefit only the Natchez.

To further belay any suspicions, the Natchez continued "business as usual" with the Fort and its outlying residents, paying their tribute to Chepart uncontested and precisely as scheduled.

Since the element of surprise was crucial, Tattooed Serpent decided to exclude the Choctaws. And for the same reason, he also did not tell anyone, not even the Great Sun or his War Chiefs, the details of his final battle plans. It was important that he show the way. If he was successful in this initial conquest, then, he reasoned, the Choctaws and other nations would not hesitate to join him in his noble campaign. His campaign, however, would not end with the French. All whites had to be eliminated. That included the English and the Spanish, too. For one was no better or worse than the other. It would be a war to end all wars. One combined army of Natchez, Choctaw, Chickasaw, Seminole, Apache, and Iroquois braves sweeping the country clean from horizon-to-horizon like one giant, red tide. The impact of such a bold undertaking would be truly astounding.

Chapter — Eleven

————

Evening — 28 November 1729....

CHEPART FELT EXHILARATED. IT HAD BEEN ONE UNUSUALLY
FAST-PACED DAY. It had begun early that morning with the Natchez
bringing in the first portion of their final tribute. Best yet, was the
fact that they had brought in more than required — at least twenty
percent more than required. Maybe that was the bastard's way of
trying to win his good graces. Of course, he accepted their meager
offerings. What fool would not? Be that as it may, there was nothing they had that could entice him to change his mind. Not their
bounty, nor the asses of their stinking bitches. There was too much
at stake. No, when he said something, he meant it. They would just
have to learn the hard way — *the ignorant bastards.* Bienville had
suggested in a letter that he should use an iron hand to keep the
Natchez in check because he felt that they would be an obstacle
and interfere with trade along the Mississippi River. Well, he had
gone a step further. With them gone there would be no obstacle.

Maybe, even after they move, it might not be a bad idea to
continue charging them tribute. A tax, so to speak, for their upkeep
and protection — and for the privilege of living on the king's land.

The money from the tribute, he would invest in a shipping
company, build a small dock, and control the flow of all the goods
from the surrounding area. He had just discussed such a project
that day with Murphy, the "Irishman". The Irish were good boat-
men with strong backs. Since they did not always align themselves
with the English, even if a major war erupted between France and
England, their business relationship would not be seriously jeop-
ardized. They both could still make a profit.

His immediate designs, however, were to start the construction of his plantation — as soon as possible. He would allow the Natchez another week, maybe two, to complete their move. Then, he would start moving in. With a little luck, everything could be accomplished and ready for production by planting season next year, especially since the Natchez's fields were already cleared. The temple would make an ideal place to store grain once he cleared it of those disgusting skulls. Yes, it had been quite a day.

"Phillipe, light the candles, then, fetch the wench, Claudette," he instructed his black manservant. "I think I need a little *amour* to settle my nerves tonight."

Phillipe trimmed the wicks and lit several night candles, placing one near the bed. When he finished, he shuffled quietly out the door.

While he waited, Chepart lifted his sleeping gown above his long, ungainly legs, walked over, and straddled a water-filled crock. Grimacing, he quickly doused its cold contents upon his privates and hurriedly dried himself. He had just dropped his gown and jumped into bed, when he heard a soft, quick knock at the door.

"Enter, Claudette. The door is not locked," he yelled.

The door opened slowly and a small-boned, early middle-aged woman entered and quickly closed it behind her.

"Cold out there," Claudette said as she removed her black headscarf and revealed a pleasing, but not exceptionally attractive face. One, however, that was heavy with hastily applied makeup. She removed her jacket, threw it on the floor, then shimmied out of her plain woolen dress. For a moment, she stood shivering and rubbing her arms, just long enough to allow Chepart ample time to admire her greatest asset — her body, adorned with pear-shaped breasts, nicely turned buttocks, and a pair of slender, shapely legs.

"Well, I'm glad to see you've already warmed the bed. I suspect there will be frost on the ground by morning. I am truly glad you called. I hate sleeping alone on chilly nights," she added as she clinched her hands between her legs and mince-stepped toward the bed.

"Wash first," Chepart redirected, nodding his head toward the crock of cold water.

"Not tonight, chéri. It's too cold. I have had one bath already today. Another would catch me a killing cold."

"Then catch it, if you must. I cannot risk having you foul the odor of my bed again. Last time, I had to air it for a week before I could rest properly."

"That was only because I was within a day of my monthly malady. There is no danger, now. My sickness is still ten days away, chéri."

"I don't care what the reason. Wash, or leave."

Claudette bristled. Reluctantly, she did as she was told. When she was done, she shivered and jumped quickly into the bed, snuggling tightly against Chepart's warm body.

"I saw you talking to the Irishman today for what seemed like ages, all hush-hush. Is there some new scheme brewing?" she asked as she slid her cold hands beneath Chepart's gown and fondled his flaccid penis with her nimble fingers.

"Only business, chéri. None of which concerns you."

"I was just wondering, trying to make small talk. I know not to pry into your private affairs. But can't a lady be even a little curious without you getting upset, chéri?"

"Prying by anyone irritates me, especially when it does not concern them. And nothing I do is of concern to you."

"Nothing, chéri?"

"Nothing."

Claudette looked at Chepart in the faint light of the candle and felt anger slowly raising its ugly head. Softly, she asked, "By that, are you also saying that I am not to be a part of your new life?"

"Depends on what you mean when you say — a part of."

"I mean, what is to happen to me once you move to your new plantation? I mean, is there going to be a place there for me or not?" she almost shouted.

"Maybe, and maybe not. Even so, I still expect to wed in the near future. Provided, of course, I am able to find a suitable wife."

"A suitable wife, chéri? Are you saying that you do not find me suitable as a wife?"

"Don't be naive, woman. Surely, even you don't expect a man of my station to wed a whore."

"I am not a whore, damn it! And I wish you would stop calling me one."

"You were a whore long before I met you."

"Chéri, that was long ago. Out of necessity. Not out of desire. If you would only look, you would see that I am really a decent person inside. All I long for is a home and a family. All I want is someone to care for, and someone to care for me. And I do not want to be called a whore the rest of my life."

"Once a whore — always a whore. It is your destiny. What, pray God, would my associates say of me, if I was to marry a stinking whore."

"Damn-it, stop calling me a whore!"

"Bridle your mouth, and your ambitions, bitch. You are trying my patience," Chepart retorted, raising his hand as if to strike her.

Claudette recoiled and covered her face with her arm.

Chepart relaxed, then continued. "I did not request you here to discuss the merits of your profession. Please proceed about your business or leave."

Claudette rose to a sitting position and stared at Chepart in the darkness, seething in quiet anger, and wishing she had the courage to knock his teeth around to the other side of his head. After a moment, she sighed, then slowly eased her head beneath the covers. At the first touch of her moist mouth, Chepart groaned eerily, his toes curling painfully like the claws of a griffon as he watched her labor at her task.

"Aw... chéri, you do your job well. Enough now. Come and finish me. I can bear this torture no longer."

Halfheartedly, Claudette rose to her knees, blew saliva into her hand, and used it to lubricate herself. When she had completed the procedure, she lifted her leg and straddled Chepart's long, rigid body. She started to say something... but then, changed her mind. Instead, she took a deep breath, reached below, then impaled herself brutally.

Chepart groaned in pain....

Once he was firmly embedded, Claudette gritted her teeth and set about discharging the duties of her ageless profession. But, it was not pleasure that was on her mind this night. It was agony and pain that she was about.

Deliberately, she set her jaws and battered down against Chepart viciously, trying her best to hurt and punish him for all the hurt and humiliation she had ever received at the hands of Chepart and all the other noble bastards of the world. As her labors intensified, she felt her own passions rising, and they rose despite the contempt she felt for the asshole who lay beneath her sweating body.

Through it all, Chepart lay submissively; grunting obscenely, accepting her wrath without contest, and enjoying the punishment offered with such an uncanny delight that Claudette's stomach turned.

Finally, a low groan swelled slowly from somewhere deep within Chepart's chest. His knees contracted, and convulsions more violent than any she had ever seen, gripped his body and shook him like a wet rag. Then, he was still....

In the flickering light of the candle, Claudette looked down at Chepart and was overcome with revulsion. *How I would love to empty my bowels in your disgusting face*, she thought as she disengaged herself and rolled to her side of the narrow bed. There, she waited patiently until Chepart was snoring deeply. Then, she took two of her fingers and used them to bring herself to a silently screaming climax. When her body finished shaking, she turned her back and snuggled deep into the warmth of the musty blankets.

———

The next morning, Claudette untangled herself from Chepart's limbs, took the top blanket, threw it around her naked body, and tiptoed over to a pot where she relieved her bladder. When she had finished, she took a moment to inspect the damage she had inflicted upon herself during the previous night's activities. Her vagina was sore to the touch and it appeared that the only person she had injured in her anger was herself. Carefully, she blotted her moist pubic hairs with the edge of her blanket, got up, and walked over to the window where she paused to watch the awakening of a beautiful, frosty morning — the frost sparkling like thousands of tiny diamonds in the first soft rays of light.

A single guard sat on a stool near the gate dozing, his chin buried deep into the collar of his long coat, his musket lying limply across his thighs. Suddenly, there was a commotion at the gate. As Claudette watched, the guard stood, stretched, sauntered over to the gate and peeped out the peephole to observe a small group of Natchez delivering their tribute. Yawning, the guard then proceeded to open the gate. When the Natchez gained entrance, they bowed before the guard as if to thank him. Then, the leader pulled out a handgun and shot him dead. Claudette screamed as the sound of the gun shot ricocheted through the countryside and ripped away the quiet of the morning.

Then, she saw them. Natchez, their bodies painted in red, white, and black harlequin patterns, swarming through the gates and over the walls like a pack of silent ghosts. In the next moment, the air was filled with loud howls, shouts of battle, and gunfire as the wild savages descended upon the still half-asleep inhabitants.

"Oh, my God! Oh, my God," was all she could say as she watched the chaos erupt.

"What is it? What is it?" Chepart asked as he jumped from his bed and rushed to the window.

"Natchez. Oh, my God, Natchez everywhere!" she screamed, pointing out the window and watching a dumbfounded Chepart, rooted to the spot, staring out in disbelief.

"Do something! Oh, my God, do something quick!" Claudette yelled as she watched her lover spin around several times in in-decision before rushing to retrieve his pants. "To Hell with your pants, you stupid ass. Get your musket and shoot the bastards. Shoot the bastards!"

Spurred by Claudette's yelping, Chepart dropped his pants and rushed to the wall to get his musket. He was too late. Suddenly, the door fell away from its hinges and several wild-eyed Natchez rushed in. Claudette screamed, dropped to her knees, and cowered. Quickly, one grabbed her by the hair and yanked, forcing her to stand while the others corralled Chepart and tied his hands behind with a leather thong. Outside, screams of terror and gunfire continued.

"Please. Please..." she begged as the one holding her hair snatched the blanket from her shivering body. "Please," she begged again. "Don't hurt me! I am not your enemy. I am your friend."

The brave laughed and jerked her head back, exposing her delicate throat. Claudette screamed again.

"Leave her alone, you stinking, red bastards," Chepart yelled several times until a gun butt plowed into his chest.

"Please. Don't kill me. Please....," Claudette pleaded as she strained to search the eyes of her captor, looking for any sign of compassion. Her captor, however, did not appear to understand. He, instead, laid his filthy, cold hands upon her breasts and tested their resiliency. She flinched. The others laughed. Then, he released her hair, squatted to his haunches, and inspected her vulva intimately. And although she was so frightened that her body was seized by a cascade of tremors, Claudette did not withdraw or hinder him in any way. For in spite of the deep humiliation she felt, she knew that the one thing that could possibly save her life was the thing all men prized the most — her womanhood. So, she let him have his way, baring herself to his curious eyes, maybe, some would say, a little too wantonly for the circumstances.

The brave looked up at her and smiled, displaying a nasty mouth filled with yellowed and blackened teeth. She smiled back, somewhat nervously. Suddenly, the Natchez howled and leaped to his feet. Claudette recoiled and hid her face in her hands, waiting in terror for the edge of a sharp knife to lift the scalp from her skull....

Moments later, she and Chepart were escorted to a place beside the stockade walls near Chepart's garden. There, the Natchez secured them with the other women, children, and slaves they had spared — all of whom were crying and wailing.

About her, the Natchez were taking their vengeance in concert, appearing like wild, screaming devils from Hell. Many of the inhabitants, she was sure, had died in their sleep without bearing witness to the famous fury of the Natchez Nation. At the hub of all this activity was a huge, club-wielding, black giant, larger than any man she had ever seen, crushing skulls and breaking bones like kindling.

Young braves, eager to prove themselves, appeared to be the most merciless. They took particular delight in scalping and lopping off the heads of their victims, stacking them like oranges into piles that numbered more than twenty.

Beside her, barely able to stand on his long, wobbly legs, stood Chepart, still dressed in his night garment, watching in silent shock the nightmare that was taking place about him. A few paces away, Marguerite was on her knees, crying and wringing at the hem of her sleeping robe until it was high above her lumpy, unsightly buttocks.

Out of the corner of her eye, Claudette happened to see the Indian woman, Morning Sun, dressed in a blood-splattered, white-linen dress, a dagger in her hand, walking like a ghost among the dead and dying as if she was searching for something or someone. A few moments later, the woman stopped and stood over the bloody body of the soldier, Maurice. Her back was to the morning sun and the sunlight that bounced off her shoulders and into her hair, created an intimidating halo that gave her the appearance of a beautiful, fallen Goddess.

Hope filled the mortally-wounded soldier's face as he tried to speak to the savage woman. His lips moved as if to say, "*Help me*," but no sounds came from his bleeding mouth.

For a moment, the Indian woman appeared to be overcome with compassion. She smiled softly, knelt beside him, took her time and carefully brushed the blood from his love-struck eyes so that he could see her face clearly. Then, she gently reached into his drawers and withdrew his penis caressingly. Suddenly, and without warning... she slashed.

When the deed was done, she held the severed penis aloft and howled like a hyena gone mad. Finally, she dropped to her knees and stuffed it into the soldier's silent, screaming mouth.

Shortly after, Claudette watched as Maurice's head was added to one of the growing piles.

Vengeance was swift. Blood was everywhere and the cries of the doomed not unlike the cries of the damned. Then, a herd of noisy children streamed through the gates and raced about the fort, beating dead and half dead bodies with sticks and clubs, and stripping away the dead's clothing which they donned in mockery. Some rushed into the prisoner-holding area and almost clubbed several of the children to death before one of their chiefs could restrain them.

Outside the gates, in all quarters, she could see heavy, black smoke rising across the sky from the burning fields and homes of several French settlers. And nearby, headless corpses could be seen hanging upside down from tall pecan and sycamore trees.

All were killed except herself, the commandant, Marguerite, twenty-seven other women, forty children, and twenty black slaves.

When the killing had been done, and the last voice of the dead carried off by the brisk, chilling wind, the litter bearing the Great Sun arrived and was placed beneath a tobacco shed attached to the wall of the fort. When he was situated, Commandant Chepart was brought before him.

"Now, Great White Chief, you who would take the land of the Natchez, who would build his house of stone upon my grave — what have you to say, now?"

Chepart, once addressed, regained some of his bravado and said with conviction, "I will spit on your grave, yet, you dog-faced heathen. You have angered every French citizen from here to Acadia. And as God be my witness, I promise, I will return with the largest army you have ever seen and strike your stinking face from this earth. And I, personally, will feed your bowels to the dogs."

Suddenly, the Indians laughed in mockery and Chepart lost his composure.

"No, Chief of the Dead, it is not you that I will fight in my next battle. My next battle will be with your king, the one who never shows his face. It is his head that will roll at my feet in the next battle. For you, your days of war are finished. You are less than the droppings from my bowels. Not worthy of dying at the hands of not one of my braves. Not even the lowest Stinkard among them.

"I have decided, however, that you will be good sport for the children. They need to taste the flavor of royal, French blood so that they will never again have need to fear a white. Cut the white Chief's bonds," he ordered.

Quickly, a brave took his dagger and cut away Chepart's bonds. Chepart massaged his wrist and looked around somewhat puzzled.

"Here, m'sieur, are your executioners." At a gesture from the Great Sun, the circle of braves parted and allowed seven to eight half-naked young boys to pass. Some were armed with hickory and oak clubs, others with stones tied to short sticks with leather strings.

The boys advanced cautiously, their faces filled with apprehensive smiles.

"Hold," interrupted Tattooed Serpent. Then, he turned to Chepart and asked curiously, "Where is your bonnet of woman's hair? This white hair that makes you a Great Chief."

Chepart looked at Tattooed Serpent sullenly, but did not reply.

"Go and get this sacred white hair," Tattooed Serpent directed a nearby brave. "No chief should do battle without his war bonnet." The Indians laughed as one ran towards Chepart's quarters.

Shortly after, the brave returned and handed the mussed, dirty wig to Chepart. Chepart took the wig, looked at it, and threw it to the ground in disgust.

Mukta No-Talk, who had been observing the proceedings in silence, lumbered over, picked up the wig solemnly, and menacingly handed it back to Chepart. The presence of the Black giant caused Chepart to reconsider. Quickly then, he took the wig, dusted it off, and set it upon his sweating head.

"Look, Serpent," Chepart said, trying to regain some authority, "this has all been a mistake, a misunderstanding of my purpose. I never intended to force you to move. I only asked that you do so in the interest of the king. But what you are about now is a total act of war. One that is certain to result in the annihilation of your whole tribe. Leave this fort now, while there is still a chance for peace. Return to your villages, and I promise, I will speak to my king on your behalf. I will tell him this was all just a misunderstanding. He will listen to me."

"The time for talk passed many seasons ago when I came to you with my heart in my hand. Today, we have no use for your words and you have no time to speak them. It is time now to defend yourself. Only your blood can quench our thirst," Tattooed Serpent replied with finality as he motioned to the boys.

The boys, encouraged by their elders who howled and shouted from the sidelines, began their advance, jabbing timidly at the commandant with their sticks and clubs.

"No.... No!" Claudette pleaded above the cries of the women and children, her heart pounding with fear. "Don't kill him. He did not mean what he said. Don't kill him.... Please!"

Chepart backed away a few steps, then decided to stand his ground. When the boys were close enough, a swift kick caught one in the abdomen. Surprised, the boy doubled to the ground in pain. Momentarily, the advance was interrupted as the boys looked indecisively at their fallen comrade. A shrill war cry from one of their elders, however, spurred them quickly back into action.

Chepart backed away again, circling as the boys crouched low and surrounded him on all sides. When they were close, he kicked out again. But this time, a club struck him mid-ankle. Chepart yelped and continued to parry and dodge while dancing about pathetically on one leg — his now lopsided wig flapping about his head like the ears of a horned beast.

Suddenly, the boys closed in and a series of quick blows to his left side toppled Chepart to the ground. Chepart got to his knees in desperation and tried to crawl from harm's way, but several well-placed blows to the head brought him down again. Chepart reeled, then he did the only thing he could. He covered his head with his arms and folded his body into a tight ball. His efforts to protect himself, however, were futile. Blow after blow, after blow rained upon his helpless body.

Claudette screamed, turned and buried her face in Marguerite's bosom. When she raised her head again to look, all that remained of her lover was a wet, bloody pulp of human tissue and stark, white bones, more white than any white she had ever seen before in her entire life. Even more white than the blinding light of the sun that filled her eyes as she fainted dead away.

———————

When the Fort had been ransacked of everything of value, it was set afire. Then, the prisoners were gathered for the return march to the village. Some of the braves wanted to take the heads back to their village, but Tattooed Serpent prevented them from doing so, stating that the war was over, and that there were none among them worthy; that their spirits could not be trusted to guard their temple walls.

Following that decree, the victorious army departed, singing and dancing joyfully like children returning from a stimulating game or excursion. Only Marguerite was further abused. She was stripped of her clothing and given to Morning Sun, who whipped her plump rump with a cane reed each step of the way back to the Great Village. Once there, she was then taken and tethered by the foot with a rope affixed to a stake in the center of a muddy, water hole — one the Natchez used frequently to relieve their body functions....

———————

Chapter – Twelve

WHEN THE COURIER BEARING NEWS OF THE ATTACK REACHED the little fort at Natchitoches two days later, St. Denis was tallying a load of merchandise in preparation for a trading expedition into Spanish Territory.

"M'sieur… Commandant… Commandant?" the courier stated excitedly as he rushed into the storeroom of the fort.

"What is it?" St. Denis replied a little annoyed.

"The Natchez, m'sieur…, the Natchez." The courier stated while gasping for breath.

"Take your time and tell me what the Hell is going on."

"*Oui*, m'sieur. I have an urgent message for you from Governor Périer. The Natchez… Fort Rosalie has been destroyed. Everyone is dead, over two hundred. You are directed to sound the alarm and secure this post. If there are any extra men, they are to be sent to His Excellency to assist in the counterattack. Trustworthy slaves are also to be armed for this event."

"Damn it. I knew it would happen sooner or later. Did Chepart escape?"

"No, m'sieur. He is dead."

"I knew that crazy lunatic would not be satisfied until he started a fucking war. Everyone told him the Natchez would never move peacefully.

"Return to New Orleans after you have refreshed, and tell the Governor — that if I am to defend this post, I need every man that I have. Tell him, I have enough food to last a month, but only enough powder to last three, maybe four days at full siege. I welcome any assistance in men and arms that he can provide. Now be gone. *Ventre a terre* (belly to the ground)."

St. Denis considered the situation grave. It was a logical assumption that the Natchez, after taking such a bold step, would systematically continue to attack other French installations. Natchitoches was the closest post to them. It, therefore, qualified as their next probable target.

The alarm was passed. Each family was instructed to bring food, bedrolls, and any weapons in their possession to the fort. The guard was doubled. The two caliber-four cannons, which had been slowly rusting away from lack of use, were cleaned and oiled. The Natchitoches, Asinai, Tejas, and other friendly tribes were contacted for support. Barrels were filled with water and stored. Old clothing was boiled, then torn into strips for bandages. Livestock was gathered and secured in a makeshift pen near the front gate of the fort where they could be brought inside quickly at the first sign of any hostilities.

During the day, the men left the Fort only to attend necessary chores, but did not wander far. At night, all returned to the safety provided by its fragile walls.

———

Etienne and his two companions, Jeanne and Alexis, were extremely satisfied with the success of their hunting expedition. Things had gone exceedingly well. They had more than seven hundred pelts between them, including a respectable number of bear hides. They had been gone almost four years. It seemed like a lifetime — a lifetime in the wilderness living like the animals they stalked and without the comforts of the fort or the enduring passion of a woman's embrace.

Now that they were back, Etienne could hardly wait. His first task, after securing their pelts at Fort Rosalie, would be to visit Morning Sun and put the peg to her until she begged for mercy.

Actually, his need for her went a little beyond the needs of the flesh. In fact, if he had taken the time to be honest with himself, he would have readily admitted that he was deeply in love with the savage woman. Her simple innocence, and thoroughly-open way of expressing her emotions, intrigued and fascinated him in ways he could not describe. If she had been European, he would, no doubt, have married her. Unfortunately, she was not. Besides, she was already married. So, he contented himself, waiting and hoping that someday he would find a wife among the girls expected to be shipped from France in the near future. For the time being, however, his heart was the property of Morning Sun.

As they drifted toward the bluff and the landing that led to Fort Rosalie, Etienne was suddenly aware that there was a lack of activity along the water's edge. That struck him as extremely odd. There was always activity there, no matter what the season.

"Things seem quiet today," he remarked to no one in particular.

"Too cold. Probably all inside," Alexis replied as they anchored and tied their boats and raft at a makeshift dock.

"We'll need help in getting these pelts to the Fort where they can be secured. Maybe, I should hurry to the Natchez village for a few extra hands to assist," Etienne offered.

"Oh… No," both his companions chorused and laughed. "You're not going anywhere near your Sun Princess until we get this raft of furs secured. That hot little piece of yours will just have to wait," Alexis stated quite firmly.

"My thoughts exactly," Jeanne added. "If he goes now, we won't see him again for a week once she get her claws into him."

"Can't rightly blame him. That Morning Sun Princess looks mighty tasty. Will you be granting your old friends a turn at the water hole, Etienne?"

"Too much woman for you, Alexis. You'll have better success with Marguerite."

"That fat-assed slob," Alexis said as he shrugged his shoulders and grimaced comically.

Everyone laughed.

"She is all either one of you have between here and New Orleans. Claudette is taken. Chepart would have your balls if he caught you sniffing after his private stock."

"That you say may be true. But, if I get half the chance, I'll have my wick up her cute little pot faster than a cat can fart. Take my chances with Chepart as they come. Tell me — just how good are Natchez wenches in bed, anyway? I hear they are pretty hot-blooded. Is that true, Etienne?" Alexis asked.

"I'm not the one who would know. I can only speak for one, and that one knows how to make a soul's blood boil."

"Well, I've had a couple of Stinkard bitches in my time," Jeanne interjected. "But for my pelts, give me a Bayougoula squaw. They will hump your balls off anytime, day or night. They never get enough. And if you really want a ball-busting ride, give them a couple of swallows of rum. Then, hang on. You'll swear you're riding a horned beast."

"*Chacun ... son gout* (Everyone to his taste)," Etienne replied with a chuckle.

All laughed again.

"Jeanne, you stay with the raft while Alexis and I go up to the fort to commandeer a beast and cart to haul our goods to the fort.

————

What greeted Etienne and his companion when they walked into the fort was something that they would never be able to describe with mere words, a holocaust of destruction — Golgotha.

"My God, what happened here?"

"Holy Mother Marie! They killed everyone!"

In a daze, they wandered about the fort among the headless bodies that lay bloated and ripening in the midday sun. Heads, that had been neatly stacked, had now been scattered by the dogs and beasts of the forest. Huge vultures half ignored them, stepped aside grudgingly with a flap of their wings, then returned to their feeding — pulling, pecking, and tugging at the fetid entrails. The odor was sickening, much worse than the smell of a thousand dead fish. Etienne doubled over and retched so hard that he thought he was going to lose his stomach.

Once the initial shock had passed, panic gripped the two solidly.

"Who could be responsible for this?" Alexis asked as he looked around bewildered.

"Natchez," Etienne replied. "Who else? They are the only ones on this continent who crave heads to this degree."

"When?"

"From the signs, maybe a week ago. No more than two."

"The bastards. Stinking, heathen bastards."

Suddenly concerned for their safety, they made a hasty retreat back to their boat in a panic.

"What the Hell is going on?" Jeanne asked as Etienne and Alexis hurriedly released the mooring and scrambled aboard their boat.

"Fort Rosalie has fallen. Everyone has been killed. Grab your oar and paddle. We need to gain some distance before they learn we are here," Etienne explained.

With that said, the trio shoved off, and headed as fast as they could for New Orleans; their knives poised to cut the rope to the raft carrying their pelts at the first sign of trouble.

Silently, Etienne searched for a reason... *Why?* he asked himself over and over again. *What on earth could have happened to prompt such violence?* And Morning Sun, what was her role in all this senseless killing? Certainly, she must have had some influence, he surmised. She must have. *Damn her dog-bitch soul.*

———

NEWS OF THE MASSACRE HAD PRECEDED THEM, and the city of New Orleans was already in a state of emergency when they arrived. The militia was being organized. Houses were being boarded. A run had been made on the arsenal by citizens seeking guns and powder. Many citizens, from the outlying areas, left their farms unattended and set up housekeeping in make-shift shanties or lean-to's, while others found refuge in alleyways and doorways. Daily, they clustered into small groups to gossip and recount the numerous folk tales they had heard concerning the ferocity of the Natchez, often adding their own cruel embellishments.

"It is said the Natchez have no fear of death. If one awakens and decides he is no longer happy in this world, he goes to a friend and asks to be relieved of his head."

"Bitou, my Indian slave, told me that they eat eyeballs like grapes."

"I never knew they were flesh eaters, too."

"No. They don't partake of the flesh. It's the heads that they crave."

"I heard, in ages past, they had killed so many people that they had three mountains of skulls stacked outside their temple."

"Do you really think they will attack us?"

"Use your head, m'sieur. They have taken Ft. Rosalie. Why should they stop there? Would you, if you were them?"

"Bunch of blood-thirsty heathens, they are. And if they do attack, they won't stop until every French head is taken."

"I say, we should kill our women and children ourselves rather than leave them to suffer at the hands of those bastards."

"And the slaves, what about the slaves?"

"Watch your back, is all I can say. No matter how loyal you think a black to be, it's my guess he'll join with the Natchez."

A few days later, several domesticated Natchez, four middle-aged males and two somewhat younger females, who had been living and working on a nearby plantation, were taken prisoner. In spite of their innocence and over the objection of their French owners, the Governor ordered them executed anyway, hoping that his actions would rally more support for his shaky militia.

They were taken, then, to the levee directly in front of the *Place de Armes*, tied to stakes, and burned alive in the sunset.

But, instead of relieving the tensions of the French citizens, the smell of burning hair and roasting human flesh permeating the night air only served as a warning preview of their own possible fate. Consequently, their fears and anxieties compounded astronomically.

Fearing an all-out revolution, and hoping to prevent the development of an alliance between the Natchez and the slaves, Governor Périer and his staff devised an ingenious plan to prevent such an event from occurring. First, he solicited the names of some thirty odd trustworthy slaves, each from a different household and unfamiliar with each other. He then had them gathered and brought before him.

"Messieurs," the governor stated as he stood before the puzzled black faces of field hands, grooms, house-servants, cobblers, levee workers, drivers, and other disciplines, "you have been brought here because you are the noblest of your lot, each of you having qualified because of your past service and devotion to your masters. As you no doubt are aware, we are at war with the Natchez. I am, therefore, offering you a rare opportunity to demonstrate your allegiance to your king. As your governor, I hereby declare that any among you, who will join us in our campaign against our enemies, will be manumitted and granted the full rights of French citizenship."

For a moment, there was silence. Then, as the impact of the offer settled, a hum of mixed emotions grew in magnitude.

"What will be our duties?" asked a skeptical slave. "Will we fight as militia?"

"As militia," the governor affirmed. "A special task force for interacting with the enemy until the main militia can be properly organized. Your first task will be to eliminate the Chouachas."

"The Chouachas are a small, peaceful tribe," one slave replied, "I know them well. They are no threat."

"Not well enough, I'm afraid. These so-called friendly people that you see walking the streets, smiling, and peddling their goods in the market are nothing more than snakes — spies on behalf of the Natchez, reporting to them our every move. We need time to prepare. For these reasons, they must be eliminated.

I say again — are there any among you who will accept this opportunity to earn your liberty?"

After some minor discussions, the governor's offer was
accepted unanimously. The men were then armed and placed
under the supervision of a French officer. With the promise of
freedom as their rallying cry, these slaves were no less merciful
than the Natchez. They fell upon the sleepy Chouachas village
in the early morning and slaughtered every man, woman, and
child in sight.

Triumphantly, they returned to New Orleans, their faces
aglow with pride and their wide nostrils filled with the sweet odor
of liberty. In cadence and stepping lively, they were marched to
the governor's quarters where they were forced to stand in for-
mation for more than an hour in the hot, sweltering Louisiana
sun. Finally, the governor came out to greet them. The slaves
cheered. Their cheering, however, soon lost its vitality once they
observed the somber expression on the Governor's face.

For several moments, the governor stood looking conde-
scendingly at the rag-tag army of slaves who would be free.
Then, he spoke. "I am relieved to see that you have all returned
unharmed. Yet, it pains me to inform you, that your zeal in
this exercise has resulted in a grave transgression against the
Chouachas Nation."

"What transgression, m'sieur?" a stern-faced, sweating
slave asked meekly.

"A crime. A crime of the worst nature. And although it
was committed through no fault of your own, it was a crime,
nevertheless."

"Please, m'sieur? What crime have we committed?

"The Chouachas were not spies as my initial intelligence led
me to believe. They, instead, were innocent and without guilt."

"But why are we guilty? We only followed your instructions. We should not be blamed for your misjudgment."

"Then, who is to blame? Certainly not myself nor anyone
under my command. The blame, I'm afraid, rests clearly on your
shoulders."

"Then, what will become of us? What of your promise of liberty?"

"Liberty, under the circumstances, is out of the question. To do so at this time will only anger the Indians more. They are already clamoring for your scalps. For the time being, and for your own safety, you must be returned to the care of your masters, there to remain until this matter settles down."

With that declaration, the slaves began to voice their objections. Some shouted in anger. Some threw their weapons to the ground and cursed, while others looked on in silent frustration.

"Lieutenant," the governor shouted above the uproar, "call out the guard and place these gentlemen under arrest until they can be claimed by their owners." Then, to the slaves, he shouted, "And should any of you decide to run away, be advised that you will find no asylum with the Indians. They, especially the Choctaw, are already aware of your crime and they are crying for retribution." With that statement, the governor returned to his quarters briskly, smiling to himself, and filled with a deep sense of satisfaction.

Word of the slaves' crime was quickly passed to the Choctaw and other friendly tribes by the French authorities with a declaration that those guilty would be sought out and brought to justice. As proof of his good intention, the governor found a recently-captured runaway, declared him to be one of the perpetrators, hung him, then put his mutilated body on public display. The tactic was effective, and strong feelings of malice quickly developed between the Indians and slaves.

That taken care of, Governor Périer spent much of his time charming the Choctaw with gifts and other material promises in an effort to solicit their assistance in the war with the Natchez. He even arranged for several prostitutes to service their War Chiefs and other key Choctaw officials. A few of the women balked. But once the Governor ordered them to sacrifice their bodies for God and country like any other citizen soldier, or suffer the consequences reserved for traitors, they complied without any further objections.

Since the Choctaws had never been close to the Natchez in their past relationship, and the fact that they were mildly offended because the Natchez had launched their revolution without them, they agreed to provide the French with sixteen-hundred braves. Their price was considerable, but the French were desperate. So, they paid without a haggle.

DURING THE SAME PERIOD, THE NATCHEZ HAD NOT BEEN IDLE. They knew, eventually, that the French would retaliate. There were many discussions by the War Council regarding the merits of taking the war to the French or waiting for them to attack their village.

"To wait is foolish," Mukta No-Talk, who was now a War Chief, stated as he addressed the council. "The French are wise in matters of war. The longer we wait, the more time they will have to prepare."

"I agree," stated another War Chief. "If we are to clear the forest, we must not stop with the first tree felled. We must continue until all the trees are felled."

After listening intently to all of the War Chief's remarks, Tattooed Serpent spoke. "I have heard your words of wisdom, and I would agree, except for several things. The post at Fort Rosalie was poorly manned. We were familiar with that place and those who resided there. Because of that, our victory succeeded without loss of life. We are not so familiar with the forts in the land of the Natchitoches or in Orleans. We do not know how many soldiers are stationed there, or what weapons and how many they have in their possession. I am also greatly concerned about who has aligned with him. We have proven to all that the French are not invincible, yet no other tribe has come forth to acknowledge our victory, or assist us in our noble effort. I am also told that the Choctaw are now offended. For these reasons, I fear that we fight this war alone — without the ability to determine who is friend, or who is foe."

"The Natchez have always acted alone," another War Chief offered. "It is best that way. We must attack, now!"

"To attack the French now is folly. If we do so, they will be perceived by all as the victims. And no matter how brave our young warriors fight, we can never hope to overcome the French and the sympathizers who might come to their aid. We must wait. We must wait and see if the French have learned to acknowledge our right to exist at this place, on this land. If so, then all is well. If not, and they insist on pursuing this war, then let them pack up their cannons and seek us out. Then, we will be perceived as the victims and they the aggressor. Maybe then, others will not hesitate to join us."

"I object," Mukta No-Talk shouted hoarsely as he jumped to his feet in anger. "If water runs from the top of one hill to its bottom, why wait to see if it will run from the top to the bottom of the next? The course of the French is already clear. They will never compromise except to their advantage. I know them, and I know their history well. Their nature is one of conquest, and they will never acknowledge our right to exist. It is not their way. They will not be satisfied until they have brought destruction upon us. When are we going to stop cowering like women and do what must be done? When?"

"It will be done when, and if, they should ever set foot upon Natchez soil," Tattooed Serpent replied calmly, but sternly.

Mukta No-Talk stood fuming at the decision for a long moment. Suddenly, he growled low in his throat, spun, and hurled his club into the sky with such a force that it went forth humming like a devil wind in pain. Then, he stalked off into the night.

When he had gone, Tattooed Serpent turned to the council and stated, "Do not be concerned for No-Talk. His heart is ruled by his passion. Tomorrow, when his blood has cooled, he will see that I have made the right decision; that with all the uncertainties, if we must fight, it is best that we fight on our terrain where the French's supply of arms and food will be limited to only what he can carry on his back."

The decision made, the Natchez again prepared for war. Tattooed Serpent had considered building a fort, but decided that there was insufficient time. As an alternative, he fortified the Great Village with trenches and surrounded it with a dirt embankment four-feet-high. They secured their food and water, then set up an early warning system so that the members of the outlying communities could seek refuge within the safety of the Great Village. There were training exercises in the use of the additional firearms captured at Fort Rosalie. Daily, the Great Sun and the Old Guardian spent long hours praying in the Temple.

Marguerite, whose head had been shaved, was now a full time slave to Morning Sun — responsible for the lowest of menial chores. Although the winter months had been quite cool, she had been forbidden to wear clothing of any sort. Her spirit broken, the spit and fire that was once part of her nature was no longer present. Her only interests now were to please her new mistress, and hopefully, to survive until the French army could muster and rescue her.

Claudette fared much better. She was taken as a wife by one of the noblemen who treated her kindly and made her feel like she was an honored woman instead of a common prostitute. She was content. She now had someone who cared for her, and soon, she would have the family she craved, for she was pregnant with his child.

Chapter — **Thirteen**

_____

March, 1730....

WITH PREPARATION FOR THE CAMPAIGN COMPLETE, the French militia proceeded up the Mississippi. Numerous pirogues and dugouts dotted the river. While some walked or rode horses along the shore-trails, others towed flat boats upstream loaded with miscellaneous supplies and weapons of war.

Natchez scouts stationed some distance from the village along the river alerted Tattooed Serpent of the approaching French Army. The alarm sounded, and the War Council convened. While the council reviewed their battle strategy, the braves, in view of their recent victory, displayed great enthusiasm, singing and dancing to torrid tempos and consuming great amounts of spirits.

Their bravado, however, was short-lived. The Choctaw arrived unexpectedly from the east the next morning and made their camp at the ruins of Fort Rosalie to await the slow moving French militia.

This caused Tattooed Serpent much concern. He had made an error in judgment. He had assumed that the Choctaw would remain neutral. He was confident that he could have defeated the French army of three hundred men, or the Choctaw, individually. But combined, he was outnumbered three-to-one. The future looked dismal. It was too late to retreat, and too late to seek the assistance of the Chickasaw who disliked the Choctaw as much as they did the French.

His greatest concern was for the women and children. Had he known what was in store soon enough, he could have sent them into hiding or to live among the Chickasaw. If he tried to do so now, however, they would be easy prey. He was despondent. For some reason, no matter how hard he tried to circumvent it, fate seemed to be against him. There was evil about. It was heavy, and he could feel its foreboding presence in every quarter.

The only apparent alternatives, under the circumstances, were to surrender and hope the French were merciful, or fight to the death. If he surrendered, he strongly suspected the French would kill them anyway. There was a chance, however, that he might be able to negotiate a settlement by offering his head and the heads of his War Chiefs as ransom. It was a long shot, but maybe a few would survive. It was worth a try.

The French, however, were delayed. Their delay being caused by the laborious task of pulling their supplies upstream and a breakdown in military discipline.

Since the pay and inducements for the militia was less than desirable, the Governor had informed the volunteers that they could keep any females captured as slaves. The men, however, were to be killed.

While traveling, the citizen's army came across a cultivated field where several Indian females were planting corn. One of the militiamen spotted them, broke ranks, and ran out across the field towards them. Several others took note and joined the chase. More followed. The Governor, on horseback, screamed orders and threats, and slashed at the troops with his riding crop. His ranting, however, was useless. His whole Army deserted before him in hot pursuit of a dozen, or fewer, females — running helter-skelter across the field and into the forest after them.

Once the females were caught, the men fought among themselves for possession. Two older females were butchered on the spot, while the remaining women were raped and ravaged by uncountable numbers. The Governor looked on in disbelief, totally bewildered by his lack of authority and his inability to control his gaggle of citizen soldiers.

"Seems that I command an army of imbeciles. Not one worth the salt in his bread," the governor stated matter-of-factly to his first officer.

"I agree. They are not the best, but they are all we have between us and the sea."

"Even the sea may, yet, be a blessing. If I could, I would shoot
the lot of them. How in the Hell am I supposed to fight a war with
this garbage for troops? Tell me? I wager that every one of the
bastards will poop blue walnuts the first time they hear a Natchez
war howl."

"I suspect you are right. For that reason, I would suggest that
we remain mounted during any affray — just in case a hasty retreat is dictated."

"Dumb asses!"

It took the rest of the day to regroup and reestablish some degree of order. By then, it was too late to proceed farther. Reluctantly,
the Governor decided to camp in the cornfield for the night.

Two days late, a nervous and distraught Governor Périer finally arrived at Fort Rosalie. Moments later, however, after seeing
the evidence of the massacre, almost every man was sick, spilling
their guts into their hands, against the trunks of trees, and upon
each other's boots.

Périer's first act was to appoint a burial detail for the scattered
remains. After that was accomplished, he rallied his army and surrounded the Great Village, interspersing his less-seasoned militia
within the ranks of the stalwart Choctaw braves.

"What do you think they will do, Coutee?" Périer asked his
Choctaw Fani Mingo (*Squirrel War Chief*).

"The Natchez will fight. It is expected. This is their land. It
has been their land for many seasons. They will fight. We have
been camped here for two days. They know why we are here, yet
they do not run. They prepare for war."

"Good. It will be the bastards' last."

"Maybe good — maybe not. We must count their women as
warriors, too. Many men will die. I fear we will pay a great price
for victory today."

"*C'est la guerre*. That's what war is about."

"Well spoken, White Chief. I hope you speak as well should they add your head to their temple wall."

Périer looked at Coutee coldly, started to say something, but then changed his mind. Instead, he stalked off a few paces and waited for his temper to cool lest he say something to offend the Squirrel Chief. After a moment, he returned and resumed his emperor stance.

"We fight now?" Coutee asked.

"How can we fight now? They are still holding hostages. We can't do anything until I make an attempt to secure their release."

———————

The Great Sun, upon the advice of Tattooed Serpent, agreed to sue for peace. For this mission, he selected the War Chief, Bear Claw. Before he became a War Chief, Bear Claw had fought with the French against the Spaniards. It was during this campaign that he had earned his many tattoos, and tattoos of every description covered his lean body. He knew the French and spoke their language fluently.

"Before you depart," Tattooed Serpent instructed Bear Claw, "place all of the French captives, except the black slaves and the white woman, Claudette, in the temple. Then, prepare it for burning. Use only the driest twigs so that it will burn rapidly. Then, go to the French chief. Tell him this has been done, and all will die if they attack. Try and negotiate a peace — one that is favorable to us. I trust in your wisdom. When you go, take one brave of your choice and the black War Chief, Mukta No-Talk."

"To take No-Talk is foolish," Bear Claw stated. "Doing so, will only anger the French more once they see that a runaway lives among us."

"That is good. Let them get angry. The root of anger is almost always fear. Take No-Talk and have him stand at your side so that the French may gauge the height and breadth of him easily."

"It will be done," Bear Claw said as he nodded in agreement.

When he had completed Tattooed Serpent's instructions and

put the French captives in the temple, he departed.

———————

"Well, seems like the Tattooed Serpent wants talk now, instead of war," Périer remarked smugly to Chief Coutee as he observed Bear Claw waving a calumet from the edge of the Natchez perimeter. "Tell him to advance."

Coutee did as he was told, and Bear Claw approached the group with long, confident strides. Behind him, bearing banners, followed two braves, one Natchez, the other black.

"*Bon Dieu*! (Good God!) What is that?"

"Black man," Coutee offered.

"I see that. Where in Hell did that ape come from?"

"I have heard of this man. Strong as ten. Fierce in battle."

"Bonjour, Chief Governor." Bear Claw said with a full smile that displayed the remnants of his decaying teeth. "I bring you greetings from the Great Sun, Chief of the Natchez."

"And greetings to you," Périer said sarcastically.

"The Great Sun asks — why have you entered the land of the Natchez with this great army? We are a small, peaceful people, content to tend our fields and raise our children. We bear no ill will toward you, or our brothers, the Choctaw. Why have you come here?"

"Surely you jest. Do you call slaughtering innocent people the act of a small, peaceful people?"

"The Great Sun expresses his regrets about the loss of the whites at Fort Rosalie. But, he begs you to understand that it was they who wanted this war, not the Natchez. It was the French — who would kill the Natchez and take our lands. The Natchez have always served the cause of peace. The Great White Chief before you stated that the king would protect the rights of all. Yet, this king did nothing to assist in our behalf. This great king turned his head away and never heard our cries. We had no recourse but to defend the lands of our homes; even as you defended yours against the Spanish. Are the whites the only people with the right to do this — to defend their homes and their land?"

"My purpose here is not to discuss politics with you, or the Great Sun. I came to free the French captives and bring those responsible to justice. And I will do that at any cost!"

"I understand. That is why I come before you — to declare that the Natchez are prepared to fight to the death. And we will do that at any cost!" Bear Claw stated with equal conviction. "If we cannot negotiate suitable terms of peace, the first to die will be your women and children — by fire. Preparations have already been made. And if you listen closely, you will hear their wailing on the wind."

Périer could not restrain a cough. "Just what did your Chief have in mind to appease one who is bent on vengeance?"

"I have two hands. In one, I hold the sacred calumet of the Natchez. In the other, I carry my weapon of war. This war you desire is senseless. Both of us will lose. As an alternative, the Great War Chief, Tattooed Serpent, proposes to give you the heads of his twelve War Chiefs — to satisfy your thirst for blood. He also agrees to release all prisoners, unharmed, and in good health. Half today, and half tomorrow. He further proposes that he will continue to pay tribute to you in corn and pelts for five full seasons. His only desire is that his Nation be spared and allowed to live in peace on this small portion of worthless land."

Périer deliberated for a moment, then called Chief Coutee to the side. "What is your opinion in this matter?"

"It is a good offer."

"Can they be trusted?"

"Can you?"

"Answer the question, Coutee."

"The blood of the Natchez and the Choctaw flows in different streams, but they have always spoke with honor. Dead, they will be of no use to anyone. This way, many lives will be preserved. You can keep your head, and their labors will benefit us both. The Choctaw, of course, will claim one-half of their tribute."

Périer bristled, visibly irritated at the Choctaw Chief's claim to half the tribute. *The gall of the greedy bastard.* Suddenly, he realized that there was no reason to be angry. There would be no tribute to share. By tomorrow, if things went as planned, there would be no damn Natchez.

For the time being, however, he decided to agree to the terms of the truce — only as a delaying tactic to retrieve the prisoners unharmed. Once they were released, he intended to make the Natchez pay dearly. He would not be satisfied with anything short of their total annihilation. He, of course, did not intend to make the Choctaw aware of his true intentions until it was too late for them to do anything about it.

"Tattooed Serpent desires a lot for so little," Governor Périer finally replied. "But…, I will agree, if — he agrees to give me his head also."

"Your terms are harsh. But, I have already been instructed to inform you that he is prepared to offer his head also for the sake of his nation, if… necessary."

"It is necessary. And him," Périer added, pointing at Big Mukta No-Talk, "I want his head, too."

"I can only guarantee you the heads of the Natchez. This man is not Natchez. I, however, will speak to him about your request."

"Speak to him? For what? That man is French property. And as your governor, I grant you my full authority to relieve him of his damn head. Without his head, we have no agreement."

"It will be done."

"Good, then it is agreed."

"Shall we smoke the calumet of peace?"

"Hell, no!" There will be no smoking *nothing* until you have complied with my terms. Sergeant, get several volunteers to go with Bear Claw and escort the captives back."

Etienne eagerly volunteered for the assignment, hoping that he might have one last opportunity to see Morning Sun. Tomorrow, in all probability, she will be dead. And even though he felt that the Natchez, as a whole, deserved no better fate, he wished that there was some way her life could be spared. Two other soldiers and a

Choctaw brave accompanied him.

———

Etienne was standing on the edge of the village waiting for the prisoners to be released when he saw Morning Sun coming toward him, swiftly but apprehensively. Suddenly, his throat went dry, and he could feel his heart beating heavily, and unevenly, like an out of tune bull drum. He was, however, quite disappointed to see that she was not wearing the white, linen dress he had given her. In its place, she wore a traditional doeskin shift. Much more disturbing was the fact that she also wore the grotesque red, black, and white colors of war upon her beautiful face. These were bad signs, signs that said she was in accord with the bloody massacre — signs that he had hoped he would never see. His heart sank. Anger gathered quickly, and now, he was uncertain about facing her. Yet, in spite of his urge to strangle her with his bare hands, he could not bridle his curiosity about her feelings now that they were no longer lovers — but declared enemies.

"Etienne," Morning Sun called as she quit her stolid pace and ran toward him.

He did not reply.

"Etienne...," she called again, much closer now, more desperation in her voice.

He still did not reply, but subconsciously, he drifted towards her as if being drawn by an unseen force. His companions fidgeted, and he knew they were waiting to see what he would do and how he was going to respond.

"Etienne," Morning Sun said as she stopped abruptly and uncertainly in front of him. "Etienne, speak to Morning Sun. So much to say — so much gone wrong. I tried. I tried to stop the war, but no one would listen. Not Chepart. Not the Great Sun. No one. Where were you? I needed you."

"You lying, blood-sucking, heathen bitch," Etienne said with venom as he drew back and struck her fiercely across the mouth with the back of his hand. Morning Sun reeled and stumbled to the ground. Quickly, Etienne drew his knife, dropped to his knees, and placed its sharp edge across her flushed, throbbing throat.

Bewildered, Morning Sun looked up at him sadly. Tears welled in the corner of her eyes. "Etienne, you too hunger for Natchez blood?"

"I do, you stinkard bitch."

"Then, do it. Use your blade. Do it quickly. Now, before the love that fills my heart with warmth turns to ice!"

"You Natchez wench, do not defile me with your stinkard love. I curse the day our paths had the misfortune to cross. Except for the truce, I would slit your heathen throat from one ear to the other."

But he did not slit her throat. Instead, he pulled her roughly to him and whispered something in her ear that made her shiver in fright. And while she looked at him in disbelief, he kissed her in a contemptuous fashion that made it clear to everyone that their past relationship was over. Then, without ceremony, he shoved her stoutly back into the dirt and blew her saliva from his mouth.

"Heathen bitch," he added as he stood and walked away. His companions found his actions curiously amusing.

———

When Etienne and the released prisoners had gone, Morning Sun lifted her aching body from the earth where she had layed crying until she could cry no more — until all the tears in her body had gone, and all the pains of the world had gathered and solidified like a hard stone in the pit of her stomach. Then, and only then, did she rise to make her way back to her lodge, trying desperately to hold her chin high, walking slowly past the women who averted their eyes and looked away — and past the children who looked at her coyly with faces that mirrored her shame without really understanding what her shame was all about — and past the braves who stood or squatted in small groups staring accusingly in her direction.

Wearily, she entered her squalid hovel. No one was there. And even if someone had been there, she would not have seen them. The hurt, the pain, and the hopelessness would not let her — would not let her see neither left nor right; neither past nor future. All she could see was *red, flaming blood — white hot in the center, boiling, and stinking of dead, rotting, smiling children.*

Exhausted, she lay down across her cot, put both hands to her head and... screamed silently, **Chicken Man... Chicker Man!**

———

At sunset, Etienne returned to the French lines with the prisoners. The Natchez had released half of the French prisoners and only those slaves who requested to be returned to the French. Most of the slaves, however, chose to remain behind. Claudette also chose to remain with her Natchez husband. The rest were to be released the next morning.

———

Shortly after dawn the next day, Governor Périer returned to the location of the peace talks to await word on the release of the remaining captives. He, of course, expected the Natchez to demand more talks to assure their safety prior to their actual release. *Crafty devils*, Périer said to himself. *Well, whatever they wanted, he would grant... temporarily.*

If all went well, today would be a great military victory for him, his *Coup de Maître*. All France would honor and praise him for his strategic ingenuity. His name would be known from one end of the continent to the other. As soon as he attained the captives' release, he would launch his attack. Those not killed in battle, he would burn alive. He reserved for himself the task of lighting the fire beneath Tattooed Serpent and the Great Sun — *the bastards.*

Arrogantly, he strutted and paced beneath a huge, live-oak tree; its gnarled trunk deeply marked with the footsteps of time. Several times, he stopped and glanced up into its asymmetrical branches and studied the reflections of the sun against the silvery backside of the newly-sprouted leaves.

After two hours, he became impatient. His impatience soon turned to apprehension when he acknowledged to himself that all was not well.

"Something is amiss," he told one of his officers. "They should have been here by now. It's too quiet. *Tour d'horizon*. Do you see anything?"

"No, Governor, nothing.... Only the March wind in the trees and smoke from the Temple. Maybe their council is still talking."

"If it was talk they were about, they had all of last night to do that. Something...

"Governor! Governor! Come quickly," a wild-eyed citizen-soldier shouted as he raced across the field.

"What the Hell is going on now," Governor Périer stated as he, his officer, and the Choctaw Chief followed the soldier into the tree line.

"Two casualties and the damn war hasn't even started," the governor declared in frustration as he looked down at the bodies of two of his soldiers with their heads bashed almost flat.

"Work of the black man," Chief Coutee offered. "Never fights with bow or lance. He fights with the root of a cypress tree."

"Damn his stinking black soul! I dare not wait any longer. We may be too late, now. Have the drummer sound the charge. *Co–te que co–te* (Cost what it may). Not one is to be left alive."

The Governor, astride his Spanish stallion, shouted orders and the French army charged, wild and rabble rousing, only to discover to their amazement that the Natchez had slipped out through their lines during the night. The Governor was flabbergasted. A whole village of over fifteen hundred heathen Indians had just gotten up and waltzed right out of his elaborate trap — leaving not one trace of the direction they took. The only humans remaining were an old Stinkard woman, the remaining prisoners who were bound and gagged in the center of the plaza, and several guardians still tending the perpetual fire and singing their moronic death songs.

Astonishment soon turned to fury, and the Governor's once-arrogant facade quickly disintegrated, leaving a comical, frustrated, and thoroughly embarrassed tyrant cursing like a one-leg sailor. Publicly, he vented his rage, beating several of his officers and militiamen with his riding crop and chastising them all for neglecting their duties. Observing the amused looks on the faces of the Choctaws did not help matters in the least, and inwardly, he wondered what role, if any, had they played in the deranged spectacle. He, however, did not risk voicing his suspicions for fear of jeopardizing their already shaky alliance. Still, he wondered. The Choctaw were a much more disciplined army than his motley crew. *How in the Hell could this have happened?* he asked himself. *The audacity of the bastards!*

Not to be outdone, the Governor ordered several men to remove the guardians from the temple. They entered. There was a yelp followed by the soft sounds of crushing bone, then silence. They waited. No one came out.

"Sergeant, get some men and see what the Hell's going on in there. I want those bastards out here now! Move!"

The Sergeant looked at the one small entrance apprehensively, then ordered two nearby soldiers into the temple. He followed.

Within seconds, there were sounds of a struggle followed by the sound of a musket discharge. Suddenly, the Sergeant broke from the entrance like he had seen a ghost, his face white as a sheet.

"Sergeant, what the Hell is going on in there?"

"Demons. The temple is full of demons."

"There are no demons, you imbecile. I want those bastards out."

"M'sieur, there are already five dead. You want to risk more?"

"Then burn it. Set the roof afire. Must I make every decision?"

Hurriedly, the soldiers collected sticks of fire and threw them onto the dry, thatched roof and into the brush the Natchez had previously stacked around the walls. Within moments, the building was blazing.

"Now, let's see what kind of demons would inhabit a Natchez temple."

Cautiously, through the smoke, several frightened guardians appeared at the entrance. The soldiers fired. The one in the front fell away dead.

"Don't shoot, damn it!" Périer yelled. "I want the bastards alive. How else can I find out where the others have gone?"

Quickly, the men rushed to the entrance, gathered the remaining three guardians, and brought them before the Governor where they were forced to kneel.

"Are these your demons, Sergeant? Are these the little demons that made you poop in your pants?"

"Hell, no. Damn it. There is another one in there taller than the head of your horse."

"The black. It must be that big black in there. I want every weapon on that door," Governor Périer shouted. "Shoot anything that appears."

The men aimed and waited, but no one came out. Suddenly, the roof of the temple caved in and caustic fumes, smoke, and debris exploded in all directions. With tears springing from their eyes, the soldiers retreated to a safer distance. Still, no one came out.

"Well, if he is in there, he is smoked meat now for certain. Coutee? Coutee!" the Governor called. The Choctaw Chief came unhurriedly. "Find out where the rest of the tribe have gone. Beat it out of the bastards, if necessary."

Coutee questioned the three remaining guardians vigorously, but his questions went unanswered. Finally, he turned away in frustration. "These men will never talk. They are guardians. They will die first."

"Then, oblige them. Kill them all," the Governor directed his men as the guardians resumed their death chants.

Amid shouts of obscenities, the old woman, her cackle-like voice pleading, was taken and hanged by the cords of her long, gray hair from the branch of a hickory tree. Her thin, frail body was then stoned until she was dead. Within moments, the flies came, buzzing with excitement and eager to partake of the rich, red nectar that gathered in pools beneath her gnarled, dangling feet.

Following the lynching of the old woman, soldiers, armed with sabers, formed a large circle. They then blindfolded one of the guardians, tied his hands behind his back, and placed him in the center of the circle. From the perimeter, other soldiers threw stones to force the stumbling soul to one side or the other. First, wagers were made regarding which side of the circle the unfortunate Indian would migrate. Then, wagers were made for and against the ability of the closest soldier to sever the guardian's head in a single blow. Two of the guardians died in this manner. The one remaining guardian was tied to a stake and burned alive with flames from the perpetual fire. When all was done, the village was then razed and burned to the ground.

The Choctaw had not remained to participate in the atrocities. Having searched the village for anything of value, they departed quietly with expression of neither joy, nor sorrow, nor pity.

At the conclusion of the activities, the Governor searched again for signs of the trail the Natchez had taken. He found none. They had simply vanished. *Probably headed for Chickasaw country*, he surmised. That was one complication he did not need. Now, he would have to fight two bands of heathens. He shuddered as he imagined how the Ministry was going to react once they learned of the fiasco. He, of course, would be obliged to make his report sound as favorable as possible under the circumstances, stressing the rescue of the prisoners as opposed to the embarrassment he had sustained. "*Damn the bastards. Damn them*," he muttered to himself.

Quite defeated and a long way from being appeased, the Governor and his citizens-army loaded their belongings and returned to New Orleans quietly and without ceremony.

———

Chapter — Fourteen

September, 1730....

S<small>T</small>. D<small>ENIS</small> <small>STOOD BESIDE A WAGON TALKING TO</small> M'<small>SIEUR</small> J<small>EAN</small> B<small>ALTAZAR</small>, a newly arrived inhabitant. Beside him, on the front seat of the wagon, sat Baltazar's wife, an overly-dark Indian with deep-set eyes. In her arms was a small, equally-dark, infant. Between the man and wife sat another boy of French ancestry who appeared to be about eight years old.

"I must warn you again, m'sieur," St. Denis said with emphasis, "the land you have been granted is some distance from this post and I cannot guarantee the safety of you and your family. I strongly suggest that you remain here until the threat of the Natchez has been removed."

"I appreciate your concern, Commandant, but the yearning to return to the wilderness is much too strong. I must proceed now if I am to complete my abode before winter sets in. We will be safe enough. I once lived among the Natchez for a short time. They are sensible. They know I have no quarrel with them."

"And neither have I. Still it is best to observe caution."

"Considering the fact that the Natchez have not shown themselves for almost a year, I strongly suspect that they are miles from here, probably with the Chickasaw. I doubt that they'll be wanting to provoke a contest any time soon."

"Even if it is as you say, I would feel a lot better if you remained close enough for me to insure your safety."

"Commandant, I know you mean well. I have tried living among my own. But, because of the wife I have chosen, it was impossible. Most people find it difficult to accept the fact that I married a woman of *couleur*. That is why we decided to leave

New Orleans. We did not belong there. We do not belong here. We'll be better off out in the wilds where we are content."

"Well, I won't stand in your way. I do ask that you be extremely careful. And if you see anything out of the ordinary, do not hesitate to take refuge at this post."

"We will do that, Commandant. My wife does not speak French, but she has noted your compassion and she thanks you. Once we get settled, we hope to conduct a volume of business with you and your neighbors. Pelts and grain."

"Your business will be most welcome, m'sieur, and I assure you, you will be treated fairly. I'll have the constable check in on you once in a while — at least every month or so. My best regards towards your new quest. And remember... should you need any livestock, I sell the finest in the country."

"Thank you again, m'sieur." With that, Baltazar tipped his black, yellow-feathered hat and snapped the reins of his two horses.

St. Denis stood watching until the squeaking wagon loaded down with accoutrements and utensils had faded into the distance. Baltazar's grant was about twenty miles south of the fort in an area that was still unsettled, and yes, he was concerned for their safety. Yet, at the same time, he understood Baltazar's dilemma. Baltazar was a typical *Coureurs de Bois*, a trapper who had lived among the Indians for many years. When he had accumulated enough wealth, he and his Seminole squaw, who was half-African, had moved to New Orleans expecting to live a modest life amidst the comforts afforded there. Instead, they found themselves in an untenable situation, ostracized and alienated at every turn. Now, after several years of trying to breach the unbreachable, they were escaping back into the wilds — leaving the petty injustices and prejudices of his fellow countrymen behind.

"Commandant!"

St. Denis spun around at the sound of his name. It was François, winded and grinning from ear to ear. "What is it, François?"

"M'selle requests that you come immediately."

"Is something wrong?"

"No, m'sieur. Everything is well, but you must hurry. M'selle has a surprise for you."

"The baby, is it the baby?'

"I cannot say, m'sieur. You must come and see for yourself."

Unable to bridle his curiosity, St. Denis returned to the fort, mounted his horse, and departed for home in a gallop. When he arrived there, his wife's maidservant, Douleurs, met him at the door with a sheepish grin.

"Douleurs, you have a strange smirk on your face. Does this mean that I have another daughter to feed?"

"What do I know, m'sieur? It was your wife who summoned you, not me. She is waiting in her chamber."

"Something is amiss here, Douleurs. I can feel it," St. Denis said in keeping with the spirit of the moment as he hurried to his wife's room.

"Commandant Louis Juchereau de St. Denis," his wife announced as soon as he opened the door, "let me introduce you to our new tenant. Meet little M'sieur Louis Juchereau de St. Denis, your first son." Then, she threw back the covers with a flourish and revealed the naked body of a strapping, six-pound, baby boy.

St. Denis yelped in joy, fell to his knees beside his wife's bed, laughing erratically, while declaring over and over again, "I don't believe it. I just don't quite believe it! My first son."

————

WINTER CAME AND PASSED WITHOUT INCIDENT. So did spring. During the summer of 1731, a band of five Indians approached the fort during the early morning and stated that they had found a white woman lost in the forest. They offered to trade her for gifts of guns and powder, so that they could hunt wild buffalo and game for their families. The Indians, however, had not done a thorough job of camouflaging their tattoos, and St. Denis recognized them immediately as Natchez. He requested that the woman be brought to him. The Indians countered and proposed that he accompany them to the edge of the forest.

Suspecting foul play, St. Denis instructed them to wait for him at the edge of the tree line. Reluctantly, the Indians departed.

When they had gone, St. Denis alerted his militia and selected four runners. "Go into the village and all the farms and pass the alarm; tell everyone to retire to this fort immediately and without delay; tell them to do this discreetly without betraying their intentions; to bring their weapons and insure that they are concealed from view."

Next, he sent for his scout, Deerfoot, and instructed him to call upon the Tejas and Asinai and tell them that their Great White Chief and friend is in need of their assistance.

When all the settlers were safely inside the post, it was well past mid-day. The gates were closed, arms were issued, and guards posted. Most of the local Natchitoches braves joined St. Denis at the post. The rest of the tribe, consisting mainly of women and children, fled for safety into Texas.

Realizing that they had been outwitted, the outraged Indians brought a naked, white-woman to the edge of the forest. It was Marguerite, the *Obese One*. Her hands were bound behind her back, and her feet were hobbled. For well over an hour, she was forced to plead for assistance under duress.

"Help me!" Marguerite screamed in a loud coarse voice. "They are going to kill me!"

"I am a French woman. Do not abandon me to these savages. Help me, please!"

To aid her in her exhibition, the Indians prodded her bleeding buttocks with arrows and sharp sticks.

When the French in the fort did not respond, Marguerite became angry.

"Help me, you shit-eating cowards! Do something.

"May dogs shit on your mothers' graves. Cowards, all of you are cowards!"

Failing to lure the French into the open, the Natchez next cut the bindings from Marguerite's feet and forced her to run with her pitiful gait toward the fort. At fifty yards, more or less, they would overtake and wrestle her bulk to the ground. Then, they would drag her, screaming and kicking, back into the tree line. They repeated this cat and mouse game several times while jeering and taunting those within the fort.

"Louis," Jalot pleaded, "if we don't do something, those bastards will kill her. Let me and François take a detail out to rescue her."

"No, hold your place. Can't you see that is their design?"

"I count no more than six, Louis. François and I could do it alone."

"Six that we see. Six Natchez would never be so bold. There must be others hidden in the trees. I cannot risk a battle in open terrain. That —"

"Holy Mother Marie!" someone shouted. "They are going to burn her alive!"

Everyone, including the women and children, rushed to the wall. Spellbound, they watched as the Natchez tied Marguerite to the base of a tall, lone pine. Then, they stacked brush, sticks, and straw grass around her until it was waist high. Their chore complete, the Natchez continued their taunting tactics — dancing, cajoling, and making mock charges toward the Fort.

Having failed again to elicit a response, they tired of the game and set the brush afire. Immediately, Marguerite's screams split the hot, summer air like a weighted hammer. St. Denis cringed, and the hair stood on the nape of his neck. Silently, he said a quick prayer, then chased the children from the wall.

Most of the women sat crying and stroking their rosaries, their eyes wild with fear, wondering if they were to suffer the same fate of those at Ft. Rosalie. Guilt tore viciously at St. Denis, and he experienced great difficulty in meeting the bewildered eyes of those around him. In his frustration, he cursed himself and wondered if he had made a gross error in judgment by not aiding the unfortunate woman. For, in spite of the vulgar sub-culture Marguerite represented, she was still a French citizen entitled to the protection of the king.

"You stinking bastards," St. Denis yelled from the wall, but Marguerite was unaware. Her screams had stopped... and all was silent except for the antics of a mischievous summer breeze that sifted through the crackling sounds of the brush fire and carried the smell of burning hair and flesh across the countryside.

Jalot could take no more. He motioned for François to follow and the two of them dashed through the gate, bent on taking revenge.

St. Denis saw them from the wall and shouted for them to return. They ignored his command and continued their assault, muskets in one hand and knives in the other. About half way to their objective, the rest of the Natchez emerged from the trees. Jalot stopped short. François stumbled and almost ran him over. Several braves saw the two, howled, and charged to accommodate their challenge. That ended the contest. Both Jalot and François turned and ran for their lives back to the safety of the fort — Jalot cursing all the way.

When they were inside, both fell to their knees exhausted. Sheepishly, Jalot looked up at St. Denis and said with a half smile, "*Mau vais quart d'heure* (That was one bad quarter-hour). There must be thousands of the bastards out there."

"You damn fool. You could have gotten yourself killed," St. Denis shouted in anger.

"Well, all I can say — it's lucky for them I didn't have my fighting stick. Otherwise, I would have beat the shit out the whole lot."

In spite of the gravity of their situation, St. Denis chuckled in relief.

The braves gave up the chase and returned to the place where the Natchez had gathered at the edge of the forest. In silence, they stood for almost an hour, staring in the direction of the fort, their miter point heads displaying numerous, bizarre-fashioned hair styles, their faces and bodies adorned in their traditional paints of war. In their midst, sitting tensely in his litter chair, was the Great Sun. Several servants stood at his side cooling him with large palmetto fans.

At an apparently prearranged signal, the Natchez launched their attack, some on foot, a few on stolen horses, all howling like a pack of hungry hyenas.

Commandant St. Denis, his confidence restored with the knowledge that he had been right in his initial analysis, called for cannon fire. They fired, but most of their first rounds were long, over the heads of the enemy, and into the trees. They were effective enough, however, to send the Great Sun and his litter party scurrying for destinations unknown. While they were adjusting their angle of fire, the Natchez closed in rapidly.

Inside the fort, there was a flurry of choreographed activity. While the men were firing from the wall, the women and slaves were reloading muskets. Young girls and boys relayed the loaded weapons to the wall and returned with empty ones.

On one trip to the wall, a high arching arrow struck St. Denis' oldest daughter, Luiza, in her upper-left shoulder. As she fell to her knees, Jalot leaped from the wall, gathered her in his arms, and carried her into the mission church where Douleurs, the maidservant, stood guard over several infants. He laid her face-down on a bench and instructed Douleurs to assist in holding her there. Then, he took out his knife. Emanuelle rushed in just as he was cutting into Luiza's shoulder to remove the deeply embedded arrow.

Luiza screamed.

"Be brave, chéri," Emanuelle whispered as she rushed to her daughter to comfort her. "We don't want to alarm your father."

"I'll try, maman, but my shoulder is burning like fire."

"Maybe this alcohol will provide some relief," Jalot offered as he held the girl's arm and poured the liquid lightly into the wound.

Luiza bit into her lips but could not restrain her screams of pain.

"All I can do at the moment, m'selle."

"You've done well, Jalot. It's best you get back to the wall. I'll bind her wound and join you shortly."

Jalot departed hurriedly to resume his post while Emanuelle, with Douleurs' assistance, proceeded to wrap Luiza's wound with a piece of muslin.

"Look after her," Emanuelle instructed Douleurs as she rushed back to her station to assist in loading the firearms.

The first attack lasted a little more than twenty minutes. When the Natchez withdrew, they left fourteen of their number dead. For the rest of the day, they remained at the edge of the woods near the still smouldering pine where they had burned Marguerite. They remained there until night fell. Then, they faded silently and cheerlessly back into the shadows of the forest.

The next day, to St. Denis' surprise, sixteen Spanish soldiers arrived from Los Adaes — sent to assist, as a gesture of goodwill, by the new governor of Texas, Captain Juan Antonio Bustillo. Equally surprising, however, was the fact that the Spanish soldiers arrived without arms.

St. Denis inquired into the matter and discovered, much to his amazement, that he had been victimized by his own boasting. It seems that in past conversation with the Spanish (*in order to intimidate them with the importance of his little fort*), he had boasted that he had enough arms to outfit a three-hundred-man army, when in fact, he only had enough arms in his possession for forty-two. In view of this, the Spanish had decided that their few, meager weapons were not required.

Thoroughly embarrassed, St. Denis cursed himself for his big mouth and assigned the men duties which did not require the use of firearms.

On the eve of the second day following the attack, a contingent of Caddo and Asinai braves began drifting into the fort, singularly, and in small groups. When questioned, none had sighted the enemy.

Throughout the lull in the war, the Natchez had been silent. And although none had been sighted, St. Denis could still feel their presence. Several times, he was almost tempted to rally his army and charge, but refrained. The few weapons he had were much too valuable to risk. Instead, he waited, watching the tree line from the wall until he knew the location of every tree that marked its irregular boundary.

Finally, on the morning of the fifth day, St. Denis decided it was time to send out a probe, hoping his actions would prompt the Natchez into revealing themselves.

When the small party penetrated the forest, they found the quite visible trail of the Natchez and followed it cautiously deeper into the forest. They were only about a half-mile from the fort when all Hell gave way. Screaming, howling Indians fell upon them from the trees. Others leaped from camouflaged holes dug into the ground, and they were forced to beat a hasty retreat back to the fort. Two of the five men were seriously wounded.

Night fell again and enveloped the little fort in darkness. While oil-soaked cattails flamed, and small fires burned, St. Denis wandered the grounds, assessing his defenses and pondering his few alternatives. The sixth day was spent watching for activity along the distant tree line.

On the seventh day, Luiza's condition worsened. Her wound was now a large, heinous, festering sore, and its offensive odor summoned every fly, mosquito, and winged vermin in the territory.

On the eighth day, at noon, during the hottest part of the day, the Natchez gathered at the edge of the forest where they awaited their War Chief's signal to attack. The signal came shortly thereafter, and the war resumed.

Well-placed cannon fire disrupted their initial advance. But with only two caliber-four cannons available, and the time required to load each, the French were unable to lay and maintain an effective barrage. Many fell. Still they came, ignoring the danger and superiority of the French militia weapons. From their actions, it was clear to all that they were fighting out of sheer desperation. St. Denis cursed as several of his men fell.

The Natchez fought fiercely and daringly. Two managed to scale the wall. One was shot in the face, point-blank. François arrested the other near the summit of the wall and threw him back to the ground.

Finally, after expending most of their munitions, the Natchez fell back. Immediately, St. Denis rallied his army and launched his offensive. Several times the Natchez stopped and tried to set up a defense, but St. Denis would not grant them any reprieve. Soon, they abandoned their efforts and fled, leaving their dead behind and dragging their walking-wounded with them.

Since he did not have the manpower necessary to both defend the fort and press his advantage, St. Denis gave up the chase. As an alternative, he dispatched Jalot, François, and his scout, Deerfoot, with instructions to trail the Natchez to their camp.

In the aftermath of the battle, St. Denis counted thirty-two dead or dying Natchez. Those near death, he dispatched straight away with a ball into the head. He found two without mortal wounds and had them brought into the fort for interrogation. After questioning them vigorously without success, and still angry over the injury to his daughter and the manner in which Marguerite died, he ordered for them a public execution. They were taken then, outside the gates, and hung from the stockade walls. Afterwards, they, along with the rest of their fallen comrades, were buried in a mass grave near the tree that had served as Marguerite's purgatory.

St. Denis' own losses totaled only nine wounded, including his daughter. Eight were attributable directly to the Natchez, and one accidental fall, which resulted in a broken leg. For that, he was thankful. He was also thankful that he had not tried to attack the Natchez on their terms. For within the forest, he found numerous well-camouflaged trenches and small log barricades laid out in a horseshoe shaped trap. If their strategy had worked, he would have charged right into an ambush. The Natchez had been well prepared.

Mid-morning, the following day, Jalot and François returned. They had located the Natchez camp in the low rolling
hills, south by southeast of the fort beside a small creek that
fed into a shallow lake. Jalot also reported that he suspected the
Natchez were starving. The Natchez were fond of pets, especially dogs since they also served as vigilant sentries. None had
been sighted, a strong indication that they had probably been
eaten. He further estimated the number of braves to be between
three- and four-hundred.

Immediately, St. Denis dispatched a detail report to the governor, summarizing the events, and closing with a request for
additional support for the war.

Luiza's condition continued to deteriorate. The fever was
relentless. Gangrene set in. Her vision failed and her arm turned
dusty-blue. And while Emanuelle prayed for her recovery, St.
Denis cursed and swore that the Natchez would pay dearly for
their part in his daughter's suffering. Yet, despite all his swear-
ing and all his raving, three weeks later, his first-born was deposited in a shallow grave in a field near his home, among the
bitter weeds, the dandelions, and crab grass, beneath the shade
of a lone spreading live-oak tree.

St. Denis was convinced now that the Natchez had to be
destroyed — like a good dog gone mad. It pained him. But now,
things were completely out of control, beyond reconciliation,
and there was nothing any human could do to change the course
of events. It was almost as if the Gods had already placed their
bets, collected their wagers, and returned to wherever it was they
went when they were not meddling in the affairs of mortals.

Extermination was no longer a matter of speculation. It was
now a matter of necessity. Something that had to be done. And it
had to be done soon.

———————

In the spring of 1732, after receiving one-hundred and fifty additional soldiers from France, Governor Périer departed with over six-hundred men in barges and pirogues up the Mississippi and Red rivers to Fort de St. Jean Baptiste des Natchitoches.

Since the Ministry had become increasingly critical of his abilities to govern and protect his charges, he had decided to exclude the Choctaws. His head was beneath the axe, and he could no longer afford to take any chances on their loyalty. This, he was sure, would be his last opportunity to redeem himself. He had to succeed, and he had to do it in spite of the Ministry's failure to provide him with the resources he deemed necessary for the task.

It was a festive occasion that greeted the entourage from New Orleans. Inhabitants gathered alongside the river singing patriotic songs and shouting greetings to their liberators. Young girls flirted with the soldiers enticingly. Casks of wine and rum kept for special occasions were dusted and offered in appreciation.

While the men made their camp outside the gates of the fort, St. Denis and Governor Périer discussed their plans for war.

"Well, what is the latest news of the Natchez?" Governor Périer inquired.

"As of the last report, they are still in their camp. I have several scouts out keeping watch on their activities. What concerns me, however, is — where are the rest? Only half of the tribe is camped in the hills."

"Maybe they have split into two camps."

"There is that chance. If they have, we have been unable to locate the second one."

"I wonder why they have not fled the country? Surely, they must know that we will counterattack."

"I suspect that the Chickasaw will not welcome them as long as their chief, the Great Sun, is alive. The Natchez probably have not yet decided to give him up. Until they do so and relieve him of his head, no tribe in the country will grant them asylum.

As far as they are concerned, there can only be one rooster to a barnyard. But then again, Jalot also reported that they are starving. So, maybe they are too weak to make the long journey into Chickasaw country. Who knows?"

"Either way, it should make for an easy slaughter."

"Quite true. Still, I am wondering, considering the circumstances, if there might be another solution..."

"Speak out."

"Well, there is a good chance that a surrender might be negotiated without a war. The Natchez are low on munitions, and in their weakened condition, once they see our numbers, they will know their cause is lost. They could be collected then and shipped to Spanish Florida in chains."

"Are you mad? Never! A crime has been committed. The bloodsucking bastards even killed your daughter. How can you suggest such a course? No. They must pay. *Sang pour sang* (Blood for blood). There is no place for them in this life. My preordained task is to rid this earth of their likes. The Ministry will accept nothing less. I am already crucified for the fall of Fort Rosalie."

"I am aware of the desires of the Ministry in this matter, but their lives are not at risk here. I don't give a damn about the Natchez. They can burn in Hell. My concern is for French lives, and I think it is foolish to expose them to danger needlessly, when our objectives can be accomplished without doing so."

"But then, you are not the one who establishes policies in these matters — are you? Your job is to see that they are carried out."

"That point is acknowledged, m'sieur," St. Denis replied, torn between pursuing what he knew to be morally right and his own selfish desire to avenge his daughter's death. After a moment, he sighed. "Well, I suppose you are right. So, how do you propose to conduct this campaign?"

"Me...? It is not I who will be responsible for this campaign. That will be your task. The Natchez are camped within your jurisdiction. You know them and this terrain. I do not. It will, therefore, be your responsibility. Its success or failure will rest squarely upon your shoulders. I, of course, will supervise and give you direct assistance where required."

"In that case, Governor, tell your men to rest well. We will depart at sunrise. The Natchez camp is a day's march from here, overland."

Once organized, the militia departed the next morning on foot, dragging cannons and other supplies by hand and with the help of a few oxen. Scouts were sent ahead to verify that the Natchez were still in camp. That night the French troops bivouacked at the edge of the rolling hills.

———

Chapter — Fifteen

THE OLD GUARDIAN SQUATTED BESIDE A SMALL CAMPFIRE, his ancient face clearly defined in its flickering light. Heavy, scabrous calluses covered his haunches and knees, making the wrinkled hide of his body appear more animal than human. Bear fat had been used to groom his silver-white hair, and although its unpleasant odor attracted numerous flies and other insects, he did not appear to mind.

In a circle, to his left and right, around the fire, sat several young boys, ages eight to twelve, talking among themselves. They had gathered to hear the old Indian tell the legend of how they came to be in this land. Behind him stood Black Hawk, the son of Morning Sun, and the one chosen to become their next Chief and Great Sun.

The old Guardian clapped his hands and the young boys quieted down. Then he began...

"In the time long ago, before my father, or my father's father, or his father; long ago and far away our ancestors lived. All the land was one, and one man could not walk its breadth. It was a good land and food was plentiful. Fruits and berries of every variety grew bountifully. The buffalo and the deer did not fear the hunter's bow. Each man cared one for the other. All things had its place, and there was a place for all things. There was peace, and the people were happy and content.

"Then one day, a man, covered with the light of the sun, fell from the sky. Everyone was frightened because they had never seen an apparition such as this before.

'*You have no reason to fear me,*' the man said, '*I come in peace, for you have honored me for many, many seasons. You have also cared for each other and honored even the smallest of*

*my creatures. For that, I am thankful. For these reasons, I have
come to you from a great distance to visit, share knowledge, and
teach you how to live upon this earth.'*

"So, the Shining-Man took a wife and lived with her while
he taught us many things — about the stars, about nature, and
how to live and govern our lives. Then, he and his wife had a
child, a female, and he adored her very much.

"When it came time for him to depart, he called all of our
people together and said, *'The time has come for me to leave
you. But in my stead, I will leave a white owl — a sign to you that
I am forever by your side. This bird is a sacred bird. You must
honor it, protect it, and always keep it from harm. I also must
leave behind my wife and my beloved daughter. In the future,
select your leaders only from the males born of the daughters of
my daughter.'*

'I must go with you,' his wife cried. *'Do not leave me behind. Please, take me with you.'*

'If this is your desire,' the Shining Man replied, *'you must
leave this world and join me in the spirit world. There is no other
way.'*

"Without hesitation, the Shining Man's wife killed herself
by tying a leather bag about her head. When she released her last
breath and her body was still, the Shining Man departed in a ball
of light that lifted him and his wife up into the sky and into the
face of the sun.

"The people rejoiced, and they protected and cared for the
bird as they had been commanded to do. In the beginning, most
of the people loved the bird. But, as time passed, some grew to
fear it. Even so, no one dared to harm it.

"One day a young warrior left the village and went on the
hunt. He was not a good warrior and his aim was poor. After
two days of hunting, he had not killed a buffalo or deer. Angry
because he was forced to return to the village empty-handed,
he took his last arrow, and at close range — he killed the little,
white owl. Holding the bird above his head, he ran through the
village shouting, 'See, I am a great hunter. I have killed the sa-

cred owl that all others have feared.'

"Those who had once feared the bird, rejoiced, while those who loved the bird went into their hovels to cry. The moon left its side of the heavens, passed across the face of the sun, and the day turned to night.

"Like thunder, an angry, great voice from the sky spoke and said, *'My people you have offended me. The arrow in the bird was like an arrow in my own heart. And because you have violated my covenant with you, you must leave this land.'*

"And so, he caused the people to leave. First, a large tribe with many numbers came with golden shields and lances, and made war against the people — causing them to flee across a small creek. Then, the creek grew and became a deep river. The river grew, and became a large lake. Then, the lake grew and became the sea. Then, the cold winds came. Everywhere, there was snow and ice. In every quadrant, ice as far as the eye could see. There were no trees, no flowers, no fruits or berries, no buffalo or deer, and no fowl — only the fish that swam beneath the ice.

"The people lived this way for a long time and many died upon the snow from the cold and hunger that cramped their swollen bellies.

"There was a noble warrior by the name of Takien. Takien was not a young man, but a man with a wife and five sons who also had five wives. Takien loved his family dearly, and he was sad because they were so cold and hungry. He knew that he would die soon, and it worried him that he would leave his family to suffer alone. He expressed his concerns to his wife and asked her, 'What can I do?'

'*Replace the white owl,*' she said to him.

'But how, when there are no fowl in this land?' he replied.

'*Then you must make one,*' his wife said.

"So the next day, Takien took a piece of ice, and with great care, he used his knife to carve a beautiful owl. Then, he covered it with snow and made the snow to look like feathers. When he had finished, he took the ice bird, his bow and arrows, and climbed for two days to the top of a high mountain. There, he sang and prayed, beseeching the Great Spirit to return the sun to the sky and warm the earth. For several days and nights, he prayed, and he waited. But, there was no response. The only sounds he heard were the howl of the cold wind and the sound of his own voice echoing from the valley below. The sun did not return.

"Saddened that the Great Spirit had not accepted his gift, he decided to return to his village. As he prepared to leave, a voice that sounded like thunder spoke and said, *'Takien, you have brought me an owl, but the owl you give me is cold and dead. I have no need for such a bird. Why have you not given it life?'*

"'How do I give it life?' Takien asked, but the sky was silent.

'Tell me,' he shouted to the wind. 'What must I do to give the bird life?'

"Still, there was no answer. Takien was puzzled, for he did not know how to give the owl life. He tried many things. He blew into the face of the owl, sang to it, prayed, and tried to make it fly. But after two more days passed, he still had not determined how to give the bird life. Takien was very sad. Because he had failed, he decided that he did not wish to live any longer. So, he knelt in the snow near the ice bird, took out his knife, and slashed deeply into his arms and across his chest. His blood fell to the ground and made the snow turn red.

"While he sang his death song, some of his blood happened to fall upon the ice owl. Suddenly, like magic, the owl came to life and flew away.

"Then, the voice spoke again, and said, *'Takien, I am pleased. You have given the ice bird life at the price of your own. For your sacrifice, I will guide your five sons and all their families to a new land. You and your wife, however, may not accompany them. You both must stay.*

"When you return to your village, stand with the setting sun to your back, lift your right arm, and spread the fingers of your right hand wide. Each son and his family must travel in the direction of a finger — one son for each finger. Their destination will be a new land.'

"Then, lightning leaped from the sky and made the arrows in Takien's quiver burn. The voice spoke again, `*The Ice owl you have given me cannot leave. It, too, must stay. For in the new land, it would melt. In its place, I give you Holy Fire from your brother, the Sun. Give each son a burning arrow. The flames will keep their bodies warm, and make their food pleasant to eat. Once they reach their new land, they must forever keep their flames burning. For as long as the flame shall burn, I shall honor them, and the children of their children will prosper.*'

"Takien did as he was told. He returned to his home and gave each son a burning arrow with the instructions of the Great Spirit. The sons and their families departed, one for each direction, leaving their father and their mother to die upon the frozen snow.

"Natchez, the son who followed the third finger, came to this land. This land given to us by the Great Spirit and our brother, the Sun.

"Now, the white man has come, not with the golden shields or lances of the ancient warriors, but with sticks of thunder to claim our land as his own. Again, we are forced to flee. The white man's numbers increase daily. He kills easily and without purpose. With his sick breath, one man can destroy a whole nation. Many people have died. Many more are yet to die. Maybe, someone again has killed a white owl. The Holy Fire, too, no longer burns, and we are a people lost and wandering. Either way, the Great Spirit is angry.

"For many moons, we have not had the benefit of a fire in our camp. But tonight I built this one so you would be better able to see our history and our future in its flickering light; so that you may remember the warmth of a fire's glow. Each night when I lay down to sleep, I can feel the chill and hear the call of the icy wind. And — each night it approaches nearer. Soon, it will be upon us, and neither mantles nor hides will keep the blood in our bodies warm...."

A moment of silence followed. Exhausted, the Old Guardian

drifted off to sleep, his chin resting gently upon his shallow chest. Slowly, the young boys got up, one by one, and quietly drifted off into the night.

A gentle breeze nursed the embers of the smoldering fire and caused it to tint the nearby surroundings with somber hues of red and yellow. A large, green snake approached the clearing, stopped, flicked its split tongue, then side-stroked its way back into the foliage. Nearby, a lone wolf howled, its voice echoing like a soft trumpet through the branches of the black, ghostly trees....

Morning Sun walked with her son, Black Hawk, along a small footpath beside a wandering stream. It was a beautiful day. Not one cloud marked the sky, and all about her was foliage that was greener than any green she had ever seen. The place was familiar, but it was not a place she had been before. This place was like a garden, lush with vegetation and fruits of every known and unknown variety, and she wondered what name had been given to this unusual place.

She followed the footpath until she came to the edge of a clearing. Beyond the clearing, she saw a large village that stretched in all directions for as far as she could see. She saw no people. *Who lives here,* she wondered. Puzzled, she entered the village and wandered through its cleanly swept, empty streets until she came to the far side. There, she saw them — a multitude of people, all gathered at the base of a huge, strange, stone structure. There were steps on all four sides and all sides led to a flat apex high in the sky. Its length and breadth awed her imagination.

As she approached, the people parted and made way for her — each bowing before her, in turn, like servants. All Indian Nations were represented. Among them were Choctaws, Creeks, Chickasaws, Seminoles, Houmas, Apaches, Cheyenne, Shawnee, Cahokians, and many of whom she did not know. They were all there, smiling and paying homage to her and her handsome son,

Black Hawk. Her chest swelled with modest pride as she acknowledged each with a small smile.

Without knowing why, and unable to restrain her curiosity, she took her place behind a line of proud women, each with a handsome, naked, male child. Slowly, step by step, she followed the women up the pyramid-like structure. At timed intervals, the people below cheered in adulation and the sounds of their volume caused Morning Sun's heart to race as she wondered what great honor was to be bestowed upon her and her beloved son.

The climb was long and slow, and the sun, exceedingly hot. It seemed like she had been climbing forever by the time she finally reached the top. Wearily, she glanced back across the majestic countryside and stared in wonder at the far off mountains and valleys, rivers and lakes. And the people below appeared so very small....*Like vermin?* Morning Sun asked herself. It was then that she realized that she and her son were the last in the line. Suddenly, a sense of foreboding cloaked her, and she decided that she did not like the place any longer.

She was about to take her son and run, when two warriors approached quickly and restrained her. Alarmed, she watched spellbound as the Shaman took the child of the woman before her and held him aloft. Then, amidst the cheers of the multitude, he walked to the center of the altar and tossed the beautiful, smiling boy into a deep, smoking pit. When the Shaman returned for her son, Black Hawk, she was shocked to see that it was not an Indian-Shaman, but a white-Shaman, French. His face was white as bone-ash with the cold, glassy eyes of a chicken, the ears of a horned beast, and a slit of a mouth that was void of teeth. Terror gripped her. She screamed for Black Hawk to run, but he only looked at her and smiled. Spurred by a mother's love, she managed to break free. She dashed to aid her son, but before she could reach him, the demon laughed and threw her beloved child into the fiery pit. She screamed in horror and fell to her knees, watching helplessly as his frail body tumbled like a weighted feather down the abyss into a pool filled with *hot, flaming blood....*

———

As the sun began its ascent into the heavens, its reflection brought life to the small bayou near which the Natchez had settled. Several older women sat in a circle cutting several small fish into bite-sized pieces. While they were so engaged, a party of seven braves, including one of the runaway slaves, gathered their equipment for the hunt.

Slowly, Morning Sun arose. The morning was cool. Yet, she was sweating, something she rarely did even in the heat of day. It was always the same whenever she had the *Chicken Man* dream — the screaming, the shaking, and the sweating.

Beside her, tossing restlessly, lay her son Black Hawk, still grieving, she was sure, for his father, Tattooed Wind, who had been killed in the attack on the Natchitoches fort. Tattooed Wind, however, was not her son's biological father. His father was the tall French Commandant of the same fort. She had mated with him during one of the Frenchman's earlier visits to their village.

When Black Hawk was born, her first impulse was to kill him. She decided later, however, that a half-breed Great Sun might be of some advantage in negotiating the political pitfalls between the two cultures. And while she felt a great deal of sympathy for her son, she felt that he bore the lighter of their burdens. For, while he grieved only for his father, she was condemned to grieve for a whole nation.

She glanced at her daughter, Red Sun, still asleep, cuddled beneath the covers near her feet, her mouth open with a saliva -soaked thumb of one hand lying nearby. In her other hand, she clutched her father's prized, silver medallion with the blood-red stone. She often wondered why her daughter was so fascinated with the object, preferring to play with it above any other item. And... she would scream like a wild she-cat if anyone dared take it from her. It was as if she knew that it was the only visible link between her and the father she would never know.

Wearily, Morning Sun retrieved several slivers of deer bone and set about carving them into fishhooks.

Her thoughts, however, were not on the chores at hand, but rather on Etienne — their last meeting, and how she regretted that she did not have an opportunity to tell him that he was the father of a beautiful daughter. That thought pained her more than anything else; the knowing that two beings so genetically linked would never come to know one another; would never know the joy of the special love that bonds the souls of a father and daughter. How she missed him and his sea-green eyes, and how she longed to see him for one last time, only if for a moment — just long enough to smell the fragrance of his leather jerkin and the sweat of his beautiful body, or to touch the coarse hairs that sprouted from his tanned cheeks.

She remembered the sweet pain of his last kiss. She had thought, surely, he was going to kill her that day. And if he had, she would have made no attempt to protect herself. In fact, if she had to die, she would have preferred it be by his hands as opposed to those of her proclaimed executioners.

His kiss of death, however, was in reality, a kiss of life... *such as it is*. For in that frightful, yet blissful moment, Etienne had whispered Governor Périer's plans to exterminate them the next day. His disclosure, of course, was meant only for her ears so that she could escape to safety. But, she was a princess. She had obligations, and she could not have walked out and left her people to be slaughtered. So, she violated his trust in her and informed Tattooed Serpent of the French governor's intentions.

Upon hearing the news, that night, Tattooed Serpent sent Bear Claw with a message of apology to the Choctaw War Chief, Coutee. Bear Claw then removed his war paint, dressed in his French scout attire, and slipped through the French sector, past their guards and over the sleeping bodies of several soldiers. It must have taken a great amount of courage on his part to restrain himself from slitting their miserable throats.

Bear Claw next located a Choctaw brave, explained his mission, and requested to be escorted to their Chief.

As he was instructed, he submitted Tattooed Serpent's apology to the Choctaw for not consulting them prior to the attack on

Fort Rosalie. He explained that he had sent a runner to them with a message five days before the attack; that apparently, the messenger was killed before reaching his destination, for the brave never returned. He proposed that if the Choctaw would let them pass through during the night, they would leave all their treasures and objects of value hidden in a convenient place for their disposal. He closed his argument with the statement:

"For many years, the Natchez and the Choctaw have lived in peace as nations that respected the other's right to exist. In all this time, even though we did not share each other's lodges as friends, the Natchez never placed a claim upon the lands of the Choctaw, and the Choctaw in all these ages have never claimed the lands of the Natchez.

"This war we fight is not a war against the Choctaw, but against the French and for our right to exist.

"Yesterday, the French claimed the land of the Natchez as their own without respect for our laws. They are men without honor, and we know that they are in their camp now planning to kill every Natchez once the prisoners are released.

"Today, the Natchez are the first to fall before the greed of this foe. A foe that grows stronger with each passing sun. I have studied them and have found that their thirst is unquenchable. Open your eyes and look. The direction of the path they follow is clearly marked, and it leads straight to the doors of your own homes. Tomorrow, when they are strong and their number equals yours, they will forget the sacrifices you have made on their behalf, and they will come to claim your lands, even as they have claimed ours.

"When that time comes, what will the Choctaws do to protect their lands? Will the Choctaw fight as men, or give it to them as a gift in exchange for more of their stinking whiskey?

"The Natchez have always respected the Choctaw as brave warriors and men of wisdom. I say — you will fight. Can you expect any less from the Natchez?"

After some deliberation, the Choctaw Chief, Coutee, replied, "It is agreed. You may pass through our lines. A path will be opened for you. Look for three feathers on the ground. From there, follow the way of the sun to the river. I must warn you, however, that we cannot be responsible for the actions of the French. If they should discover you while in the process of passing through, we will be obliged to honor our original commitment to them. Expect no more from us."

When Bear Claw returned, he informed Tattooed Serpent of the Choctaw's terms and conditions. In response, Tattooed Serpent gathered everyone in the plaza and informed them of his plans for their escape.

Every precaution was taken not to disturb the French. They wrapped their feet in portions of cloth and animal hides. Small children were gagged so they could not be heard if they cried out. All children, less than four-years-old, were carried on the backs of parents or others. They took no food or personal belongings, only their weapons. For the first time since the beginning, a Great Sun left his litter behind and walked beside his mortal subjects.

A scout located the three feathers and the procession passed through the way made for them by the Choctaw without an incident. A small war party led the way, followed by the women and children. The rest of the braves followed. When they had passed through and were a safe distance away, the black man, Big Mukta No-Talk, took his club and returned in the direction of the French lines, for what — she could only imagine. She just closed her eyes and prayed that Etienne would be somewhere safe, far away from No-Talk's path.

Two days later, Mukta No-Talk rejoined the procession, his body burned badly in several places and a gunshot wound in his arm. But… the smile of satisfaction on his wearied, black face told all, and she knew that somewhere there were several dead Frenchmen with their skulls bashed to tiny bits. No-Talk was a fierce warrior, and where she once looked upon him with disdain, she now admired him greatly for his awesome strength and courage.

First, they traveled north, parallel to the river for two days as if they were headed toward Chickasaw country. Then, under the cover of darkness, they crossed the river to the west side and turned southwest, traveling overland and off the beaten trails, eating nuts, grub worms, and anything else edible that they could find. Finally, they came to a group of gentle, rolling hills. It was there beside a small stream that they made their camp.

They were in the area almost a month before they realized that they were only a day's march from the fort at Natchitoches.

Throughout their exile, they subsisted meagerly on nuts, fish, and wild game. What powder and balls they had were soon expended. In order to protect the location of their campsite, no fires were allowed. So, they ate their meat raw. And when winter came, they were forced to huddle in tight groups within their temporary, hastily-constructed hovels to keep their bodies warm. Food was at a premium, and they were on the verge of starvation, reduced to eating any vermin that they could catch. Small children fought for scraps and poked the brush for insects.

Even after the winter passed, there had been no relief. There were no seeds to plant because the grain they had harvested the previous year had all been left behind. Many were sick, and death visited their camp daily, wandering aimlessly and wantonly through their village indiscriminately snuffing the life from men, women, and children.

In desperation, Tattooed Serpent left for Chickasaw country to arrange asylum for them. Mukta No-Talk and a third of the Natchez Nation went with him in the first wave. He did not take the Great Sun because the Chickasaw, like most tribes, did not normally welcome the chiefs of other nations. In most cases, as a precaution, they were killed. If all went well, it was Tattooed Serpent's intention to negotiate for the Great Sun's life, then return for the remainder of the tribe when suitable accommodations were secured.

It was during his absence, that a lesser War Chief grew impatient, called the Council together, and proposed that they attack the Fort at Natchitoches to obtain food, and powder for their weapons.

Morning Sun warned the council that such a plan would surely provoke the French to renew their war against them. The War Chief argued that Tattooed Serpent was late in returning; that maybe the Chickasaw did not care to accept so many refugees; that the fort was poorly manned and once it was captured they would have food and a place to defend themselves. Wisdom took second place. The council agreed, and the fort was attacked.

Now, they lived in fear with few weapons and little food, and she knew it would only be a matter of time before the French came. Each night, she prayed that Tattooed Serpent was safe, and that he would soon return to lead them to safety.... *Etienne, my one love — where are you?.... The fire of my dream is alive. It sears the flesh from my bones. Do you know of my pain? Can you hear my cries upon the wings of the wind.... Do you know of my love for you, and my fears? Will you be among those who will come to slaughter me and your beautiful, little red-haired daughter?*

———

At the first shot, or maybe the second, a ball of hot metal tore through the side of Morning Sun's hovel, shattering thatch and branches, and striking her in the chest. The sickening thud accompanied by the sounds of gunfire and screams jerked Black Hawk from his reverie. His first thought was of his mother. He called her name, then watched as she toppled forward, still clutching her chest with a bloody hand. Her mouth was open as if she wanted to speak, but Black Hawk knew instinctively that she was already dead.

Then, the cannons roared with a sound he had never heard before. A sound so loud and unearthly that the ground beneath him trembled in fear. Red Sun screamed. He reached for her, but she scurried to her mother and burrowed her head deep beneath her limp, bloody arms.

"Stay here!" Black Hawk yelled to his sister as he jumped to his feet and dashed out of the hovel and almost into the path of three warriors who raced toward the French troops on horseback. He watched as they were shot down by a volley before they ever reached the edge of the compound.

For several seconds, Black Hawk stood rooted to the ground in confusion. Suddenly, he turned and dashed back toward his hovel to retrieve his father's bow. He was within fifteen feet of the entrance when a ball struck him in the upper thigh and knocked him to the ground. He glanced over his shoulder and saw the Old Guardian shuffle to the center of the village with his lance raised in open defiance. His final act of bravery drew the fire of a third of the French riflemen as bullet after bullet ripped his ancient body apart.

The fall of the Old Guardian appeared to serve as a prearranged signal. For within seconds, the French launched their charge and fell upon them like a dark cloud raining blood and terror. Amidst the screams and the deafening commotion, Black Hawk could hear the voices of the French officers shouting orders and instructions while, at regular intervals, the cannons continued to belch their black smoke and blazing death. The French were all around him firing at anything that moved. So, he lay on the ground pretending he was dead and hoping his little sister would remain inside his mother's hovel. Fortunately, she had.

The Indians fought bravely, but were soon forced to retreat until their backs were against a small lake. With their arrows and lances expended, they were soon reduced to throwing rocks and large stones. It was like shooting turkeys in a barnyard. Some stood their ground, others tried to swim away, but the French gave no quarter. They stood on the banks and fired at will until the lake was red with Natchez blood. Years later, this infamous lake would come to be known as *Lake Sang pour Sang* (Blood for Blood).

In the aftermath of the battle, most of the adult male warriors were killed. Also killed, were the females who had sustained serious wounds. Claudette, who was in the last stages of her second pregnancy, had survived. But when an attempt was made to separate her from the rest of the Natchez prisoners, she suddenly attacked the French soldier nearest her. She, in turn, was shot at close range. Then, her ripe abdomen, swollen with life, was punctured, and the infant who resided there impaled on the end of a sharp lance.

The Great Sun was found seriously wounded, sprawled on the ground near his makeshift Temple. He was brought before the governor and forced to kneel. Governor Périer looked down at the half-naked man who would be a God and sneered. He was about to administer the *coup de grâce,* when St. Denis intervened. Angrily, the Governor ordered him back. Then, with great ceremony, he pointed his handgun at the Great Sun and shot him in the head, point blank.

The single shot that killed the Great Sun, however, frightened Red Sun and she emerged from her lair crying, and still clutching her mother's silver medallion. Black Hawk wanted desperately to aid her but his shattered leg would not allow him to do so. Suddenly, a huge hand from above snatched his sister aloft. In the process, her mother's treasured ornament fell to the ground near Black Hawk's hand. When the moment was right, he took it, placed it between his chest and the earth, and resumed his death-like posture.

"Well, look what we have here," a large brawny soldier said, "a redheaded half-breed. It seems some low life has been bedding one of these heathen wenches. It's the scum of the earth who would dishonor his country in times of war." At which point, he hurled the young girl to the ground and prepared to run her through with a lance. François caught the lance mid-thrust, snatched it away, and shoved the soldier aside roughly.

Angered by the intrusion of a slave, the soldier yelled, "Dupart, give me your weapon. We have one more heathen for the funeral pyre."

"Hold, both of you," St. Denis intervened angrily, "or I will instruct my heathen to break every bone in your damned body. We are not here to murder children. Back off!"

"These are the bastards who killed my father at Fort Rosalie," Dupart shouted in anger. "None deserve to be spared."

St. Denis looked at the seventeen-year-old boy and said quite solemnly, "This child is not guilty of killing your father. And although the Natchez did, they never shed one drop of any child's blood. Should we be any less compassionate? Go your way. This war is over."

Sullenly and reluctantly, the two Frenchmen backed off. Glaring angrily, they watched as François lifted the child from the ground and handed her to one of the female captives who nodded her thanks and gathered Red Sun into her arms.

A commotion within the ranks of the Natchez prisoners drew the attention of both Governor Périer and St. Denis.

"What is it?" the Governor asked his interpreter.

"This woman," the interpreter said, pointing to a middle-aged woman dressed in a filthy, but highly-decorated robe, "she is the wife of their chief. She says, she must be allowed to accompany her husband."

"Is the wench crazy?"

"No, m'sieur. Not crazy. It is their custom. The Great Sun's wife and his servants are all expected to accompany him into his next life."

Both the Governor and St. Denis were aware of the custom, but neither had ever witnessed such an event.

After some thought, both agreed to the request, but for different reasons. St. Denis agreed out of respect for their customs and beliefs. The Governor agreed out of curiosity, and his desire to satisfy a deeper, darker urge.

The Governor nodded his approval and a thin, gawky guardian named Two Dog was escorted to the remnants of a makeshift temple where he retrieved several doeskin bags and an equal number of leather strings. The bags were issued to five persons. One was given to the wife of the Great Sun, three to his servants, and the Guardian, Two Dog, kept one for himself.

When the dispensing of the bags was complete, the Natchez prisoners, male and female, began their ritual with a low, throaty howling that grew in crescendo until the heavy vibrato of their chorusing voices echoed among the low, rolling hills like that of a pack of lonely wolves.

Although all took bags, it was obvious that one of the servants was reluctant to consummate her sacrificial duty. To her, the wife of the Great Sun said —

"I see you take a bag, yet you hide your face so that I may not see your eyes. I say to you, cast your bag aside. It is not good that you depart this world in body and leave your heart behind. No person can dwell in two places at the same time. Stay here. I will tell my husband that you are delayed — that you will follow at a later time. He will understand."

The servant, in spite of her shame, let her bag slip to the ground and shuffled to the side where she sat down and lowered her head in disgrace.

To her people gathered there, she said —

"There is no need to weep for me. I make this journey full of hope and joy. It is I, who weep for you. You who are condemned to struggle beneath the yoke of the white man. Never again to know the peace and purpose of our fathers. Never again to know your place upon this earth, or the true warmth of our brother the Sun. Do not weep for me — it is I who weep for you."

To the Frenchmen gathered, she lifted her regal head with great dignity, and said —

"And you, brave men who sail distant seas and build great temples of stone — you, who say we are different, vermin of the earth, not worthy to hold up our heads and declare that we are a people. A people who know the pain of birth, the joy of love, and the sadness of death. For all your wisdom and knowledge, have you never wondered why the color of blood is red? Or asked yourselves — why is it that heathens know the art of planting seed, harvesting the grain, and grinding it to make a simple loaf of bread, even as you do?

"I see you now with sticks that spit fire and great cannons that hold the powers of the wind, but I know all too certain, that your hands once held the bow and pulled its thong, even as we do.

"Have you never asked yourselves why this is so — or searched the words of your talking marks for the answer?

"I, the lowest of the low, a heathen Stinkard, have. And I say to you that we are the same, from the same place... the same teacher.

"And you, great White Chief of the Natchitoches, the man we once called a noble friend, today while you were killing my people, you also killed your son, Black Hawk, the son of Morning Sun. If you do not believe me, find his body, look into his face and you will know that I speak the truth.

"But such is the way of both the living and the dying. For in spite of all your power and magnificent weapons of war, you too must depart this land even as I do, and leave behind your riches and robes of many colors.

"And when you reach this new land, it will not be as king or queen, or master, or slave, but as sister and brother.... And you, the noble ones, will reach for my hand, the hand of a lowly Stinkard, even as I will reach for yours — not in war, not in sadness, but in love and joy. For there, all men will again be equal and all will dwell within the warmth and protection of our brother, the Sun, and his father, the Great Spirit....

"And so, I must go. Time passes, and my husband awaits me."

With these final words and as much dignity as she could possibly muster, the Stinkard woman knelt and placed her bag firmly upon her royal head. Two Dog, the Guardian, sealed it tightly around her neck with one of the leather strings. He did the same for the two remaining servants, and then for himself, hoping that his feeble gesture would atone for his regretful act — the one committed by a young, curious boy who in his innocence had failed in his attempt to protect the Holy Fire of his nation.

Their voices muffled, each knelt and joined in the singing of their haunting, songs of death....

In silence, the French soldiers stood watching in utter amazement as, one by one, the entourage gasped for breath and tumbled to the ground. When the last body was stilled, the mournful howling of the remaining Indians faded into a few faint sobs that throbbed softly and anonymously.

"Well, this spectacle is over," Governor Périer said to the officer next to him. "Muster every able body and get this mess cleaned up." Then to St. Denis, he said, "Was that Stinkard woman correct about you having a Stinkard son?"

"The woman was delirious in her anguish. Her words were only meant to offend me for my actions against them. I assure you, I have never bedded an Indian female in my life, so how could I conceive a child. It's all rubbish."

The governor accepted the reply guardedly, and then proceeded to supervise the cleanup activities.

While some of the soldiers aligned logs in a clearing for the pyre, others collected the dead bodies and stacked them on top. Those that were still alive with mortal wounds were executed while the ones not mortally wounded were restrained and corralled with the women and children.

François worked solemnly and mechanically while large tears streamed down the taut cheeks of his dark face. As he went about his duties, he happened to discover the still alive body of the half-breed. Instinctively, he knew that it was Black Hawk. There was no mistaking his master's features in the young man's face. Without fanfare, or an announcement of his discovery, he carried the boy to the holding area where the Natchez women could attend to him. As he resumed his duties, he found one of the leather bags used during the suicide ritual lying on the ground. He picked it up and stuffed it into his pocket to keep as a souvenir.

In the meantime, St. Denis wandered over to a large tree, sat down upon one of its exposed roots, and rested. He could still hear the voice of the Stinkard woman and her words weighed heavily upon his mind. *Had he unknowingly killed his own son?* he wondered as he remembered a special night and the mind-shattering experience of making love to an unknown Natchez princess. He had a strong urge to search among the bodies for the truth, but concluded that such an attempt was not in his best interest considering the current circumstances.

And... was it a coincidence that the ancient beliefs of these heathens included an afterlife in a place similar to that called Heaven by Christians? Could it be that Christ, in years past, also walked upon the soil of this new land? Was their reverence to the Great "Sun" symbolic, or equal to their belief in the "Son", Jesus Christ?... *And just who did teach these heathens the complicated process of baking a loaf of bread?*

These thoughts, he knew, would plague him for the rest of his life, long after the dead bodies were gathered and burned on the roaring funeral pyre.

————

PART III

The Silver Medallion and A Slave's Quest For Freedom

Slave Cabin,
(Cane River, Natchitoches, Louisiana)

Chapter – Sixteen

IT HAD BEEN A GOOD WAR — IF YOU COULD CALL ANY WAR
GOOD. There were only fourteen dead and twenty-two seriously
wounded out of some six-hundred-odd men. Yes, St. Denis supposed, it had been a good war. Still, for some reason, his victory
was hollow and empty. Where he should have been overcome
with joy, he was filled with something that was a cross between
penitence and despair, as if he had committed some unpardonable sin. He had never seen so many humans killed in any one
battle before in his life.

Maybe age had something to do with his insecurity and the
way he felt. He was not sure. He had noticed lately, particularly,
since the loss of his daughter, that the value of a life was growing more important to him. With her death, he suddenly realized
that no person was immortal, not his daughter, not the Great
Sun, and certainly, not himself. To put it bluntly, he was just
getting a little too old for the stresses of war and the other tasks
necessary to survive.

After their return to the fort, there was a celebration to commemorate their victory. St. Denis participated in the activities
briefly as a matter of courtesy. Then, he left to seek the comforts
of his home, Casa de Sombrilla. Emanuelle tried several times
to get him to tell her about the battle, but soon gave up once she
observed that he had no desire to discuss the details with her.

The next day, St. Denis held a burial ceremony for those
who had given their lives for their king. Afterwards, the militia
spent the rest of the week building log rafts for their trip back to
New Orleans. While the men worked, many of the local inhabitants took the opportunity to visit the prisoner stockade area.
While most came solely out of curiosity, a few came to jeer and

taunt the frightened and helpless victims. He chased those away whenever he caught them in their act.

When the rafts were complete, the prisoners and the militia, along with their cannons and equipment, were loaded aboard for the trip downstream to New Orleans. There, the prisoners would be paraded through the streets to show the citizens that their grand governor and French justice had triumphed once again.

Afterward, the women and female children were to be parceled out as slaves. Males under the age of fifteen would be relocated to Haiti and used as slaves. Potential warriors over fifteen would be released in the swamps of Spanish Florida.

Once loaded, the flotilla shoved off amidst shouts of farewell and the ringing sounds of gunfire from the shore. St. Denis, with François as his oarsman, followed behind in his pirogue to escort them a portion of the way.

Sometime after they were underway, the Natchez boy, Black Hawk, managed to free himself. When the convoy reached the tip of the Isle Brevelle, a long strip of land surrounded on all sides by two branches of the same river, he summoned all of his strength and slid over the side. Even wounded, he was a good swimmer, and his strokes carried him swiftly towards the muddy shore.

Dupart, first to be aware of the escape, sounded the alarm, took aim, and fired his single-shot weapon. Other shots were fired, but none found their mark.

While the rafts were being poled to the side, Dupart dove into the river to chase the youth down. Shouts of encouragement from the others cheered him on.

"Get him, Dupart. He's one of the bastards that killed your father at Fort Rosalie!"

"Let fly his stinking scalp."

"*Vive la Dupart!*"

The Natchez boy reached the shore, struggled up its muddy banks, and hobbled into the forest. Dupart soon followed, close at his heels, brandishing a wicked dagger.

While the flotilla waited expectantly for Dupart to return either with the Indian boy or preferably his scalp, mosquitoes and large, green flies wreaked havoc upon the lot. Several curious alligators which had been disturbed by the unusual activity slipped into the water and floated lazily toward the barges.

"Damn these vermin," Périer remarked as he smashed a large, blood-filled mosquito on his arm. "I shall be dead before I can inform the ministry that the king's dominion has once again been secured."

"Ignore them. That seems to make it easier," St. Denis suggested.

"Ignore them? How in the Hell can I do that? These vermin are more ravenous than a pack of hungry wolves. I do not know how you endure. They antagonize me even more than do the Natchez. If we had an ounce of sense, we would give the whole damned country back to the stinking heathens and go home."

Thirty minutes or more passed beneath the hot sun and the suicidal attacks of the insects before the Governor became unduly concerned. "Sergeant," the Governor yelled, "question the prisoners. I want the name of that young heathen."

A few moments later, the sergeant reported, "It was Black Hawk, the son of Morning Sun."

"Take a search party and find them. Dupart should have returned by now. Kill the Natchez boy."

"Rather than risking the delay of a search party," St. Denis interrupted while trying to conceal his anxiety about the identity of the boy, "let me send my slave, François. He is a good tracker, and he knows this area well."

"*D'accord — d'accord.* Just get him moving so we can be on our way before the lot of us fall victim to this foul smelling swamp."

François departed quickly, loping along the trail of blood and heavy boot prints made by Black Hawk and Dupart. Suddenly, his eye caught the reflection of the sun on a metal object lying on the floor of the forest among the leaves. He stopped and picked it up. It was a silver medallion with an embedded red stone. He studied it for a fraction of a moment, placed it around his neck, and proceeded deeper into the forest.

About four hundred yards inland, he found them. Dupart was dead. A sharp stick had been driven through his mouth and into his head. A few feet away, Black Hawk lay shaking, barely conscious from the heavy loss of blood. Besides the wound in his leg, he was now bleeding from a four-inch cut along his hair-line. There was also a deep gash across his left eye. Apparently, Dupart had attempted to take the boy's scalp while he was still alive. Carelessness in the process evidently cost him his life.

When François approached, the frightened boy lifted Dupart's knife defensively. François growled softly and dis-armed him with little effort. Acting quickly, he gathered mud from a small water puddle, mixed it with a hand full of spider webs that he collected from some low-hanging branches, and packed it on the boy's wounds. He then tore the sleeves from his shirt and used them to bind the mud in place. Nearby, he saw two logs lying almost parallel on the ground. He picked Black Hawk up, laid him between them, placed the knife at the boy's side, and covered him with moss and brush. When that was done, he gathered some of the blood covered leaves and scattered them for about fifty paces along a trail that led to the opposite side of the island.

After a quick survey of the area, he lifted Dupart's body to his shoulder and carried him back to the river.

"What's this? What happened?" Périer inquired with frustration.

"This boy is dead. The Indian drove a stick into his head."

"I see that. Where is the damn Indian?"

"I do not know. From the signs, the Indian was wounded badly. There was blood everywhere. I followed his trail for a short distance, but decided I should return the French boy to your care."

The Frenchmen were angry. Some wanted to pursue the boy and bring him to justice, but it was getting late, and the Governor wanted to get underway before another mishap could occur. All he needed now was for something to go awry and rob him of his finest moment, a moment he was sure would be reflected in the annals of history as a brilliantly-executed military maneuver. In fact, he would guarantee it. Every periodical in France would receive a personal copy of his report.

Somewhat reluctantly, the flotilla pushed off again to continue its slow journey downstream.

St. Denis and François sat in their pirogue watching silently until the last craft rounded the bend of the river. Then, the Commandant nodded, and François turned their pirogue for home.

After a moment, St. Denis' voice broke the silence.

"What happened in the forest?"

"In the forest, m'sieur?" François asked self-consciously.

"Yes, in the forest, damn it. I want the truth."

Taking a deep breath to fortify himself, François reluctantly replied, "It is true that I found the body of the French boy dead in the forest, as I said. But, I also found the Indian boy. He was close to death and defenseless. He is but a youth, and I could not bring myself to kill him. So, I left him to the mercy of the forest."

"That medallion, where did you get it?"

"I found it on the floor of the forest. Probably dropped there by the Natchez boy. You may have it, if you like," François said as he moved hastily to take it off.

"No, you keep it. What I want to know about is your chemise," St. Denis asked, his voice swelling in anger. "What happened to the damned sleeves?"

François cleared his throat, and then replied hesitantly, "I used the pieces to cover the wounds of the boy — to prevent the flies and mosquitoes from antagonizing him while he waits for death. Did I offend the Commandant?"

"Yes, damn you. You have! What you have done is punishable by law. In fact, I have a good mind to turn you over to the governor for justice!"

Fear gripped François. The penalty for lying and assisting the enemy was severe. In many cases, it could even mean death. "Please, m'sieur, you must not do that. I am sorry. It just seemed like the only humane thing to do. I have seen enough death to last a lifetime. I saw no reason to kill a boy who is already dying."

"Damn it, I am not talking about the damn boy. That was a perfectly good chemise you destroyed. Chemises like that cost money. With that one destroyed, what will you do for another? Can you buy one? I certainly cannot. I have other expenses. That chemise would have lasted at least another two years."

"I am sorry about the chemise," François said with relief. "I will work harder so that you can buy me another. If necessary, I will work both day and night."

"Never mind! But next time, mind you, you'd better think twice before you go about destroying my property."

François nodded his head in agreement and released a long sigh of relief.

After a moment, St. Denis asked calmly, "Do you think there's a chance the boy might survive?"

"I do not think so. In his condition, it would be a miracle."

"You know, that boy, Black Hawk, is a Natchez prince. He was to be their next Great Sun."

"Are you certain that this boy would be chief?"

"He is the one. I heard of his selection several years ago."

After a long moment of silence, François asked softly, "Commandant?"

"Yes."

"Is that boy your son?"

"How the Hell would I know. Well... there is a chance he could be."

"Should we go back and assist him?"

"No! Absolutely, no! We cannot. Leave things as they are."

"Then, that is sad."

"Well, maybe the little bastard will get lucky. However, I suspect that he will be dead by nightfall. Alligators are hungry this time of year.... And François, do not speak of that boy as my son again. To do so would only create more problems between me and the governor. And... never say a word about this to anyone, especially my wife. You understand?"

"Yes, m'sieur. I understand. I will not speak of this to anyone.Do you believe the words of the Natchez woman — about the next life?"

"Yes, I suppose so," St. Denis replied solemnly.

"I pray it is so," François added. "Yes, I pray it is so." Then he, too, was silent.

François knew that the commandant was silently wishing the Natchez boy well. If not, he would have turned them around and gone back to make sure that he was dead. The commandant, of course, would never openly admit his concerns to anyone, or provide the boy with any direct assistance. That was his way.

François admired his master. He knew he was a slave and knew his place as a slave. However, at times like this, when they were alone in the wilderness, just the two of them, he felt a much more deeper type of bonding with his master — one that was infinitely more satisfying.

"You see this land?" François said with excitement as they passed the northeastern edge of the Isle.

"Yes. What about it?"

"I hunt on this land. This is good land. It is the best land in the territory. If I were a free man, I would buy this land, build a farm, and become a great farmer. I would be the best farmer of all."

"You know, I think you are right. It does look like good land. Would probably be an excellent place for a *vacherie* (pasture) where I could graze my livestock. With rivers on all sides, I won't have to worry about them straying too far. In fact, as soon as we get back, I think I will register a claim for it. An excellent suggestion, François."

François looked at his master befuddled. The point of his statement was not about farming or a pasture. It was his liberty that he wanted to discuss. He thought for a moment about how he should go about pursuing the subject, then decided to let the matter rest. Someday soon, when the time was right, he would bring the matter up again.

———

That evening, as with every evening following the war, the inhabitants of the little French settlement of Natchitoches hurriedly put their plows away, fed their chickens and livestock, then gathered in small groups on stoops, around small fires, or in each other's sitting rooms to talk. Recounts of the battle remained the preferred topic, and the story was told and retold a thousand times with as many variations, each version resulting in still more subtle departures from what actually occurred.

François sat on the side of his bed with his feet resting on the dirt floor of the cabin that he shared with Gilbeau. Gilbeau was lying across his bunk staring up into the thatched ceiling. No one knew exactly how old Gilbeau was. He was, however, too old to do much work. It was his wisdom that endeared him to everyone. Gilbeau knew a lot about many things, especially about horses and livestock. He also knew a little about root medicines and had passed that portion of his knowledge to Marie Françoise's mother to add to her already extensive library of remedies. Because of his wide experiences and his recollection of events, dates, times, and places, he also served as a living history book. Consequently, he was the first to be consulted whenever anyone encountered a problem of an unusual nature.

Gilbeau, for all his wisdom, however, did not know from which place in Africa he came. Whenever he was asked, he would simply reply, "From the land where the sun rises from the sea."

"Gilbeau, have you seen death before?"

"Yes, many times. Death is a constant companion, and I expect he will probably visit me soon."

"I'm talking about war-death. So many people, all dead.

Blood everywhere. Men, women, children, all gone. The entire lake was red with their blood."

"*C'est la vie.* That's the way of the living."

"I know. I just feel like talking about it to someone.... Gilbeau, is there no other price for freedom saving death? Is that the only way I can gain my liberty?"

"Only the snake knows, but he only speaks to a chosen few."

"Are you chosen?"

"Maybe. Maybe not. Only the snake knows."

François wondered exactly what Gilbeau meant as he studied the yellowed eyes of the old man in the candle light, waiting for him to offer an explanation. Gilbeau's mind, however, seemed to be somewhere else at the moment, somewhere far away and inaccessible to mortal man.

Realizing that an explanation would not be forthcoming, François sighed and lowered his chin to study the silver medallion that hung from his massive neck — the one he had found in the forest. He wondered how such a young boy had obtained such a beautiful and delicately-crafted ornament. Maybe, it once belonged to one of the unfortunate souls at Fort Rosalie, he reasoned. He would probably never know. Still, he wondered. And as he wondered, his thoughts turned to the Natchez boy he had left lying between the logs, half-dead, and bleeding badly. If the boy was not already dead, he doubted that he would last much longer. He would be easy prey for alligators or bobcats, not to mention the bears. Why the commandant had refused to lend assistance to his own son troubled him greatly, and he felt a surge of anger fill his heart. For if his master had no compassion for his own flesh and blood, how could he, a slave, expect his master to be sympathetic toward him and his quest for freedom.

With some effort, he reached beside his bed and lifted the leather suicide sack he had taken as a souvenir before the dead bodies were piled on the funeral pyre. Exactly why he had taken it, he was not sure. He just thought it might be useful sometime — for something. As he stroked its soft texture, his thoughts turned to the Stinkard woman and the remarkable words she had spoken with such an undeniable conviction, as if it were only a casual stroll from this world into the next. He prayed it was so.

Wearily, François returned the bag to its place beneath his bunk, took off his clothes, blew out the candle, and retired for the night. Outside, he could hear music coming from the cookhouse where some of the slaves had gathered to sing and dance. He listened intently to the rhythmic pulse of the drums and felt himself drifting slowly back to a better time, a better place, a place far away across the sea. A place that now existed only in the farthest reaches of his memory — and that memory was slipping away fast....

Slave Cabin,
(Cane River, Natchitoches, Louisiana)

Chapter – Seventeen

THE NEXT MORNING, A FULL HOUR BEFORE SUNRISE, FRANÇOIS AROSE, packed a bundle of food, mostly biscuits, chicken, and a small chunk of dried fish that he had stolen from the kitchen. When he had finished, he quietly walked down to the river. He had not rested well. All night, he had been plagued by nightmares of the previous week's activities while wondering if the Natchez boy was dead or alive. It was something he had to know. Otherwise, he would have no peace of mind.

When he arrived at the river's edge, he pushed his pirogue into the water, climbed in, and let it drift downstream until it was safe to use his oars.

In the twilight before dawn, he found the spot where he had left the Natchez youth. The boy, however, was not there. Suspecting the worst, he knelt down beside the logs and carefully studied the area. The leaves were still warm, which meant, more than likely, he was still alive. *Probably hiding in the brush*, he reasoned. He was tempted to call out, but decided against it.

After searching the immediate area and finding no other signs, François sighed, took the bundle of food and placed it between the logs. Somewhat disappointed, but filled with hope that his assumption was correct, he took a last glance around, then headed back to the river just as dawn was breaking across the horizon.

When he returned to the fort, Zolare, the cook, was starting her fires. Quietly, he pulled the pirogue up on the landing. There was a splash about twenty-feet away. He paused and scanned the river. *Probably ole Slimy Green*, he thought to himself as he hurried to his quarters.

The next day, he repeated his trip down the river with another bundle of food, all the time, fearful that the commandant might discover what he was about. For although the commandant was indulgent concerning many matters, he was certain that the commandant would not support him in this particular project, especially since the boy was a Natchez. The very sound of the word had a way of irritating all Frenchmen, and his master, in many respects, was no different from the rest.

As he suspected, the Indian could not be found. But, the cloth from the bundle of the previous day was there, folded neatly. The food was gone. François was elated. *So, the boy was alive.* Without searching further, he put the empty cloth in his pocket, and carefully deposited the second bundle between the logs and departed.

The third and fourth day, he did the same. Each time he returned, he found the food gone and the cloth folded neatly beside the logs. On the fifth day, however, he was surprised to find that the food was still there, just as he had left it. Concerned and clearly expecting the worst, he searched the area frantically, this time much deeper into the forest. He called out several times, trying to mimic the Natchez howl. There was no reply. He did find a single primitive arrow without a stone head. It had been recently carved, and this led him to believe that maybe the boy was alive and apparently, well enough to venture out. He would have felt a lot better, however, had he known for sure.

Feeling sad and a little unappreciated, he walked slowly back to the river, regretting that he did not have an opportunity to talk to the boy to give him hope, or maybe, even encourage him to build another Natchez nation. But then, he surmised, how could one boy build a whole nation. His driving need to communicate with the boy wasn't about rebuilding a nation, he was being driven by a conscience that demanded that he do something to atone for his part in all the killing that had taken place. Well, he decided, maybe the boy will find a home with another tribe. The Tunicas and the Caddos lived nearby.

Suddenly, François realized that he had tarried too long. The sun was brushing the tops of the trees. Quickly, he dashed for the river, jumped into his pirogue, and headed for home.

"François!" It was Zolare, standing at the landing, her arms crossed, and her eyes cutting like daggers. "Where have you been? The commandant has been looking everywhere for you."

François frowned as he tied up the pirogue. For the moment, he ignored Zolare, watching her out of the corners of his eyes as she waited impatiently for an explanation. He, however, saw no reason to give her one. As he started walking toward home, Zolare followed.

"Did you not hear me, or have you lost your senses?"

"Zolare, do not antagonize me this morning. Shouldn't you be about your chores? It's morning food time."

"The commandant has eaten already and he is angry that you weren't in your quarters. I only came to warn you, just trying to be helpful."

"Well, be helpful by addressing your own affairs," François replied curtly.

"Maybe I should. And just maybe, I should also tell the commandant that this isn't the first morning you have stolen his meat and biscuits and slipped off down the river. Where is it that you go? Are you slipping off to see Cleotis, too, or is there some other woman down there — one whose master is so poor that you have to feed her the commandant's food every morning?"

François took a deep breath, strongly tempted to drag Zolare back to the landing and toss her into the river. Instead, he stopped, turned, and stared at her contemptuously.

"Yes, I think the commandant would be very, very interested," Zolare continued smugly. "And I don't think he would tell me to address my own affairs, either."

That did it. François had enough. "Then maybe," he said, emphasizing each word with his finger, "the commandant will also be interested to know that you did not wait to get married, that you have been getting pegged by his scout, Deerfoot, in the moss nest you have near the big tree in the pecan grove."

Zolare stopped in her tracks, her mouth agape.

François smiled in satisfaction. "Oh, yes. I know about your visits there. Sometimes two or three times a week. Late in the night when everyone else is asleep. That's probably how you found out that I was gone. What happened? You and Deerfoot spent the whole of last night in the grove?"

For a moment, Zolare was speechless. Suddenly, she lashed out. "You bastard! You are the lowest creature on this earth. You have no cause to start spreading lies about me. Anyone could have been in the grove with Deerfoot. For all you know, it could have been your little bitch, Marie. And, yes, I know you have asked to marry her."

"It could have been, but I cannot agree since I saw you meet him there with my own eyes."

"You bastard. You disgusting, low down-to-the-earth bastard. You have no right sneaking around spying on people."

"No worse than you."

"That is a lie. I was not down here spying on you. I only came down because I did not want to see you get into trouble. But, maybe I was wrong. Maybe, I should tell the commandant so I can watch him put the whip to your black ass."

"The whip fits yours, too. Come, let us go quickly and tell the commandant what has been happening. My ass can take the whip. Can yours?"

"Wait a damn minute — François. I didn't say I was actually going to tell him. I only said, maybe I should. And how come all this talk about whipping? You don't understand anything," Zolare said, clearly on the defensive.

"No, I do not understand." François said, pressing his advantage. "It is not my place to worry about such things. But, I am curious to know how the commandant will feel once he knows you have been going to the grove to get humped by a heathen — clawing the dirt on all fours and bellowing like a cow in the field."

"My God, you sonofabitch! You have been sneaking and spying on me!"

"Oh, and now I am a sonofabitch, too. Well, we shall see,"

François said as he turned to walk off.

"Wait, François! Wait! You know I don't really think you are a sonofabitch," Zolare said as she grabbed him by the front of his sleeveless chemise. "Please, you just don't understand. You don't understand nothing at all. You tell me. What would you have done if you were me. If you look, you will see I am no longer a young girl. I grow older each day. I am human, same as anybody, and I have these feelings that come over me from time to time — feelings that torment me in the night, feelings that you do not understand. They just come, and they come especially when I think of you. What was I supposed to do? Sit around and wait for you to assist?

"François, I have loved you since the day you first came. And I loved you even though you were standing in the yard, looking stupid, and smelling like a horned-goat. All I have ever wanted was to be your wife and to have your children. But you ignored me, laughed, and caused others to laugh, too. You never took one minute of time to see me for who I really am. Too busy sniffing behind that little snot-nosed wench, Marie. That's who you want, isn't it? Isn't it?

"Well, you want to see something? You want to see what a real woman looks like? Here, you bastard, look!" Zolare screamed as she ripped open the front of her bodice. "Take a good look so you won't have to sneak and spy on me from the bushes."

"Zolare... "

"Go ahead and look," Zolare said again as tears started to cascade down her tense cheeks, her body shaking with emotion. "Look and see what I was forced to give to a heathen. This is the body of a woman, m'sieur. Not that of a piss-tail child.... I only wanted to love you. Wanted you to be my first, but you, you made me do foolish things, then laughed. Do you know how it feels when someone you love laughs at you? Go ahead, wood-head! Don't you want to laugh some more? Go ahead, let me hear you. Your stupid laughing doesn't bother me anymore."

François was slightly amused at the whole affair and was about to smile. But suddenly, Zolare reared back and sent a round-house swing in his direction. He ducked just in time. Quickly, he grabbed her arms and pulled her close to hinder any further attempts.

The moment she was in his arms, Zolare relaxed and let the tears flow. François comforted her and let the sobbing run its course, fully conscious of her huge, quivering breasts and her fast hardening nipples. Suddenly, he felt arousal. It was not the right time or the place, and certainly not the right woman. But no matter how hard he tried, he could not restrain the swollen organ that reared its head and thumped boldly against the front of his well-worn trousers.

Zolare felt it, too, bumping lightly against her upper thigh, a response that both surprised and delighted her. Careful not to disturb the magic of the moment, she pressed in closer and adjusted her stance for the best advantage.

"Forgive me, Zolare." François whispered as he detected Zolare's pelvic brushing against him in a barely perceptive undulating motion. "It was wrong for me to say such things. I know life has not been easy for you. And, I am not blind, and had I not fell in love with Marie first, I would have been honored to be your man. I never intended to cause you misery. You are a good woman and you deserve a good man — someone older and more worldly. Deerfoot is not the one for you. The commandant would be furious if he knew. I wanted to speak to you before about Deerfoot, but did not know how. You must wait. He will find you a good husband. I am sure."

"François, I suppose you are right, and I, too, am truly sorry. It just seemed that I had no other choice. Don't you see? After a time, I became afraid that I would die without knowing what life was all about. You understand now, don't you, François? Believe me, there was no one else. Deerfoot came, and I relented."

"Now that you know about life, I suggest that you restrain yourself in the future. Just like I found out, the commandant could have also."

"François, I must be honest. I will try, but I don't know if I can — not alone. Now that I have tasted the forbidden fruit, I will be forever tempted to taste it again. But with your help, it would be an easy task. Will you help me François? It would be so easy if you would consent."

"I don't know what I could do to help. You must do it by yourself — alone."

"Don't you understand? I cannot do it alone. It's like a malady, stronger than me, a kind of sickness that torments me. Death is the only way I can escape its power. François, I am tormented now. Without your help, what shall I do?"

"Zolare, I do not want to hurt you. I understand, but... I cannot assist. It would not be right, not as long as there is a chance that Marie will be permitted to be my wife. Am I being unkind?"

"Yes, damn it, you are being unkind. But, I understand. I know that you are tormented, too. I can feel the evidence of your torment even now as we speak. It will be a long time before the commandant gives Marie to you. Don't you see? Together, we could help each other — make the nights easier and the waiting less harsh. All that need be is for you to visit me from time to time. Keep Deerfoot off my mind. No one need ever know. Just you and me, friends, helping each other along the way. That's all — nothing more. I would be thankful for that. I know that you love Marie. And even though I shall continue to pray with all my heart that you will choose me in the end, I promise, I will not disturb your chances with Marie. I will trust in the judgment of the Good Mother and pray that She favors me. And, if it is my misfortune that the commandant should grant you Marie, I will accept my fate, and I will make you the most beautiful blanket in all the territory for your wedding bed. I promise, chéri. I promise."

François sighed and Zolare could feel that he was losing his resolve. Smiling to herself, she pressed in tighter against him, consolidating her position, and trapping the wild animal that strained between them with her thigh.

"Zolare," was all François could say at the moment. Her subtle grinding motions were driving him insane. The thumping was now frantic and out of control. Her nipples, hard as stones, pricked him and caused the hair on his chest to rise. The heady aroma of desire filled his nostrils. They flared and he breathed deeply. Had it not been for the light of day, he would have thrown her to the ground and taken her right there.

Totally immobilized, he closed his eyes as he felt Zolare's hand slip from his shoulder and wander slowly down his abdomen to rest nervously upon the front of his trousers. There, she caressed him lightly with the tips of her feather-like fingers. François groaned again, this time loudly.

"*Cette nuit*," Zolare said with a hoarse whisper. "François, you come for me tonight."

"I don't know, Zolare — maybe."

"No maybe, damn it. Tonight, you come for me. Tonight, in the early evening, in the pecan grove. You come. I will be there... waiting," she said through gritted teeth as she squeezed his crotch firmly for emphasis.

Suddenly, François winced and released a deep moan that terminated with strained trill. His knees buckled and a wet spot suddenly appeared and spread rapidly across the front of his trousers.

"*Cette nuit*," Zolare whispered for verification.

"Tonight, yes. Tonight — I will be there…. Zolare?"

"Yes?"

"No one must know."

"No one," Zolare affirmed, beaming with pleasure as she kissed his chest with several quick pecks.

François pushed her away gently. "Alright. I will be there. We will meet after the lamps are out," he said as he adjusted his trousers, and she, her blouse. "We must get back. Everyone is probably looking for us."

"I know."

"As for my trips down river," François explained as they started up the trail that led back home. "I have been taking food to a Natchez boy that I rescued during the war. He was seriously wounded and close to death. The commandant must not know. I pray you will not reveal me, as I will not reveal you or Deerfoot."

"Do not fear, François. That is a good thing that you do. I will say nothing. By the way, I told the commandant this morning that you were out early trying to catch Slimy Green. That's what I call that old alligator that browses around the landing at night."

"You scoundrel," François playfully admonished.

Zolare laughed, then dashed ahead to get back to her chores.

Satisfied with the turn of events and thoroughly anxious for night to arrive, François hurried to the storage shed to assist St. Denis in transferring a load of grain from sacks to barrels for shipment to the Spanish.

———

"Well? Did you catch the damn alligator or not?"

"No, Commandant. Old Slimy Green is a wise old 'gator, that one. But, one of these days his luck will run out. Then, he will be all mine."

"Do it soon. The slimy bastard is getting on my nerves — getting more adventurous everyday. Pretty soon, he'll be demanding to lounge on my damn gallery. I wish I could get rid of them all, every damned one of those contemptible, foul smelling creatures. You can smell the effluvia of their excrement from here to Mexico. I'd give anything if I could breathe a breath of fresh air one time before I die. Is that asking too much? Is-that-ask-ing-too-damn-much!"

François did not reply. He knew his master did not expect him to answer. All he wanted was someone to shut up and listen whenever he was in one of his ranting, raving moods. That was the way he relieved himself whenever something was troubling him. And when he asked for your advice, the worst thing anyone could do was to give it to him. Knowing this, François busied himself, humming as he went about his tasks.

———

St. Denis had been struggling hard to maintain some degree of stability within his monopoly, but it had been difficult. He suspected that a few of the younger farmers had been trying to cut around him by slipping up river during the night to trade their produce directly to the Spanish for a higher price than he offered. The older farmers would have never challenged his authority in this manner. They knew of his hardships and the time he spent in the rat-infested prisons of Mexico kissing Spanish asses just to make trading possible. The young ones, however, were another problem. Well, he would just have to make examples of a few of them, and he would keep doing it until they respected his position and authority. Didn't they realize that he deserved to make a small margin of profit? For as long as he could remember, it seemed like all of his hard work served only to benefit others, leaving nothing for himself. He felt drained and tired — an empty shell, half the man he once was, and all for naught. Time was crowding him. He was getting older and slipping further behind. It was dreams that kept a man alive, and he dreaded the day he would awake and discover that his dreams were nothing more than a figment of his imagination. Yet, he knew that day was fast approaching.

But the young ones, the ones standing at the threshold of life, they still had a lifetime of living ahead to make their fortune. *Didn't they know that?* Didn't they understand that a man his age needed to enjoy some of the fruits from his labors before he died? *No, they didn't.* They didn't give a good God-damn. Too greedy. In too big of a hurry. Well, a few busted asses would slow them down a bit....

"François!"

"Yes, m'sieur," François answered as he raised his head and watched his master wipe the sweat from his face with his forearm.

"Have you noticed anything suspicious going on during the night."

"Like..., like what?" François stammered, wondering if he, Zolare, or both had been discovered.

"I mean like anyone going up the river at night — late, hauling grain to the Spanish."

"No... no, m'sieur."

"Well, some bastard is! And if I catch him.... Damn, it's hot in here. This heat and the smell of alligator dung is enough to drive any man insane. You finish packing these barrels. I'm going to the fort."

When the commandant had gone, François slowed down his pace. He was finding it increasingly difficult to concentrate on his duties. His accidental discharge that morning had done nothing to diminish his appetite. If anything, it had only excited him more. And having had a preview of what was to come, he was impatient for the day to pass. Consequently, he found himself perceiving everything he saw with a sexual connotation. Even Three Tooth, the overweight Indian slave woman, tempted him as she bent over her task of washing the family's clothing. Occasionally, she would look at him over her shoulder and smile... knowingly.

Trying to work with an erection hampering his movements proved to be quite frustrating. François, however, did not become alarmed until Emanuelle summoned him to run an errand. Too embarrassed to allow her to see him in his condition, he tried everything he could to make his erection go away. He doused his head with water — tried to will it away by thinking about Eula and other nonsexual things. He even thumped it, hoping the pain would arrest its rambunctious behavior. Nothing seemed to work.

Emanuelle called again, more impatient this time. So, François gave up and hurried to answer her call.

When he entered the house, he immediately dropped into a half-squatting position.

"What is it, François? You feel faint? Are you malaise?" Emanuelle asked, quite concerned.

"No, Madame. It is my back."

"Well, squatting is the worst way to relieve a back pain. Come here and stand with your back up against this wall. It's the best way I know to obtain a measure of relief."

"It is only a very small pain, Madame. It will pass."

"The wall works well for both. Large or small. Now, come here," Emanuelle directed as she took him by the arm and led him to the wall. "Don't stoop. Straight up. Back flat."

Reluctantly, François did as he was told, trying inconspicuously to conceal his real problem by covering it with his hands.

"Doesn't look like no back problem to me," interrupted Marie's mother, Douleurs, as she stood in the doorway. "There's no wall in all the world that can cure his problem."

François started to sweat profusely.

"Come now. Why do you say that, Douleurs?"

Douleurs nodded and pointed with her eyes.

Emanuelle glanced down. Immediately, her mouth dropped, and suddenly, she was embarrassed, too. "Oh my God...." was all she could say before François bolted and ran for the door.

Douleurs laughed loud and hard. Emanuelle joined her.

"That boy needs a wife," Douleurs added.

"Absolutely, and soon. But from the size of him, that will be a chore for anyone who undertakes that duty."

They both laughed again.

"Why hasn't the commandant married him to Zolare?" Douleurs asked with a puzzled look on her face,

"He has tried. But, it is still your daughter, Marie, that François wants to marry. Of that, he is quite adamant."

"Oh no, m'selle, absolutely not. I will not allow it. You must make him marry Zolare."

"Believe me, the commandant has been trying to do just that."

"Trying? Did I hear correctly… trying? That boy is a slave — a good for nothing slave. Who is running this damn place, anyway? Him or the commandant?"

Emanuelle laughed.

"M'selle, please do not laugh. I am worried. When he first asked for my daughter, I said nothing. I never thought he was serious. You must do something quick. Either make him marry Zolare or order the services of the next *Courrier de Amour* who passes this way. They have women who are trained to endure. The club that boy wields would cripple a decent woman."

"Come now, don't be so modest. Surely in your time, you have tested one of equal stoutness."

"Not me, m'selle. One like that would bring a horned beast to its knees."

"I agree. I agree… but wouldn't it be a beautiful way to die. One foot already in heaven…"

"Speak for yourself, Madame. I'd just as soon keep both my feet planted firmly on the ground and him far away from me."

Both laughed again.

————

Chapter – Eighteen

FRANÇOIS ARRIVED EARLY AND WAS WAITING AT THE APPOINT-
ED PLACE beneath a pecan tree in the grove when Zolare arrived carrying a woolen blanket across her arms.

"François," she whispered as she approached, "you came."

"Yes," François replied, watching nervously as Zolare spread her blanket upon the ground and sat down.

"Good. I was a little worried — afraid you might have changed your mind. Come, and sit beside me."

A little hesitantly, François joined her on the blanket.

"Are you nervous?" Zolare asked.

"No, I am not. Why do you ask?"

"You just seem a little uneasy. You aren't frightened, are you?"

"No," François retorted with the bravado of a young boy. "Why would you think I am frightened?"

"Oh, I don't know. I know I was frightened my first time."

"Well, I am not."

"Then, that is good," Zolare said as she took François by the hand and pulled him toward her.

Eager to get to the business at hand, François groaned, shoved Zolare back, and scrambled clumsily upon her body.

"No, François. Stop... wait!"

"Stop? Why...?" François asked as he paused.

"There is no need to rush. We have all night to explore each other. Besides, we are human, not animals. Just hold me in your arms for a moment and let me enjoy the nearness of you."

Still quite eager, François encircled Zolare's heated body within his arms and pulled her close against his chest. As they lay caressing each other beneath a high summer moon, François nuzzled her neck and touched her skin lightly with the tip of his tongue, enjoying its mild, salty taste and the odor of her that reminded him of over-ripe persimmons. He kissed her neck again, then held his breath as he slowly moved his right hand from the small of her back and cupped the underside of her full breast. At the first contact, Zolare shivered, and suddenly, her nipples hardened and burrowed into his chest like two sharp-pointed, river-washed stones. It was then that Zolare took him by the back of his head and pulled his mouth down to hers in an unfamiliar and strange kiss that startled him and yet, made him sweat profusely with passion.

"François?" Zolare asked softly after the kiss had been broken.

"Yes?"

"Do you like my breasts?"

"Yes," François replied, staring hungrily as she opened the top of her chemise with her free hand.

"Here," Zolare said in a deep throaty voice, "take it. Take it and kiss it for me."

Eagerly, François buried his face in her bosom, took the large, dark nipple of the nearest breast in his mouth, and gnawed. Zolare groaned. Then, he felt the palm of her cool hand sliding down his taut abdomen and into the crotch of his damp pants. She touched him, and they both groaned.

"Remove it," Zolare commanded. "I must see it first."

Quickly François sat up and lowered his pants with boyish pride.

"*Magnifique*," Zolare said as she gaped at the quivering mass with unbelieving eyes. "Truly *magnifique*.... Would you like to see me?"

"Yes," François replied expectantly. But as soon as Zolare lifted her skirt and revealed the dense growth of hair between her shapely, dusty-blue thighs, he forgot that he was not an animal — forgot that he was a God-like creature of the highest order. He, instead, bellowed loudly and fell upon her like a beast in the wild. He felt Zolare resisting, but his passion was now in control and it was not to be denied. Suddenly, Zolare abandoned her efforts, threw her legs wide, and assisted in the impalement with an eagerness that equaled his own. He showed no mercy, and neither did she. She held him in a vise-like grip, surprising him with her strength and the manner in which she used the backs of her heels to drive him even deeper into her moist warmth. It was like Heaven. It was like Hell. Like fire and ice, sunshine and rain.

In his delirium, he heard Zolare scream softly between her clenched teeth, and the sound of her passion caused the hair on his neck to stand like the hackles of a hound. Immediately after, he folded into a knot, vacillating and filling her abundantly with the rewards of their efforts....

When it was over, they sat for a moment, breathing heavily, holding each other, listening to the night, and enjoying the fragrance of a nearby magnolia tree.

"François," Zolare said with delight, "that was the best ever. Was it as good for you?"

"Yes, for me, too. I never want to stop. We must do it again, and again."

"It delights me to hear you say that," Zolare said with a chuckle. "Making love takes on a new perspective when it is done with the one you truly love."

"We are not in love. Yet, it was extremely pleasurable. Why was it so?"

"Because of me, I suppose. I love you enough for us both. Maybe that is sufficient," Zolare said pensively as she reached and took his reawakening manhood gently in her hand. "You know — if we were married, I would take this creature's care in my charge, and I would insure that he was never without. We could live like this for the rest of our lives — just you and I, and him, of course. Wouldn't that be wonderful?"

"Well..., yes. I suppose so," François said in a strained voice as he took a deep breath.

"You suppose? Don't you know? What kind of answer is

that?"

"It was not an answer to offend you. I..."

"Oh, never mind," Zolare said in frustration, "I know exactly what you intended."

While François was trying to decide upon a suitable response, Zolare stood, straightened her clothing, and prepared to leave.

"You are leaving?" François asked with concern.

"Yes, I am," Zolare answered coldly.

"But, why?"

"Obviously, it is time to go."

"It is early yet. You said we had all night."

"Well, I was mistaken."

"Zolare, please. Don't be angry. We should do it again."

"Why? It meant nothing to you. Besides, you still think I am too old to be your wife."

"I never said that."

"Of course, you did, chéri. You said much, much more. More than you will ever realize. You just stated that my quest was hopeless. You also said that making love to Marie will be better for you. You stated it quite clearly, and I hear very well."

"Stop talking in riddles, Zolare, and sit down."

"I suppose not, chéri. Another night... maybe," Zolare answered as she turned and walked away into the night.

"Zolare?" François called after her, but Zolare only lowered her head and continued on her way, leaving him to grapple with his re-awakening passion alone.

When she was out of sight, François sighed audibly in frustration, then buried his face in the blanket where he wrestled with his conscience, unable to acknowledge his growing feelings toward Zolare, and equally unable to breach the wall of tradition that excluded her as an eligible wife. For a long time, he lay pondering his predicament, savoring the odor of their recent activity, waiting, and hoping that Zolare would return to corral the unmerciful beast that she had inadvertently released upon the world. But the footsteps he had hoped to hear remained silent. Finally, he grew tired waiting and decided to relieve himself with his hands.

While he was adjusting his clothing, he was suddenly overcome with a feeling that he was being watched. He paused and glanced about, but saw nothing. Quickly then, he picked up Zolare's blanket and headed for his cabin, stepping lively.

———————

Marie Françoise had known for some time that François had asked for her hand in marriage. There were not many secrets that escaped the slave's intelligence network. She, of course, was delighted. François was an exceptional man, and he was in good graces with her master. That was good. That would help make their lives as slaves a little easier — for them and their children. But she, like everyone else, also knew that both Zolare and Eula also wanted him. While she was not worried about Eula, Zolare posed a real threat. Besides being attractive and seductive, *or so everyone claimed,* Zolare was also aggressive. For that reason, she usually got her way.

Since by nature she was rather shy, she would sometimes hide or do whatever was necessary to avoid being in François' presence for any length of time. She hated herself for being that way, but she just couldn't stand being near him for long without getting the urge to rush to the privy and relieve her bladder. Excitement had always affected her in that manner. One time, when she was much younger, her mistress, Emanuelle, had said, quite speculatively, that she could accompany her on her next excursion to New Orleans. Although the statement was made partly in jest, her excitement at the thought of that possibility was so intense that she never made it to the privy. The dam broke immediately, and all she could do was to stand there while the warm liquid ran down her legs and into her oversized shoes. She would die if something like that was to happen in front of François. So, she lived in constant fear that Zolare would snare her prince away before she became of age.

At the moment, her fear was well founded. A week earlier, she had seen them both coming from the landing in the early morning. She had been standing near an opened shuttered window washing fruit jars. Instinctively, she knew that something out of the ordinary had happened. Zolare was too happy, running down the pathway from the landing, jumping upon the gallery like someone half her age, and switching her derrière all over the house. And she had the scent, too. That special scent a woman gets when she's in need of a male. The mating scent, that's what she had overheard her mother call it. Anyway, anyone with a nose could smell it, and her switching around the way she switched only served to make it worse. And she could, at the very least, keep her chemise closed. It was shameful, no — sinful, the way her voluptuous parts bounced around like that. It wasn't fair.

A little self-conscious, Marie lowered her eyes and looked down at her own budding breasts and felt somewhat inferior. They were growing, but at a pace much too slow for her and no amount of pulling seemed to help. Zolare was gaining ground, and she was saddened.

Normally, Marie spent most of her time feeding the livestock or helping with her mistress's youngest children, and sometimes out in the fields with the other young adults. The rest of her time was spent helping her aging mother attend her mistress's flower garden and trying to learn the ancient art of root medicine. Knowledge of that skill, she knew, would guarantee her a position on the household staff. Otherwise, she would be destined to work in the fields for the rest of her life — among the snakes and thousands of other detestable creatures. She grimaced at the very thought of that possibility.

As it was, her mother was the only source of medical assistance readily available to the household. She served as midwife, performed light surgery, and provided concoctions for any ailment from clubfoot to the common cold. Miraculously, her elixirs appeared to work on any number of occasions.

But unlike Gilbeau, her mother did not place the same amount of faith in the unnatural as the old man did. She relied more on God and the natural things of life — the things the Almighty had placed on this earth for man's benefit — the things her mother had once learned from her mother.

Her mother loved plants, and she was especially fond of roses. As for herself, however, she could do without them and their sharp thorns. When she told her mother this, her mother had replied, "*I wouldn't fret over the thorns, chéri. God put them there for a purpose. Once He created the roses and saw how brilliant and beautiful they were, He realized that they were too alluring to survive unprotected. So, He decided to guard His handiwork by adorning their stems with sharp, pointed spurs.*"

As time passed, she came to believe her mother's words. For quite often, the most perfect blossoms were those deepest within their protective barrier.

On slow days, she and her mother wandered through the forest and along the edge of the swamps and bayous, studying and collecting different plants and roots. Her mother explained each, the good plants and the bad, and how to prepare them. Rose hip, sunflower seeds, mullein, and currant for colds. Calamas, cayenne, Jesuit's bark, and wild quinine for fevers. Asafetida, a vermifuge for worms. Willow bark for headaches. Ergot, belladonna, and black snake roots for the pains of labor. Ginger for whooping cough. May apple for purging the bowels. Basil, chicory, and anise for love potions. And for the nerves, when the love potion did not work, a double dose of Indian Winauk (sassafras), catnip, and menthe.

Marie studied hard and applied herself to learning the art. It was one way to keep her mind off François, and off Zolare, too — *the strumpet!*

———

Fall arrived. Marie was standing in the doorway looking out

at a flight of wild geese scrambling up from the river where they had stopped to refresh themselves before proceeding on with their journey further south. She was lost in her reverie when her mother's voice broke the silence and startled her.

"Marie?" her mother called.

"Yes, maman?"

"Watch the house. I am going out to attend the garden."

"Summer is gone, maman. There is no need with everything dying or already dead."

"That is why I must go. This is the time of year when plants need our compassion the most. It is a small price to pay for all the pleasure they brought us when they were alive and well."

"Maman, you talk like plants and flowers are human — like they have souls."

"Who is to say they do not, chéri? I do know that we all trek the same path. We are all born of the earth. We mature, give birth, then... die, if not from old age, then from illness, or even the woodcutter's axe. Some of us leave this life modestly without a whimper while others cry out miserably in despair. Nothing's different — all the same. Yet, of all the living varieties, I think it is the roses that scream the loudest. Can you smell their aroma?"

"Yes," Marie replied as she lifted her nose and sniffed the air lightly. "It smells overly sweet, almost like rotting fruit."

"That, chéri, is the cry of a dying rose. Watch the house, I'll be back in a moment."

While her mother was out in the garden, Marie picked up one of her master's books and leafed through its heavy and worn pages, searching for drawings or anything else that might give her a clue as to its contents. How she wished that she could read. If she could, she would not hesitate to explore every book in her master's possession. Occasionally, her mistress read to them from her Bible. And while she found this enjoyable, it did not satisfy her yearning to discover for herself the secrets hidden within its text.

Suddenly, a strange feeling of uneasiness overcame her. She put the book aside, walked to the door, and peered out into the garden. She did not see her mother. With curiosity prodding her, she left the house and went straight for the garden, passing through the evergreens and stepping around the small fish pond. She had just passed the banana tree, when she stopped dead in her tracks and screamed... "Maman? Oh, no! Maman. Maman!"

Her terrifying screams brought Emanuelle, the children, and several slave hands running. When they lifted her mother from among a clump of crushed elephant ears, they found her hand clutched close to her heart. In it was the tiny bud of a late blooming rose.

The next day, François dug the grave, and Gilbeau spoke the words as they buried her mother in a small grave adjacent to the garden that she had loved and cared for so well.

———————

With her mother gone, Marie's world lay collapsed about her. Everyone, especially her mistress, attempted to console her. She acknowledged their efforts, but nothing they did was adequate enough to fill the black void. Alone now, she went about her work listlessly and without purpose. When her chores were done, she would wander down by the river to sit among the willows and ponder her losses, her mother and — François. For by then, she was well aware of his afterhours affair with Zolare.

First, it was the two of them coincidentally being away at the same time, both missing dinner, and other things. Later, she saw them for herself, going off toward the pecan grove. She had followed quietly, like a thief in the night, and watched while they rutted among the fallen leaves. It was a painful sight to see and it hurt her deeply. One mind told her to turn and walk away, and she would have, except for the fact that she was trapped by a bold mixture of confusing emotions — one that pierced her heart like a knife, and the other that made her spasm and sweat with her own unfulfilled needs. She was sure that everyone else knew what was going on, too. But no one said anything about it to her, she supposed, because of their respect for her feelings. She knew, anyway. She didn't need them to tell her what was going on in the grove. She knew.

So, out of respect for their respect for her, she kept her silence, played ignorant, and said nothing about her true feelings. She had no right. It was common knowledge that the commandant wanted François to marry Zolare. So, let him have the big-tit cow. Besides, no one seemed to give a damn about how she felt, anyway. They were all too busy worrying about Zolare. *"Well, she's ready for bedding and breeding,"* her mother used to say. As if that made everything alright.

Yet, in spite of all the negative signs, she still continued to hope that, somehow, things would resolve in her favor. Now, it appeared that she had fought a losing battle, a battle she had lost without ever getting the chance to strike one blow in her own defense.

———————

Shortly after her mother's death, Marie was officially appointed to her mother's former position as a full time attendant to the commandant's wife, Emanuelle. The cabin she and her mother had shared was given to Eula, and she was instructed to sleep on a pallet in the bedroom with her mistress' daughters, Rosa, Douleurs, and Petronille. Since Rosa was only one year her senior, the arrangement proved to be quite satisfactory. They had a lot in common — boys. A subject they frequently discussed late into the night, long after the candles had been snuffed. And while Rosa set her sights for princes and men of noble birth, Marie set hers for François, the slave.

This change in living and working arrangements also had some other benefits. Since her mother was no longer there to protect her, François now found thousands of excuses to visit with her at the big house using one pretext or another. As a result, she gradually lost much of her shyness and gained better control of her bladder. She also noticed that since their friend-ship was now more open, François did not go to the pecan grove as often. This pleased her.

Soon, it was apparent to everyone, including St. Denis, that a courtship was in full progress. Not wanting this to happen, St. Denis again decided it was time to prompt François into marry-ing one of the two older females.

"François," St. Denis said as they stood in the yard near a cauldron, "I have done my best to be patient. I have offered you a wife, and you have yet to come forth and claim her. What must I do to remedy this situation?"

"Permit me to marry Marie, m'sieur."

"Have I been talking to the wind around here? I told you before, Marie is not available!"

"I understand your concerns, and I agree. For that reason, I am willing to wait."

"You'll wait?" St. Denis asked like he did not believe his ears. "I'll be damned and crucified, if you will wait. You're to choose between Zolare or Eula. I am not running an operation here for your damned benefit."

"You must understand, Commandant. I cannot marry those old women. They are good women, the very best, but they are senior to me. I already have one master. I do not need two. I beg of your consideration in this matter."

"My consideration? Why, you do have some nerve. The problem here is that I have tried to treat you like a human, and now, you're trying to tell me how to conduct my business."

"I am sorry, m'sieur. If I cannot have Marie, I must choose none."

François' reply infuriated St. Denis. As if the problems of the young farmers were not enough, he now had a slave who did not respect his position of authority either. *What is the world coming to?*

"You black gorilla," St. Denis shouted, "I am master here

— not you. I am in command here — not you. Do-you-un-der-stand? Starting this day, you are hereby relieved of your duties in the wood shop. I desire your services in the field with the other dumb asses clearing the forest. You will not set foot in this house under any circumstances, or for any reason, or I will have your head and Slimy Green will have your black carcass. Now, get the Hell out of my sight!"

With that, St. Denis stormed into the house and went to his room, almost slamming the door off its hinges in the process. His actions frightened both Emanuelle and Marie who were into their needlework at the time.

"What was that about?" Marie asked her mistress.

"I don't know," Emanuelle replied even though she suspected her husband's anger had something to do with François' marriage to Zolare.

She had seen her husband angry before, but never to the degree where his body shook from sheer rage. He was changing. He was now fifty-five, and the more he aged, the shorter his patience grew. She suspected that a lot of his frustrations were rooted in their financial problems, and that was one thing she found difficult to understand. How could a man who had faced so many dangers and plodded so many uncharted paths let a few meager *livres* take him to an early grave? Money had become an obsession with him. It was all he talked about, and his madness was starting to affect everyone, including the children.

———

Months passed, and while François worked in the fields, Marie went about her chores absentmindedly and filled with hopelessness. Sometimes, she found herself daydreaming, standing by the window gazing out across the fields toward the tree line where the slaves worked, listening to the echoes of their axes biting into the trunks of the willows, hickories, oaks, and pines. Then, she would hear a loud voice yell, and she would wait expectantly for the frightening snap which preceded the thundering crash as the trees fell — like the walls of Jericho tumbling down....

From time to time, they sang work songs and she would listen intently, trying to discern François from among the many melodic voices that drifted on the winds across the fields. Other times, she would hide behind the chicken coops which were between the house and the fields. There, she would scan the horizon until her eyes blurred, hoping to catch a glimpse of him in the distance.

In the evenings, she kept her eye on the grove, watching helplessly as François resumed his nocturnal relationship with Zolare.

———————

Two weeks before the arrival of a joyless Christmas for Marie, Louis, the cobbler, ran away. Anyway, that was the conclusion of everyone concerned after Louis had remained missing for several days. Nadine took his running badly, cursing him for not taking her with him in one breath, and begging the commandant to fetch him back in the next.

Then, one week before Christmas, François discovered Gilbeau dead upon awakening from a miserably cold night's sleep. That evening, after the coroner had completed his inspection, the slaves gathered again to lay another of their numbers to rest. As Cecil, the slave, spoke the words, Marie stood beside her mistress, Emanuelle, looking out across the grave site, staring longingly at François, and he at her. Suddenly, she realized that François was speaking to her silently. She asked him to repeat what he had said with her eyes. He did, saying... *I love you,* soundlessly with his lips. At that moment, she lost her composure and was seized by a fit of crying that quickly summoned several slave women to her aid.

Emanuelle had observed the exchange between the two. And being a romantic at heart, she decided it was time to approach the commandant about the plight of the two slaves. She

did so that very night following the burial and after their evening's meal.

"Louis," Emanuelle said after clearing her throat, "how can
a man as wise and compassionate as you be so insensitive where
it concerns matters of love? When you were a prisoner of my
Grandfather, was not our situation similar to that of François
and Marie?"

"I fail to see the similarity," St. Denis replied. "Ours was
a matter of the heart. François is a slave and his is a matter of
finance. I have two wenches. Both need mates. Both, by now,
should have been bred several times.

"At a considerable loss of revenue, I have attempted with
patience, mind you, to let François choose. For almost eight
years, I have been waiting. I think I am well within my rights to
force him to take the wife of my choice."

"My dear husband, don't you realize that forcing François
to marry will not guarantee an increase in your stock. His heart
yearns for Marie, and hers for him. I predict, that if you permit
this marriage, the two of them would have a young one every
year — maybe, even two or three a year, if that were possible."

"That is not my concern. Marie is only sixteen. In the meantime, I have two perfectly healthy wenches and one bull-headed
stud going to seed and telling me how to run my damn business. Time is money. I have a labor base to maintain. Douleurs is
gone. Louis and Gilbeau are gone. Must I lose another two years
before something is done to replace them?"

While Emanuelle searched for a suitable reply, St. Denis
continued, "And what am I to do about breeding the other two?
Zolare is rubbing up against fence posts now. The law requires
that they be married, and once married — not separated. I cannot, in my position, ignore the law, marry François to one wench,
then later, send him to bed another. What else can I do? I have
no other males available and no money to buy any." Then as an
afterthought, he added, "Of course, if you agree, I could perform
that service myself. That is exactly what Bectel did. He bought

all black wenches, six of them. Not one male. Yet, he must have a hundred little bastard children scrambling about all over the damned place. Every one of them looks exactly like him. Well... all except the one that looks like Louis. Bectel's stamina amazes me."

As St. Denis appeared to entertain the thought, Emanuelle walked casually to the wall next to the hearth and took down her kitchen knife. With the knife behind her back, she returned and knelt meekly between St. Denis' legs. Then, with cat-like quickness, she grabbed him in the crotch. This act solicited peals of laughter from St. Denis as he doubled over and squirmed. Very sternly, Emanuelle said between clenched teeth, "If ever I learn that you placed this (squeezing his manhood for emphasis) between the legs of some black wench, I will carve it from your body and feed it to Slimy Green. Maybe, he will choke on it."

At that, they both laughed. It was the first time they had enjoyed a sound laugh together in a long time, and it felt good to them both. St. Denis yielded and gave his permission for the two to marry — when Marie reached the appropriate age, of course.

———

Upon hearing the commandant's decision the next morning, Marie was overjoyed. She danced about and squealed like the young girl she was. Unable to wait, she pleaded to be excused, so that she could go to the fields and tell François the good news. Emanuelle agreed and stood in the doorway, watching as the young girl raced across the fields toward the tree line. The sight filled her with satisfaction, and her heart swelled with pride knowing that she had just made two people very, very happy.

———

That evening, François returned to his cabin and fell across his bunk. Although he was elated about the recent turn of events, he still had a grave problem to solve. It concerned Zolare and how she would react once she heard the news. There would be a confrontation. That was for certain. It was just a matter of time. He just hoped Zolare would accept things as they were without creating a scene in the process. That, however, was doubtful.

How he wished Gilbeau was there to give him some advice. But, the old man was gone, and there was no one around who could fill his shoes. When he was alive, it had been good to come in from a hard day's work, relax, get the old man to talking, then lay back and listen to his tales of wonder. It was a kind of escape for him; one that allowed him to leave his miseries behind for a moment or two and visit other worlds less hostile than his own. Now, there was nothing left of his youth but a memory. Soon, that would be gone, too. He thought about the crude, wooden grave-marker he had constructed for Gilbeau and wondered how long it was going to last. Maybe, he should have made it out of stone.

He tried to sleep, but sleep would not come. So, he concentrated on his shaky future with Marie while listening to the night noise from the river — the droning of the swamp, alive with the sounds of frogs, katydids, and crickets with an occasional bellow from a restless alligator. A lone mosquito flared its wings, buzzed, and then was silent. He waited for the sting, but it did not come. He heard what he thought might have been a mouse scrambling across the dirt floor. But, he wasn't sure.

———————

Chapter — Nineteen

MORNING CAME IN THE SAME MANNER AS IT HAD ON THE PREVI-
OUS DAY AND THE DAY PREVIOUS TO THAT. The sun rose and blasted
its trumpet like thunder across the tops of the tall, thinly-limbed
pines — spurring life in all its forms into action. Birds fluffed
their feathers and prepared for flight. The cock crowed and re-
established authority over its domain. Alligators slipped silently back into the streams and bayous, and searched the banks
for sunlit expanses to warm the cold blood in their bodies. The
cooks lit their fires while the horned beasts in the meadows bellowed to be milked.

A ray of light slipped between the shutters of the little cabin,
wandered about the room for a moment, then nudged François
awake with its brilliance.

Wearily, François rolled into a sitting position and scratched
his wooly head. He had endured a restless night. He was still
tired and every bone in his body ached like he had been tram-
pled by a herd of wild mustangs. With some difficulty, he forced
himself to get up. He stretched, stepped into his breeches, then
walked lazily out the door to the mulberry tree that stood at the
rear of his cabin. There, he leaned with one arm against its trunk
and relieved his bladder of its weighty burden.

As he watched the liquid spatter and soak into the thirsty
soil, he noticed a large, green beetle ambling unpretentiously
among the leaves in the nearby grass. Carefully and with a mali-
cious intent, he took aim and tried to drown it — following the
scurrying creature as far as he could and bombarding it with a
high, yellow, liquid arc.

When he had finished, he walked around to the east side of
his cabin and stopped before a crock filled with water. He turned

his back to the warmth of the morning sun, then doused his head and face with its cool contents. Still not fully awake, he negotiated his way back into his cabin and pulled on his tattered, work chemise. He then lifted the lid on the wooden box that secured his meager belongings, found his bruised, tin eating bowl, and departed slovenly for the cookhouse, hoping that Zolare had not yet heard the news.

He was wrong. Eyes sharper than daggers greeted him the moment he stepped across the threshold of the cookhouse. He avoided looking directly at her and took his place in the slow moving line. When he was standing in front of her, he took a deep breath and held out his dish timidly. Zolare hesitated for a long second, then with a small angry sneer, she dug her spoon into a pot of cornmeal and bacon-grease sagamite and slammed it onto his plate with such a force that his plate was ripped from his hands. With that, she turned on her heels and stalked out of the cookhouse door. Several people behind him snickered. He ignored them, picked up his plate, served himself, then went outside to sit at the wooden eating table.

François labored in the forest with a lot less enthusiasm than that displayed the previous day. He worked mechanically, his thoughts still preoccupied with his future. When his day's work was done, he bypassed the evening meal and went straight to his cabin where he laid across his bunk. The chain that secured the silver medallion had begun to irritate his neck. So, he carefully took it off and studied its intricate, fascinating design. One day soon, he decided, he would have to revisit the site where he found it — just to appease his mind and satisfy his unabated curiosity. Within moments, he was fast asleep....

———

A somber, light fog caressed the terrain as François launched his pirogue to go down river once again to search for signs of the Natchez boy. It was a moonless night, but for some reason, he could see quite clearly.

When he arrived there, he secured his pirogue and rushed to the site where he had last seen the boy. The area had changed. It had aged and everything about him was in shades of gray, as if a blight of some sort had robbed the forest of all life and color. The earth was mushy and damp, and the pungent odor of mildew and rotting vegetation, which hung heavy in the still air, caused his nostrils to twitch.

He found the two logs between which he had placed the boy. He was surprised to find that the area was now covered with moss, lichen, and spider webs — not unlike a cocoon.

Is there a body encapsulated here? he wondered. Afraid of what he might find, François picked up a small stick, dropped to his knees, and rubbed his hands up and down his thighs apprehensively. His pulse quickened. Very gently, he peeled the moss back with the stick and laid it to one side. Spiders and worms scrambled frantically for safety while large green flies took to flight, humming noisily with anger.

Sure enough, there was a corpse there. And although the corpse resembled the boy, François noted two things. The body was now that of an old man, and its once youthful face was painted for war in the traditional Natchez fashion with blackened eyes and bizarre patterns of red and white colors about the face.

Cautiously, François reached out and touched the carcass lightly. There was no warmth, and the cold, hard skin was as brittle as parchment. When he withdrew his hand, some of the dried skin fell away.

Well, at least, he had his answer. The boy had not survived. The last in a long line of the Great Suns was gone and with him all hopes for rebuilding a Natchez Nation. As he mourned the fate of the fallen prince and studied his primitive, troglodyte-like face, he slowly realized that the wounds in the corpse's thigh and hairline had begun to bleed. *How can this be?* he wondered. Puzzled, he leaned closer to get a better view. He thought he saw an eye flicker — he froze.

Without moving a muscle, he watched the face of the Indian intensely, wondering whether or not his eyes were playing tricks upon his harried mind.

Suddenly, the blackened eyes opened and François groaned in unrestrained terror. He closed his eyes to clear his head, failing to notice the rotten arm that was slowly rising from the grave. In the next moment, an icy hand clutched his throat in a viselike grip. *No..., this can't be. I must be dreaming — must wake up*, he told himself with deep urgency.

François awoke, jumped out of bed, and hurriedly lit his waxberry candle. When his nerves had settled, he sighed with resignation and climbed back into his bunk where he waited patiently for the morning sun to rise. Silence awoke, saw the labor of his restless breathing — then laughed, or so it seemed.

———

For a couple of weeks, François went out of his way to avoid Zolare. Avoiding Zolare, however, also meant that he had to avoid Marie, too. For, it was rare when the two were not in close proximity of each other. Even so, he stayed away from the cookhouse, missing meals and surviving on fruits and vegetables. On the occasions he did choose to eat a regular meal, he sent Cecil or someone else to the cookhouse to fetch it for him. On one such occasion, he went to Cecil's cabin and found him sitting on his porch, his dark face cloudy and etched with deep lines of worry.

"Something's stomping in your cornfield, Cecil?" François asked with concern.

"I suppose you might say that," Cecil replied solemnly.

"What?"

"Trouble, and plenty of it."

"What this trouble look like?"

"Probably best that you don't know."

"Does it concern me?"

"No."

"Then, you must tell me. I promise to keep your confidence."

"Well... between you, me, and that black crow yonder, it looks like M'sieur Bectel."

"What about Bectel?"

"Bectel killed Louis. Louis didn't run away. He's dead — blowed away by the worms by now."

"Who says so?"

"Can't tell you that. Gave my word not to reveal names."

"How did it happen?"

"Seems Bectel caught Louis with his bed wench, shot him, then hauled the body off somewhere nobody knows. He come back, almost beat Cleotis to death, and swore he would kill any one of them that breathed a word."

"We should tell the commandant. This man must be brought to justice."

"Justice? What justice?" Cecil replied angrily. "If there was justice, we would not be here in the first place. If there was any fucking justice, there would be no yokes around our necks. No, telling the commandant would be the worst thing we could do. Besides, it won't help matters in the least. It won't bring back the dead and will just make things worse for the living.... What we say here, has to die here. You understand?"

"I understand," François said, still quite concerned about the revelation.

"It's best. Not right, but best. A slave's life means nothing in a white man's eyes. They are more concerned about the loss of a dog than one of us. Things need to change. But nothing is going to change until we get tired of living the way we do, band together, and take our fate in our own hands."

"Cecil, are you talking war? A revolution?"

"I'm talking worse. A massacre. If it was left to me, I would kill every one of them, man, woman, and child — the way the Natchez did at Ft. Rosalie. Their mistake was not finishing the job."

"You would kill the commandant, too?"

"Him, too."

"I agree that the rest could die, and I would aid, if that time came. But, I do not think I would be willing to kill the commandant or any member of his family."

"I understand your feelings. But if you would be unwilling to do so, then I would have to kill you, first. There can be no middle ground. The commandant's allegiance is to his own kind. Not to us, his slaves and property. He would rally with his countrymen. He would leave us no choice. Still, you mark my words, the time is coming, and it is coming soon."

"Who else knows about Louis?"

"No one. I only told you because a secret of this nature is too grave for one person to contend. You want me to get you some food?"

"Well, I was going to ask that of you, but now, I'm no longer hungry."

"Me either. But I must go anyway to get something for my wife. She is ill. Hasn't been feeling well now for several days. It's no trouble to bring something for you, too."

"Just look after your wife. I have some dried fruit if I get hungry later on."

"You know, you can't run from Zolare forever."

"I know," François replied as Cecil walked away.

The circumstances regarding Louis' death weighed heavy on François' mind for several days following Cecil's disclosure, as did Cecil's troubling remarks about a revolution. Cecil was the first person to ever speak to him about such a forbidden subject, and now, he wondered if a revolution was the only solution to his problem. He had wanted to believe Gilbeau, had wanted to believe that the commandant would grant him freedom in return for his services. But much time had passed, and he had not seen any visible inclinations on the part of the commandant to grant freedom to anyone, not even unto Gilbeau. And Gilbeau, in his opinion, was one of his most devoted. All white men are the same, he concluded. All selfish, greedy people without respect for the feelings of others. People who will do anything as long as it serves their own purposes.

That fall, Cecil's wife died of the consumption. Marie did all she could in her inexperienced capacity, but her efforts were in vain. However unfortunate, the incident proved to be one of salvation for François. For shortly after, the commandant offered Zolare to Cecil.

Cecil, in turn, proposed to Zolare. Zolare, however, did not accept immediately. And while the population gossiped and waited expectantly for her decision, several days elapsed. Then, late one evening on a day of rest, while François was sitting on the porch of his tiny cabin, he saw Zolare walking in his direction. He pretended not to notice and did not lift his head until she was standing before him.

"François," Zolare said with a serious tone.

"Yes, Zolare."

"We must talk."

François sighed and nodded his head in agreement.

"I suppose you've heard that the commandant has offered me to Cecil."

"I heard that. Are you going to accept?"

"That is what we need to talk about. What about you and Marie? It is important that I know."

"Nothing has changed."

"Well, I suspected as much. I just wanted to hear it from your own mouth. That being the case, I suppose I don't have any other choice."

"Cecil is a good man."

"I know," Zolare replied as tears welled heavily in her eyes. Somewhat ashamed, she turned her face away and tried to stem the flow with the back of her hand. After several unsuccessful attempts, she abandoned her efforts and allowed them to flow freely down the taut cheeks of her dark, troubled face. "Yes," she continued, "Cecil is a good man. He is kind, and the commandant is very dependent upon him for his knowledge in the fields. He is most certainly a good man. But I, in all truthfulness, can never love him nor can I forget the past. Our times were sacred, and it saddens me to know that our paths are no longer joined."

"Zolare, as difficult as it may be, we must forget the past."

"François, Heaven knows I will try. I will do the very best I can to rid myself of the torment you have brought into my life. I just wish you would have given us a fair chance. I would have spared nothing to make you happy."

"In time, you will learn to love Cecil. I am undeserving. He is worthy. Give him an opportunity. Things will work out."

"Nothing you say can ever make me love another man, François, not as long as you live and breathe... only you," Zolare said without fanfare as she turned on shaky legs and walked sadly away.

François watched until she had entered her cabin. When she had done so, he hung his head in despair as strong feelings of guilt tore viciously at his insides.

———

A simple marriage ceremony performed in front of Cecil's cabin made Zolare his wife. Cecil, of course, was quite happy with his good fortune. He was well into his middle age and Zolare was a refreshing addition to his otherwise somber life. She was young and considerably more passionate than his previous mate, a fact that did not escape the eyes of his small circle of friends.

Many mornings, Cecil found it difficult to begin his daily task, often complaining about his back and a lack of energy. The men, in turn, took every advantage to tease him.

"Eh..., Cecil, another rough night, last night?"

"*A` bon chat, ... bon rat* (To a good cat, a good rat)," Cecil would reply.

"If you need any help in straddling that big, pretty derrière, you can always call on me, Cecil."

"Don't you worry, son. Old Cecil been straddling derrières

for almost forty years. Didn't need no help then — don't need none now."

The men would laugh some more. Then, someone would start a work chant....

"Wax your shoes, tip your hat,
Ain't no work ever hurt like that.
Wax your shoes, tip your hat,
We know how you hurt your back...."

It was all in good fun, and Cecil took great pleasure in their envious attentions.

Zolare's outlook was not as enthusiastic. Her outlook was more one of resignation, of having accepted her fate, of trying to make the most of a lesser situation. In doing so, she avoided François whenever possible without being too conspicuous. When it was not possible, she said what she had to say, and did what she had to do without frivolities, and she did it without letting him look into her eyes and into her soul. For her eyes were the eyes of Judas — they told all.

In 1733, Bienville returned to Louisiana and resumed his former role as Governor of the territory. A dispatch, received by St. Denis from Bienville, stated that he had been sent back to bring the Natchez to full justice and restore tranquility among the heathens, and that he was soliciting St. Denis' support in this undertaking.

During July of that same year, St. Denis' second born daughter, Marie Rosa, who was eighteen, received a proposal from Monsieur James de la Chaise, an older, but prominent newcomer to the colony. Marie was serving hot café and teacakes when she overheard M'sieur la Chaise ask St. Denis and Emanuelle for their daughter's hand. As soon as she was finished, Marie hastened to inform Marie Rosa of the news. Then together, they watched and listened from behind the doorway as the negotiations proceeded.

"Will you accept?" Marie asked Rosa in a whisper.

"Yes, I think I will."

"But you know nothing about him."

"Oh, but I do. I met him in the market several weeks ago. He is newly arrived. A business man of means with influential friends both here and on the continent."

"How do you know all this?"

"I asked questions, silly."

"Well, why you never mentioned this before?"

"You never gave me a chance. You were always too busy talking about François," Marie Rosa replied with a snicker.

After M'sieur la Chaise had departed, St. Denis called for Marie Rosa and told her officially of the proposal. She accepted and word of her acceptance was sent to M'sieur la Chaise in a formal letter.

Since this was the first wedding in the household, Emanuelle and St. Denis went through great pains to make it a noteworthy affair. In many ways, they tried to duplicate the gaiety of their own wedding in Mexico. All of the local Indians were invited, as were the Spanish population at Los Adaes. Beasts were killed and roasted over open fires. The forest was picked clean of flowers. Wine, tangy cheeses, and linens for new dresses were hauled in from New Orleans.

The marriage took place in the mission church and the festivities on the banks of the river. And although the affair was costly, it was one time that St. Denis truly enjoyed playing the role of host to his many friends.

———

During January, 1734, St. Denis' bookkeeper, Derbanne, departed on a trip to New Orleans to arrange for the purchase and shipment of stores for the settlement. He, however, did not return alive. His body was found floating in a small bayou on the edge of the city. The coroner's report, received by St. Denis, mentioned a bruise to his head suggesting foul play, but the death was ruled accidental due to the lack of more conclusive evidence to the contrary. Fortunately for the colony, Derbanne had concluded his business prior to his untimely death.

With the coroner's report in hand, St. Denis personally assumed the responsibility of informing Derbanne's family and assisting them in the transfer of Derbanne's estate to his two sons, still commonly known as the *"Derbanne Boys"* even though they had grown into industrious young men. Of the two boys, Jeanne was the more outspoken and leader of the clan. His brother, Gaspard, was more passive and quite content to follow.

Without a bookkeeper, St. Denis was forced to assume these detestable duties until he could solicit a replacement from New Orleans. This essentially tied him to his office. And although this additional duty aggravated him, it was one of the least of his worries. He was more concerned about the activities of the Chickasaws and their renegade Natchez companions who were growing more daring and making more frequent raids into French Territory. There were several reports that Tattooed Serpent, much older now, was sighted among them. Still other reports spoke of Chick war parties under the command of a giant, black runaway who raped and killed his victims unmercifully.

St. Denis' concern was that they would eventually seek out his post in retribution for his part in the Natchez war. With this in mind, he requested that his post be augmented with twenty additional soldiers. Bienville, however, denied the request, stating that the Chick's efforts were concentrated along the Mississippi River and were of no immediate threat to him. Not totally convinced, St. Denis beefed up his fortifications, anyway.

The following spring, his worst fear was realized. A trading party he had dispatched to the Spanish mission was attacked by a small band of Chicks under the leadership of the large Black War Chief within six miles of his post. The party, consisting of two French traders, one soldier, and two Indian slaves, managed to escape with their lives. But in the process, everything in their charge was lost, including their mounts. A large percentage of these goods had been consigned to him by his constituents. When word of the loss reached the post, the Derbanne boys were among the group of venders who stormed his office seeking reimbursement and demanding that something be done about the Chicks.

"Gentlemen," St. Denis addressed the group, "I believe this was an isolated incident. Instead of worrying about a few sacks of grain, we should be thanking the Good Mother that no lives were lost. Armed guards, however, will be utilized to escort any future shipments. Other than that, there is nothing more that I can do."

"There should have been armed guards all along, and certainly before today," Jeanne Derbanne offered. "The Chicks have been pestering us for several years. Now, they are being joined by runaways, and no one seems to be concerned."

"Jeanne, we are all concerned. In fact, I just received a dispatch from Governor Bienville last week stating that since the Chicks have ignored his request that they turn over Tattooed Serpent and his band of renegades, he is strongly contemplating launching an all out war against them.

"A war? A full scale war?" Derbanne asked, visibly alarmed.

"Are you deaf? Yes, a full-scale shooting, killing war — one that just may involve you and your companions. And since you're all such concerned citizens, I am sure that you will want to do your part when that time arrives, won't you?"

"Well..., yes," Derbanne stammered. "But surely, you don't expect us to walk off and leave our farms. We're farmers, not soldiers."

"Well, a little training will remedy that shortcoming. In the meantime, I suggest you let me attend my duties. I was just in the process of drafting a reply to Bienville with my assessment when you interrupted me. As you can see, we are concerned. But planning a war takes time and resources. And no one should start a war without first trying diplomacy. In the meantime, you must learn to take the good with the bad — as I do. Now, go home so that I can attend my chores, and give thanks for the small blessings we have already received."

A little reluctant, and still far from being satisfied, the group departed, then stood outside where they milled around talking among themselves. The subject, of course, was the forthcoming war and the role they might be expected to play in that event.

After a moment, St. Denis sighed, then sat down to complete his draft to Bienville, informing him of the Chick's raid in his territory and advising him to continue his diplomatic efforts to resolve the crisis. He also stated that, if war was inevitable, he would participate, but suggested that the few soldiers under his command be left in place to guard his outpost.

Talk about the raid remained on the lips of every citizen for several weeks. And although they spoke of the runaway's involvement with a guarded tongue, word about the black war chief's rampage soon reached the ears of the slaves.

"Have you heard the news?" François asked Cecil as they worked beside each other in the field.

"What news do you speak of?"

"About the black war chief."

"I have," Cecil replied.

"Do you think the revolution has begun?"

"I am not certain, but it is a sign that the time is near. He may be the one we've been waiting for — the one who will rally our cry for freedom."

"I think he must be a very brave man, this war chief. The whites fear him. And although I have had no reason to speak of it before, I am one who would follow him when the time comes."

"It may mean we will have to kill the commandant."

"I know. But as you stated before, if there is a war, neither the commandant nor I would have a choice in the matter."

"What about Marie? You're to be married soon."

"I would take her with me. She would go."

"I wouldn't be too certain of that. She is young, a house

servant firmly bound to her mistress. Her bond will be difficult to break."

"I suppose I should talk to her and discover her opinion."

"That would be foolish. House servants cannot be trusted. She would betray you."

"Marie would never do so."

"Still, it is too risky to confide in a mere girl. She may get you and me both hung should she disclose what we are contemplating. You should wait. Wait until the time is right. Besides, there is no need to cause her alarm over something that may never take place. Just wait, and see what the future holds."

"I will do that," François replied as he savored the special feeling that comes with the anticipation of liberty.

And while François openly condemned the conduct of the black runaway and the Chicks for his master's sake, inwardly he took great pride in their audacity. Thoughts of liberty grew like a spark in a box of dry tinder causing him to reflect and ruminate. And in his deliberations, he decided that if things did not go well for him, maybe he would give up his hopes, take Marie, and join this brave black warrior in his noble efforts....

———

Chapter – Twenty

September, 1735

"MARIE," ST. DENIS SAID, AS HE SAT WATCHING HER FOLDING CLOTHES BESIDE A SMALL WOODEN TABLE, "my wife has reminded me that you will be eighteen in a few days."

"Yes, m'sieur," Marie replied as she paused in her task.

"Is that so, Emanuelle?"

"Well...," Emanuelle said as she put her needlework aside, "I am not at all certain. Maybe, I am mistaken. Maybe, it is next year. I seem..."

"No, m'selle," Marie interrupted, her voice filled with concern. "You are not mistaken. Next week for sure, on the 24th day of September."

Suddenly Emanuelle laughed. "I am only jesting, chéri. Yes, Louis, she will most definitely be eighteen in a few days."

"Does that day have any special significance to you?" St. Denis asked with a small, hidden smile.

"Yes, it does, m'sieur," Marie replied. "That is the day François and I are to be married."

"Then, don't stand there. Go and fetch him. I need to discuss this matter with you both."

Before he had ended his sentence, Marie had already dashed for the door. Within a few moments, she returned, dragging François by the hand, both hardly able to contain their excitement. "Here he is, Commandant," Marie stated between breaths. "I found him in his cabin."

"Well now, François, do you still want to marry this contrary, young lady?"

"Yes, Commandant, I do."

"Then, you both have my full blessing."

"Merci, Commandant," François replied as Marie squealed and almost crushed his fingers with her tiny hand. "I shall always be grateful for your compassion in our behalf."

"Then, all is well. As of tomorrow, you may return to your former duties. I suspect you will need time to ready your cabin."

"Merci..., Commandant?"

"Yes, François."

"How soon will this marriage take place?"

"Oh, I don't know. I suppose we will let you pick the date."

"Good. With your permission, I choose tomorrow."

"Of course not," Emanuelle interrupted with a mischievous smile. "That is too soon. This is a special occasion, and it must be planned like one — very carefully. First, we must..."

"First, we must get you baptized," St. Denis interjected in a manner that startled Emanuelle.

"Baptized?" Emanuelle asked for clarification. "I assumed that you had taken care of that matter years ago when you purchased him."

"Well...."

"Oh, never mind," Emanuelle said before turning her attention back to François. "Well, since my dear husband has ignored your salvation, we must first get you baptized. Then, we shall select a date — one at the convenience of the priest. Then, there are the preparations and a thousand other things to do."

"With so much to do," François offered, "I should go and fetch the priest now, so that we can proceed without undue delay."

"I'm afraid that is impossible. The priest is in New Orleans on business. He will be gone for at least a month — maybe more. But..." Emanuelle added after noticing the distressing look on François' face, "I promise, we will proceed with all dispatch, the moment Father Vitry returns. You have my word on that."

"Thank you, m'selle," François replied halfheartedly as he and Marie excused themselves.

When François and Marie had gone, Emanuelle resumed her needlework. Suddenly, she stopped, looked at St. Denis curiously, and asked, "Why have you delayed in your duty to have François baptized?

You are usually very prompt about such matters."

"I should have done it long ago, and would have, except for a certain problem...."

"I'm listening."

St. Denis paused. After searching for the right words, and deciding that there were none, he stated quite bluntly, "The truth is — I purchased François shortly after he had killed another slave in a bitter duel."

"What? Our François?" Emanuelle asked in alarm. "Surely you jest."

"I'm afraid not."

"How? And for what reason?"

As Emanuelle listened with concern, St. Denis recounted the event for her benefit; explaining the circumstances which ignited the duel between François and Mukta, how they fought, his wager with the Englishman, and how Mukta died.

"...When I purchased him, I was not certain of his character, did not know if his soul was salvageable or not, and I certainly did not want him confessing his sins to the wrong ears. That would have destroyed his value had I decided not to keep him."

"And you have kept this a secret all these years?"

"Not intentionally."

"It seems to me, it was clearly a matter of self defense — a mere boy, stranded in an unknown place, and forced to fight for his life. Enough to drive any person insane. You must attend to this affair the moment Father Vitry returns. Promptly. Do you hear me, Louis? Promptly."

"Yes, of course, chéri."

————

Finally, two days before Christmas, the priest returned, and François was baptized the day after, on the 26th day of December, 1735. With that taken care of, the wedding date was set for the 8th day of January, and the preparation for the event resumed amidst the gaiety of the holiday season.

"Well, chéri, you will soon get your chance to become a woman.

Are you excited?" Emanuelle asked Marie as she finished the last stitch
in the hem of a dress she was giving to Marie for her wedding.

"*Oui,* Madame. I can hardly wait," Marie said with unbridled
excitement.

"Come now, stop your fidgeting long enough to try this dress on."

Emanuelle sat and watched as Marie quickly slipped the dress over
her head. She wished that it could have been white, but unfortunately,
she had nothing else available. Still, it was a beautiful dress. The bodice
was made of black velvet, pointed at the front with an exceptionally low
décolletage. The lower part was of blue satin, and it shimmered like
thousands of diamonds as it flowed out into a full circle with a modest
train in the back. Alternating black, and white ribbons circled about
the skirt at different levels with a tasteful amount of lace near the waist.
Emanuelle loved the dress and had worn it many times as a young girl
to the social functions given by her grandfather in Mexico. But as she
grew older, she began to spread in several unforgivable places, partly
due to the rich foods that she loved, and partly due to the burden of
child bearing. At the moment, she was pregnant again, and hoping that
this would be the last time.

Yet, in spite of the fact that she could no longer wear the dress,
she continued to treasure it. She had hoped to pass it on to one of her
daughters, but Luiza was dead, and Rosa had refused to wear it when
she got married, preferring to take her chances on obtaining the latest
fashions from the Continent.

"I must say you look beautiful. You must never let François see
you this way until the day of the wedding. Otherwise, the commandant
will have to lock him in his workshop to protect your chastity."

"M'selle, after all the time spent waiting, I would hardly run if
François came through that door right now to take me away."

"I wouldn't be too anxious if I were you. After you see what hangs
between his legs, you might find yourself begging to be readmitted into
my house," Emanuelle laughed.

"Surely, you jest."

"No, chéri. I've had occasion to witness the monster that resides
there, and I dare say — if you survive the first day, yours will be a life
of contentment and Heavenly joy."

"M'selle, is it your intent to frighten me?"

"No, chéri. Just a word of caution. Believe me, there is enough there for both you and Zolare," Emanuelle said before she realized what her words implied. "I'm sorry, chéri. I didn't mean that the way it sounded."

A little unnerved, Marie replied smugly, "I am not offended. Besides, I am twice the woman Zolare is. She does not worry me. After we are married, François will forget that she ever existed."

"That's the spirit, chéri. Now look in my armoire, and bring me two of my petticoats."

Two weeks later, on the appointed day of 8 January 1736, the marriage took place in the small mission church at the Post of Natchitoches. They were a handsome couple. François, the noble fisherman, and Marie Françoise, the beautiful maiden in whose eyes one could still see the reflection of the ancient Nile.

The ceremony was brief with only a few persons in attendance. Included were the priest, St. Denis, his wife, Emanuelle, and the surgeon, François Goudeau, who had served as François' godfather during his baptism.

After the official wedding, the slave couple was taken by wagon back to Sombrilla where Marie and François repeated their vows again for their friends and the rest of the slave population. At the conclusion, Zolare rushed to Marie, hugged her enthusiastically, and presented her with a gift.

"Marie, this is my gift to you and François. Something I started years ago just for this occasion."

"Merci, Zolare," Marie said, quite surprised, as she unfolded a beautiful quilt made of woven swan's-down.

"I do hope you will like it."

"Oh, Zolare, but I do. It is beautiful. How can I ever thank you enough?"

"No thanks are required. This is my attempt at a peace offering — my way of wishing you and François all the happiness in the world."

"Zolare, I know how much you..."

"Don't say another word, chéri. François was never meant for me.

Just remember how fortunate you are, and think of me warmly — as you would a friend."

"Merci, Zolare. I will. I truly will."

"Now, let me help you move your things to your new cabin. Your husband is growing impatient."

While François waited anxiously at the door to his cabin, Zolare helped Marie to collect her bundles, and together, they hauled them into Marie's new home. A group of well-wishers followed them — teasing and singing chants as it was customary to do in their native land. François greeted her at the steps and escorted her in.

While their friends celebrated the event with the help of a crock of liquor provided by St. Denis, François carefully put Marie's belongings away. While he was doing so, Marie completed a silent inspection of her new home, then sat shyly upon François' bunk and waited. For several minutes François stalled, arranging, then rearranging Marie's things among his own. Finally, he finished.

"This is a small cabin," he said, a little too loud, "but we will not live here long. Tomorrow, first thing, I will start on a new cabin, one much bigger, maybe three rooms. Four — if you like. I promise, it will be the best cabin in the territory. I..."

"François, I like your cabin just fine."

"I know. But this cabin, this is not the best cabin. This one is old. It smells old. Nothing seems to help, not even the mint leaves I threw about the floor. You deserve a much better, maybe, even one as large as the big house."

"Really, François, your cabin is fine. We do not need more. Besides, any place can be beautiful as long as it is filled with love and joy."

"Then, if that is true, this must be the most beautiful cabin in the whole world because I am overfilled with joy this day.... Marie, I have waited a long time for this moment, and now that it has arrived, I can hardly believe my good fortune."

"I feel the same, chéri...."

An awkward moment followed as François stared down at his new wife. Self-consciously, Marie averted her eyes and pretended to inspect her skirts. Finally, unable to stand the suspense any longer, she squealed, leaped from the bed, and threw her arms around François jubilantly.

Laughing heartily, François quickly gathered her into his shaking arms and embraced her with a gentleness that both surprised and tantalized her. For several moments, they said nothing, content just to be touching, embracing, and enjoying the warmth of each other's body. Without realizing what they were doing, Marie suddenly realized that they had been slowly spinning around, almost dancing a somber minuet. They stopped. Then, François lifted her face delicately with his huge hands and kissed her full, moist lips tenderly. "I love you," he said simply and with finality.

"And I, you," Marie replied

"It seems like I have loved you all my life — since the first day I saw you, standing on the gallery, hiding behind your mother's skirts."

"And I loved you, too. Even though you were unclean and ungroomed. I said to myself, what a handsome, unclean man, Zolare's man is. Zolare will be very happy."

"Zolare's man?"

"Yes. Everyone called you Zolare's man. So, I did too, for many years. But later, I overheard maman say that you had asked for me, and you know what?"

"What?"

"I wet my clothes."

"You did what?" François asked again as he doubled over in laughter.

"I did," Marie said between laughs, "standing in the next room eavesdropping, and before I knew it... my bladder just let go. All over maman's freshly scrubbed floor. My maman wanted to kill me."

When their laughter had subsided, Marie stated seriously, "Later, I noticed how you looked at me. And each time you did so, I could feel something pulling at my heart, and I had a strong suspicion that our destinies would run along the same path. From that moment on, I stopped calling you Zolare's man. Sometimes, there was doubt, and sometimes I cried. But that time has passed, and now, I know nothing but complete joy."

They kissed again, at first gently, then with a growing intensity as they pirouetted around and fell upon the bed with the fever clearly upon them both. Not long after, their marriage was consummated. Finally, they were one, and they were content....

"Chéri?" Marie said softly after they had rested.

"Yes."

"I was just wondering..."

"What, chéri?"

"I was just wondering... did I meet your expectations?"

"Each and every one. You were *magnifique.*"

"Better than Zolare," she asked pointedly.

"Zolare?"

"Yes, Zolare, and speak truthfully," she replied as she felt the pace of his breathing change.

"Marie," he said, then cleared his throat. "I love you, and you alone. You have no equal, and certainly not Zolare."

"It makes me happy to hear that. You must forgive me if I ask you that each and everyday — just so that I can feel this way for the rest of my life."

"That pleases me, and my reply shall always be the same, for I shall love you forever."

"And I, you. Forever," Marie said quietly, then closed her eyes to rest.

For a long span, François lay looking up into the ceiling, listening to the even breathing of his new wife, strongly tempted to wake her and solicit her opinion about running away and joining with the black war chief. *What will happen if she does not desire to go?* he asked himself. *Would she betray me?* The more he pondered the question, the less secure he felt in his own mind. It was not anything that Marie had said, done, or failed to do that was responsible for his sudden loss of faith in her devotion. And what was responsible remained vague and unclear in his mind. That being the case, he decided to follow Cecil's advice, keep his silence, and pretend that he was content with his lot. The time was not right. Not yet, he acknowledged as he fell away to sleep. *Not yet....*

Emanuelle sat beside her husband, on a bench beneath the barren branches of a sycamore tree in their backyard, staring forlornly in the direction of François' cabin, wondering how her maid servant, Marie, was faring. Tensely, she listened as she adjusted the light shawl about her shoulders, expecting at any moment to hear her young servant cry out in pain. The cry never came, and for some unexplainable reason, she felt a little disappointed. But then, she reasoned, maybe African women were designed to accept large phalluses. God knows, she did not think she could. Still, the idea was extremely titillating, and she felt a warmth spread through her lower body.

While Emanuelle was lost in her private thoughts, St. Denis rose and stretched.

"Where are you going?" Emanuelle asked pointedly.

"To the fort. I have some business to attend there."

"Not this day, chéri. I have an urgent need for you in my chamber," Emanuelle said with finality as she got up and led the way back to their house. St. Denis followed her meekly.

Outside, the revelry continued. Cecil had constructed a stringed music box which he plucked in cadence with the drums and the clapping of calloused hands. And while the merrymakers sang and danced their impromptu versions of French reels, Emanuelle shucked her clothing, preened her breasts, then directed her husband to their bed and drew the netting. There, she prepared for a long, tortuous, voyage. One, however, that was absolutely necessary.

———

"What we need, Marie," Zolare said, a few months later, as she and Marie sat on stools near a steaming cauldron plucking feathers from a hen, "is a good shower to cool this earth and make life bearable. The April winds have forsaken us, and summer is yet to come."

"I agree. Still it is the summer that I prefer."

"It isn't that I dislike summer. Summer has its good points.... Oh, my God, here comes Eula," Zolare said with mock disgust and turned her head in the opposite direction. "Is she coming this way?"

"No, she's turning into Nadine's cabin."

"Thank God. She is starting to get on my nerves."

"In what way?"

"I swear, I think she watches my cabin and waits until she is certain that Cecil and I are making love. Then, here she comes."

Marie laughed.

"I could have killed her the other night. I was moments away from popping my cork — reaching for it. And what happens? She knocks on the stinking door. A hammer couldn't have been any louder."

"Well, I'm glad she is your friend and not mine."

"Thanks, Marie. That doesn't help me at all. That wench needs her own man. That's why she eats so much. If the commandant doesn't pair her off soon, he will need two carts just to haul her fat ass from one end of the field to the other."

"I suspect you're right about that," Marie said with a giggle.

When the plucking was done, Zolare held the hen over the fire to singe off the small feathers they had missed. While she was doing so, Marie leaned over and whispered secretly, "Zolare, guess what?"

"What, chéri?"

"I think I am *enceinte.*"

"*Enceinte?* Oh, Marie, I am truly happy for you. François must be a very happy man. How long?"

"Two months, going on three."

"You are blessed. If Cecil doesn't make me pregnant soon, I'm going to give him back to the commandant to sell for dog meat. Well, I must go. I'll cook the chicken while I'm preparing m'selle's meal. When I'm finished, I'll send Cecil to fetch you and François."

As Zolare headed for the cookhouse, Marie returned to the big house to attend her own chores, feeling content in the knowledge that she would soon be a mother, never realizing that she and François were well on their way toward fulfilling their mistress's prophecy.

———————

Chapter – Twenty-One

Mukta No-Talk squatted at the edge of the forest peering out between the branches across a recently harvested field at a lone cabin. He and several Natchez and Chickasaw braves had been observing the cabin for several hours in an attempt to determine the number of occupants living there. So far, they had identified four, an adult male, a raven-haired woman, and two young adults. One of the youths was a young girl about fourteen with yellow hair. The other was a slightly older boy. He thought he had caught a glimpse of a fifth person inside, but he wasn't certain.

He spent most of his time, however, watching for the raven-haired woman. From the distance, she appeared to be about thirty-five to forty years old, mature, but still shapely. From the manner in which she went about her chores and the tone of her voice when she yelled instructions to her family, Mukta decided that she was a little too overbearing for his own personal taste. She was, however, an improvement over most of the ones he had encountered on his previous raids into French territory. Usually, they were nothing more than fat, hooked-nose pigs. Those of that type, and those with yellow hair, he dispatched straight away, either by shooting or crushing their skulls with his trusty club. He detested women with yellow hair. Yellow was not a natural color for creatures. For that reason, they frightened him even worst than Diablo. This young girl, however, intrigued him despite the fact that she had yellow hair. This one, he concluded, was interesting, maybe interesting enough to become his woman. He would see.

Yes, this would be the place where he would start this particular skirmish of his continuing war against the French. They were about as deep into French territory as he cared to go. From here, he would leave a fiery trail back north, attacking several targets that he had selected on the way in. That was the best way. Attack on the way out. That way, even if the results of their raid was discovered, they would already be moving out and away from any army the French could muster.

In the beginning, he had experienced some difficulty in convincing the Indians to use this type of battle strategy. He finally succeeded after they were almost trapped behind enemy lines. On that occasion, a passerby found one of the cabins they had burned while on their way deeper into French territory. The passerby mobilized a group of settlers and almost caught them in a trap as he and his war party were withdrawing out of the French's territory.

While he had been able to sell the Indians on that part of his strategy, he was never able to persuade them to fight at night. For some reason, which he could not understand, they insisted on fighting by the light of day, preferably at the break of dawn. And trying to get them to fight in the winter was like trying to yank hair off a bear's balls.

It was late evening now, and the cabin he was looking at would have made a perfect target for a night attack. By morning, they could be miles away. But with the situation like it was, the only thing left to do was rest and wait for the morning sun. Quietly, he signaled his band and they withdrew deep into the forest to wait for morning.

The air was getting chilly, so Mukta removed a blanket from his pack and settled down beneath a huge tree. Wakanee, a seasoned Natchez brave, came and sat beside him.

"How many will we take this time, Mukta No-Talk?"

"Two," Mukta No-Talk replied in a coarse, but barely audible voice.

"We selected more on the way in."

"I know this. But, one is too close to this place. The smoke of this fire will be easily seen. We must pass it by and take the next."

"Two is not so many. We have twelve braves. Two will not

provide enough bounty for twelve. The last time we took four. We should take four this time."

"Last time there were many cabins along the path we travelled. There are not so many along this path, and we are already deep in French land. This time, we take two. Next time we will choose a better path."

"I do not think the braves will be very pleased with only two."

"I am not concerned. I am the commander of this war party. We take two. Bounty is not the only reason we fight. We fight to avenge our dead, or have you forgotten?"

"I have not forgotten."

"Good. The last time out together, you did forget, and our enemies escaped while you and the others abandoned me to chase after their pack-mules — all loaded with nothing but worthless rubbish."

"We will take two," Wakanee stated, although it was clear that he did not agree. Without another word, he got up and stalked away.

When Wakanee had retired, Mukta threw his blanket about his shoulders and stretched out his colossal body to rest, caressing the hideous skin that covered his badly burned arms and chest, and remembering the night several survivors of the battle at Natchitoches stumbled into camp a few years ago....

At the time, he was into his milk and honey, kneeling behind the upturned buttocks of a slightly overweight Chickasaw female. Suddenly, there was a commotion outside. He stopped his rutting and listened. There were loud shouts followed by weeping and wailing. Hurriedly, he shoved the woman aside, threw his loincloth about his nakedness, and rushed out the door of his lodge.

"What is it? What has happened?" he asked Bear Claw, straining to make his voice heard over the noise.

"The French. They found the village and killed everyone there. Only four men and nine women escaped."

His heart pounding with excitement, Mukta searched the crowd until he spotted the silver hair of Tattooed Serpent leaving the gathering, walking slowly toward his lodge, his head bowed. He rushed after him, calling out, but was unable to make himself heard. He quickened his pace, caught up with Tattooed Serpent, and tapped him on the shoulder.

"Yes, No-Talk," Tattooed Serpent stopped and replied.

"Now, we fight. Yes?"

"Yes. Now, we fight. But first, I must counsel with the Chickasaw, tell them of our intentions, and seek their assistance in building a fort. This war will not be an easy one."

"You build the fort. Me — I cannot wait. I wish to take a war party, now."

"I will not stop you or any of those who care to follow. I ask, however, that you wait until the fort is complete before you do so."

"How long must I wait?"

"About four months."

Elated, Mukta hurried to his hovel and retrieved his war club. He then raced to the totem in the center of the village and struck it several times about the base, causing it to resonate with a dull, thumping sound. This act, by custom, announced to all interested warriors that he was organizing a war party and soliciting volunteers.

When the gathering of warriors was large enough, he howled in a voice that sounded more like the screeching of a caged feline rather than that of a man who stood almost seven feet tall. The crowd hushed.

"I, Mukta No-Talk," he shouted, "will take a war party against the French in four months. We will take much bounty. The time has come to make the white dogs pay for the deaths of our people. Any man with the courage to follow me, stand at my side."

Several Indians howled and joined Mukta at the totem.

"Are there any others? I seek only the bravest. Join me if you thirst for French blood. There will be bounty for all. What is theirs today, will be ours tomorrow. Weapons, women to tend your fields by day, and women to warm your beds by night. Thousands of French heads for your stakes!"

Quickly, the numbers at his side grew. When he had selected twelve of the best, he called out to the drummers who lifted their sticks and struck their hollowed out logs in a rhythm that was both solemn and intense. Women and young maidens joined them, chanting and shaking their rattlers in cadence. Warriors gathered in a line, four abreast, dancing and stomping their feet as they circled a small fire in the center of the village.

And while the warriors danced to the passions of their ancestors, Mukta No-Talk, the giant, danced to the passions of his, alone and apart, intense and pagan, his huge body shuffling awkwardly and yet intricately to a dark rhythm born of Africa — a rhythm that only his ears could hear — that only his heart could feel. And when his body was wet with sweat and his veins filled with racing blood, he called for the Black Drink, *Ilex vomitoria*. Then, he threw up his guts along with Diablo and all the other evil spirits that had found refuge within his huge, aging body.

The Chickasaws agreed to the plan without modifications, and four months later, Mukta No-Talk and his braves donned their war paints and departed on their first raid into French territory screaming fire for fire, killing, and burning everything within their reach.

When he returned, another War Chief and his party departed, then another. This was Mukta's seventh raid over the last three-year period. It would not be his last. It would take a thousand fires and a thousand screaming Frenchmen to pay for the damage done to his weary body and soul. And even that, he feared, would not be enough.

———

The moistness of the morning dew and a heavy bladder awoke Mukta early the next morning. Several of the braves were already up, talking quietly with bridled excitement as they freshened their war paints, and cleaned and loaded their muskets. Mukta got up, wiped his weapon dry with a small piece of doeskin, and replaced the damp flint with a new rock. He, however, did not don his war paint for this occasion.

When he had finished, he motioned to the others to follow him to the edge of the forest. There, they waited until the smoke from the morning's fire lifted and rose from the chimney of the tiny French cabin. Mukta waved his arm, and the braves scurried from the trees, across the open fields, and took their places behind outhouses, fences, and woodpiles.

When they were in place, Mukta threw the butt of his musket across his shoulder and started walking toward the house whistling a French folk song that he knew was familiar to all.

At the cabin, he stepped boldly upon the gallery, knocked, and called out, "*Bonjour*" several times as he waited.

Cautiously, the door opened. The raven-haired woman peered out. "*Oui*," she replied.

"M'selle, I am lost. Can you tell me where I am?"

"One minute," she said as she turned and called to her husband. "Pierre, there is a black man at the door. Says, he is lost."

Mukta heard the rustle of covers. Shortly after, a still half-asleep man appeared at the door and stated, "You are lost?"

"*Oui,* m'sieur."

"Where did you come from, and who is your master?"

"Mukta No-Talk has no master, m'sieur," Mukta replied as he lifted his musket, kicked in the door, and blew the face of the man away.

That was the signal. Immediately, the rest of the braves stormed the house, scrambling in through battered down doors and unopened shutters amidst the screams of the women. The teen-aged boy jumped from his cot and raced for his father's musket which hung on two wooden pegs embedded in the wall. He was shot in the back. He fell away dead. The young girl also tried to run, but Wakanee caught her and dragged her back by the hair.

"Bind her," Mukta instructed.

While the young girl was being bound, Mukta ripped the clothing from the raven-haired woman, forced her to her husband's bed, and tied her hands to the headboard.

"Who shall be first?" Mukta No-Talk asked as he appraised the luscious body of the quietly, weeping woman, ignoring her not so attractive face.

"No one. Kill her so we can move on," Wakanee demanded.

"Not this one. No-Talk needs pleasure. Who shall be first?"

A young warrior by the name of Small Crow howled, dropped his loin cloth, and dove between the woman's legs. She kicked and fought like a wildcat, but Small Crow finally mastered her and completed his vigorous, unskilled assault. While the others watched in amusement, Wakanee walked away in disgust.

When the boy finished, he jumped from the bed and howled his delight, grinning from ear to ear.

"Anyone else?" Mukta asked as he pulled aside his loin piece and stroked himself menacingly above the head of the frightened woman.

"There is no one else, No-Talk," Wakanee stated with contempt. "Finish what you must, so we can move on."

Mukta nodded, crawled upon the bed, and took his pleasure. *Milk and honey*, Mukta said to himself. *Milk and honey*.

When it was over, Mukta got up breathing heavily, and released the woman's bonds. He was about to assist her up, when the woman released a muffled scream and came at him with her claws bared. Like one would swat a fly, Mukta backhanded her angrily and sent her naked body sprawling across the dirt floor. Then, while the woman's bawling daughter watched, Mukta took a loaded musket from one of his party, placed the tip between the woman's legs, and fired.

The woman's daughter suddenly went berserk, screaming hysterically. Mukta turned and started towards her, but the girl fainted dead away. Mukta chuckled lightly, reached down, and picked up her limp body.

"Take what you want of this man's possessions," Mukta instructed Wakanee, "Then set his cabin afire."

While Wakanee did so, he threw the girl across his hip and headed for the horses.

———

Mukta No-Talk and his party rode north by northeast the rest of the day without stopping, following little-used foot paths through the dense forest and along small streams, unhurriedly, but steady.

As he had decided, they bypassed the second cabin and proceeded towards the third, the last one on the edge of the French territory. By then, it was quite clear that Wakanee did not approve, and Mukta could sense that the young warrior was on the verge of challenging his authority. That being the case, Mukta decided he would kill Wakanee at the first opportunity, the first time they were alone without witnesses, and certainly before they returned to their village.

The young girl, still in her sleeping clothes, rode with Mukta. She sat in front, holding tightly to the mane of the russet-colored horse with her bound hands. She had cried profusely upon awakening to find that she was a prisoner. But, once the tears and dust had dried and caked upon her parched face, she rode silently with a blank stare that was not of this world. One, however, that said quite clearly that she had finally come to terms with her fate. That was good. Because she had done so, Mukta felt himself developing a certain fondness for her, and the color of her hair seemed less important.

He was growing old, and with his age came a weariness that he had been reluctant to acknowledge even unto himself. Yet, acknowledge it he must, for he was over forty-eight years old, maybe fifty, and the time to father and raise children was departing fleetly. Time had passed him by like a raging river, swift and turbulent, cutting into his body like a knife, and taking with it all memories of his youth, his homeland, and the young girl he was to have married. Now, he could not even remember her face or what she looked like. And he could not imagine what about her was so special that he had found it necessary to leave his small, interior village and travel the many miles it took to reach the coast, where he planned to procure the worthless conch shells that her parents had demanded. *All in vain. All for nothing.*

The slave girl aboard the Marianne, however, still rested gently on his mind. He remembered her well. She had feelings for him — feelings that he had been unaware of until that fateful day in the Slave Market of Algiers. The day he had heard her scream in despair when Diablo placed a rusty spike in the hands of his evil-eyed son and directed it deep into his throat. Her howling and weeping while the others laughed at the sight of his blood would remain with him forever. He often wondered what had happened to the girl, had even hoped that she might be among the slaves that he might liberate. But so far, that possibility seemed highly unlikely. Slaves were difficult to liberate. Many chose to fight and die with their masters, while others ran away from him to hide in the brush like frightened animals. The few that did join with him hardly made it worth his effort. And the evil-eyed boy, well... he would like to meet him again, too. Just one more time, so that he could liberate his bastard soul from the world of the living. *Just-one-more-time.*

There were occasions when he had considered taking an Indian wife. But deep inside, he knew that such a decision would have never granted him the degree of satisfaction necessary for him to settle down and abandon his war with the French. Maybe, nothing would. But since, in his mind, he blamed the whites for the misfortunes that had denied him a life of his own choosing — what would be more befitting than to take one of their own, their pride and joy, and use her to propagate his strain, the bloodline of a lowly slave. And so, in his reflections, the presence of the young girl grew steadily in importance to him, Mukta No-Talk, War Chief, and liberator of the oppressed....

"What will you do with this girl?" Wakanee interrupted as he pulled his horse up beside Mukta.

"I have not yet decided. Maybe, I will take her as my woman," Mukta replied as he reached out to steady the shaking, frightened girl.

"It is best to kill her. She is crazy. She has snakes in her head. She is no good for a mate."

"That will be my decision," Mukta replied as he spurred his horse two lengths ahead of Wakanee.

That night, they made camp near a river where they washed and prepared their meals. When that was done, Mukta took the dazed girl to his pallet, forced her to lie down, then joined her beneath the warmth of his blanket. Nearby, he was conscious of the other braves who sat watching him and whispering quietly. *Not good. Is there a mutiny afoot?* he wondered.

Feeling suddenly alone, Mukta reached for the shivering girl who lay with her back to him and pulled her close against his groin, holding her tenderly and protectively like a tiny bird on a string. He felt his manhood stir, and for a moment he was tempted to take her. Tonight, however, was not the best time. *Something was amiss — something not good.*

It was clear to him that the threat of Wakanee had to be removed before he could devote his full attentions to those of pleasure. *Diablo, hear me, and hear me well. Go on your way. Mukta is too old to survive another of your encounters....*

Two hours before midday of the next day, they tethered their horses to several trees, gagged and bound the girl to another, then proceeded on foot to scout their next target.

They were half-way to their destination when they encountered a black slave. He was sitting on a log eating cold biscuits from a small, canvas sack. In another sack was the carcass of a small animal. When the man looked up and saw them, his black face turned ashy-white with terror. Mukta started toward him. But to his dismay, the man leaped to his feet, dropped his musket, and bolted like a frightened deer. Wakanee was faster. He overtook the man, leaped across his back, and they both tumbled into the dense undergrowth.

Wakanee was about to drive his knife into the man's throat when a winded, lumbering Mukta, shouted, "No."

"Back away. This kill is mine," Wakanee contested angrily.

"Kill him and I will snap your neck."

"This man is an enemy. He would sound the alarm," Wakanee stated as Mukta approached.

"I must talk to him. He may be of some service."

"This man can be of no service to us," Wakanee said as he drew back his knife to finish the job.

With a growl, Mukta struck Wakanee across the neck with the backside of his forearm and bowled him over and to the ground.

"I must talk to this man," Mukta said as he stood over Wakanee. "If he can be of no service, you are welcome to his head. I must talk to him first."

Wakanee recovered, placed his knife back into its sheath sullenly, and stalked away.

"What is your name?" Mukta asked the still frightened slave.

"Modeka."

"Do you live at that place beyond the trees?"

"*Oui*, I live there."

"How many black men live there with you at this place?"

"About six."

"Are there any black women and children there?"

"*Oui*. There are four women and six children."

"How many of these people do you think would go, if I was to give them liberty?"

"I do not know, m'sieur. Maybe, all."

"Would you go?"

"Yes. I would go."

"I am Mukta No-Talk, a Natchez War Chief. If you will assist me, I can give you liberty. I can also, if you wish it, give you a place to live in my village among the Chickasaw. If you refuse,

however, I will be obliged to give your head to Wakanee. Which,
do you prefer?"

"I prefer liberty, m'sieur."

"Then tell me, how many white men live at this place you
live, and how many weapons do they have among them?"

"There are five. My master, his three sons, and his brother.
They live there."

"How many weapons do they have?"

"They each have muskets, and there is also the one that I
use for hunting."

"How much black powder, balls, and wadding do you have
in your possession?"

"I only have enough to load three, maybe four times."

"That is not enough for our needs. Keep it for yourself. You
must go back to this place where you live. Tell the black people
they must not interfere. Tell them that they will not be harmed;
that Mukta No-Talk, their brother, brings to them the gift of liberty; that from this day forth their lives will be their own to live
as they choose. After you have done so, and if it is possible, you
must take your master's black powder and hide it in a safe place
until I have conquered him. Are you willing to do this small service in exchange for your life and liberty?"

"*Oui*, m'sieur. I will do as you ask gladly."

"That is good. I will wait here for three hours, until you have
done as I have requested. Then, we will attack. At the sound of
gunfire, take your musket and use it in my behalf. Liberty shall
come quickly, like a thunderbolt from the sky."

"*Oui,* m'sieur. Merci. I will do as you ask. *Merci*, m'sieur."

When the slave had departed, Wakanee came to Mukta as
they walked back to their camp. "What words did you speak to
that man?"

"Many things. Among them, his promise to assist us."

"That was unwise. That man cannot be trusted. I felt his
heart, and his was the heart of a coward. We should leave now.
It is better to return to our village empty-handed like frightened,

old women than to remain here."

"If you are frightened, then you return like an old woman. Mukta No-Talk will stay and fight."

"Mukta No-Talk will stay and die."

At their camp, Mukta released the leather thong that bound the girl to the tree, then used it to secure one of her ankles to one of his own. When he was finished, he sat down beside her at the base of the tree and rested....

Almost two hours had passed while the warriors milled around, waiting in anticipation for Mukta to give them the signal to attack. Suddenly, gunfire erupted, seemingly from everywhere, on all sides. Several braves fell in the first volley. Mukta jumped to his feet to run for his horse, but found his leg still anchored to that of the girl who lay on the ground screaming horribly. He pulled his knife and had just finished cutting his bonds when another shot rang out at close range. A ball tore into his gut almost spinning him around. He yelled in pain and covered the gaping wound with his hand. He glanced around, and in the near distance he saw the intense, black face of the man he had rescued, on his knees, and reloading his smoking weapon with shaking hands. Mukta cursed and hobbled for his horse. He was trying to lift his bulk astride it when Wakanee who was already mounted, looked at him in disgust and spurred his horse in his direction.

Mukta assumed that Wakanee was coming to aid him. But to his dismay, Wakanee came along side, howled, then suddenly kicked Mukta's horse in the side, causing him to bolt. As Mukta tumbled back to the ground, he saw Wakanee galloping off with several white riders in hot pursuit.

Seconds later, a severely wounded Mukta lay looking up into the angry, red faces of several men who stood pummeling his body with the butts of their muskets and kicking his groin with muddy, knee-high boots. *Diablo, vile demon of Hell, curses to you. Victory is yours at last...,* he said to himself as the butt of a musket drove its iron heel into his face. He saw nothing more, save the blinding redness that welled and filled his fractured skull to overflowing.

———

Chapter — **Twenty-Two**

———

IT WAS A FESTIVE OCCASION THAT GREETED ST. DENIS, JALOT, AND FRANÇOIS as they docked their pirogue on the wharf in the City of New Orleans. Bienville had finally declared war on the Chicks, and they had been summoned to participate. Reluctantly, St. Denis had done so after passing his command over to a newly- arrived officer named Lieutenant Taillefert.

"I wonder why there are so many people about today?" Jalot inquired as they threaded their way through the narrow streets filled with black and Indian hawkers, tourists, seamen, soldiers, servants, and fancily-dressed women carrying a variety of brightly-colored parasols.

"Could be in response to the war effort," St. Denis replied.

"Well, there's one way to find out.... Pardon, my friend," Jalot asked the next person to collide with him, "what is the meaning of all the activity today?"

"Haven't you heard?" the stranger replied. "They captured the black war chief. There will be a hanging this afternoon. On yonder post is the public notice."

At the mention of the words "black war chief," François flinched as if he, himself, had been struck by the heavy hand of fate, completely stunned by the distressing news

"Well, I'll be damned," Jalot said, shaking his head in acknowledgement. "It's about time they caught the black bastard. Let's see what the notice says, Louis."

To the front, thirty paces away on a post, was nailed a sign that read "TRAITOR" in bold letters. Below, on the same post, was a public letter that several people stood reading. As St. Denis and Jalot shouldered for a position among their ranks, François stayed close behind, his eyes bewildered, and his stomach turning from an abundance of green bile,. Patiently, he waited, hoping that St. Denis, Jalot, or both would read the sign aloud and satisfy his mounting curiosity. They, however, chose to read in agonizing silence, taking their own good time. When they had finished, François waited for an explanation, but his companions ignored him and turned to walk away.

"What... what did that paper say, m'sieur?" François inquired plaintively as he hastened to catch up with his master.

"It is not a matter that concerns you, François. We must go. Bienville is waiting."

"Please, m'sieur," François pleaded, "you must read that paper for me. I must know what it says about this man."

"If you insist," St. Denis said with resignation as he led the way back to the public sign post. It says —

"Be it known to all men that the slave, who called himself a Natchez War Chief, is guilty of having committed grievous crimes of the most barbaric nature against the people, and against the King of France. For these crimes, he is to be affixed with an esparto grass halter and dragged by the tail of a pack-horse through the streets of the city to the gallows where his hands and feet shall be struck from his body, and hung until dead. There, he is to remain hanging from the gibbet until his body and all his parts are consumed by the birds and the elements.

All shall bring their slaves and cause them to bear witness to this execution so that they may observe the fate reserved for those who, in their disobedience to their masters, desire to run away and commit crimes against the sovereignty of France.

A punishment equal to that of this criminal awaits any person who violates this ordinance and removes the said body."

"Who made the words on that paper?" François asked.

"Who else, but our good friend, Bienville," St. Denis said as they headed for the governor's quarters.

———

"*Bonjour, mon ami.*"

"*Bonjour, Governor,*" St. Denis said as they embraced somewhat formally. "I stopped along the way and read your public notice."

"Good. The black's capture was purely a stroke of luck. The timing could not have been more perfect. With the state of war that exists with the Chicks, we hardly need the distraction of a slave rebellion, too."

"What happened?" St. Denis asked, then stepped back to take a second look at Bienville's expertly-groomed … *la brig-adiére* wig.

"The son-of-a-bitch was ambushed while he and his band were waiting to raid a German farm north of here. The bastard had even tried to talk the slaves into revolting. Fortunately, one of them he had contacted had the forethought to warn his master, and they kicked the bastard's ass and took him prisoner. When I heard that they had captured him, I had him brought here to stand trial."

"I'm surprised they did not kill him."

"Believe me, they wanted to. However, I convinced them that a public hanging would serve a far greater advantage. Then, I arranged for the nuns to maintain his health just for that purpose."

"Will you be officiating this afternoon?"

"No, the judge and the hangman will do that. My role will be that of an observer. Why don't you retire to the barracks, put your things away, and refresh yourself. Then join me back here at four glasses past noon to see the grand finale... and bring your black manservant. He should see this execution so that he can relay the news to the benefit of others."

"I will do that. *Bonsoir.*"

At the appointed time, four hours past noon, the governor and his entourage from the backwaters of the Red River, followed the gauntlet of gawkers that lined both sides of the streets that ran from the guardhouse to the river, then along the levee to a site on the outskirts of the city. There, the governor directed them to a place, previously reserved for him, where they had an unobstructed view of the hastily constructed gallows.

The crowd, for the most part, was relatively quiet except for some subdued conversations punctuated, once in a while, by fits of forced laughter. Suddenly, after what seemed like an eternity beneath a hot, unforgiving sun, the crowd roared in the distance, their roar preceding the laboring gait of the sweating packhorse like a wave at the front of a flat-bottomed boat. Behind the horse and rider, affixed in a coarse, grass halter, was the body of the once stalwart Black giant, rolling and tumbling in a cloud of dust like a huge, irregular log at the end of a taut rope.

François stood watching the spectacle in silence, his mouth agape, his knees weak from fear, his heart heavy and filled with a combination of rage and sorrow. When the players in the tragic ensemble were almost abreast, he closed his eyes in despair. When he opened them again, the sweating pack horse was almost directly in front of him. Suddenly, he gasped, and his eyes widened in a state of sudden awareness.

"It's him," François shouted in alarm to his master. "I know that man. It's him."

"It's who?" St Denis asked.

"Mukta. That man is Mukta."

"Your servant knows this man?" Bienville asked suspiciously.

"I doubt so," St. Denis stated cautiously. "Still, he does resemble the rogue he killed several years ago."

"Yes, it is him. I am certain. It is him, Mukta," François insisted.

Frantically, François parried his way through the crowd with a sense of urgency and ran toward the fallen giant just as the winded horse faltered to a halt. St. Denis and the governor followed, both equally curious.

For several seconds, François stood, leaning over the prone, bloody, mud-caked body of the giant, stripped of skin by the razor sharp seashells that permeated the soil of the city. In silence, he studied the bloated face, looking for signs of recognition, and listening to the labor of the dying man's heavy breathing — the volume and rhythm of which was not unlike that of a fallen mastodon.

"Mukta," François stated with quiet confidence as tears flowed liberally from his eyes.

Slowly, one glassy, blood-shot eye opened and stared back at him intensely. "Snake Eyes," Mukta said passively without malice or anger. "My God has forsaken me. If your heart allows you to do so, pray to your God on my behalf." Then, the blood-shot eye retreated again from view.

But in that one fleeting moment, however brief, François had discovered all that he needed to know. He knew that the end of an era was at hand; that their lives had come full circle; that he had no further need to fear the ghost of his past; that all between them had been forgiven, each unto the other.

"Well, is he the one?" Bienville asked impatiently.

"Yes, m'sieur," François stated pensively as he stood erect and backed away. "It is him, Mukta."

"Executioner, proceed with your duties," the governor announced theatrically.

With his heart in his mouth, François watched while several robust men dragged Mukta's bulk up the stairs to the gallows where, to his horror and the maddening roar of the crowd, the executioner, with great ceremony, lifted a freshly sharpened wood chopper's axe above his head and struck the limbs from Mukta's body. Then, like a butchered beast, the limbless-body of Mukta, the giant, was hoisted high above the crowd where it flew heavily at the end of a firmly-knotted noose. Throughout the whole ordeal, and although his lifeless body jerked spasmodically like that of a headless chicken, Mukta never once cried out in pain.

Not long after, while the nuns sang hymns of liberation and the priest mouthed his hollow words, many of those who had gathered, dispersed with the setting sun to congregate in nearby taverns where they fortified their bodies with vessels of potent spirits, danced jigs, and flirted outlandishly with the ladies of the night.

"I do not understand," François said with concern as he and Jalot trailed the governor and his master back into the city. "Mukta was dead. I killed him, yet he returned to be a war chief. How can that be?"

"Apparently, you did not do your job well," Jalot offered. "Why are you so concerned? You should be pleased."

"It is not natural for a man who was dead to return from the grave."

"Well, he is dead now," the governor stated, "and that is for certain."

"We shall all worry if he should return for a second time," St. Denis stated with a chuckle.

"Commandant," Jalot spoke, "if it's all well with you, I think I'll do myself some tomcatting. Excitement like we had today makes the *fillies* a little more amorous than usual, and old Jalot wouldn't want to be missing out on anything to be had."

"Be about your mischief, Jalot. Just don't do anything to antagonize the seamen."

"Can't enjoy myself without breaking the nose of at least one of them," Jalot stated with a laugh as he headed for the nearest tavern.

When he had gone, St. Denis turned to François, "While the governor and I are attending our business, you return to the garrison and stay there. It's not healthy for a black to be wandering the streets after dark."

"Yes, m'sieur," François replied solemnly as he headed for the garrison, walking quickly with an uncertain step, trying to sort things out in his mind and put them back into perspective. He, however, was unsuccessful. Disappointment, guilt, and a host of conflicting emotions blocked all his efforts. He was disappointed because the black war chief he had held so high in reverence was nothing more than a myth, a mere figment of his imagination. And now, liberty for him and his family was more elusive than ever.

Now, he was about to partake in an unholy Indian war, a war designed to destroy the very people who had offered sanctuary to the oppressed. Both, he and Mukta, traitors. Both, victims. Both, hostages of fate. Both, like two rudderless ships being swept along toward destinations that neither aspired. Yet, despite the tragic circumstances, he was relieved to know that he was not guilty of having murdered Mukta.

As he entered the gates of the garrison, the vision of Mukta's gently-swaying body came to mind, and he was suddenly overcome with pity for the aged giant. For no man, regardless of his crime or station in life, deserved to die in such a horrible fashion, alone and without honor. No one, not even the likes of someone like Mukta....

As St. Denis and Governor Bienville entered the governor's quarters, a young boy entered the room, nodded to the governor' then departed without speaking a word.

"I see you have guests aboard," St. Denis stated as a matter of fact.

"I suppose you could say that," Bienville replied. "His parents, who are friends of mine, encouraged me to bring him along for an excursion.... Well, Louis, it delights me to have you with me on this campaign — to know that you have responded like a true patriot. It will be like old times, you, me, and the wilderness."

"Of course, you knew I would come. The call to duty is hard to ignore. Still, I must admit that I was somewhat reluctant. You and I, Governor, are far past our prime. And for me, the call of adventure is not as strong as it was in my youth. I yearn only for the comforts of home and the warmth of a small fire. Do you realize that I am almost sixty years old?"

"That is what you say now. Wait until we are combing the forest and killing Natchez and Chickasaw vermin. Then, you will come to life. In spite of our age, we are still the men who will chart this country's destiny."

"Surely you jest. Our time has long passed. Walked off and left us both. No one cares for the wisdom of old warriors and statesmen."

"That is where you are wrong. Sure, there are a few who doubt our abilities. But we, you and I, will prove them wrong. Wait until we return with a barge load of Chickasaw and Natchez scalps. Then, they'll know who still holds the reins on this country."

"If you will permit me, Governor, may I speak plainly without offense?" St. Denis said as he took a seat and crossed his legs.

"Of course, you may. I have great respect for your advice in these matters."

"Well, what concerns me, Governor, is — why, at this point in time, do you feel it necessary to start a war with the Chicks? Don't we have enough problems to sustain us for the time being?"

"What is wrong with everyone?" the Governor almost shouted as he leaned over St. Denis. "All of a sudden, my motives are being questioned by everyone. What has happened to French honor since I left? The honor of our country has been soiled by a band of ignorant savages — burning, and raping, and killing. And no one seems to give a damn. You, of all people, should be the last to promote complacency in these matters. Complacency breeds contempt. French blood has been spilled and those responsible have not been brought to full justice... or should I just say, *C'est la vie*, and let the damn Natchez continue to escort the Chicks down the Mississippi at their will?"

"Well... no. But, I am of the opinion that justice was served when we destroyed most of the Natchez population in 1731."

"That was a half-assed job. Justice will not be served completely until every Natchez responsible is dead. Tattooed Serpent is still alive, and I still subscribe to the `eye for an eye` doctrine," Bienville stated quite dramatically.

"I would agree with you if the Natchez had been the ones guilty of provoking the war. But in this case, one of our very own was responsible. The Natchez had no alternatives. They fought to protect their lands like anyone else would have done.

"It has always been my position, from the beginning, that our cause is better served through diplomacy rather than war," St. Denis said, his voice modulating to almost shouting in order to get his point across.

"Lower your tone, m'sieur," Bienville admonished. "Do you deny that all the land about us belongs to the King of France? That not one arpent belongs to any heathen? The Natchez, like everyone else, are and were subjects of the King, and as such — whether right or wrong — they were obliged to comply with any decisions or proclamations declared by his duly appointed agents."

"Governor, all I am trying to say is that we should offer them their land back as a sign of good faith. There can't be more than two-hundred still alive, and that's counting the women and children. That would accomplish two goals. It would separate them from the Chicks, and it would put them in a location under our jurisdiction where we could keep an eye on them. Doesn't that make sense?"

"Hell, no. I'd rather eat cow shit first."

St. Denis stopped talking and looked at Bienville with thorough disgust, wondering how he had come to develop such an unrealistic point of view. So, with a lot less enthusiasm, he attempted to approach the subject from a different angle.

"Then, tell me, Governor, are we to ignore the English? They are aligned with the Chicks and have provided them with numerous weapons. Don't you realize that an attack could provoke a war with both of them? Should we risk a war with the English, too, when we can't even protect ourselves against a child with a stone?"

"Numbers do not matter to a shrewd statesman. That's something you evidently have not learned yet. I have fought many battles and never once did I lose a single French life. It's all a matter of using your wits," Bienville said, thumping St. Denis on the head with his finger annoyingly.

St. Denis brushed the governor's hand away and re-groomed his hair with his fingers.

Unnerved, Bienville continued, "It's all a matter of using one person's greed to counteract another's — of getting one greedy heathen to fight another. A few worthless beads and those dim-witted Choctaws will fight anyone."

"Times have changed. Those dim-witted heathens are not so ignorant anymore. While you have been away, they have discovered that your damn beads are worthless. They now desire things of greater value, like guns, and powder, and even gold coins. Is the treasury so fat now that we can pay their price, while the soldiers in my garrison have to grub for worms to supplement their diet? I, personally, have been providing for their upkeep out of my own resources, and you, like all the rest, have ignored my requests for reimbursement. "

"*Co-te que co-te*. I don't give a damn what it cost."

"I have been hearing that phrase a lot lately, but never one *livre* have I seen to support it. My position is — if we have the resources to purchase the aid of the Choctaws, I am of the opinion that it would be a far better exchange if we used such resources to purchase peace rather than run the risk of losing even one Frenchman to the cause."

"But then, no one gives a damn about your opinion, does one?" Bienville shouted at the top of his cracking voice. "While you have gone soft in your old age, my resolve has consolidated. I was sent back here specifically to govern this colony and restore its tranquility. And I will accomplish that task even if I have to kill every barbarian on this continent. Louis, do not contest me in this matter.

"Sometimes, I seriously wonder about your motives. Are

your opinions driven by the fact that you are the father of a son with a stink-ass Natchez she-bitch?"

"I will ignore that insult out of respect for you. I have no knowledge of the matter about which you speak, and I resent your accusation."

"I find that questionable. Everyone else in the colony knows about your indiscretion."

St. Denis sighed, then decided to surrender the argument. Besides, battle plans had already been initiated. Bienville had ordered Pierre d'Artaguette, a Commandant in Illinois, to gather an army of fifty men and meet him in Chickasaw country for an offensive to take place in the following month of May. He had also contacted the Choctaw, showered them with gifts, and dazzled them with his statesmanship until they finally agreed to furnish him with a third of the braves he desired. Hopefully, with cannons to supplement the combined force and a little luck, maybe they could win a decisive victory over the Chicks.

"Shall I serve tea, now?" Jason asked as he entered the room timidly.

"Merci, Jason," St. Denis answered promptly. "I would love to partake of…"

"Belay the nourishment, Jason." Bienville interrupted. "St. Denis is just leaving."

"I suppose that was my cue," St. Denis said candidly. "If you need me, I will be lodging in the barracks."

"You are not required to participate in this endeavor, Louis. It's better that you return to your post. I need no enemies in my ranks."

"Do not assess me wrongly, Governor. In spite of our differences, I am still a loyal French subject. I will do what is demanded."

The Governor did not reply. Instead, he turned away in silent frustration and withdrew into another part of the house.

"M'sieur," Jason offered, "I must apologize for the governor's behavior. He is not himself these days."

"That won't be necessary, Jason. Still, I have never known him to be quite so difficult."

"And neither have I. These days, he spends most of his time bitching, and the rest, making new enemies. Nothing pleases him anymore, and he trusts no one. I blame it all on age, m'sieur. Nothing more. Age has conquered us all."

"Well, at least, I see he had the forethought to augment you with some assistance."

"If you're referring to the student the governor brought back from France to assist me, well... he is worthless. Nothing but a contemptible, little freeloader who sits around on his ass, reading, and powdering his porcelain face all day."

"Well," St. Denis said with a laugh, "I suppose I shouldn't tarry. Thank you for your concern, Jason."

"And you, for yours, m'sieur. *Bonsoir.*"

"*Bonsoir.*"

———

Two weeks later, a flotilla of rafts, flatboats, broad-horns, and keel boats departed up the river once again. Men on foot, some on horseback, and others driving oxen with carts of supplies followed close behind, weaving along the footpaths and trails bordering the river. The weather was less than desirable for such a task, and for two days the clouds threatened rain. The humid heat was unbearable and the mosquitoes, marsh flies, and mud daubers tantalized and aggravated everyone in the procession.

St Denis, Jalot, and François rode together in their pirogue.

"What's wrong with that old bastard, Commandant?" Jalot asked after having noticed Bienville's curt and discourteous behavior.

"Hell, if I know. Just getting old, I suppose."

"I have never seen him this way before. He's acting worse than a frustrated, old-wench."

"He has problems. Things have changed, and he hasn't yet

found a way to cope with them."

"What he needs is a piece of ass. Good, old-fashioned, woman's ass. Not some young boy's."

"That's an unkind thing to say, Jalot," St. Denis said with a small chuckle.

"Well, you tell me, what other reason could there be? He has never married. I know all the whores in New Orleans, and they say he has never touched even one of them. And an Indian squaw or a black wench would scare the screaming dog-shit out of him."

"He claims to be a dedicated man, living for his country with no time for carnal pleasures."

"You can believe that shit if you want to. Me, I think he's popping his valets."

"I doubt it."

"Well, there is one way we can find out. I say, you invite him to visit Natchitoches, then lock him in the powder house with that black wench of yours, Zolare. She'll find out where his interests lie. And my money says — he'll be kicking down the damn walls to get out."

Everyone laughed at the idea including François. And although he did not fully appreciate Jalot's inference about Zolare, he had to admit that the statement did contain a measure of truth.

"Well, whenever you like," Jalot offered, "just give me the word and I'll see if I can't fit my boot up his fat ass."

Everyone laughed again.

Suddenly, in retrospect, St. Denis stopped laughing and looked at Jalot suspiciously. "Jalot, have you been slipping around my slave quarters?"

"Now, Louis, would I do a thing like that?"

"Where a split-tail is concerned, I have my doubts. But hear me well, Jalot. I'll not have any half-breeds with the looks of you running around my place."

"Who me? Nothing to worry about there. I am well aware of your desires concerning that subject. You'll not catch me tipping through your cornfields in the night. But, I must admit, that one has a mighty tempting body for a black wench."

Two days later, they arrived at the landing on the Mississippi River that led to the ruins of the Natchez village. St. Denis decided to stop and survey the site. In the vicinity of Ft. Rosalie, settlers were slowly rebuilding. The Natchez village site, however, was now void of life, where at one time it was filled with thriving activity. This was François' first opportunity to see the site, and he could only imagine what it was once like. Now, all that remained were the walls of the Great Temple, remnants of a few lodges, and an assortment of wind-scattered debris. The only other visible signs of life were manifested in a flock of blackbirds and crows. While some circled overhead, others nested in the fruit trees as if standing vigil over the decaying remains of the ancient empire. Soon, these signs, too, would be gone, and with them, all evidence that a noble race once occupied this tiny space within the infinite universe.

Seeing the sight reminded François of the Natchez boy, a proud prince, now dead, or at best nothing more than a forest-scavenger. He supposed his feelings for the boy were so profound because of his own circumstances. For he, too, had been uprooted, deprived of his heritage, and forced to survive in unfamiliar surroundings. Now, everything that the Natchez had was gone — like a mark in the sand. And if he wasn't careful, his mark would be gone, too. Acknowledging this, he promised himself that he would do everything within his power to leave his mark upon a rock as Gilbeau had suggested. And those tasks that he could not accomplish during his life, he prayed that his children would have the strength and courage to carry on in his stead.

Everything he wanted to do, however, depended upon whether or not he could gain freedom for himself and his family. But now, since the spark that could have ignited a rebellion on his part had been quenched, his hopes again rested with the generosity of his master. Freedom, of course, was a delicate subject and one not easily discussed. Yet, he knew he would have to discuss the matter with the commandant soon, before he succumbed to old age or some other unfortunate event — like an unnecessary war with the Chickasaws.

About midday of the fifth day, dark clouds gathered in the south and stalked their trail like a hungry pack of wolves. Within two hours, the rain was falling in torrents, and the journey upstream became more laborious. Jalot noticed that the wind had started to kick up miniature white caps.

"Shouldn't we be pulling onto shore until this squall has passed?" Jalot asked St. Denis.

"It wouldn't hurt. It may get worse. Pull up next to the Governor's boat," St. Denis directed.

Once alongside, St. Denis shouted, "Governor, don't you think we should pull onto shore until this squall passes?"

Bienville frowned and looked up into the sky casually. Then, he turned to St. Denis and replied, "No, we are already running late, and I have no time to spare. A little rain won't hurt anyone. Return to your place."

St. Denis was flabbergasted. He stared at the Governor in total disbelief as he allowed his pirogue to drift back into its place within the column. "The fat-headed bastard," he said aloud.

Bienville's cutting remarks had angered Jalot, too. "Look at that old bitch, perched up there like the Queen of Sheba. What I should do is shoot a hole in his bloody boat, then give him a damn dipper — keep his ass busy until we get where we're going."

Minutes later, the wind attained gale proportions, whipping the swells in the river up to four, sometimes five-feet. The wind, rain, and spray effectively reduced the visibility to zero. Lightning struck close by, so close, you could clearly hear and smell the air burning as it knifed through the dark, overcast sky. That was all it took. Pandemonium reigned as the fleet hustled for the shore.

In the process, a wave caught the keelboat carrying the two cannons broadside. It was lifted, then rammed into the corner of a log raft in the convoy. The cannons ripped their mooring, tumbled to the low side, and crashed through the gunnels. The boat with its supply of balls and powder sank immediately.

Once ashore, the men huddled beneath makeshift shelters of thatch and brush. François found a small, shallow cave which he shared with St. Denis and Jalot. They built a fire and rested. A short distance away, they could see Bienville wrapped in his blanket beneath his lean-to, shivering in the rain, his once highly powdered wig hanging limply about his ears like a waterlogged rat.

But, in spite of Bienville's obvious discomfort, they did not invite him to share the warmth of their fire — nor did he ask.

"It's a bitter world, isn't it Governor?" Jalot said to himself as he collected a wad of mucus in his mouth and blew it in the direction of Bienville's shelter.

The rain lasted for three days.

———————

Chapter — Twenty-Three

TEN DAYS LATE, BIENVILLE FINALLY ARRIVED AT THE PLACE he had arranged to rendezvous with d'Artaguette. Commandant d'Artaguette and his army, however, were nowhere to be found. That being the case, and speculating that he was detained, Bienville decided to start the war without him.

When he arrived at the first village, he was delighted to find that d'Artaguette had preceded him. After surveying the damage inflicted by d'Artaguette at the site, he remarked smugly to St. Denis, "This is the way it's done. This is the way a true French Commander puts the fear of God into a bunch of stinking heathens. D'Artaguette knows his art well. If he accomplished all of this with only fifty men, I dare say, we will be departing for home tomorrow. Yes... looks like our work here is done."

François looked at the dead, mutilated bodies of the Indians and became violently sick. His sickness grew worse when he observed the body of a fetus which had been carved from the womb of a pregnant female.

Elated and confident of an easy victory, the gallant militia proceeded to the second village.

The scene that greeted them there, however, was one of absolute horror and disappointment. While it was evident that a fierce battle had been fought, it was also equally evident that brave d'Artaguette had not been successful. There were bodies of Frenchmen everywhere. Several had been mutilated, others burned at the stake. The stench was overwhelming.

Bienville cursed. St. Denis checked his supply of balls and powder. Jalot found a quiet place, sat down, and crossed his legs, while François said a silent prayer.

Without warning, a swarm of arrows suddenly filled the hazel blue sky. Several men fell; the rest took cover, firing blindly into the surrounding forest at an unseen enemy. Then, there was silence....

While the militia regrouped, Bienville sent for his Choctaw scouts and directed them to locate the Chick stronghold. Four hours later, they returned and reported that the Chicks were preparing their defense within the walls of a large fort.

"A fort?" Bienville asked with disbelief etched deeply upon his face. "What kind of a stinking fort?"

"A big, strong fort with many braves," the scout affirmed.

"There are no forts in this country. The lazy bastards don't have enough initiative to build a descent hovel."

"Maybe the English assisted them," St. Denis offered.

"This fort is not English — not French. Chickasaw fort."

"An Indian fort. You must be crazy!"

"This fort is not like your fort," the scout reported. "Different, but big and strong."

Bienville walked away. This information came as a complete shock to him. He never suspected that the Chicks had enough intelligence or industry to undertake such a task. But, since the Natchez normally included fortifications in their strategy, he concluded that the fort must have been the result of Tattooed Serpent's influence. All the more reason why the Natchez renegades had to be brought to justice.

It was becoming quite clear to Bienville that the frontier and its mode for war was changing, and changing rapidly. If this continued, soon he would need the full complement of a regiment to settle even the simplest of disputes. He, however, kept his assessment private, for he had no intentions of admitting his concerns or anything else to anyone, and certainly not to St. Denis.

The next morning, Bienville marched on the Chick's fort. As he approached, he was greeted by the tortured cries of several

French soldiers that filtered through the canopy of the forest, their voices filled with terror and pain. At the edge of the clearing that surrounded the fort, he saw them — three Frenchmen tied to stakes with brush stacked around their feet. One was Commandant d'Artaguette. Knife wounds had been slashed across their chests and lower torsos.

Bienville halted his column and paused to evaluate the situation. He had a problem. A problem of extraordinary concern.

Looming high before him was the most abominable defense structure he had ever seen. It was constructed of upright logs at least thirty-feet high, placed close together. The irregular intervals between them had been filled with mud. Five-feet from the top, heavy, sharp pointed lances had been embedded.

It was clear that the wall had not been constructed by engineers, nor had its builders used the tools of that trade. The wall was not square, but more like a lopsided parallelogram, almost diamond shaped. At each corner, a projection had been constructed which enabled archers to defend its lengths.

There appeared to be three levels. The lower two were fitted with small round portholes for their riflemen. The third and top level was for their archers and lance throwers.

Fifty yards in front of the wall was a trench. This was the Chicks first line of defense. The outer and forward edge of the trench that formed their perimeter was vertical and served as protection for any defenders stationed there. The rear wall of the trench, however, was sloped back towards their fort at a degree that permitted them to easily retreat, and at the same time, prevent their enemies from using it as protection should it be captured.

The dirt excavated from the trench had been packed around the base of the fort in such a manner that the fort appeared to be resting on the top of a high mound. This added additional support for the walls and also made it difficult to set them afire. "*Damn Tattooed Serpent*," Bienville said to himself, "*and me with not one cannon.*"

As he contemplated his battle plan, Bienville was acutely

aware of the fear and uncertainty etched on the faces of his less seasoned troops. To prevent this condition from spreading and affecting the rest of his men, Bienville decided he could not afford to delay any further.

So, amidst the bloodcurdling screams of his countrymen, he launched his attack. At that moment, the Indians stuck torches to the brush around the stakes that supported the three Frenchmen, then scurried back to the safety of their trench.

The combined army of French and Choctaw fought bravely, but their efforts were fruitless. They never made it beyond the Chick's first line of defense. On the ground level, the Chicks were firmly entrenched, while above, others fired their weapons through the strategically placed portholes. The French were sitting ducks, and their losses were heavy. Soon, Bienville was forced to retreat.

That night, beside a campfire, Bienville, St. Denis, and the Choctaw War Chief sat discussing their battle tactics.

"Have you any suggestions?" Bienville asked St. Denis.

"Without cannons, our courses are limited. We could send a party back to New Orleans."

"No. That would take too much time."

"Then, if you're willing to risk the casualties, we could try to fight our way to the wall long enough to plant a charge. That, of course, would reduce the supply for our muskets."

"That may be worth a try. What do you suggest Coutee?"

"I have seen this wall. There are many braves inside. It is foolish to puncture the nest of the hornet when all one has to defend himself with is a stick."

Bienville ignored Coutee's remark and redirected his attention to St. Denis. "Tomorrow, see if you can get close enough to plant the charge."

With renewed determination, Bienville regrouped and prepared to attack again the next morning. But first, he was forced to watch again as the Chicks burned another of their thirteen remaining French captives. That pattern set the pace for each battle. The French would approach, the Indians would burn another one of their captives, and that would signal the start of the day's activities.

Thus incited, the French would charge angrily, only to retreat shortly thereafter with their dead and wounded.

Although he attempted several times over the next four days, St. Denis was never able to reach the wall.

"Damn.... What I would not give for just one cannon — if I had just one cannon, I could turn the tide of this battle," Bienville said at the conclusion of the day's activities.

"The word, *If...*, to my knowledge, Governor, has never won a battle," St. Denis replied half-jokingly and half-sarcastically to Bienville's remark.

"Well, what do you suggest?"

"Our next course seems apparent to me."

"Well, speak up!"

"We do not have a cannon. Without one, we will never be able to breach their walls. Our losses are great. Our food and ammunition are low — need I spell out the obvious."

"Say what's on your mind, Louis."

"To be blunt, Governor, I suggest we pack up what we have left and take our asses back home. We are wasting lives and resources needlessly. Later, if you desire, we can try to negotiate a peaceful settlement to our differences, or regroup and try again."

"I suspected that would be your solution. Louis, you are a disgrace to the country that bore you. You're nothing but a Indian-loving, shit-eating coward."

"In spite of what you think of me, even you must recognize that we have only one logical choice."

"No. I quite disagree. I am not yet ready to turn tail and run. Tomorrow, we will hit them again with everything we've got — with every man we have, including the cooks. I want Tattooed Serpent in the worst way. If we lose this battle, every heathen tribe in the country will be building forts and showing us their ass. Next, they will be building their own cannons. We attack at first light."

The next morning, a weary group of apprehensive citizen soldiers gathered at the edge of the forest and halfheartedly charged the fort. Again, they were defeated. During the melee, St. Denis was seriously wounded, struck in his upper thigh near the hip by a well-thrown lance. Jalot tended him.

"Devils almost got you that time," Jalot said as he wrapped the gaping wound.

"Could have been worse. I saw it coming, but I just couldn't get out the way fast enough."

"We're getting too old for these sort of games, Commandant. In your younger day, I've seen you ballet through a hail of lances without getting one scratch."

"Well, those days are gone. From here on, I guess I'll leave the fighting to the young ones. I'm finished."

"And I say the same, Commandant. To Hell with this thankless shit. The only war I'll be wanting to fight is between the legs of some wench."

In total, Bienville lost over a hundred French soldiers, not counting his wounded. How many Choctaws were lost, he did not know — and did not care.

With his supplies running low, and his troops demoralized and intimidated by the formidable wall, Bienville finally decided to withdraw and return to New Orleans.

The bitter and humiliating defeat did not set well with Bienville. It was his first loss of any significance. As a result, he became paranoid and vented his rage indiscriminately on everyone, especially St. Denis — accusing him of being an Indian lover, a traitor, a Spanish collaborator, and anything else that came to his mind.

"I suspect a lot of the problems I am having today are probably due to the complacency you nurtured in my absence," Bienville said as he packed his accoutrements beneath the lean-to that served as his headquarters.

"My complacency? When was I appointed Governor of this territory? You and your handpicked successors shared that responsibility. Now, you blame me — and call me an Indian lover when it was I who defeated the Natchez?"

"Oh yes, you defeated the Natchez, alright — but only after they kicked you in the balls first. With all your so-called Indian friends, I can't see how they were able to camp on your doorstep without you being aware. The way I view it, harboring criminals borders on high treason."

"Governor, you are truly playing the part of a bastard, and I resent your remarks. I have never harbored a criminal in my life and certainly not a Natchez. I was never aware that they were camped in my jurisdiction, probably because the Indians in my area, as everywhere, sympathized with their plight. They had a legal grievance, and that grievance was conveniently ignored by you and the Government."

"The Natchez are nothing but a stinking pack of dingo-dogs. Why should the Government have protected them? They never once supported the Government. When I asked the Great Sun for assistance in fighting the Spanish, the old bastard told me to fight my own *fucking* war."

"Can you blame him after the treacherous manner you employed to kill over half of his War Chiefs."

"What do you mean, Louis?" Bienville asked defensively.

"You know very well what I mean. No man of honor would ever use a flag of truce and promises of peace to trick an enemy into his camp, then torture him until his ransom is paid with the heads of his war chiefs. I also know that the account in your log spoke nothing of this, but rather of your great ingenuity and superior strategy. Snakes are known to have more integrity."

St. Denis' knowledge of the episode was too much for Bienville's shattered ego. "Get out! Get out... now, God damn you!" he shouted, enraged by the revelation. "Get out and go back to your pepper-shitting, Spanish whore, and the Indian dogs you love so well." Then, he paused for effect and added acidly. "You, my friend, have just dug your own grave, and I will be the one to push your ass into it. Now get out — before I have you thrown out."

These words coming from an old friend hurt St. Denis to the quick, especially the words that implied his wife was a Spanish whore. Quite angry, St. Denis got up stoutly, grabbed his walking stick, and hobbled off toward his shelter.

"Well, what has the old wench got to say now?" Jalot asked as St. Denis hobbled up and threw his stick to the ground.

"The man is insane. A bucket of manure has more brains than our fair Governor. I came that close to wrapping this stick around his flat head."

"Well, I wouldn't let the old bastard worry me, if I were you. Best thing you can do is turn your back and walk away."

"I wish it was as simple as that. But knowing Bienville, he'll never let me just walk away — not in this life, he won't," St. Denis said solemnly as he eased himself down upon his pallet. He was, however, quite concerned. Bienville could be a formidable enemy, and he was sure that he had alienated him past the point of reconciliation. Exactly what that and Bienville's threat meant — only time would tell....

––––––––

For the trip back, extra rafts were constructed for those who had walked or ridden horseback on the way upstream. While they worked, Chickasaw scouts watched openly from a distance but did not attempt to press the attack.

"What do you think they are up to?" Jalot asked St. Denis.

"Nothing, just making sure that we are leaving."

With all their equipment loaded, the French shoved off. As they approached the first bend of the river an alarm sounded. A contingent of Indians sat on horseback in their ceremonial dress observing their departure. From his bonnet and regal posture, St. Denis was able to discern Tattooed Serpent sitting majestically upon a dappled-gray stallion, his silver hair blowing in the wind, and his ceremonial lance raised high in a victor's salute to an old enemy.

Suddenly, a single shot from the lead raft sounded, and instantly, the old Natchez Chief slumped forward. The horse reared, and Tattooed Serpent tumbled heavily to the ground.

"Good shot, Sgt. Terreborne! Good shot!" Bienville shouted jubilantly, while the men cheered. "From all appearances, you got the old bastard right between the eyes. What a shot — you salvaged the day."

The shot was unexpected, and St. Denis, who was riding several rafts behind Bienville, had stood up in shock as the old Chief was felled, ignoring danger as the angered Indians howled and fired back at them until the French flotilla drifted out of range....

When the French had gone, Wakanee leaped from his mount to assist the old Natchez War Chief.

"Save your strength," Tattooed Serpent instructed. "You will need it to fight the French dogs. I know my old foe... he does not give up easily. He will return — next time with his cannons. The hammer of his cannon can master our fort. To prevent this you must strengthen your defenses. Build another trench out beyond the range of his iron cannon. The trench will not stop him — but it will make his way slow and narrow. His cannon will be vulnerable at this time... but, do not attack the cannon. Your arrows cannot harm it. Attack the wagons that carries the cannon's black powder. Without powder, his cannon becomes a burden.

"I regret that I will not be able to assist you. The work will be hard... but, you are young and I see in your eyes the strength and wisdom of a great chief. My days of war are finished... and now, I long only to see the lands of my ancestors.

"For this reason, I command you — do not commit my body to the air, or to the earth, but to the river — so that I may drift pass my homeland and look upon the green fields of my forefathers a last time."

Shortly after, Tattooed Serpent was dead.

Saddened, Wakanee took the old warrior's ceremonial lance and tied it to his arm. Then, with the assistance of another, they cast the body of Tattooed Serpent into the river. The body sank, then slowly floated to the surface further down the stream, the first leg of its long journey to the sea and past the ruins of its birthplace —the village of the Natchez Nation.

On the evening of the fourth day following their departure, Bienville stopped his convoy to allow his men to take care of their personal hygiene and cook a warm meal.

While they were so engaged, he removed his shoes, sat on the side of his raft, and dipped his weary feet into the cool comforting waters of the muddy Mississippi River. In solitude and amidst the evening noises of the river and its creatures, he studied the setting sun that hung low over the horizon and wondered what phenomenon caused it to generate such an array of beautiful colors — purples, reds, blues, yellows, grays, and all hues in between. He had seen a great number of sunsets in his lifetime, but for one reason or another, he had never taken the time to contemplate the majesty of its daily ritual....

"The sun paints a beautiful picture, doesn't it, Governor?" asked a nearby soldier.

"Yes, it does… beautiful," the governor replied.

Suddenly, out of thin air, a silvery, glowing sphere appeared on the northwestern horizon and hovered there, in the sky, for several minutes like a second moon. As the French stared in silence with bewildered eyes, the object's color changed to a shimmery red, then sped off like lightening toward the northeastern horizon where it disappeared.

"What the Hell was that?" a nearby soldier asked Governor Bienville.

"How the Hell would I know?" Bienville replied sarcastically. "You saw it as well as I — some kind of a weird flying object."

"Well, it was no meteor. They do not stop still, mid-air, then race off like a cat with his tail on fire."

While still staring intently up at the night sky, something in the water brushed lightly against Bienville's leg. Without thinking, he kicked the object with his foot. Suddenly, he screamed in pain, jerked a bloody foot out of the water and scurried backward on the raft.

His anguish brought several soldiers to his side, and with some effort, they assisted a delirious and shaken Governor attend the wound to his foot. Then, they searched the water to determine the cause of the Governor's alarm. And there, beside the raft, bobbing gently in the muddy water was the bloated, half-eaten body of Tattooed Serpent, still holding his sacred lance with a smile etched clearly upon his ghoulish face... or, so it seemed.

While the Governor huddled in the center of the raft, one of the soldiers shoved the body back out toward midstream with a long pole. Then, the entourage stood watching as the remains of the last of the Great War Chiefs resumed its journey to destinations unknown.

"*Bastard — heathen bastard*," Bienville murmured to himself several times as night stepped impetuously upon the horizon and sent its intimidating shadows scurrying across the land and across the face of a very tired and weary, old statesman.

———————

Jean-Baptiste Le Moyne de Bienville
(Public domain, Great South by Edward King,1875)

PART IV

Bienville's Revenge

The African House,
(Melrose Plantation, Natchitoches, Louisiana, Herb Metoyer)

Chapter — Twenty-Four

"ILL WINDS HAVE VISITED HERE, LOUIS," Jalot stated with some concern as he, St. Denis, and François proceeded up the Red River toward their beloved post.

"Probably the same winds that capsized our cannon boat," St. Denis added as he noted water marks, five-to-six-feet above river level on the trunks of the trees, and the extensive wind damage in all quadrants. Still hanging heavy in the air was the pungent odor of dying marine life, excrement, and rotting vegetation.

"Well, they say that trouble and sorrow travel together, hand in hand."

"That they do, Jalot. That they do. *Faire force de rames*," St. Denis ordered as they dug in their oars with an increased sense of urgency.

An hour later, they were drifting into the small dock near the post. With some relief, they noted that, although weathered, the fort was still standing.

St. Denis extracted his aching body from the confines of the slender pirogue and stretched his wounded leg as he observed Lieutenant Taillefert, his second in command, and several others rushing out to greet them.

"Welcome, Commandant. Good to have everyone back alive. How went the war?"

"Not in our favor, I'm afraid. We were the fortunate ones. We left a great number dead on the battlefield. Some planted, and some at the mercy of the elements."

"How serious is your wound?" Lieutenant Taillefert asked.

"It could have been worse. Fortunate for me, Jalot is a good surgeon. What happened here?"

"The worst storm we have ever had. A horror," Lieutenant Taillefert reported. "Cook houses, trees, barns, and wagons took to the clouds like flights of wild geese. Rain, and ice, large as your fist, fell like missiles. Within hours, the river rose faster than a man could walk and laid siege to the post for more than seven days. Only those on the high ground escaped its wrath. At last count, over sixty horned beast and seven horses were lost."

"Any lives?" St. Denis asked, fearing the worse.

"Only four. One drowned, the rest from cholera. Your wife and family are well. The Indians faired worse."

"How much damage to my farm?"

"High ground saved your home, but the river claimed most of your fields."

"This may be a lean winter. Take a survey of each household and determine the potential yield of the undamaged fields. It may be necessary to enact restrictions in order to preserve us over the coming winter. If you need my assistance, I will be at home tending my wound."

When St. Denis and François arrived home and stepped upon the gallery, Marie was the first to hear them. She came to the door to investigate, and suddenly screamed, "My God, it's them. M'selle? M'selle? Come quickly. They're back! The Commandant is back!" Without waiting for a reply, she rushed out the door, curtsied to St. Denis with a quick, excited "Welcome home, Commandant," and almost leaped into François' arms.

"François, She answers prayers. The Blessed Virgin listened and brought you safely home. I...," Marie was saying when she suddenly burst into tears.

"Yes, she does," François replied as he consoled his wife, holding her and their unborn child as close to him as possible.

While the two embraced, St. Denis dropped his bag and leaned his walking stick against the wall beside the door. While he was doing so, a slow-moving, very pregnant Emanuelle opened the door and threw open her arms with another squeal of joy.

"Thank Providence, you're home safe and in good health."

"Almost did not make it back this time," St. Denis declared as he embraced his wife.

"What is it, chéri?. What happened?"

"I sidestepped the wrong way and caught a lance in the hip."

"Thank God, you are alive. Come inside. Let's get you off your feet and into a decent bed.... Marie?"

"Let her be," St. Denis interrupted. "She is quite busy now. Zolare can assist me. And how is my new son?" St. Denis asked as he placed his hand gently on Emanuelle's swollen abdomen.

"Kicks like a mule, and keeps me flat on my back." Then to François, she yelled, "And you, François, are you well?"

"Yes, m'selle. I am well."

"I am so relieved. You and Marie take tomorrow as a day of rest. I'll send for you if I need anything."

"Merci, m'selle," François replied as he and Marie slowly walked off toward their cabin.

"François?" St. Denis yelled after them.

"Yes, Commandant."

"If we're lucky, we'll both be celebrating the birth of sons in a few months."

"Yes, m'sieur. We must pray that it happens just that way."

"And Marie," Emanuelle added, "tell Zolare to find the girls and tell them their father is home."

"Yes, m'selle."

Everyone was overjoyed that the Commandant and François had returned from the war safely. The excitement of the moment passed quickly to the young slave children who suddenly became overactive with spontaneous activity. While they raced about noisily playing "Dodge the Bull," their parents milled around the back gallery, waiting anxiously to pay their respects, and welcome their master back home.

Finally, after Zolare had cleaned and dressed his wound, St. Denis limped out onto his rear gallery to the roaring cheers of his well-wishers and the festive sounds of clapping hands. And although Zolare's vigorous scrubbing had aggravated the pain in his hip, he waited patiently until each adult and child had an opportunity to acknowledge his return. When the activities were over, he waved farewell and retired for the evening.

Later that night, in the light of a late rising moon, François tapped lightly on Cecil's window. "Cecil," he called. "Cecil?"

"Who is it?" Cecil asked in a gruff voice.

"François. Come out. I need to talk to you."

A few moments later, Cecil stepped out of his doorway still dressed in his sleeping clothes. "It's good to have you back," Cecil said as he yarned and scratched his head. "Zolare told me you were well, but I never expected to see you this late at night. Is something wrong with Marie?"

"No. She is well. Asleep at the moment."

"Then, what?"

"Dreadful news. The black war chief is dead. He was captured, and the governor had him hung in New Orleans just at the start of the war. There will be no revolution. Cecil, they struck the limbs from his body before they hung him, and he never once cried out or begged for mercy."

Then, François told Cecil the details about how he came to know Mukta, how he thought he had killed him, and his disappointment in discovering the real identity of the fabled war chief.

"This Black War Chief was not the one to lead us to freedom." François stated sadly. "He was once my enemy, still, I am angered and pained by the way he died. Cecil, they kill hogs with more compassion than they do when they kill one of us."

"What you say is true, and I doubt that they will ever change. Why don't you pick up the torch?" Cecil inquired.

"I do not think I am capable. I am not a leader, only a fisherman... and a carpenter."

"It's just as well. Things have changed now, for you and me both. Your wife is expecting. Me, well... I'm too old to partake in a revolution. No chains can be more binding. Still, in spite of what you say about this war chief, I believe he served a purpose. Maybe that will be enough to convince the whites to reconsider and set us free. Who knows?"

"Maybe, but I don't think so."

"Well, worrying our minds won't help. Go home and rest. You must prepare for the arrival of your new child."

———

In August, 1736, three weeks after his return, Emanuelle gave birth to her sixth child, another girl. She named her *Marie des Neiges de St. Denis*, Marie of the Snow, because a light snow had fallen on the night that she was conceived — a snow that had fired her passions beyond customary limits and sparked a delightful night of marathon lovemaking....

St. Denis' wound healed quickly, but it left him with an impaired leg and a noticeable limp. Slowly, he resumed his business. He had lost a great deal of momentum. But again, with renewed determination, he set about in pursuit of his fortune.

In November of the same year, Marie and François had their first child, also a girl. Since she was François' first-born daughter, and in accordance with the customs of his homeland, he named her Dgimby.

St. Denis, who did not care for African names, promptly had her renamed Marie Gertrude. This, of course, did not bother François; he continued to call her Dgimby, anyway. To commemorate her birth, François took his hunting knife and carved her a beautiful set of wooden rosary beads.

About the same time, St. Denis was also informed that his daughter, Marie Rosa was expecting. This news brought him a great measure of joy. He was sixty-one years old, not in the best of health, and had often wondered if he would live long enough to see the birth of his first grandchild. Consequently, such an event prompted him to take time from his busy schedule for a small celebration in her honor.

Most of the prominent families of the area attended the festivities. While the women sat around gossiping and eating from a wide variety of foods, the men drank rum, discussed business, and listened to St. Denis' plans and expectations for the growth of the area. Who could ask for more. His assets were growing. He had good friends with whom he could share a glass of wine, and a brand new grandson — on the way (*he hoped*).

Other than routine administrative inquiries, he had not heard directly from Bienville since the war. He knew through other sources that Bienville, stubborn to the last, had continued to send small raiding parties of Choctaws to harass the Chicks. His efforts, however, only resulted in even greater losses. Consequently, the efficiency of his office was impaired, as was his rapport with his administrators and former supporters.

In March of 1737, St. Denis made another trading visit to the Spanish Post of Los Adaes. He anticipated great things during the coming year. The economy was suddenly booming, most of his charges had now turned to farming, and the air of the community was charged with expectancy. All of which meant that there would be an increase in the volume of business conducted, especially with the Spanish.

So, in anticipation of this expected increase in activity, and after obtaining the concurrence of the Spanish Commandant, St. Denis directed François to build him a cabin suitable to serve both as a storehouse and a place where the two of them could rest during their trading visits. The sight selected was near the Spanish mission in an open field surrounded on three sides by a grove of trees. To assist him in his tasks, St. Denis further arranged for the services of several Tejas Indians.

As François went to work, St. Denis, in the company of five Nachitoches braves, departed on a trading venture further into Texas to obtain horses and other livestock from the Asinai Nation.

Two months later, he returned. With him, he had in tow, nine fine horses, one a black Spanish stallion which he claimed for himself, twelve goats, and five milk cows. He stopped first to visit with the Spanish priest.

"Well, Commandant, I see that your venture was quite successful. The black stallion suits your stature well. Does he have a name?"

"Yes, he does, padre. Meet M'sieur Diablo."

"Diablo? Why would you give such a handsome animal such a detestable name?"

"A name is nothing more than that — just a name, padre. But at the moment, I'm too exhausted to discuss the merits of a horse's title. It's been a long, tiring journey."

"Then, you may get to make ready use of your new cabin. Your black servant has worked diligently. It is almost quite complete."

"Good... and, of course, you know the cabin is available for your use as well as mine. That it benefits us both should keep Commandant Gonzales happy. Has he expressed any misgivings since allowing me to build it?"

"Well... not exactly."

"Well? What did he have to say?"

"I'm not sure exactly how to say this... but, it just wasn't quite what he had in mind."

"Not what he had in mind? What the hell did he expect? I never promised to build him a damn castle — only a small, modest cabin. A storehouse." St. Denis stated, getting just a little testy.

"It is not that, senor. I just think he would have preferred something... well... maybe, a little less flamboyant."

"Less flamboyant? I would have thought just the opposite. François is quite skilled. It puzzles me that Gonzales is not pleased. Exactly what is wrong?"

"For me, nothing. I find it quite adorable. But I suggest you wait and judge for yourself."

Thoroughly puzzled, St. Denis departed immediately for the site, following the trail that led around the thick grove of trees, talking to himself, and still trying to figure out what could have possibly caused Commandant Gonzales to be so concerned about a damn one-room cabin. Suddenly, he stopped dead in his tracks — looking, but unable to believe his bewildered eyes.

Before him stood one of the most peculiar structures he had ever seen in all his life. Awesome. Like something from another world. Shaking his head with his mouth fully agape, he slowly walked toward it as if he was stepping from one dimension of time into another.

The cabin itself was suitable enough. It was fashioned by standing logs upright in the ground with the spaces between them filled with *bousillage*. This was standard practice. What was non-standard — was the enormous thatched roof that dwarfed the little one-room structure, looking to all the world like a mushroom with eves that projected ten-to-twelve-feet beyond the outside walls on all sides.

The Commandant's first reaction of astonishment passed quickly, in one stage, to silent, blinding anger. He did not like it. That was no cabin. Hell, it was a hut, a damned *African* hut.

St. Denis quickened his steps and stormed toward the alien structure, his scarlet breeches whistling in cadence with his long, limping strides. He had every intention of ordering François to rip down the repulsive, aboriginal appendage. But, when he observed his servant standing in front of it, his face beaming with obvious pride, the Commandant did not have the heart to do more than complain.

"M'sieur Commandant, you see? I have built us the most beautiful cabin in all the world. You like it?" François asked, his smile broadening.

"Well... yes, François. But why in the Hell is the confounded roof so damned large? Are we to be crushed beneath?"

"The roof?" François turned and looked up at the roof a bit puzzled. "The roof is for the rain, so the rain will not wash away the mud from the walls," François replied, a little confused that the commandant did not understand such an elementary principle. François continued, "Everybody likes this cabin, especially the Indians. One day more than twenty came to sit in the shade pro-vided here. I had to send them away so that I could finish my work.

The Spanish, they like it, too. Everyday, they come in groups, look at our cabin, then stand beneath the trees talking for long hours."

Since François did not speak Spanish, St. Denis knew he would have had no way of knowing what was being said. But he spoke Spanish quite fluently, and he had a pretty good idea what they were saying about François' abominable creation.

After a moment, he sighed audibly and made a mental note to provide François with more specific instructions in the future — especially about how he wanted his roofs built. For the time being, however, he decided the cabin would serve its purpose, just as long as Bienville never chanced to lay his beady eyes upon it. All he needed now, in addition to his other charges, was to be accused of being an African lover, too.

But as days passed, St. Denis discovered that the extended roof was not such a bad idea after all. It provided a large area for storage in the loft, and no matter what the position of the sun, there was always at least one shady side. When the sun shifted, all one had to do was slide his chair around the corner.

After spending several pleasurable days there with François beneath the shadows of the structure, St. Denis decided that the extended roof design might be useful when he built his next home. He, of course, could have done without the company of the local Indians who arrived promptly each day as the sun reached its zenith to share in the comforts afforded there.

Usually, St. Denis would nap while the Indians smoked their calumets, relaxed, and conversed quietly with one another. As soon as the sun changed its position, the one closest to him would nudge him in the ribs, point at the sun, and ask, "We move now?"

St. Denis would frown, open one eye drowsily, look up at the sun, and nod, "Yes."

Then the group, in concert, would pick up their seats and shift to another side of the cabin. St. Denis would lean back, resume his nap, and leave the Indians to their musings.

Fate sometimes has a way of devastating a person's hopes. Especially, it seems, when that person drinks too full of joy's measure, or takes too great a pride in its offerings. And so it was with St. Denis.

Unexpectedly, fate stepped in again during the month of June, 1737 and dealt him another devastating blow. His daughter, Marie Rosa, and mother of his first grandchild, died during childbirth. She was barely twenty-one years old. Both she and the child were lost.

Three days later, he, Emanuelle, and his daughter's husband, M'sieur la Chaise were forced again to make a solemn trek to the family plot to bury another of their beautiful daughters. Her grave, and that of his first grandchild, was dug beside that of her older sister, Luiza.

No words can explain their sorrow. Long after everyone, including M'sieur la Chaise, had departed, he and Emanuelle sat near the stones weeping, consoling one another, and remembering all of the unforgettable moments that occurred in each of their daughter's short lives.

———————

Gradually, St. Denis was able to lay aside the trauma of his daughter's tragic death and resume his activities. In June, 1738, much to his delight, François and Marie presented to him their second child, a boy, that they named François Kiokera, Jr.

The year of 1740 also brought two more additions to the St. Denis household. Although he had expected another girl, Emanuelle surprised him with a second son in January of that year. He was named *Pierre Antoine Juchereau de St. Denis*. Then, slightly more than a month later, Marie Françoise presented François with his second son, *Jean Baptiste*.

During this same year, St. Denis received an official dispatch from Bienville stating that peace had been negotiated with the Chickasaw and the war was over. St. Denis chuckled to himself, for he knew from his sources that Bienville was still quite frustrated because he had been unable to win a decisive victory over the Chicks. He posted the dispatch for the public to read, but did not arrange for any activities to celebrate the event.

And so, it appeared that St. Denis was again within the good graces of fate. Farmers were working their fields aggressively. Crops of several varieties were growing in abundance, and food was plentiful. He had an excellent pasture out on the Isle with an adequate supply of horses and livestock, and trading with the Spanish was exceptional. As a result, his liquid assets expanded considerably, and he now had enough funds to make some needed improvements to his homestead.

This task, he gave to Emanuelle, granting her full reign to use her own judgment in redecorating their home. Excitedly, she, her maidservant, Marie, and François, loaded their carriage and departed for New Orleans with Jalot as their guide and two armed soldiers for protection.

Emanuelle had never visited New Orleans before. As a result, she was totally unprepared for the sights and sounds that greeted her and filled her with the excitement of a child. It was as if she had died and gone to Heaven.

With Jalot's assistance, they found accommodations in a small boarding house. Then, for several days, she and Marie wandered the crowded, narrow streets filled with quaint shops and street venders, thoroughly awed by the strange smells of exotic foods and herbs, and the unfamiliar dress and accents of people from an assortment of far-off places. At the market place, near the levee, they sampled the foods, drank café, and marveled at the sight of the large ships — some standing idle along the river, others loading or unloading their goods, and still others, gliding silently into and out of the harbor like as many weaver shuttles on a sheet of ice. In the late evenings, they sat on the balcony of the boarding house above the banana trees and scented arbors filled with the aroma of magnolias, gardenias, and honeysuckles, discussing the day's activities, and reviewing and updating their shopping list.

Once she had become accustomed to the city, she spent

the rest of the month shopping and ordering stylish furnishings. Included were a marble console, some fine china, two beautifully woven wool rugs, a gilded table with scrolled legs decorated with leaves and flowers, a broad-back chair dressed in rich velvet, several gilded bronze figurines, a tapestry from the royal factories of les Gobelins, and three beautiful paintings by a noted artist for her drawing room.

For her children, she purchased a couple of books, a slightly used clavecin, dresses, and jeweled combs. For herself, she purchased several delicate pieces of jewelry that happened to catch her eye.

It was while she was shopping for the jewelry that she was befriended by a very handsome young man.

"*Bonjour*, m'selle," the young man said with a small bow.

"*Bonjour*, m'sieur," Emanuelle replied.

"I could not help but notice that you appear to have an eye for beautiful stones. I, too, am fascinated by the finer things of life, especially beautiful jewelry, and beautiful, Spanish women. May I be of some assistance to you with your shopping?"

"I suppose so, m'sieur. And who do I have the pleasure of speaking with?"

"My name is M'sieur Robert Trevor. My father was a jeweler, so I know jewelry very well."

"In that case, of course, I would appreciate your advice. My name is Emanuelle de St Denis. My husband is Commandant at the Natchitoches post."

"I know exactly who you are. Word of your beauty preceded you."

"You are making me blush, m'sieur."

"My words mirror my heart, m'selle."

"Well, although I can rarely afford it, I love jewelry. But, since I do not have the experience or the expertise to determine the quality or appropriate value of an item, I shop only by looking at its color, size and design."

"Well, there is one item here that you should try on. It caught my eye several days ago. I am very surprised that no one has purchased it yet." Saying that, Trevor reached into the jeweler's display cabinet and withdrew a beautiful green emerald stone mounted on a butterfly with gold filigree wings and suspended on a delicate gold chain.

"Now turn around," Trevor ordered.

Emanuelle did as the young man requested, then raised her chin as he placed the necklace around her neck. He then ushered her to a mirror. As Emanuelle inspected her appearance, she watched as Trevor approached from the rear and placed his head close to hers. In the mirror, their eyes met and locked, and his hot breath on the back of her neck caused a shiver to pass quickly down her spine.

"M'selle, I am smitten by your beauty," Trevor stated.

"*Merci*, m'sieur. Thank you for your kind words," Emanuelle said with a small laugh. "They do brighten an old lady's spirits."

"I enjoy seeing you laugh, m'selle. Still, I have expressed to you my true feelings. Your age has no bearing upon my heart."

Emanuelle was a little unsure about what to say under the circumstances. So, she purchased the necklace without saying anything further.

When her transaction was complete, the young man insisted on escorting her with her packages back to her quarters.

At the door, as Emanuelle turned to express her thanks, the young man pulled her into an embrace and quickly kissed her moist mouth passionately. Her knees went weak and she folded into his arms.

"Please, m'sieur," she stated without conviction.

"M'selle, my passion has overwhelmed me. Invite me in and tell me that you desire me as much as I do you."

"Please, m'sieur. I am flattered by your attention, but I am a married woman and cannot respond to your, or my, desires. Forgive me. I must retire."

"No offense, m'selle."

"None acknowledged, m'sieur."

"If it pleases you, I will be happy to assist you in making the arrangements to ship your goods back to your post."

"*Merci*, m'sieur. That would be a great benefit to me."

"Consider it done, m'selle. *Bonsoir.*

"*Bonsoir, m'sieur.*"

When the young man had gone, Emanuelle hurriedly took off her clothing and climbed into bed, her blood boiling and wondering what would have happened had she taken advantage of the opportunity to be ravaged by such a young, virile, and passionate young man. She was almost tempted to call him back, but could not convince herself to betray her husband. Instead, she shoved her hands between her legs and caressed herself until she satisfied her inner cravings. Then, quite exhausted, she fell fast asleep.

True to his word, the young man returned two days later with his servant and assisted in the packing and tallying of her goods for shipment. It was a delightful experience for her to discover that she could still capture the attention of a male's eye. And as they went about their chores, they each used every opportunity affordable to caress or brush up against one another. When their tasks were done, she found herself longing for want of an opportunity to let him kiss her again. That was, however, impossible as long as her servants were near.

The next day, still glowing from the attention of the young man, and quite exhausted from her shopping ordeal, she reluctantly departed for home in the company of two mule teams and wagons loaded to overflowing. She and Jalot traveled with one team, while François and Marie travelled with the other.

Chapter — Twenty-five

WHILE PROSPERITY BOOSTED THE LOCAL ECONOMY, it also boosted many of St. Denis' administrative duties and made it more difficult for him to maintain absolute control of his monopoly.

Normally, St. Denis bought corn from the farmers at one peso a *fanega (about 2 bushels)*, which he, in turn, sold to the Spanish for three pesos. When the Spanish priest suddenly rejected his price on one of his visits, he became more than a little suspicious.

"So, what is wrong with this grain that it is not worth three pesos a fanega, padre? This is fine grain. None better in the territory."

"Senor, it is not the grain. It is the price. Much too expensive for my feeble treasury. Besides, our bins are quite full at the moment and there is no pressing need for any additional grain."

"How have you come by this additional grain? Your meager little fields would hardly feed my goats."

"Oh, we have our resources," the priest said, smiling gently.

"Well, where does this leave me — you sanctimonious, old bastard? We had an agreement. Now that I have gone to the expense of packaging and transporting my goods here, you choose not to honor it. Just what am I supposed to do now? I have a lot of time and money invested here."

"I am sorry for the inconvenience, senor. But since our granary is full, the best I can offer you for your troubles is — one and a half... maybe, two pesos at the absolute most."

"Never — never, you treacherous, little coot! Have you gone mad? Three pesos or nothing! I'd rather dump it in the river and feed the fucking alligators."

"That would be regretful. But then... it is your corn."

"You damn right! It is my corn!" Highly miffed, St. Denis stormed from the mission and reloaded his grain. Then, as an afterthought, to appease his anger, he jumped the fence into the priest's chicken-yard and chased down two of his chickens. Amidst the squawking, flying feathers, and the shrieking of the priest, he held the chickens aloft and yelled, "As recompense for my troubles, you thieving old goat." He then jumped back across the fence, climbed into his cart, and applied the whip to the oxen, cursing like a dry-docked seaman all the way back to Natchitoches.

The priest stood by and watched his departure thoroughly appalled....

As soon as St. Denis reached the fort, he parked his cart at the gate and instructed François to return it to his barn. While François was preparing to do so, the two Derbanne boys happened to pass by. Both rode a single horse. They smiled knowingly and shouted, "*Bonjour*, Commandant. I see you have an abundance of corn this season. Would you like to purchase some more?" They then galloped off, laughing wildly.

For several moments, St. Denis stood watching and fuming with rage. When the boys were out of sight, he threw his jacket to the ground in a fit of anger. "Damned little guttersnipes. Damn those little, ill-conceived urchins. Sergeant... Sergeant!" he screamed as he headed toward the barracks in a huff.

"Sergeant?" St. Denis called again as he kicked open the door to the barracks.

A half-asleep soldier jumped from his bunk and reported, "Yes, Commandant?"

"Get up off your lazy ass and park it along the trail to the Spanish mission. And stay there until you discover who is hauling grain to the Spanish. Keep an eye on the bayous, too. I want the bastards caught, or I will have your stinking balls. You hear me? Do it now. This minute!"

"Yes, Commandant," the soldier replied as he quickly went about packing his gear.

Three nights later, on a Friday, the Sergeant returned with the Derbanne boys in tow. He had caught them red-handed, traveling along the trail at night loaded down with grain which they were planning to sell to the Spanish for two pesos a fanega. With a little more force than necessary, the Sergeant threw them into the guardhouse and proudly reported his success to the Commandant.

The following Monday morning, at the conclusion of a very relaxing weekend, St. Denis arrived early and had the boys brought before him.

"So, it seems that I will have the last laugh after all," St. Denis stated quite smugly. "I should have the constable take you to the square for a public ass-whipping. And I would, too, if not for the respect I have for your deceased father. If he was alive today, I suspect he would do the same. What do you have to say in your defense?"

"We have nothing to offer," the older replied.

"That being the case, I will forego the whipping — just to prove that I am a compassionate man. Your goods, however, will be confiscated and sold, and the proceeds therefrom will be placed in the post treasury."

"But, Commandant, that is all the grain we have. We work hard for our produce, and it isn't fair that you should only pay us one peso a fanega while you sell it to the Spanish for three. We should get at least...."

"Damn it, boy!" St. Denis interupted. "Do not tempt me. Get the Hell out of here and be thankful you're leaving with the skin on your backs."

Sullenly, the two boys left. It was clear, however, that they were quite dissatisfied with the turn of events, and St. Denis suspected that his troubles with the two were just beginning.

A month later, in October, St. Denis laid his former valet and friend to rest. Jalot had spent his latter years drinking and gambling frequently, brawling occasionally, and mounting one wench or another almost daily. It was during the latter activity that he expired.

Because he considered Jalot to be one of the founding fathers of the colony, St. Denis ordered a full military burial for the occasion. He, however, was quite disappointed when so few of the inhabitants turned out for the ceremony. He mentioned this to Emanuelle as they stood beside the gravesite beneath an overcast sky. She suggested that maybe it was because of the weather which was threatening rain. And although it did rain torrents just at the conclusion of the activities, St. Denis was not at all appeased. Besides being a steadfast friend, Jalot had been an invaluable servant to the colony, and he felt that despite the weather, every man, woman, and child should have been there to bid him a befitting farewell.

As Christmas approached, the gaiety of the season heightened with each passing day. Strings of lanterns were hung along the banks of the river. The forest was picked clean of holly, pinecones, and other seasonal decorative items. Vendors in small shops, and along the streets, displayed their wares enticingly and hawked curious citizens.

Within a week of the Holy Day, a special messenger from New Orleans arrived and presented St. Denis with an unexpected and unwanted petition, the impact of which caused his blood to boil and utterly destroyed his festive mood. The administrators of the Company of the Indies were demanding payment for the goods that he had lost on his initial trading adventure into Mexico — an adventure that had taken place more than twenty-five years earlier.

Since he and Bienville had parted ways during the Chickasaw war, he was certain that his old friend, the Governor, had allowed the matter to resurface in a premeditated act of malice.

Convinced that the demand was without foundation, St. Denis decided to pursue the matter in the courts. He requested, and was granted, a hearing which was set for March 5, 1741 in the City of New Orleans.

On the appointed day, St. Denis entered the court somewhat apprehensively. His apprehension grew as he sat watching the Company's lawyers dressed in the latest fashions from the continent, thumbing through their papers and conversing secretly. There were three of them, and now, he regretted not having hired his own. The number of documents in their possession also caused him some concern, for he had none. His documentation had either been lost or misplaced over the years. As a result, his growing apprehension crystallized quickly into something bordering absolute terror.

The court opened with a formal and ominous air. After the docket was read, the Company's lawyers presented their case, stating that St. Denis, acting as an agent of the Company, had accepted, on consignment, goods of a sizable value for trading; that the goods had been given to St. Denis in good faith, trusting that he was an honorable man; that several years had passed and St. Denis had not yet reimbursed the Company or properly accounted for the disposition of the said goods.

In reply, St. Denis argued that he had gone to Mexico on behalf of the colony; that a portion of the goods were lost during an Indian raid that almost cost him his life, and the rest was confiscated by the Spanish; that he spent more than two years of his life in a Spanish prison, for which he was never compensated; and that, instead of him, the Company should have pursued the Spanish for the loss.

The Company lawyers led by one, M'sieur Robert Trevor, argued that the goods had been consigned to St. Denis, not the Spanish; that St. Denis, who was aware of the risks involved, did not make these risks known when he solicited the consignment; and that St. Denis, under those circumstances, was liable for any losses incurred as a result of his poor judgment and failure to protect the interests of the Company.

St. Denis declared that he had not purposely solicited the consignment; that he was approached by an agent of the Company who convinced him to undertake the project, whereupon, he then submitted his formal solicitation; that since he was an emissary of the government, it was his understanding that the government was underwriting the total cost of the expedition.

In rebuttal, M'sieur Trevor produced an affidavit, signed by Bienville, stating that St. Denis was never officially appointed as an emissary; that the consignment project was a private business transaction between St. Denis and the Company; and that St. Denis had pursued the project despite his widely proclaimed objection.

St. Denis retaliated by charging that the Company was part of a conspiracy against him, and the fact that they allowed twenty-five years to elapse before bringing the matter to his attention was proof of this; that this reason alone was sufficient grounds to dismiss the case and release him of any further obligations.

M'sieur Trevor countered that the Company had not pursued the matter because of their compassion for St. Denis' financial inability to satisfy the debt during that time; that St. Denis' status had improved and the Company felt that he was now in a position to honor the debt without an undue hardship upon him and his family. Then, as proof of his position, M'sieur Trevor presented the court with an itemized list of all the articles recently purchased by St. Denis' wife, Emanuelle, and shipped to Natchitoches.

As the court reviewed the list, St. Denis' hopes for absolution vanished quickly, leaving him filled with frustration and anger. After several moments of deliberation, the white-wigged magistrate announced his decision and declared St. Denis liable.

As a final argument, in a desperate effort to reduce the amount of his liability, St. Denis reminded the court that he had been forced to finance the cost of the Natchez war out of his personal assets — all without compensation from either the government or the Company; that the court, in the interest of justice, should reduce any liability held against him by an equal amount.

His eloquent plea fell on deaf ears and St. Denis was held liable for the full amount, much to the pleasure of his old friend Bienville — he was quite sure.

An auditors report, read to the court, disclosed an inventory of twenty-seven mule loads consisting of the following:

1. 50 muskets, 100 pounds of black powder, and 24 sacks of balls.

2. 120 pieces of narrow Brittany linen.

3. 50 pairs of red woolen hose, 24 pairs of blue, of the best quality,

4. 179 bundles of Flemish thread.

5. 60 pieces of green twill.

6. 56 half-bolts of fine laces, the widest from Aberia [sic].

7. 42 pieces of blue twill, and several remnants of 16 1/2 varas.

8. 51 pieces of wide Brittany linen and 17 pieces of Rouen linen.

9. 12 pieces of fine French satin and 18 pieces of light camlet.

10. 24 wigs, half Brittany and half Parisian.

11. Miscellaneous articles, parfums, couleurs, and iron and copper utensils.

The goods were assessed a value of eighteen thousand, three hundred livres and eleven sous, and St. Denis was ordered to pay or have his property auctioned to satisfy the debt.

Without any further options, St. Denis agreed to honor the debt and departed New Orleans a broken man, both spiritually and financially.

———

When St. Denis returned to Natchitoches and disclosed the strange turn of events, Emanuelle unleashed her Spanish temper and ranted loudly about the greed and selfishness of the governor and the rest of his henchmen.

"I hate them. I hate them all. You are the only honorable Frenchman I know. This was all a conspiracy to punish you for marrying me."

"I suppose you are right. But, what puzzles me is how in the world did M'sieur Trevor obtain a list of everything you purchased in New Orleans."

"Trevor?" Emanuelle asked visibly concerned. "Would you be speaking of a young man named Robert Trevor?"

"Yes, I am. He was the lawyer who represented the Company?"

"*Fils de salope*" (son of a bitch). Now I know why the sick bastard was so eager to help me with my shipping arrangements."

"You allowed him to assist you?"

"Yes, I did. He offered, and stupid me, accepted."

"Assisting you was a very convenient way for him to obtain information about my affairs."

"Oh, Louis, I am so sorry I let this happen."

"It wasn't your fault. Bienville and his friends are expert manipulators. They would have found other ways to obtain what they wanted to know."

"Your friend, Bienville, is a dog — a jealous dog who can't stand to see you get ahead. He only kept you around because he needed you. Apparently, he doesn't need you anymore. Louis, you have always exercised more control over the frontier than he, even in the beginning. He knows that. That is why he never recommended you for Governor.

He doesn't want the ministry to discover who has been behind his success. I never trusted that beetle-eating derelict, anyway. But you, you kissed his little, fat ass just like the rest of his slimy, male whores."

"That's not true, Emanuelle. You have never seen me kneel before a man's ass in all your life, and you know it."

"Say you."

"Well, I do say. If you want to accuse me of trusting him... yes, I am guilty of that. And yes, maybe I was naive. But it wasn't always that way. There was a time when we had each other's confidence."

"*Folie de grandeur*. Don't humor yourself. He has always been the same, a snake in the grass. A stinking, man-loving snake at that. You were just too stupid to see it. He used you the same way he uses the stupid Indians — to do his dirty work for a few worthless beads. *N'est ce pas*? Isn't it so?"

"No, that is not so. Besides if you had used some of the foresight that you accuse me of lacking, maybe I wouldn't be in this predicament."

"Just what are you speaking about, Louis?"

"I am talking about M'sieur Robert Trevor, about you playing the grand dame, and how he was able to obtain an itemized list of all your purchases to present to the court. That is what I'm talking about. How a gullible old woman allowed herself to be duped by a treacherous, young scavenger to the detriment of herself and her family. That is what sealed my fate. And you call me stupid?"

"Oh, my God, Louis," Emanuelle said as she broke down in tears. "Forgive me. I never suspected his true intentions. Maybe, we are both equally stupid without the wisdom to deal with those treacherous bastards in New Orleans. I hate them. How I wish that God would hammer down their levee with his fist and drown every son-of-a-bitch in that wicked city."

"Emanuelle," St. Denis said on a lower key, "what's done, is done, and us at each other's throats will not help matters. There is not one thing you or I can do about it at this stage."

"Yes there is, damn-it!" Emanuelle admonished as she fell to her knees before him. "Yes, there is. Pay the debt, chéri. Give him back his damn fort. Then, tell him to kiss your ass. We could move to Mexico and live there in peace with my family and start our lives over."

"At my age? I fear it's much too late for that."

"It is not too late. If the money is that important, then, let's keep our damn money. Don't pay the bastards one sou. Let's sell what we have, escape to Mexico, and live the rest of our lives in leisure. The older children can fend for themselves.

"Louis, you know I love you. I love you more dearly than anything on this earth, and it pains me to see you suffer in this manner. If this continues, you will be dead before spring. I could not bear that. Please, take me home to the land of the painted hills and beautiful sunsets. And away from these hellish mosquitos!"

"Emanuelle, you of all people, should know that I cannot abandon my duties and flee like a thief in the night. That is exactly what Bienville would like to see me do — run, so that he can lay a charge of high treason against me."

"Then, you sit down right now and write the good Governor. Tell the bastard you resign and to take his ragged fort back. We don't want it anymore. Do you hear me, Louis Juchereau de St. Denis? Do it now. Today. Let's be rid of this misery. Please, chéri, for my sake. I have not seen my family for more than twenty years and I long for them. Grant me this one humble request."

St. Denis wrote the letter....

My Dear Friend and Governor,

By now, I am sure you have heard that I was caused to reimburse the Company of the Indies for the goods that were lost during my mission to Mexico, a mission that I undertook as an emissary for my country at the Company's request, and for the benefit of the colony. Even though it has caused a severe hardship on me and my family, I have agreed to honor this unjust debt, even as I have always honored you and my country.

Yet, in spite of my hardships and sacrifices, it seems that my country has chosen to dishonor me. Since there is a loss of faith between my country and me, and between me and my country, I now request that I be relieved of my trusted duties so that I may retire and live the rest of my few days with my wife's family in Mexico. She is desirous of returning there before her age prevents her from undertaking such a strenu-

ous journey.

I will sell my properties and use the proceeds to settle my debts prior to departing. Your utmost attention is required so that I can proceed with a timely transfer. Because of my health, time is essential.

I received a letter from my sister, and your sister-in-law, two months ago. She is still in Canada and doing well. She sends you her warmest regards.

Respectfully,
Louis Juchereau de St. Denis

Almost three months later, while working at his post, St. Denis received a casual reply from Bienville informing him that his request had been forwarded to the Ministry in France for their approval. In the meantime, he was to continue in his capacity as Commandant of Poste de St. Jean Baptiste des Natchitoches until a decision is received.

When St. Denis read the reply, he slumped into his chair and closed his eyes to blot out the anger and frustration that threatened to consume him. There was no need for Bienville to have forwarded his request to France when it was within his authority to release him.

"Damn him," St. Denis said aloud as he struck the top of his desk with the base of his fist.

After he had calmed, he opened his eyes and read the letter again, hoping that he had misread or misinterpreted Bienville's true intention. Nothing had changed. Bienville's intentions were quite clear. The old bastard was trying to provoke him into deserting his post so that he could register charges of treason against him. The fat-headed ass.

Wearily, St. Denis got up, placed the letter in his pocket, and headed for home, wondering how he was going to break the news to Emanuelle. Any way he chose, he knew, would surely break her heart.

Chapter — Twenty-Six

NEWS OF BIENVILLE'S REPLY UPSET THE HOUSEHOLD. For days, Emanuelle stormed around the house displaying her fiery temper and challenging her husband to abandon his post and take flight to Mexico. To escape her condemnations, St. Denis confined himself to his room and closed the door where he remained for several days, ignoring both his wife and his duties at the post.

François, too, was extremely concerned. While he sympathized deeply with his master, he wasn't at all too thrilled about him moving to Mexico. Such an unauthorized flight, while eliminating certain problems for his master, would in all probability generate other problems for himself and his family. Under those circumstances, he could hardly expect the commandant to take him, his wife, and all their children with them. This meant, quite clearly, that his family would have to be divided and parceled out to whomever had the necessary funds in ready cash. For him that would be a fate worse than death.

The future looked truly dismal, and François spent several days brooding over its questionable outcome. Then... a brilliant idea occurred to him. Hurriedly, he found St. Denis and presented to him a proposal.

"Commandant," François said with excitement, "you have a pasture on Isle Brevelle — the land I found for you after the Natchez war. Do you remember? It is the land I said I would farm if I were ever a free man."

"Yes, I remember. But it is worthless. I couldn't sell it for two warm farts on a cold day."

"You must not sell it. You must give it to me. With your permission, I would take this worthless land and work it with my family. I will build a cabin, live there, and farm. I will work hard, clear the land, and sow the seeds. I promise you a bountiful harvest each season. With this worthless land, I will repay your debt to that fat-assed, homo-governor. If..."

"Be careful how you speak of the governor, François," St. Denis warned with a mild scowl.

"No disrespect for the governor, m'sieur. But if I can do this and repay your debt, then you will have no further need to move us to Mexico. We can all stay right here at this place."

"Who said anything about moving "us" to Mexico," St. Denis said quietly amused.

"Well..."

"I think it's a wonderful idea," Emanuelle interrupted. "You and Marie could live and work there as a family, and at the same time, assist the commandant."

"Emanuelle, don't go promoting foolish ideas. François doesn't know one thing about farming."

"Not at this moment, Commandant. But I can learn. Cecil can teach me. Before, I was a great fisherman. Today, I am a great carpenter, yes?"

"Well... yes."

"Then, you see? Tomorrow, I will also be a great farmer. The very best, m'sieur."

St. Denis considered the proposal. What François suggested was not a normal practice. Many things could go wrong. But then again, it could work. Finally, after a long pause, he announced, "I agree. Start next week. Take Cecil and Hebert to assist you. Also, take two oxen and anything else you need to get started."

"Commandant,...."

"Yes, François."

"There is another part to my proposal — a most delicate part."

"Well, let's hear it."

"This debt you have is very large, *beaucoup*. Do you agree?"

"Yes."

"Would you say this debt you have is more larger than all

the money in the world?" François asked, using his hands for emphasis.

"Well... I suppose you could say that."

"Such a large debt will demand that I work both day and night without pause. If I am willing to do this in your behalf, will you consider granting liberty to me and my family when it is done?"

"Liberty?"

"Yes, m'sieur."

Why do you need liberty? You and Marie already have as much liberty as anyone in the territory. Besides, what would we do without you and your skills, or without Marie and her concoctions?"

"You will lose none of these things, Commandant. In gratitude for your generosity, my family and I will continue to provide you the services you require without charge. And if you allow us the privilege to continue to live on your land, we will also give you a generous portion of any profits generated there."

"It doesn't make sense. Why ask for liberty if you're going to continue in the same manner as without it?" St. Denis almost shouted. "No, I cannot, and will not, agree to such a request."

The last remnants of hope quickly disappeared from François' face and gave way to silent frustration. After a moment, he replied solemnly, "I must beg you with all compassion to reconsider my petition. Without liberty, I am like a man who walks apart from his own shadow. You have been a good protector. The best in all this land. But without full liberty, I am still bound to the chains of the slave ship, Marianne. I have a family. What is to become of them if you should die or move to Mexico? I must think of them even as you must think of your own family. I cannot bear the thought of them being taken from me and sold the way you sell your horses and horned beasts.

"You have named me François, the slave. But inside, within a place that you cannot see or touch, I hear the name Kiokera, a free man. I was not born a slave. I do not wish to die a slave, even if I have to exercise the one act that is certain to sever me from this station."

"François, listen and listen well, if you're planning to run. Be aware, I will..."

"Louis," Emanuelle interrupted again. "Shut up, and listen to what François is saying. His proposition has merit. After all this time, you know as well as I, that François and Marie would never dishonor us. Everyone desires liberty, why shouldn't he? He is not planning to run. He is offering to purchase his liberty, and I believe he and Marie should have the opportunity to do so."

After a long pause under the scrutiny of Emanuelle's glaring eyes, St. Denis finally released a sigh of resignation and agreed to François' demand. Liberty would be granted to him and his family once they cleared his debt and the courts released control of his assets.

Just South of the fort, the Red River split into two streams. Thirty miles further south they rejoined. The flat land between the two streams was the area commonly referred to as the Isle. Although not an island in the strictest sense of the word, it was bounded on all sides by water. The left fork which formed the western boundary was called the Red River, and the right fork and eastern boundary was called the Little River.

The Isle was further separated into two halves by a small stream or bayou that ran generally east and west. The upper portion was called *Cote Joyeuse*, and the bottom half (where the Natchez prince, Black Hawk was last seen) was called the lower Isle.

It was in the upper eastern half of the Isle (*Cote Joyeuse*), on a plot of land beside the Little River, that François installed his farm.

First, he built two thatched hovels, one for himself and Marie, and the other for Cecil and Hebert. Next, he built a chicken house and fenced in a small livestock pen for his cow and four goats.

Then, they set about clearing the land.

It was not an easy task, but the work was different this time. This time, there was a purpose. This was going to be *his* farm, *his* land, and most of all, *his* home. For this reason, he gladly endured the swollen joints, aching muscles, and blistered hands that he protected by wrapping them with small pieces of muslin.

At day's end, when the sun had completed its falling arc across the southern skies, he dreamed. He dreamed of success on a grand scale. And in his visions, he saw a grateful master bestowing liberty upon him and his family; saw his modest farm grow into a sprawling empire with fields that stretched from horizon to horizon; and amidst the green of the soft rolling hills, he saw his children and grandchildren living in comfortable splendor, protected, and far removed from the dark shadows of slavery.

Fall came and changed the colors of the landscape. Then, the rains took their turn with winter close behind. Still, François labored — chopping, sawing, burning, and felling trees, and digging and burning out large stumps and meandering roots. The straight and sturdiest logs, he laid aside to be used in the construction of his cabin. He kept some to build fencing, and some for firewood.

In December, Marie left her children with Zolare and moved to the Isle to assist. Shortly after the move, however, she found herself pregnant with her fourth child.

By spring the next year, under Cecil's guidance, François had cleared and prepared ninety arpents, ready for planting.

When the seeds had been sown, François left the fields and started construction on his cabin. Marie, although hampered by her condition, assisted wherever she could, helping Hebert to mix the mud, deer hair, and moss, while Cecil and her husband dug holes and stood the sturdy logs upright. And while the men trimmed and set the saplings for the roof, she busied herself tying thatch into bundles which she then strung together on long slender poles.

Building the cabin was a task of great love for the slave couple, for this was to be the place where they would live and enjoy the fruits of liberty. For this great privilege, they mentally prepared themselves to make whatever sacrifices necessary to insure that their master never regretted the decision he had made on their behalf.

Nature took its course. Soon, the seeds sprouted and the once stark, barren rows that marked the landscape were now sprinkled with fresh colors in a multitude of shimmering greens and yellows. It was a beautiful process, one that François and Marie, both, observed in wonder and with renown respect. It was as if God had gotten up one morning before sunrise and waved His majestic hand over their fields. For when they awoke and looked out of their door, life had sprung from the barren soil like magic.

During this period, François worked the land during the day, removing unwanted weeds, aerating the top soil, and carefully nursing each plant. In the evenings by the dusty light of the setting sun, and at night by the light from clusters of oil soaked cattails, they worked on their cabin, or their *chateau* — as they fondly called their modest abode. And when the cattails dimmed and the night sounds settled into a contented drone, they retired to their hovel and put their weary bodies to rest.

"François," Marie said as she sat up on her pallet and nudged her sleeping husband. "François, wake up."

"Yes, chéri?" François said sleepily.

"Something is outside."

"Outside? Are you certain?"

"Yes, I am certain. The shadow of a man passed across the doorway."

François got up, went to the door, and peered out into the bright, moon-filled night. "I do not see anyone. Maybe, it was Cecil or Hebert."

"No, it wasn't either one of them. I would know. This was someone else's shadow."

"Well, I don't see anyone now."

"Probably gone. Come back to bed."

When François was again settled, Marie said softly, "François, do you believe in spectres?"

"I suppose so. Why do you ask?"

"I think it was a ghost that I saw tonight — for a third time."

"You have seen this thing before?"

"Yes. The first time was one night about three weeks ago when I got up and went outside to urinate. I was squatting just outside the door when I saw someone out in the fields walking slowly along the rows, touching, and looking at the plants. Just as I was about to call out to him, he turned and walked off into thin air. Scared me to death. I dropped my robe in a hurry."

"Why didn't you wake me?"

"Well... after I came back inside, I wasn't all too certain that I had seen anything. Maybe, just my imagination, I said. But then, last night, while you were resting, he came to the door and looked in. He seemed to be staring at your medallion. I sat up. Then, he just vanished right before my eyes. Just like a puff of smoke in the wind. But tonight, I am certain that whatever I saw is real."

"What did this ghost look like?"

"He had the body of a youth, but his face was tortured and aged. And... eyes that were gentle, but sad. The most saddest eyes I have ever seen."

"Did it look like Gilbeau?"

"Gilbeau? No. This was an Indian ghost, but not like the Natchitoches or Tejas. He was different. I have never seen an Indian who looked like this one — one with a loincloth of animal fur. Do you think we have built our farm on sacred ground?"

"Could be. There are many things I do not understand about the dead. Sometimes, when I am out in the fields I, too, get a strange feeling that I am being watched. It could be Gilbeau's ghost. He was strange enough to cause such an apparition."

"In what way?"

"Like this," François growled as he jabbed at Marie playfully. Marie squealed and doubled into a tight ball. "Stop it,

François," she said with a laugh. "You're frightening me."

"Well, go to sleep. It will be morning soon."

Marie, however, was unable to sleep. Her senses were suddenly acutely sharpened, and she was able to discern hundreds of strange sounds that she had never heard before. All of which, now frightened her.

Outside, through the door of their hovel, she watched as low clouds slipped beneath the moon, constantly changing their liquid shapes like an opaque, panoramic kaleidoscope. Changing, then changing again, and again — like ghosts? Goose bumps suddenly covered her arms and shoulders. Quickly, she snuggled closer into the security of François' arms and pulled the covers tightly over her head.

———————

By early August, 1742, their *chateau* was complete in all its splendor. A second structure, foreign to the shores of this continent was now in place boldly displaying its theatrical, thatched, mushroom-roof.

Inside, François had constructed a small fireplace with a hearth to provide warmth for their bodies and to cook their meals. To one side was a small altar that was added at Marie's insistence so that God would have a proper place to dwell. The floor was of dirt which François had soaked with water and packed with the end of a log until it was as hard as stone. There were two windows and two doorways. Later, he would build and install the contrevents and doors.

Along one wall was a small stairway that led up to the second floor. The floor space there was almost as large as that of the lower level. Here, he would build beds for his children so they could rest comfortably, high above the ground and the radiant heat of the scorched earth.

As François and Marie stood back and surveyed their handiwork with pride, Cecil and Hebert approached and stood along side.

"You see this cabin, Marie? You see it, Cecil? Hebert? It is much better than the one I built in Los Adaes. This cabin will stand a long time — forever."

"It is a beautiful cabin, chéri. Truly beautiful," Marie said as she looked up at her husband admiringly.

"You see, Gilbeau," François cupped his mouth and shouted into the wind. "This is my rock. When the mountains fall into the sea, my rock will stand.... Do you hear me, Gilbeau?" he shouted louder, his voice echoing through the pines and rolling hills. "You hear me, old man. This is my rock... *rock.. rock!*"

Overjoyed and forgetting that Marie was pregnant, the four slaves danced, circling round and round, and clapping their hands in rhythm. Then, they did their version of the Indian tick dance, moving in and out, and stomping their feet at the imaginary insect.

Suddenly, Marie groaned in pain and slipped to her knees.

"What is it, Marie," François said as he and Cecil rushed to her side.

"The baby, I think the baby is coming. I guess he didn't like our little tick dance," Marie tried to joke, then grimaced as she endured another sharp pain.

François gathered her in his arms and started towards their temporary hovel.

"No, chéri, not there," Marie pleaded, "...in our *chateau*. Our baby must be born in our new home."

Three hours later, on 24 August 1742, while his wife squatted over a cane-straw mat in the middle of their empty, one-room cabin, François assisted in the delivery of his fourth child, a girl. Because she was his second born daughter, he named her Coincoin in accordance with the custom of his homeland. Then, as an afterthought and to rob St. Denis of the pleasure of renaming her with one of his Christian names, he named her Marie Thérèze "Coincoin".

"François?"

"Yes, chéri."

"Will you also carve a rosary for Coincoin?"

"Yes, I will."

"Then, her rosary must be different from all others. It must be special, for she is a very special young lady."

"I will do that tomorrow, chéri. Right now, I need to move our belongings into our new home."

While Marie rested, François left and went to his hovel where Cecil and Hebert were waiting.

"A boy or girl?" Cecil asked solemnly.

"A girl."

"You are a blessed man."

"Yes, I am. But, so are you, Cecil. We are all blessed."

"That is what everyone says, but I have my doubts," Cecil replied with an air of distress.

"Are you troubled, Cecil?"

"No. Just tired, I suppose."

"I understand. We will rest tomorrow. Meanwhile, will you and Hebert assist me in moving my belongings into my new house. Hebert, you may live here in my old hovel, and Cecil you may keep the one you have."

After the move was completed, and Cecil had retired, François said to Hebert, "What is wrong with Cecil?"

"It's Zolare. Cecil says she will be angry at him once she learns that Marie has another baby."

"Well, let him rest. Starting tomorrow, I will see that Cecil gets to visit his wife more often."

"*Merci.* I am sure he would like that."

"Good night, Hebert. I hope you like your new quarters.

Chapter — **Twenty-Seven**

———

DURING THE LATE EVENING OF THE NEXT DAY AS THE SUN SLPPED FROM ITS PERCH, François went out beyond the fields to a certain ancient oak that grew near the river in search of a branch suitable for carving a rosary. He was in the process of detaching a long, slender branch when something moved in the shadows near the water's edge. He paused. It moved again.

"Halt! Who moves there?" François shouted with a slight tremor in his voice.

There was no reply.

"Who moves there?" François repeated.

There was a noise. François backed away, ready to bolt for his cabin at the first sign of hostility.

After what seemed like an eternity, a crippled creature dressed in a loincloth of animal fur limped from the shadows carrying a heavy bundle across his back. As François watched apprehensively, the being walked to a clearing beside the river, lowered the bundle to the ground, and squatted submissively.

"Who are you? What do you want?" François asked as he approached cautiously.

The creature replied in a language unfamiliar to François and pointed toward the bundle with animated gestures.

Realizing that the being was of no threat, François approached and squatted opposite him and his bundle. "What is it that you want?" he asked again as he surveyed the hapless, beast-like creature whose eyes glowed yellow in the light of the half-moon night.

Without replying, the being bared his jackal-like teeth with a soft snarl and pushed the bundle toward François. As François lifted and inspected the smelly animal hides, the creature pointed toward the silver medallion that hung from his neck.

"My medallion? You want to trade for my medallion?" François asked as he lifted the medallion over his head and handed it to the creature. It was then, while the creature was examining the medallion forlornly with small, wounded animal-like howls, that the thought suddenly occurred to him. *Could this be the Natchez youth?* he asked himself. *Is this the reason for his strange behavior?* For a moment, François forgot the furs and studied the creature's face for signs.

"Black Hawk. Are you Black Hawk, the Natchez?" François asked with expectancy.

At the sound of his name, the creature looked at François and gently nodded, "Yes." Then, he quickly averted his tear-filled eyes.

"I thought you were dead," François shouted as he laughed heartily. "I thought the alligators had swallowed you whole. You're one lucky Indian. Wait until I tell my wife about her ghost." And although François assumed that Black Hawk did not understand a word he said, he rambled on in his excitement for several minutes. When he quieted down, the creature nodded in solemn self-satisfaction, then placed the medallion gently on top of the hides.

"No. It is a fair trade. You keep the medallion. Take it. It belongs to you, anyway," François instructed as he took the me-dallion, placed it in the palm of the creature's gnarled hand, and closed his fingers about it.

For several moments, the creature looked at the medallion in indecision. Then, he set his sad eyes, shook his head negative-ly, and carefully placed the medallion back on top of the bundle. Then in a gentle voice, the creature said in broken French,

"I see you as I see the sun, with great honor. These are my gifts for you and your family. *Merci, mon ami.* Thank you, for letting me live. As you protected me at a great risk, so shall I stand vigil over you and your family."

Without another gesture or sound, the creature stood and limped away, dragging his lame leg behind him.

"Wait, do not go. You are welcomed here! Black Hawk!" François yelled out several times, but an instant later, the Natchez had vanished into the dense undergrowth of the forest.

When he had gone, François counted the pelts. He had seven, all of which were the hides of adult bears. Hurriedly, he gathered the pelts and rushed home to share the news of his encounter with Marie.

"Marie? Marie?" François shouted as he rushed into his cabin and dumped the pelts to the floor.

"Yes, chéri. What is it?"

"You were right. You did see someone. But, it was no ghost that you saw. No ghost."

"Then, what?"

"It was Black Hawk, the Natchez boy."

"The Natchez boy?"

"Yes. The Natchez boy I rescued during the war."

"And what did this Natchez boy want?"

"He brought us a gift — pelts. Seven of them," François declared with unrestrained excitement as he pointed to the bundle he had dumped in the middle of the floor.

"He knew. The spectre knew," Marie stated with a sudden awareness. "He knew!"

"Knew what?"

"The spectre knew that our daughter would be born last night. Don't you see? This gift is his blessing for her. I told you he was not a bad spectre. We must use it in her behalf."

"Marie, what can a baby do with seven, stinking hides. We can make better use of them by purchasing the things we need for the farm."

"The farm will take care of itself. We must sell them and hide the money away for Coincoin. And should our plans for liberty go awry, then at least, maybe we can purchase her liberty when she is of age. Don't you see? The gift is a sign. We must use it in this fashion."

With some reluctance, François agreed, then said solemnly,

"Marie, I need to share a secret with you."

"A secret?"

"Yes. This Natchez, Black Hawk, is the Commandant's illegitimate child with a Natchez Princess. You must never mention this to anyone, not even Zolare, and certainly not to m'selle."

"This is surprising, but I understand."

"Remember, no one must know."

"Your secret is now mine, chéri."

When Marie was again resting, François stepped out the door, took a seat, and proceeded to carefully carve a very special rosary for his newborn daughter. Mosquitos plagued him, but tonight he did not mind. It had been a good day. He had a beautiful, new daughter, and by the Grace of God, Black Hawk, the last in a long line of Great Suns, was alive and well. Yes, it had been a good day.

He looked out over his dusty but thriving fields and wondered how much his harvest was going to help the Commandant. The very thought of him and Emanuelle moving was still a matter of grave concern, and he knew he had to succeed. Anything less, and his worst fears would be realized.

But for now, all was well. So, he leaned back in self-satisfaction and watched the fireflies darting and flickering in the night, their effect like an un-choreographed dance of wild northern lights. He sat quietly enjoying their cavorting until he heard his newborn daughter cry. He then went inside to help his wife attend to her. He had a feeling — an uncommon feeling that Coincoin was a good omen. All the signs said it was so.

The harvest had begun. Cecil had left earlier for the fort with their first load of produce. He was to remain in Natchitoches for a two-day visit with his wife before returning. Meanwhile, François and Hebert continued to work the fields.

"I hear voices," Hebert said as he rested his hoe and listened intently.

François paused and listened. He heard the voices, too — coming closer. Putting aside their tools, they walked across the field to the bank of the small river that adjoined the farm and watched as two white men in an Indian birch-bark canoe paddled lazily towards them.

"Who are they?" Hebert asked.

"I don't know. Sounds like they are speaking *Anglais*."

"Can you speak English, François?"

"*Non*," François said as the boat landed on the bank in front of them.

"*Bonjour, Messieurs*," François and Hebert said in concert.

"*Bonjour*," the tall-one replied as he and the short-one walked up the bank carrying their muskets.

"*Parlez vous Anglais?*" the short-one asked.

"*Non.*"

"You speak a little French Simp, ask him where the best trapping grounds be," the short-one said to the tall-one.

The tall-one, in turn, asked François the question in broken, but understandable French.

"I am not knowledgeable about such things, m'sieur. I am a farmer. But, most trappers hunt much farther north."

"Where is your master, maybe he can be of some assistance," the tall-one asked as he spat tobacco juice over his shoulder.

"My master is at Fort Jean Baptiste, about twelve miles north, up the river. This is my farm," François said proudly.

"What he say, Simp?"

"He say his master ain't here. That this is his farm."

"He ain't lying, Simp. Look over yonder. Don't that look like an African house?"

"Well, damn me soul. Now ain't we done seen all. That's a black hut, alright. Ain't no white man what would be caught dead in a cabin like that one. I say all the time and I say it again, the French ain't got sense God gave a hoot owl. What one in his right mind would be letting a slave have his own farm and all like a free white."

"Yeah, they not quite right in the head no matter what end you looking at."

"Heh, Charley. Is that a cook's fire I smell in the air?"

"Smells like it, Simp."

"Maybe, if we ask kindly, we might get ourselves an invite to dinner. You ain't scared to eat black folk's cooking are ye, Charley?"

"Anything is better than this salt pork."

"M'sieur," Simp said to François, "I know you're not expecting any guest, but me and my friend have been in the wilds more'n four months. We'd consider it mighty friendly if you shared your cooking with us."

"*Tout a vous* (at your service). We do not have much, but what we have, you are welcome to share."

"*Merci*, amigo," Simpson said as he started walking toward the hut. The rest followed.

As they approached the cabin, François called out to his wife. A moment later, Marie stepped timidly out of the door to greet the strangers. She had not been prepared for visitors and wore an old cotton dress given to her by Emanuelle. Because of her recent pregnancy, her breasts were extraordinarily full and much too large for the uncomfortable confines of her tight bodice. As a result, she could not secure the top clasps and her full breasts were somewhat exposed. She covered them modestly with her hands.

"Hey, Simp, you see the teats on that black sow?" Charley whispered wild-eyed.

"Yea, and that's one pleasing ass what she got, too."

"You ain't just smoking. I think I'll be having me a taste of that, afore we leave."

"Maybe, we ought t'just eat. These French blacks is different from the ones back east—spunky, and that one might not like you fooling around with his woman. Besides, we don't need trouble with no Frenchmen around here, condition being what they is between us and them."

"That don't worry me none, not with the hurting I got in me balls."

"Best you forget it, Charley. I don't want no iron in my gut on account of ye stinking balls."

"*Ma femme, Marie*," François interrupted and introduced his wife. "Marie, these two travelers will be eating with us."

Marie nodded courteously, then motioned the men inside to sit at their small handcrafted table. The men, in turn, nodded their thanks and took their seats on two of the four small, backless stools.

While Marie busied herself, François watched proudly as the tall one completed a visual inspection of his home.

"Nice cabin you got here," the tall one stated. "What is your name again?"

"Kiokera, but my master prefers to call me François."

"Well, François," Simpson said with emphasis, ignoring the reference to the African name, "I like your house, and that's from me heart."

"*Merci.*"

At that moment, Simpson glanced at Charley and was immediately disturbed. Charley had said nothing since entering, he was too engrossed watching the black woman, his attention focused on her breasts, as if waiting to see if one or both of them would fall out as she went about her tasks. A moment later, the woman leaned over the hearth and inadvertently displayed her ample buttocks, causing Charley to groan audibly.

"What are you grunting about, Charley? You say something?" Simpson asked, a little annoyed.

"Didn't say nothing, Simp. Just coughing me cough," Charley replied, then coughed twice for effect.

Marie served a modest meal consisting of wild duck, corn, lentils, and fig preserves. Then, she took her place at the small square table with François to her right, Charley to her left, and Simpson on the opposite side.

"So, this is your farm?" Simpson said to François, trying to force a small conversation.

"*Oui.*"

"I'm surprised a man would let his slave live so far away without watching. Must be one fool, all I can say."

"I do not understand?"

"Excuse me. I just meant that you have a very understanding master."

"Yes, I agree. He is the best master in the territory. Maybe, you have heard of him, Commandant Louis de St. Denis."

Simpson coughed at the disclosure and looked around quickly, hoping Charley had heard so that he would not start any trouble. Charley, however, was still engaged.

"You have heard of him?" François inquired again.

"Well... yes, in a manner of speaking — from the Indians. They say he is a great warrior."

"One of the best, m'sieur. I have fought with him several times. He is one who knows no fear."

Simpson nodded in agreement as he focused one nervous eye on Charley. He had known Charley for more than ten years, and he could tell from the twinkle in Charley's eyes that he was going to get them both thrown out on their rears, the same way he had gotten them thrown out every tavern they had ever dared to frequent. What bothered him most about Charley was his unreal lust for black women. Black women fascinated him in ways no one could describe. *The darker, the better* — is what Charley always said. If white women ever discovered the depths of Charley's lust for black, heathen bitches, they would take him with all expediency to the nearest tree and let him fly by his balls.

He glanced at the woman and had to admit that she was comely. He was about to compliment her on the meal, when suddenly the woman got up, scowled at Charley, then went to the hearth where she pretended to tend the fire. Instinctively, he knew that Charley had done something offensive. With some alarm, he nudged Charley under the table with his knee as a warning, but Charley chose to ignore him.

When the woman returned, Simpson smiled in an effort to put her at ease and stated, "M'selle, you must be the best cook in the territory. This meal, although modest, is fit for a king. I..." Suddenly, there was a tremor. He felt it just before a wild round-house slap resounded and sent Charley sprawling off the back of his stool to the floor where he sat trying to focus his eyes on the furious woman who stood over him with a threatening glare.

Everything happened so fast, that both François and Simpson were caught off guard. It took only a moment, how-ever, for them to analyze what was going on. Simpson looked at François, and François looked at Simpson, both undecided about what to do next.

But when Charley leaped to his feet angrily and started stoutly towards Marie shouting, "You black bitch, I'll break ev-ery bone in your stinking body." That broke the spell.

Quickly, François jumped up, caught Charley by the arm, pulled him back, and planted a right cross to his cheek. Charley reeled, stumbled into the pile of firewood, and went down again. Hebert, who had been sitting on the woodpile, abandoned his post and leaped through the window, his eyes big as two Spanish doubloons. Simpson dashed for one of the weapons standing near the door. Just as he was reaching for it, a short chop to the back of his skull caused his knees to buckle. He stumbled back into the cradle, almost overturning it, and started the baby to crying.

Charley got up and attempted to re-enter the fracas, but instead, found himself dodging the life-threatening blows of a stout piece of firewood that Marie was swinging like a battle axe, making sure that she stayed between Charley and the baby who was still screaming.

While Charley was cursing and ducking, François took up one of the muskets and leveled it at the two Englishmen. Immediately, they both froze, then slowly backed towards the door.

Charley's arm was severely bruised, and he was angry.

Simpson only wanted to get out alive.

"What you gon' do with that musket, m'sieur?" Simpson asked with concern. "You wouldn't be shootin' two lone travelers for nothin' — now would you? Charley was only jesting. He didn't mean you and your lady there no harm."

For several seconds François glared at the two indecisively, his body shaking with anger. "Scum," he finally said through the edges of his teeth.

"You black sonofabitch. You don't be talking to me like that."

"Shut up, Charley!" Simpson instructed.

"To Hell with you. No black wench can slap me in the face and old Charley don't be doing nothing about it."

"Bridle your damn tongue, Charley. Can't you see him with a musket?"

Charley shut up, but he was still fuming.

François saw the hate in Charley's narrowed eyes, the same hate he had seen in the eyes of Captain Fortierre and the rest of his slimy crew, the same hate that stripped black men of their souls and raped black babies while still in their mother's womb. The same hate that prodded black men to the hanging trees and struck the limbs from their abused bodies. *The same. All the same*, he said to himself as he leveled the gun at Charley's head and drew back the flint hammer. Charley went bug-eyed and backed away.

"No, François. No!" Marie pleaded. "Please, don't do it. They are not worth the agony."

"Get off my property," François said, still shaking in rage. "The stench of your leathers is fouling the odor of my home."

"I'm sorry about the misunderstanding, m'sieur. We'll be leaving on our way," Simpson stated as he grabbed Charley by the arm and led the way back to their canoe. Marie picked up her baby and followed several paces behind.

"Before you depart, swine, I think it best you both enjoy a good bath — compliments of me and my wife."

"What the Hell he saying, Simpson?"

"He wants to see us take a bath."

"What? Are you crazy, you black bastard? That water is freezing. Shoot if you will. I'll not be obliging ye."

"Into the river or you both will be leaving minus your balls," François instructed as he lowered the musket and aimed it at Charley's groin.

"Into the river Charley and cut out your tongue," Simpson reprimanded as he led the way towards the cold water.

"Messieurs, any fool knows you can not take a proper bath with your clothes on. Please remove them."

"What's he saying now, Simp? What the Hell he saying now?"

"Just shut your mouth and take off your clothes."

"Goddamnmit, Simp," Charley stomped at the ground and bristled at François.

François lifted the musket and pointed it at Charley's groin again.

Grudgingly, Charley slowly dropped his pants. Whereupon, Marie doubled over in laughter, pointing in mockery at his shrunken penis. Charley looked down self-consciously, then sprinted for the river.

As they stood waist deep in the water shivering, François emptied one of the muskets and tossed it to them. Simpson caught it.

"Messieurs, be thankful that I have spared your lives. You have been very fortunate this day, especially since you're so far from home. Now, get into your canoe and get off my land. If I ever set eyes upon you again, I will bury you in my fields."

Charley acted like he wanted to challenge François again, but Simpson hurriedly grabbed their clothes and shoved him toward their canoe.

As the two paddled away, Marie came and embraced her husband proudly.

"Are you well, chéri?" François asked.

"Yes."

"What happened?"

"That old horned-goat was taking liberties with my leg."

"I thought so. Damned Anglais dogs. The scourge of the earth, they are."

"Think they will come back?"

"I think not, chéri. You hit too hard. I must be careful in the future. I did not know I had such a little wildcat on my hands."

Marie laughed. "I'd just as soon not see the likes of those two again."

"I think they are gone— *passe, ventre ... terre.*"

"I wonder what happened to Hebert?"

"Probably still running."

"Well, let's go home. The fields can wait. I think we've had enough excitement for one day."

They both laughed heartily as they turned for home.

————————

"Simp, we can't be letting them black devils get away with what they don' done," Charley said after they had managed to put on their clothing without upsetting their tiny canoe.

"Shut up. I told you not to start trouble, we being on foreign soil and all. I should shoot you myself. Them folks is the property of that fellah, St. Denis, Commandant of the whole French militia and half the Indian tribes in this area, and you out here trying to start a war. I tell you, Charley, this is the last time for me in the wilds with the likes of you. Next time, you find you somebody else to partner with — somebody who don't mind getting their ass shot full of iron."

"I don't give a damn, Simp. I don't need you, either. But right now, we got us another problem. What are we going to do about my musket? We need that musket. What can we do without it? I say we go back and get what's our own. We could get it and be in Chickasaw country before word got to that St. Denis fellah or anyone else."

"Well, what you suggest — we just walk up and ask him politely to hand it over."

"Hell, no. We don't ask him for shit. He's got to be killed —
and her too, once I get my fill."

"Kill them both?"

"The boy, too. We can't be leaving no witnesses, can we?"

A little hesitant, Simpson had to admit that the musket was
an invaluable asset. Travelling without it presented certain risks.
Finally, he agreed and instructed Charley to steer the canoe to
the side where they debarked and walked overland back to the
edge of the forest near François' cabin.

"This looks like a good spot," Charley said quietly when
they reached the edge of the tree line. "You want to do it, or
me?"

"No. You the best shot," Simpson stated. "Just don't miss."

"Don't worry. I don't miss nuthin' at this range," Charley
said as he found a good spot and stretched out prone upon the
ground. "Come on outta there you black bastard and have a taste
of me English balls.... Simp, you know what I'm gon' do?"

"What, Charley?"

"I'm going to put me pole right up her rear. That's what I'm
gon' do. Put it right up her ass. Next time, she won't be so quick
to laugh when she sees a white man what's naked and all."

"Let's just get the musket, Charley."

For several hours, they waited patiently in the bush, one
or the other dozing and both fanning away insects continuously. The sun had sunk low on the horizon and its long shadows
had started to meander slowly across the barren cornfield when
François finally stepped out the door of his cabin.

"There he is! Right there, coming out the door," Simpson
whispered urgently.

"I see him. I see him," Charley said, leveling his musket and taking a measured aim. "He's all mine... the black
son-of-a-bitch."

Suddenly, a dark-toned, whistling noise startled them both.
A split second later, there was a deadening thump, and Charley

keeled over with a cane arrow buried deep in his back.

Simpson yelped, leaped to his feet, and turned to run just as another arrow flashed through the foliage and drove its barbed end completely through his neck. Simpson stumbled and pitched headlong into a tree. He was dead before his body came to rest upon the bed of dried leaves that blanketed the moist floor of the forest.

————

Chapter — Twenty-Eight

WITH THE FINAL HARVEST OVER, FRANÇOIS WAS FILLED with a deep sense of satisfaction and pride as he headed back to his farm alone in an empty wagon. Cecil had been instructed to remain at Sombrilla to assist the commandant. He had accomplished a lot during the past year. Yet, despite this, he also knew that he was a long way from securing his dreams. All he had to do was look at his master's face, see the deeply etched lines of worry, and know that the future of him and his family was still a matter of uncertainty and grave concern. How he wished it wasn't so.

The only time during the past year that he had observed the commandant even attempt to smile was today when he and Cecil brought in their last load of corn, beans, and tubers. It was a small smile and would have gone unnoticed by anyone other than himself — a smile so small that it never reached his master's dried, cracked lips. It appeared suddenly and quickly, and lodged weakly in the corners of his tired eyes. It left the moment he said, "Thank you, François. Thank you for all your tireless efforts." However brief, it was still a smile — one large enough to fill him with overflowing pride.

In November, 1742, Emanuelle sent a message instructing Marie to return to Sombrilla; that she was not feeling well and was in need of her medicine. Somewhat unwilling, Marie packed a few personal items and did as she was told.

Marie's return to Casa de Sombrilla with her new baby created a great deal of excitement. Everyone, it seemed, was happy to see her, especially Zolare who rushed out to assist her as soon as Hebert brought the cart to a halt.

"*Bonjour, chéri,*" Zolare said with a squeal. "*Bienvenue* (welcome)!"

"*Merci,* Zolare. And how are my children?"

"They are well and growing like weeds. And what is this we have in our arms? Is it a baby or a melon for m'selle?"

"A baby girl, I'm afraid."

"Well, I do declare. Won't m'selle be delighted. How is François?"

"A little worn, but in good health."

Well, give me your sack and let's go inside. I have a thousand questions, all that require detailed and unhurried answers."

Emanuelle met them at the door, smiling warmly, and reaching out to take the baby from Marie's arms. While Zolare went about attending her chores, her mistress's children, Douleurs, Marie des Nieges, and little Juchereau, joined them, giggling and jostling, each trying to get a peek at the new baby.

"Oh, Marie," Emanuelle said, "she is adorable. She looks just the same as you when you were born. Same big, bright, eyes and tiny mouth. What is her name?"

"Coincoin, m'selle. Marie Thérèse Coincoin."

"Coincoin? That's unusual. What does it mean?"

"It means, my second born daughter. Dgimby is my first."

"How absolutely clever."

"Let me see, maman," Emanuelle's seven-year-old daughter, Marie des Nieges, insisted as she tugged at her mother's skirts.

"In a moment, chéri," Emanuelle replied as she walked across the room to her settee and sat down heavily. "I am truly glad to have you back. I did hate to send for you, but I am all drained. Don't know from one day to the next if I will live to see the morning sun. Besides, I worry about you and François so far out in the wilderness alone. I don't know what I would do if something happened to you and robbed me of your concoctions. Why just a few weeks ago, some travelers found two Englishmen floating in a canoe with both of their heads missing. My..." Emanuelle stopped mid-sentence as she noticed the uncommon expression that suddenly appeared on Marie's face. "What is it Marie?. Are you well?"

"Yes, forgive me, m'selle. I am fine. I am just glad I was not around to see such a spectacle."

"Seems that you were on the verge of fainting for a moment. Well, as I was saying, my husband said it was the worst job of butchering he has ever seen. They brought the bodies here, and Louis had them buried. He strongly suspects that a few renegade Natchez are responsible. You know, they never did catch them all. I..."

"Maman.... Maman?" little Marie des Neiges pleaded to get her mother's attention. "I want to hold the baby."

"Alright, chéri. Sit here beside me if you want to hold the baby."

Quickly, the little girl scampered upon the settee and stretched out her arms.

"Now, be careful," Emanuelle instructed as she placed the baby in the child's arms. "Remember, she is just a wee, tiny baby and very fragile.... Marie, your farm has been a blessing indeed. With your contribution, Louis expects to have his debts paid off in five or six years at the most by his own calculations."

"That news will make François a very happy man, m'selle. He works day and night for that very purpose."

"Well, you can tell him for me, he has exceeded all expectations. You must be tired from your journey... Zolare," she yelled over her shoulder. "Come and assist Marie to her cabin."

"Yes, m'selle," Zolare said as she sauntered into the room and attempted to take the baby from the seven-year-old.

"No! This is my baby."

"M'selle...?"

"Give the baby to Zolare, chéri. The baby must rest now."

"No, maman," the young girl shouted as she began to cry. "I want it. You said I could have the next baby the alligator brought in from the swamps."

"Now, don't be difficult. You're too young to have a baby now. When you grow up, you can have as many as you like. Now, give the baby to Zolare."

"No. I don't want some other baby. I want this one."

"M'selle," Marie interrupted, "it would please me if you consented. I think they will make a good pair."

"Well, that suits me fine. I agree. They will make a good pair." Then, to the child, she said, "Marie has agreed to let you have her baby, your own little maidservant, but only under these conditions. Until baby Coincoin is old enough, you must assist Marie with her care; that means taking care of her toilette and helping to feed her when she gets hungry. You treat her kindly, and she will be a devoted servant to you. Do you understand?"

"Yes, maman."

"Now, let Zolare take your baby to Marie's cabin for you. You go along and assist."

With twinkling, moist eyes, the young girl nodded in agreement and relinquished the baby, not certain that she understood the full scope of her duties, but eager nevertheless — never realizing that her decision that day marked the beginning of a bond between the two that would endure a lifetime.

"Marie," Zolare said as they walked toward the cabins with little Marie following close behind, "you are truly a fortunate woman."

"In what way?"

"Well, you know..." Zolare paused as she adjusted the baby in her arms, "I mean having your own farm and a good, strong, healthy man to attend your needs."

"In that respect, I guess you're right. François is a good provider. But the farm, well... it's almost more than I bargained for. Managing a farm is much more difficult than cleaning up after m'selle and her children."

"Oh, I'm not talking about things like work or providing. I'm talking about more pleasurable things. Things like making love. It must be nice to be able to stop and do it anytime you have a mind to without having to worry about who's watching or being afraid m'selle will call just about time you're ready to crack your eggs."

"No, I don't have that problem," Marie said with a chuckle, "but there are other things that interfere just as much. Most of the time, we're too busy to even think about making love and too tired once day is done."

"Well, that's your fault. I say, first things first. And François would have to brush my cat, first thing, before I'd let him set one foot out the door — each and every blessed day."

"Zolare, you're crazy as a loon. Don't you ever think about anything else besides sex?"

"Absolutely not. What else in this world provides the same degree of pleasure. Just talking about it gets me all wet."

"Oh, my. Sounds like Cecil is going to be in for an arduous night." Marie chuckled again.

"Don't even mention that old goat's name. Sometimes, I feel like stealing the Commandant's musket and running him off to Point Coupee or somewhere."

"What has Cecil done now?"

"Nothing, the old buffoon. Completely worthless as a lover since he returned from your farm. What did you and François do to him out there?"

"Nothing, except maybe... we worked him too hard."

"I doubt that. Cecil has never been one to overwork himself for anybody."

"No, it's his knowledge that is of value."

"Well, at the rate I'm going, I may never have a child. And here you are with four already. Half the time, his rising part won't rise. And the other half, he's either too tired or sleepy. It gets worse by the day. I swear, I'm being driven mad. Just thank the Heavens that you don't have the problems I have."

"Well, as soon as I'm settled, I'll prepare you an elixir. Give it to him and see if it helps."

"Heaven will bless you if it does. But do me one favor."

"I will, if I can. What do you want?"

Zolare leaned close to Marie's ear and whispered, "Make it with double portions."

Marie laughed heartily.

They had arrived at Marie's cabin, so their conversation ended as Marie dropped her bags at the door to embrace her three other children.

Now that Marie des Neiges had a real baby to care for, she quickly cast her playing dolls aside and devoted her full attention to the care of baby Coincoin. She hovered over the baby constantly. Sometimes, when Marie Françoise was busy with her chores, she would lay out a pallet on the floor for them, and there, Marie des Neiges would spend hours on end playing with Coincoin or singing the one French lullaby that she knew from memory. On one occasion, before Marie Françoise realized what the child was doing, she found her trying to nurse the baby with her own immature breasts. That the child loved the baby was quite evident, and whenever she referred to Coincoin, it was always as her *"noir enfant chéri."*

In early spring, 1743, Marie left baby Coincoin in the care of Zolare *(and Marie des Neiges)*, gathered her two oldest children and Cecil, and returned to the farm to assist her husband, François, with the planting. By late spring their fields were again in bloom with what promised to be another record crop.

While St. Denis was more than pleased with François' success, he was too occupied with other problems to fully express his appreciation. France had declared war against England, and although the colony was not directly affected at the moment, St. Denis still had to divert many of his valuable hours toward the preparation and organization of the local militia. This meant taking a census, inventorying supplies, answering verbal and written queries, and ferreting out all the young men of fighting age. It also meant a constant stream of drafts and reports between his post and New Orleans, and a thousand other items necessary in the administration of his post.

Throughout this period, direct communications between St. Denis and Bienville were held to an absolute minimum, and even then, only under circumstances where it could not be avoided.

In May, 1743, after a two week trading visit with the Spanish, St. Denis returned home. As soon as he saw Emanuelle's face he knew that something was amiss. She, however, did not reveal what was troubling her until they were seated at the dining table waiting for Zolare to serve their evening meal.

"Have you heard the news?" Emanuelle asked solemnly.

"What news?"

"That your friend, Bienville, has decided to retire again."

"I was unaware."

"Well, that's the latest."

"How did you come by this news?"

"The priest returned from New Orleans while you were away. He informed me two days ago. Of course, you must write him and inquire about your own request to retire. Surely, he will answer you favorably now. If you wait until he is gone, it may be necessary to submit a new appeal to whoever replaces him. That could mean another unnecessary delay."

"I suppose you are right. I have nothing more to lose at this point."

St. Denis penned the letter that very night and dispatched it the next morning. He waited patiently, but after three weeks had passed, his hopes for a speedy reply began to fade.

Then, in June, 1743, he received a dispatch which stated that Pierre Rigaud Marquis de Vaudreuil had been installed as the new governor of Louisiana. Shortly after, in mid-August of the same year, St. Denis learned from a visiting boatman from New Orleans that Bienville had packed his valises and sailed for France — leaving like a thief in the night without one word regarding his request to retire. This news devastated St. Denis. The point of a sharp sword driven through his heart could not have been more damaging than was Bienville's contempt and total disregard for his welfare. Angry and quite frustrated, St. Denis closed the doors of his office and remained there in seclusion for the rest of the day and a greater part of the night.

It was late when he finally decided to go home. Emanuelle was waiting for him when he stepped wearily across the threshold.

"Emanuelle... I,"

"I already know. The news preceded you. He has gone."

"Yes. Left a week ago on the frigate, South Winds."

"Then, he has won. Your dear friend has sealed our fate in stone."

"Emanuelle..."

"Well, it doesn't matter," Emanuelle said with an air of resignation. "You're too old and I am too tired to undertake the long journey to Mexico, anyway. So, let it be. We'll survive. Come to bed. You need your rest."

The fact that St. Denis had lost favor with the authorities in New Orleans soon became general knowledge and within a month after Bienville's departure, St. Denis detected a growing uneasiness among his constituents. It began with eyes that avoided his own, self-conscious gestures and comments spoken in his presence, and whispered conversations that terminated as soon as he was within listening range. Gradually, many of his closest friends stopped visiting his office to chat or discuss the news. And in the evenings, they also neglected to invite him to their gatherings in Bertrand's tavern where they often congregated to gossip and share a glass of wine. Several times, out of curiosity, he stopped by anyway and invited himself to sit at their table. And although he was not rebuffed, he found their conversations contrived, and utterly uninteresting.

He realized, of course, that their actions were only a reflection of his own insecurities and the loss of his own self-esteem. As time passed, he made a half-hearted attempt to re-assert his authority, but soon realized that the sails that he had once depended upon to propel him through the barrier reefs of similar waters were now too torn and tattered. As a result, he found himself well off his intended course, drifting, and floundering dangerously in a sea of jagged, hull-crunching rocks.

As the circumstances worsened, several local creditors who had lost goods consigned to him during a Chickasaw raid several years earlier became bolder, challenging his authority, and clamoring for restitution. Their clamoring reached its peak during the month of May, 1744.

One such creditor was young Jeanne Derbanne, son of his deceased bookkeeper. Except for one or two mischievous incidents when the boy was younger, St. Denis had come to admire Jeanne and his daring nature. In many ways, he reminded St. Denis of himself at that age. For like himself, young Derbanne had fallen in love with and married a Spaniard, the seventeen-year-old daughter of Spanish Commandant Gonzales. He accomplished this despite the objection of Commandant Gonzales by slipping quietly under the cover of darkness into the Spanish Fort of Los Adaes and abducting his bride to be. Then, he brought her back to the fort and married her the next morning in the mission church — just minutes before the enraged Commandant arrived with a detail of five soldiers.

That happened in 1736. Now, the boy was nothing but a pain in the ass, and he was testing St. Denis' patience severely.

"Jeanne, why do you insist that I am liable for your goods? It is general knowledge that everything was lost during the Chick raid. Do you think my couriers deliberately handed them over? My lost was three times your amount," St. Denis stated as firmly as possible.

"That is a moot point. The point being — I entrusted my goods to you to trade to the Spanish in my behalf since, by your law, I was forbidden to do so myself."

"Still it was not through my neglect that they were lost. I never agreed to act as an insurer for losses resulting from circumstances beyond my control."

"Apparently, the courts feel differently."

"Exactly what are you trying to say, Jeanne?"

"Just this. Tell me, did the courts rule you negligent for the Company's losses during your Mexico venture?"

"Well.... Yes."

"Did they not also hold you liable for those losses?"

"Yes, they did. But..."

"That, m'sieur, is the point. In my sight, it appears that these same principles apply in my case."

"In the case you speak of, the court's decision was made

with malice and wholly administered on behalf of my enemy, the Governor — not on the basic principles of justice."

"Justice? You should flee from the word. Where was justice when you confiscated my corn, sold it, and kept the proceeds for yourself? Where was justice then? And why are you the only person who can legally trade with the Spanish? Are you not a French citizen, the same as I? Is this a concession granted only to you because you have a Spanish wife? Well, my wife is Spanish, as well. No, Commandant, something here has a foul odor, and I think the courts will be more than pleased to rule on this matter. They may even entertain the thought that there never was a raid—that you planted the story just to hide the true disposition of my property."

"Why you young, ungrateful son-of-a-bitch. If your father had not neglected your education, you would know that as commandant of this post it is my duty to manage all business affairs of this settlement. You would also know that no common citizen is at liberty to establish monopolies and conduct international trade; that rights of that nature are limited to a few responsible men of stature — those who either purchase said rights from the king, or granted such rights by his office. That is the French way. As for me, that right came with my appointment as Commandant, and while I have not interfered with your, or anyone else's, interior business affairs, it is my duty to establish laws regarding international trade. How else can the king, or this colony, be assured of getting their just due in taxes? It is taxes that maintain the soldiers in my garrison and pay the wages for the administration of this colony. The only area where I may have exceeded my authority was in my decision to initiate trade with the Spanish at a time when our countries were at war. The threat of war no longer exists, and even if it did, I would still do anything necessary in order to insure this colony's well-being. How dare you accuse me of thieving."

"Me? That allegation, m'sieur, never passed from my mouth. I know nothing of the matters you speak. I was born here on this soil — not in France. And since I am unknowledgeable about what is right or wrong with your international trade laws, my only course is to petition the court for their opinion."

St. Denis' frustration with his inability to convince the young man that he was a man of honor overwhelmed him, and for the second time in his life, he lost control of his commanding composure. He coughed once, then twice, then several times in rapid succession.

"Since you were my father's friend," Derbanne continued, "I will give you four weeks to make good the debt. Beyond that, I will not only seek payment for my losses to the Chicks in the courts, but just to complicate matters, I will also seek retribution for the manner in which you exploited the labors of your faithful and defenseless subjects — to include interest for the grain you confiscated under questionable authority."

"Jeanne..., what must I do to convince you to the contrary?"

"Pay the debt, m'sieur." With that exchange, Derbanne turned and stormed out of the door.

Moments after Derbanne departed, St. Denis felt himself growing sick. His head was spinning and he was nauseous. There was no way he could repay the debt. He felt certain that he was on firm ground where his monopoly was concerned, but not quite so certain about his obligations to insure the goods of his consignors — and considering the way things had gone the last time he was before the court, he was absolutely sure that they would rule against him again. That act, of course, would open the door to everyone else with a similar claim and leave him in total financial ruin.

Wearily, he arose slowly and made his way home. Several times, he felt needle sharp pains in his chest, and twice, he almost slipped from the back of Diablo, his prized Spanish stallion.

Emanuelle was feeding her chickens when she observed her husband's stallion approaching at a somber, uncertain pace. Instinctively, she knew that all was not well. Without another thought, she dropped her sack of corn and rushed to assist him.

"What is it? What is wrong?" Emanuelle inquired with alarm.

"Just a small malady. It will pass. Send someone out to the Isle to fetch François and Marie."

"Let me put you to bed first. I will send for them in the morning... at first light."

"No. Send for them tonight."

After putting her husband to bed, Emanuelle did as she was asked. She sent a runner to the Isle, and while she was doing so, she also sent one for the surgeon.

Day was just awakening when Emanuelle heard the approach of a fast paced horse and wagon. Anxiously, she arose from her sitting chair beside her husband's bed and went to the door.

"M'selle, we came as fast as we could," François stated with visible concern. "Is the Commandant well?"

"No, he is not," Emanuelle replied simply. "He is waiting for you. Been asking for you all night. Come along. He is in his chamber. Maybe, he will rest better once he knows you are here."

François and Marie followed Emanuelle into their master's chamber and paused beside his bed.

"Louis, are you awake?" Emanuelle asked softly. "François and Marie are here."

"I know," St. Denis replied. "Light my lamp, then leave us. I need to talk to them about a private matter."

Emanuelle lit the lamp solemnly and left the room, closing the door quietly behind her.

"Are we alone?" St. Denis asked.

"Yes," François replied. "We are alone."

"Good. I do not want to cause your mistress anymore grief. I am dying. I sent for you because I have a petition to place before you. It concerns you both."

"We are willing, m'sieur. What do you desire?"

"First, I have not forgotten your quest for liberty. But now, it seems that our most Gracious Lord has decided to summon me before our agreement can be consummated. Under the circumstances, and as long as the courts have command of my property, which includes you and your family, my hands are bound. I can do nothing to assist you. This is grievous.

"Yet, in spite of this, and because my children are young and unknowledgeable, I am compelled to ask that you and Marie continue to serve my dear wife as you have served me — to protect her and insure her well-being for so long as she may live; that you should do this even though you both may later obtain your liberty and be under no legal obligation to do so. I place this petition before you not as master to slave, but as a father to his most trusted son and daughter."

"We are honored, m'sieur."

"I also ask that you continue in your efforts to assist my dear wife in disposing of my debts. And should you be fortunate enough to accomplish this goal, I have commanded her to honor my pledge of liberty to you. I know that my request is a task of great responsibility. I ask because I know of no other to whom I can entrust her care. Will you accept the terms of my petition?"

"Yes, we will. We would have done so even had you not asked. Marie and I will never leave m'selle's side. But," François replied on a lighter note, "you must not worry about such things. You need to rest so you can hurry and get well. You are like a rock, and rocks live for many, many years."

"If only that statement were true."

"Well, maybe this news will cheer you up."

"What news?"

"I know you won't believe me, but your son, Black Hawk, although he is crippled, is alive and well."

"Are you sure?"

"Yes. He is still on the Isle. Exactly where, I do not know. He is like a ghost. He has visited me on several occasions. If he was able to survive, then so can you."

"The next time you speak to him, tell him that I was unaware that I had a son, and let him know that I wish him well."

"I will do that."

"... François?"

"Yes, m'sieur."

"Do you remember the words of the Stinkard woman — what she said about the afterlife?"

"Yes. I remember them well."

"I will soon know if she spoke the truth."

"I believe she spoke the truth."

St. Denis sighed then drifted off to sleep. Quietly, Marie and François excused themselves and left the room.

It was clear to everyone that the commandant's condition was grave; that death was never more certain. Emanuelle found it hard to believe that her once stalwart husband was now as helpless as a baby. His face which was once so full of life and vitality was now gaunt and withered, and his once thick, auburn hair, now thinned and gray. Still, he was her love. So, she and Marie sat by his bedside and waited patiently with him for the inevitable.

Finally, on the eleventh day of June, 1744, less than ten months after Bienville's contemptuous departure, death stepped across the threshold of Casa de Sombrilla, silently, and in the calm of the early morning. St. Denis felt its ominous, but not unfriendly, presence and understood. He had played life's game with gusto, and now that it was time, he experienced a great sense of relief.

He had led a full life, fished the waters of a thousand streams, dined among nobles, and slept among the most savage of savages. He had walked the fertile earth almost from sea to sea sustained by the love of a special woman of immense stature. No, he had no real regrets. There was, however, one place that he never had the opportunity to visit — a place in the far northwest with mountains that stretched high into the heavens like majestic thrones covered with caps of pure, white snow. He had heard of this place many times during his travels and he wondered now, if by chance, he might happen to pass there on the final leg of his journey.

Soon, he would know if the Stinkard woman was right in her vision of the afterlife; if she and the Great Sun would welcome him as their brother or shun him as the enemy who had destroyed their nation. Soon, he would know. And now, he was anxious to start his new adventure....

Suddenly, a cold, thorny hand struck him violently in the chest and took his breath away. Gasping, he raised slightly, coughed, then collapsed.

Emanuelle stirred from her slumber, touched her husband — and screamed... "*Ma vie est finie!* (My life is over!)"

———————

Word traveled fast through the countryside to every village and every hamlet that the Great White Chief had passed away. Soon, the trails and the waterways were filled with processions of country-men, Indians, trappers, and Spaniards... all en-route to pay their last respects to the noble Frenchman.

On the day he was laid to rest, their combined numbers filled the little mission church and all roads that led to its doorsteps.

Indians in colorful bonnets and costumes, and *Coureurs de bois* (Frenchmen who married and lived among the Indians) in their doeskin jerkins mingled freely with French gentlemen and their la-dies dressed in their finest garments and multicolored robes — their faces painted in various shades of rouges and lavenders.

Emanuelle, dressed in the *couleur* black, acknowledged each of them as she followed the procession serenely to a small stone and mortar vault behind the mission church at Post de St. Jean Baptiste des Natchitoches. She acknowledged those she knew, and those she did not know; those she saw and did not see; those who spoke and those who did not speak. And when the procession had reached the edge of the world, she watched stolidly as François and Cecil bur-ied her husband in a grassy plot — a plot hidden among the grave stones and crypts where small children often played after church, where old men gathered in the evenings to sit and pass the time away, and where young lovers met in the night beyond the sight of their parents to frolic, and occasionally — to make love.

Emanuelle had watched the proceedings in silence, staring blankly as if she was looking out across the void that separated one life from the next. And when the ritual was over and all the flowery words had been spoken, she departed unwillingly, leaving behind a sizable part of herself to be sealed in the crude crypt along with a small note which she had tucked in her husband's pocket. She had penned the note during the night following his death. In it were the following words...

>*Farewell, my love,*
>*May God speed you on your way,*
>*Keep warm, travel light,*
>*and do not be concerned for me.*
>*And when you get to that final place,*
>*whether it be Heaven or Hell,*
>*Build you a large fire,*
>*one that I may see from a great distance,*
>*So that I may find you easily,*
>*and take my place again by your side.*
>   *Dieu vous garde — my beloved.*

>   *Eternally, Emanuelle*

—The End—

E p i l o g —

~ ~ ~

THAT EVENING FOLLOWING THE FUNERAL,   AND WHILE
EMANUELLE'S CHILDREN PLAYED A GAME OF STICKS on the floor of the
sitting room, François sat outside on the gallery steps gazing out at
the setting sun, watching intensely as it struggled to remain aloft.
Louis, his master's son, had left earlier to go carousing in town with
other boys his own age. Behind him, his mistress sat in a weathered, split cane chair, absentmindedly fingering the ends of the light
shawl that hung loosely about her shoulders. Beside her, his wife,
Marie, stood cooling their mistress with a small, palmetto frond fan.
They, too, were watching reverently, the last rites of day....

"M'selle?"

"Yes, François."

"How many fires do you think there are in the sun — one, or
many?"

"Many, I suppose."

"I agree. I, too, think there are many — all small. I think that
there are so many, that from a distance they only appear as one. Has
anyone ever tried to follow the sun — to see where it goes and what
happens once it arrives at its destination?"

"I'm sure there are those who have tried, but the sun is fleet
of foot and nothing living, not even the fastest horse, can match its
stride."

"An eagle could do it, if he was smart. If I were an eagle, I
would station myself on the evening side of the world. There, I
would wait. Then, when the sun arose the next morning, I would
precede it with all haste so that I could be at the appointed place at
the appointed time."

"There are those who say the world is round, that the sun travels in an arc and never sleeps."

"Who are those who say this?"

"Scholars and men of learning."

"Maybe, these scholars should ask the Dogans. They would know for certain."

"The Dogans?"

"Yes. An ancient tribe in Africa whose camp is near the river Niger. I have never seen these people myself, but the elders of my village say that these people can see what no man can see; that they know the stars, their names, and the paths they travel well. They also say that the Dogans worship a black star, a dead star that moves about a larger star once each sixty years; that they have celebrated this event for more than three thousand years with a festival called *Sigui*. Yes, I suspect that they would know."

"The stars are beyond me. I am satisfied just to marvel at their beauty."

"If the world is round, as these scholars suggest, maybe the Commandant is not dead. Maybe, he has just dropped from our view to arise again on the other side of the world. Maybe..."

"François...," Marie said with an air of caution. "You're disturbing m'selle."

François glanced back, saw the last rays of the sun flicker in the moist eyes of his mistress, and was immediately sorry for having spoken his clumsy words. This had not been the intent of his conversation. He had only intended to entertain her, and maybe, lighten her burden. Now, he wished he had kept his mouth shut, stayed out of it, and let time cure her broken heart. The sun had vanished from both of their worlds, and no man living had the knowledge or the strength to draw it back into its place, and certainly not him. He could be of no further assistance here. It was time for him to prepare himself — like the eagle he spoke of. For if an eagle, or a man, could outwit the sun, then either could claim the greatest reward of all — the fulfillment of a dream.

With a sudden sense of urgency, François stood and approached his mistress.

"M'selle?" he said softly.

"Yes, François." Emanuelle replied solemnly.

"Forgive me. I did not mean to disturb you with my foolish talk."

"*Ne vous en faites pas* (Do not worry). Your talk was not foolish. It was very endearing."

"M'selle, there is nothing more I can do here. With your permission, I will be leaving. I must get back to my chores. Marie will stay to tend your needs."

"Must you leave tonight?"

"Yes. My fields have gone unattended for too long, and there is much to be done."

"I understand and agree. M'sieur Leblec, the overseer, is quite capable of overseeing my interest here. Marie, tell Zolare to pack a sack of food for François, and François — take my husband's horse, Diablo. He will be of more service to you than to me. I will send Marie to join you in a few weeks — as soon as things are settled here."

"*Merci*, m'selle."

While François went to the barn to saddle up Diablo, Marie instructed Zolare to pack him a sack of food. Then, she went directly to her cabin to gather François' personal belonging.

"My, what a handsome pair of black stallions the two of you make," Zolare said softly from the shadows as she entered the dimly lit barn with a small food sack.

"Damn, Zolare. You scared the Hell out of me."

"Zolare chuckled as she sauntered towards Diablo's stall and stopped in front of François. "That was not my intentions, chéri. There are things more desirable that I would like to do to you."

"Zolare, be careful. I have no time for mischief."

"I am not interested in mischief. I am on a mission with a purpose, and it concerns you."

"What?"

"François, I want a child," Zolare said with a serious tone as she closed in and took his hand in hers. "I want a child more than anything else in all this world."

"As much as I would like to, I cannot assist you. Give Cecil an opportunity."

"François, you know, as well as I, that Cecil is not capable. Despite all his bragging, he is an old man and not capable of fulfilling his manly duties. You are my only hope. I…"

"Sorry, I'm late," Marie interrupted as she entered the barn with another sack containing François' clothing.

François coughed, stepped back from Zolare, and hurried back to his tasks.

"I did not intend to startle you." Marie added sarcastically. "I was delayed by the children."

"Oh, Marie," Zolare replied self-consciously, "I was just telling François that when you leave to rejoin him on the Isle, I would like to accompany you to see my husband. If m'selle allows me to do so, won't that be wonderful — the four of us in the wilderness?"

"Yes, it would," Marie replied as a matter of courtesy even though she felt a little ill at ease about what might have transpired in her absence. Then to her husband, she said sternly and somewhat curtly, "You go directly home and straight to bed without delay, and stay there. I will join you as soon as m'selle releases me."

"I will be waiting anxiously, chéri."

"And be watchful of the Natchez boy. Remember — he kills."

"You worry too much. The boy is no threat to us. The Englishmen received exactly what they deserved."

"Still, he is a savage, and one cannot be too cautious. You heed me, do as I say, and stand your guard."

"I will do that, chéri," François answered. Then, he kissed her, climbed aboard Diablo, and departed with a wave of farewell.

When he had gone, Marie turned to Zolare and said quite sternly, "Whatever you may have on your little feeble mind, forget it."

Then, she left a speechless Zolare standing uncomfortably in the shadows of the barn as she walked briskly back toward the house.

As Marie retrieved her fan and resumed her post, Emanuelle released a long, audible sigh and flipped her shawl angrily at several unwelcome mosquitoes. In the distance, above the pines, several birds of an unknown variety circled the purple sky as if searching the night for a place to roost. A tiny jack rabbit wandered leisurely across her front yard, saw her, then darted quickly, deep into her flower bed near the roses. She followed it with her eyes, wondering how it, and the other vulnerable creatures of the world, managed to survive in the midst of so many predators like wolves and alligators, lawyers and judges, and powdered male scavengers who passed themselves off as governors.

Soon, Lieutenant Taillefert would come with his cadets and clerk to inventory and appraise what was left of her husband's assets, and it irritated her to think of them pulling, plucking, and rummaging through her things with their filthy hands. If they would but ask, she could save them a considerable amount of time for she knew the count of every worthless item in her possession.

There were six chests of linen and clothes, twelve of her husband's surtouts — some a little better than others, but all with beautiful gold and silver braids and tassels. Beneath the house there were forty-two sacks of last year's pecans and four hundred and fifty pots of stinking bear oil waiting for shipment to New Orleans.

In her care, were sixteen adult slaves, twelve African and four Indian. And among them were seventeen little slave children, twelve African and five Indian — all darlings and especially dear to her heart.

On the land of Casa de Sombrilla, there were twenty-two arpents of corn. There were also fifteen arpents planted with beans, and eight with indigo. In the meadows, they had exactly one hundred and eleven horned beasts, twenty-seven fine Spanish horses, four wagons, two carts, and one carriage with a loose wheel.

She had ten slave cabins in various states of repair, a barn, a weaving house, a curing shed, a cookhouse with three iron cooking pots and a cauldron, and she had a modest home. Inside, she had twelve forks and spoons, twenty-four plates, a speckled blue Chinese vase, two silver goblets, some utensils, five mattresses, two pieces of printed calico, and a few jewels, some given to her by her grandmother, and a few that she had purchased for herself in New Orleans. And, if they insisted — she also had seven pairs of drawers to cover her naked ass.

It seemed like a large estate, but even if they sold everything she owned, she knew it would never satisfy her debts. She supposed most of it would go toward paying the nine thousand livres she still owed the Company of the Indies. If that wasn't enough, she suspected they might even confiscate her home. They could. *And what about Marie and François?* She loved them dearly, and she knew that they loved her; that they would work their fingers to the bone in an attempt to save her and salvage their dreams of liberty; that they would do this in spite of the fact that time was clearly to their disadvantage.

With the estate in such disarray and tied to the courts, she doubted that they would ever realize their quest. But, they would try. Of that, she was never more certain. How she wished her husband had listened to her. They could have sold what they could, taken the money and ran — back to Mexico. Her beautiful, beautiful Mexico. Debts be damned.

Bienville — you old, fat-assed heifer... I salute you. You did your dirty work well.

"Marie?"

"Yes, m'selle."

"Let us retire. I'm ready for bed."

Without answering, Marie took her mistress's arm gently and escorted her into the house. Once inside, Emanuelle paused above her daughter, Marie des Nieges, and baby Coincoin. Both lay fast asleep on the floor of her sitting room.

"They are adorable, aren't they, Marie?"

"*Oui*, m'selle. Yes, they are."

— ~ ~ ~ —

A Cane River Saga

References:

1. Barnett, Jim, *The Natchez Indians*, Division of Historic Properties, Mississippi Department of Archives and History, Natchez, MS, 1998.

2. Conrad, Glenn R. (Editor), *Louisiana History (Volume XXI, No. 3)*, The Louisiana Historical Association, summer 1980.

3. Cross, Ruth, *Soldier of Good Fortune*, Banks Upshaw and Company, Dallas, TX, 1936.

4. Davis, Edwin Adams, Raleigh A. Suarez, & Joe Gray Taylor, *Louisiana, The Pelican State*, Louisiana State University Press, Baton Rouge, LA, 1985.

5. d'Iberville, Pierre LeMoyne, *Iberville's Gulf Journals*, translated and edited by Richebourg Gaillard McWilliams / University of Alabama Press, Tuscaloosa, Alabama, 1981.

6. Du Ru, Paul, *Journal of Paul Du Ru*, February 1 to May 8, 1700, Translation by Ruth Lapham Butler, The Caxton Club, Chicago. IL, 1934.

7. French, B. F., *Historical Memoirs of Louisiana*, Lamport, Blakeman & Law, New York, NY, 1853.

8. Kniffen, Gregory and Stokes, *The Historic Indian Tribes of Louisiana*, Louisiana State University Press, Baton Rouge, LA, 1987.

9. Le Page du Pratz, Antoine, *The History of Louisiana* (facsimile reproduction of the 1774 edition, edited by Joseph G. Tregle, Jr.). Louisiana State University Press, Baton Rouge, 1975.

10. Lorenz, Karl, The Natchez of Southwest Mississippi. In *Indians of the Greater Southeast: Historical Archaeology and Ethnohistory*, edited by Bonnie G. McEwan, pp. 142-177. University Press of Florida, Gainesville, 2000.

11. Mignon, Francois, *Plantation Memo, Plantation Life in Louisiana 1750-1970, and other matter*, Claitor's Publishing Division, Baton Rouge, LA, 1972 / 1981.

12. Mills, Elizabeth Shown and Gary, *Tales of Old Natchitoches*, The Association for The Preservation of Historic Natchitoches,

Natchitoches, LA, 1978

13. Mills, Gary B., *The Forgotten People*, Louisiana State University Press, Baton Rouge, LA, 1977.

14. Penicaut, Andre, *Fleur de Lys and Calumet*, Penicaut narrative of French adventure in Louisiana / translated and edited by Richebourg Gaillard McWilliams; foreword by Robert R. Rea / University of Alabama Press, Tuscaloosa, Alabama,1953.

15. Phares, Ross, *Cavalier in The Wilderness*, Pelican Publishing Company, Gretna, LA, 1976.

16. Sansing, David, Sim Callon and Carolyn Smith, *Natchez, An Illustrated History*. Plantation Publishing Company, Natchez, Mississippi, 1992.

17. Swanton, John R., *Indian Tribes of the Lower Mississippi Valley and Adjacent Coast of the Gulf of Mexico.* Bureau of American Ethnology Bulletin 43. Smithsonian Institution, Washington, D.C., 1911.

18. Brandon, William, *The American Heritage Book of Indians*, American Heritage Publishing Co., Inc., New York, 1961.

19. Hall-Quest, Olga, *Old New Orleans, The Creole City; Its Role in American History 1718-1803*, E. P. Dutton, New York, 1968.

20. Neitzel, Robert S., *Archeology of The Fatherland Site: The Grand Village of The Natchez*, Mississippi Department of Archives and History, Jackson, MS 1997.

21. *Estate holdings of Louis Juchereau de St. Denis*, June 12, 1744, Document #151, Northwestern University Library Archives.

22. *Journals written by Louis Juchereau de St. Denis* , September 30, 1731, relative to the Natchez Indian attack on his post, 6 documents #1 thru 6, 14 pages, Northwestern University Library Archives. (*Translated by Herbert Metoyer, 1996.*)

23. *Will of Louis Juchereau de St. Denis,*March 26, 1744, document #132, Northwestern University Library Archives.

What Some Folks Say

"Herbert Metoyer's new historic novel, *Small Fires in the Sun,* is a wonderful, engaging, historical and well-crafted novel that is essential and important to understanding the history and struggles of the deep south and America. This well-written novel is a page turner filled with toil, humanity, love and war. If the Academy Award nominated film, *Beasts of the Southern Wild,* peeked your interest in Louisiana, Mr. Metoyer's epic novel will fill in the history of the why and how. *Small Fires* is a stunning achievement for a first novel by a very talented American writer." — **M.L. Liebler**, *Professor, Wayne State University, Detroit Poet and Editor* of ***Working Words: Punching the Clock and Kicking Out the Jams***. *St. Clair Shores, MI.* www.mlliebler.com.

_____

"This book must have been a work of passion on behalf of the author. This is evident considering the amount of research it must have taken to develop such an intriguing and pulsating story about the cultures that evolved during colonial Louisiana. Informative and easy to read." — **Robert Williams**, *New Orleans, Louisiana.*

_____

"Get ready for a thrilling ride through an explosive period of history! With heartfelt sensitivity and a touch of humor, Metoyer unveils the winding tale of a Louisiana family's love, passion, and tortured past. Skillfully mixing fact with fiction, he pens a vivid description of a bloody uprising aboard a slave ship crossing the Atlantic Ocean, the family's early ties to a powerful Natchez tribal community, and their aspirations while serving as house slaves on a plantation ruled by a French slave master. The journey that unfolds is both compelling and shocking. This book is a must read!" — **Denise Crittendon**, *Publisher and Editor, Esteem Multi-Media, Detroit, MI.*

_____

"This book is educational, intriguing, and even jolting at times. A very good read!" — **D'Anna Savage**, *Ladies Literary Society Book Club, Southfield, MI.*

_____

"This book is an emotional roller-coaster ride. How the author was able to blend such believable and true-to-life characters into one story is a testament to his abilities as a first-time author. It was an easy task for us to identify with all of his characters and share in their aspirations and disappointments. Like us, I am sure you will laugh and cry right along with them. As a bonus, we also learned a lot about the colonial history of Louisiana. Very interesting." — **Dr. D. B. Walker** and **Prof. Diane M. Lockett**, *President and Vice-President, Detroit Writers' Guild, Detroit, MI.*

_____

"After reading this book, I am now a believer in the term that — '*Life is stranger than fiction.*' I salute Herbert Metoyer for the masterful manner in which he took actual historical events and wove them into such an awesome and intricate plot. You will not be able to put this book down!" — **Hattie Jean Holmes**, *Ft. Worth, TX.*

"For some reason, I always examine a new book by reading the ending first. In this case, I started with the epilogue. By the end of the first page, I was hooked." — **Tammy Mason**, *Columbus, OH.*

"When I first read a draft of *Small Fires in the Sun*, I knew it had the ingredients of a best seller. Also, its colorful characters and the way it is constructed makes it a great candidate for an action-packed movie." — **Linda S. Manuel**, *School Teacher, Retired, Gahanna, OH.*

"Undeniably compelling and exceptionally rewarding. This novel is supremely rich in language and uniquely blessed with genuine originality." — **D. Marlene Thomas**, *TMC Consulting, Ft. Washington, MD.*

"Fantastic! I was emotionally involved from the beginning to the end. And... the words in the note penned by Emanuelle to her beloved husband, St. Denis, upon his death, touched my heart and spirit. It should serve as a reminder to lovers everywhere to tuck a smile away today, and learn to appreciate that bumps in the road can be made smooth tomorrow."—**Zelda E. Irby**, *Federal Government, Retired, Gaithersburg, MD.*

"Good historical fiction that educates and entertains. Herb Metoyer has managed to combine actual history with suspense, intrigue, and romance to create a one-of-a-kind story. Especially interesting was the manner in which he incorporated the unique matrilineal society of the Natchez Indians (*believed to be of Phoenician ancestry*) into his narrative. The novel is descriptive of the setting and beautifully written. *Small Fires in the Sun* is a must read! — **Pamela Llorence**, *Southfield, MI, (native of Natchitoches, Louisiana).*

"What an exciting movie this novel would make. Vivid descriptions, memorable characters, and an action-packed plot. Need I say more?" — **Melanye Finister**, *Actress, Philadelphia, PA*